SNOWED IN WITH THE MOUNTAIN MAN

O'SULLIVAN SISTERS BOOK 4

SOPHIA QUINN

FLP

Cover art (copyright) by Tugboat Design
www.tugboatdesign.net

ISBN: 978-1-99-103405-2 (Paperback)
ISBN: 978-1-99-115939-7 (Kindle)

Forever Love Publishing Ltd
www.foreverlovepublishing.com
2022 - USA

———

Dahlia O'Sullivan did not do tears.

But when her sister Rose wrapped her in a hug in the kitchen of their deceased father's Montana ranch home, her throat felt suspiciously tight.

Maybe pregnancy hormones were contagious.

"Thank you for coming," Rose said in a high, watery voice.

Rose's baby belly was a bumper between them, and Dahlia fought a fresh wave of emotion at the reminder that her little sister was going to be a mother.

That *she* was going to be an aunt.

Dahlia squeezed her sister tighter. She still couldn't quite believe it. Dahlia swallowed hard, but even so, her voice sounded too raspy when she answered, "Always."

Rose's arms tightened around her like she knew precisely what Dahlia meant.

No matter what, she'd be there for her and the baby...

Even if she was about to get on a plane back to New York City.

Emotions were trying to get the best of her, and Dahlia

was keenly aware of their audience. Rose's boyfriend, Dex, was hovering nearby, and their newfound half sister Emma and her fiancé, Nash, were right behind her, waiting their turn to say goodbye.

Oh, and JJ was here too.

Finally.

The ranch hand who was supposed to drive her to the airport had kept her waiting forever this morning.

All of them were watching, so Dahlia did what she'd always done best. She pulled it together. Chin coming up high, she took a step away from her baby sister.

Goodness. How could her baby sister be having a baby of her own? No, she wasn't technically a child, but after having raised Rose for most of her life, Dahlia wasn't sure she could ever see her as a grown-up either.

Rose's lips wobbled with unshed tears. Dahlia had to glance away to keep her voice even. "Now…" She went for firm and businesslike. How else was she supposed to stay in control? "I expect updates on your health and the baby's."

"Of course." Rose nodded.

Dahlia pointed at Dex. "And I expect you to look out for her."

"Always." Dex lightly squeezed the back of Rose's neck, and she grinned up at him.

Ugh. That dreamy look they were sharing, it was like watching one of those sappy Hallmark movies.

Dahlia's insides rebelled against a flash of yearning that tried to rise in her chest. As if! Romance was the last thing she was interested in. It was great that her baby sister had found the world's sweetest man, but that kind of thing was not for her.

Dahlia had learned her lessons the hard way, and a

love like Rose and Dex shared was simply not in the cards for her.

And she was absolutely fine with that.

Dex's smile shifted from Rose to her, changing to a different kind of warmth as he stepped forward and surprised her with a hug.

And while her answering hug wasn't exactly enthusiastic, she tried her best not to draw away too quickly.

She hadn't exactly been the nicest to Dex when they'd first met, and if he was willing to move past that for Rose's sake, then she supposed she ought to as well.

Still…

She didn't really do hugs, just like she didn't do tears.

But of course, that didn't stop Emma from rushing her the moment Dex stepped aside.

Dahlia tried not to roll her eyes at her warm wishes and requests for her to come visit again soon. Not one of them was going to shed a tear at seeing her leave, that much she knew.

But they loved Rose. It was obvious. She might have been just as much a stranger to Emma and her sister Lizzy as Dahlia had been the day she'd arrived, but they'd taken Rose in and looked after her.

They'd looked after Rose in a way Dahlia never could.

Her chest grew so tight she wasn't sure where to look or what to do. Instinct had her glancing toward the door— toward her escape from this emotional scene.

But JJ was standing in the doorway, blocking her path, and what was worse…he was watching her. Everyone around her was talking over each other, emotions being aired out like wet laundry, and yet JJ was staring straight at her with that unreadable expression of his.

So quiet, so calm, so seemingly unfazed by anything

going on around him, JJ looked like a quiet port in the eye of a hurricane.

Dahlia pulled her gaze away quickly, but not quickly enough. His look rattled her. And she'd already been on edge.

When she turned, she found herself swept up in a bear hug from Nash. "I hope you make it back for the wedding."

Dahlia gave his back an awkward pat in response.

She wasn't sure how she was supposed to act around the guy who was about to marry a sister she'd never met until their father's ridiculous will forced them to. Not to mention the guy who'd actually known their father, who'd worked this property for him…

A man who knew more about their family than she did.

The thought had her backing away from Nash the moment he set her free.

Emma gave her a sappy smile—the kind totally befitting a small-town kindergarten teacher who apparently moonlighted as a saint on the weekends by the way Rose talked about her.

"We really are glad we got to meet you," Emma said.

Dahlia nodded. She would have forced a smile, but her twin sister, Daisy, had long ago informed her that her fake smiles resembled a sneer.

"Yeah, well…" Dahlia backed away. She could all but hear a ticking clock in the back of her mind, counting down the seconds until her flight. "Congratulations on the wedding."

But don't expect me to be there.

She didn't say that, of course. She was smart enough to know that people thought she was callous and hard-

4

hearted. She was sure they whispered words just like that behind her back. But she did have some manners.

Honestly, though, if Rose wasn't dead set on living in this Podunk little town of Aspire, Montana, Dahlia would likely never return.

But Rose would be here, along with her new baby. So of course she'd have to come back for visits.

She cast one last glance over at Rose, but her sister was making eyes at her boyfriend—again. Dahlia had never truly understood that phrase until these two. But if humans could have little heart emojis in their eyes like cartoon characters, then Rose and Dex would absolutely be sporting them right about now.

"All right, well, I guess we're off." She turned to head to the door and—*bam*. There it was again. That jolt when her eyes locked with JJ's.

She wasn't sure how or why, but every time her gaze collided with his, it felt like a mini explosion. It'd been that way since the very first time she met him, right here in this kitchen the month before, during her first trip to see her baby sister, and it had only grown worse on this second trip to be with Rose when they found out the baby's sex.

It was annoying.

She looked away quickly, but not quickly enough, because heat was surging into her cheeks like she was some prepubescent tween who'd never seen a handsome man before.

And yes, he was handsome—if you liked that whole bearded, scruffy, might-not-have-showered-in-a-week sort of look.

Which she didn't.

She arched her brows in a prompting look as he stood

there eyeing her from where he leaned against the door-frame. "Well?"

His lips quirked up on one side, his eyes sparkling with amusement, the way they did every time she spoke to him.

It was irritating. She couldn't tell if he was laughing at her or not.

But of course he was. After all, it wasn't like he was laughing *with* her.

Speaking of being laughed at... Dahlia caught Emma's giggle and didn't have to look over to know she and Nash were laughing too. Again.

So stupid.

She reached for the handle of her luggage, but somehow JJ got there before her. Which was startling because only a second ago he'd been leaning against the doorframe.

"You don't need to—" She started but stopped as he ignored her, hefting the luggage easily as she hurried after him. "JJ, I can carry my own bags."

He led the way into the entry hall, the sounds of laughter following in her wake.

Oh, they were just so amusing, laughing just because she'd gotten a little flustered a couple times.

Whatever. She didn't care.

When he paused to open the front door, she made another grab for the luggage, but all that earned her was an indulgent smile. One that said, *Nice try, but I don't think so*, without him saying a single word.

He was good at that, she'd discovered. Saying a lot without saying anything at all.

From what she'd gathered from Emma and Lizzy, JJ didn't talk much in general. None of them seemed to know much about where he came from or how he'd come to be working at the ranch. They just knew he was a good friend and "had a way" with the animals.

Whatever that meant.

He set the luggage in the back seat of his truck and opened the passenger side door for her before she could do it herself.

"I should have hired a rental car," she muttered.

She hated being at the mercy of other people. More than that, she hated being late.

He slid into the driver seat and started the truck. Country music immediately began to play, and she found herself relaxing slightly.

At least now she was on her way.

At least the goodbyes were over with.

Dahlia didn't do goodbyes. It was right up there with hugs and tears.

She looked out the window, the warmth from the heater soaking through her puffy winter jacket, and a scent that was so very JJ seemed to permeate the air.

It was a nice scent—a mix of pine, peppermint, and leather. It was clean and homey, and she wondered if he had a mint addiction or something.

She sat up straighter. What was she doing obsessing about his smell? Gah, it was a good thing she was leaving this rural nightmare.

Shifting her focus to the long dirt road that led away from the ranch rather than the man beside her, she sniffed and set her jaw, deciding that a quiet ride to the airport was exactly what she needed.

"You okay?" he asked when they'd pulled onto the long, one-lane road leading to the highway.

She glanced over at him. Like always, he looked

7

absurdly laid-back. For a second she wondered if he'd even said anything at all.

"Of course I'm all right."

There was that irritating hitch of his lips, the one that said she was amusing him. "Okay, then."

She turned back to face the road. Another long silence passed before his low, gravelly voice filled the truck's cab.

"You seemed a little on edge, is all."

"If I was on edge, it's because you were running late," she snipped. "I can't miss my flight."

"That's it, huh? I thought maybe you were sorry to be leaving."

She scowled at his easy reply. Was he being sarcastic?

She *was* on edge about making this flight. Her bosses at the marketing firm would be livid if she asked for more time off.

And yet…her jaw grew tight and her heart ached at the memory of Rose's wobbly lower lip when she'd started to say their goodbyes.

Rose would be fine without her. She had Dex, and Emma, and Lizzy, and Nash, and Kit…

A humorless laugh escaped her as she turned to look out the window. Rose would be just fine without her.

And Dahlia…well, she had a life to get back to.

"They're gonna miss you too." JJ said it so quietly she almost didn't hear.

Which made it all the easier to pretend she didn't.

2

E veryone liked to say that JJ was good with animals. But that wasn't the truth. Or...it wasn't the whole truth.

It wasn't like he was some mystical Dr. Doolittle type, speaking some secret code that horses and dogs could understand.

Nah, he just knew how to be quiet. And when a person was quiet long enough, he learned how to listen and not just hear. How to see and not just watch.

With all the talking and the laughter and the emotions running high back there in the O'Sullivans' kitchen, it was no wonder no one else noticed that Dahlia was having a hard time of it.

And right now, as they sat in silence, some old-school country music easing the tension and the soothing land-scape sliding by, he could feel hurt seeping out of her.

As one familiar meadow blended into the next and the mountain range he'd come to think of as his home came into view, he took in the beauty of the snow-capped peaks as he let Dahlia calm down. This world was a far cry from the one he'd grown up in, but it felt more like his home than any place on the East Coast ever had.

Especially his cabin up there in the pass between those two mountains. It was the one place in this world that was truly his own.

He cast a glance over at his uptight passenger. She was staring but not really seeing, judging by her distant gaze. He thought to point out where his cabin was located but changed his mind. He kept silent the rest of the way to the airport.

Mostly.

"The snow makes it real pretty this time of year, don't it?" he said after a full hour had passed in silence.

Mainly just to give her an opening in case she changed her mind and wanted to talk.

"It makes it look cold." Her tone was matter-of-fact but not barbed.

That was progress.

He knew what the others thought of Dahlia with her tough demeanor and her sharp tongue. But he liked her.

Not *liked her,* liked her like Nash and Kit teased. He'd had a taste of love and marriage once, and while it hadn't lasted long, it had been long enough for him to know that lifestyle wasn't for him.

So no, he wasn't pining away for the tightlipped, surly brunette in the passenger seat. But from what he'd seen of her during her last two stays at the ranch, he liked her enough that he didn't mind if she took out some of her hurt on him.

Unlike the others, he knew her anger wasn't meant for him. If anything, he suspected her anger was aimed at herself, though why that might be he didn't know. Mostly, he suspected she was an awful lot like his horse Zion. That colt had given everyone a run for their money before JJ came along.

The other ranch hands claimed he'd tamed Zion. He hadn't. He'd just been patient with the skittish horse. Everyone thought Zion had a temper or was wild and erratic. But Zion had just needed time to get to know people. He was wary of newcomers—still was to this day. But if you showed up every day and spoke to him kindly, showed him you meant no harm…

Well, then, you couldn't find a more loyal and loving horse.

Not that Dahlia was a horse. He had a hunch she'd clock him right in the nose if he were to suggest it.

But she wasn't some mean-spirited harpy either. That much he knew for certain after watching her take care of her sister in her own unique way.

She shifted in the seat beside him, wrapping her arms around herself.

"You cold?" He reached for the air controllers. "I can make it warmer."

"No." After a pause, she added, "Thanks. I'm just nervous."

He glanced over. He knew better than to try to put words in her mouth again. That'd only send this skittish colt shying away from him.

The image had him swallowing down a laugh, and her look pierced him like an arrow. "What?" she snapped. "Why are you laughing at me?"

He shook his head. "Just laughing, that's all." He made sure to meet her gaze. "Not at you. Never at you."

There was that wariness again.

What on earth had happened to this woman to make

her so strong yet so suspicious? A muscle ticked in his jaw as his mind raced to fill in the blanks.

He wasn't an overly possessive man by nature, but he was protective. The idea of this woman facing danger made his insides coil and his muscles tense.

"What are you nervous about?" he asked.

"Missing this flight." Her hands were still in her lap, but she was gnawing on her lower lip, a crease between her brows.

Would it really be so bad to be stuck here with your sisters a little while longer?

He knew better than to ask.

She glanced over. "What?"

He looked back to the road, a little startled as he realized he'd been staring again. She was entertaining to watch, that much he could admit. But right now she wasn't so much entertaining as...well, fascinating.

No one could deny that Dahlia O'Sullivan was a beauty. Unlike Rose and her other two sisters that he'd met, Dahlia had dark hair, and it was thick, sleek, and shiny like silk.

His fingers shifted on the wheel as he wondered what it'd feel like to run his fingers through it. He shook off the thought just as quickly.

He felt sorry for the lady, that was all.

And yet he caught himself sneaking another glance in her direction. Just like her personality, her looks were another form of riddle. She had the smoothest, softest-looking skin, but her jawline and cheekbones were sharp enough to cut glass. Her eyebrows and nose were narrow and...well, *dainty*, for lack of a better word. But her lips were full, her eyes dark and observant.

They were getting close to the airport, and it was a

good thing. The woman couldn't seem to sit still for more than a few seconds. She kept crossing her legs and recrossing them, fidgeting with her zipper and then fussing with the contents of her purse.

For a lady who was so eager to be on this flight and out of the state, she sure seemed nervous.

"Don't like flying?" he guessed.

She shot him a sidelong glare. "What?"

"You seem on edge again," he offered.

She shrugged. "No. Yes. I mean…no one really loves flying, right?"

He didn't answer. She wasn't nervous about flying. "You looking forward to being home?"

She nodded, but her words came a second too late. "Yes. Yeah. Of course. It'll be nice to get back to normal."

He nodded but kept silent, inwardly counting as he waited for her to elaborate. She was too keyed up to stay silent for long. *Three, two—*

"It's just… My job is stressful, you know? They weren't happy about me taking more time off, and I need to finish up work tonight before I head into the office tomorrow."

He nodded as she trailed off, shooting him a dubious glance that had him battling a smile.

So wary, this one. But what he'd discovered he liked best about her was that she knew how to speak her mind. He lost the battle with his grin when she demanded, "Why are you just nodding like that? If you want to speak, speak!"

He smiled over at her, which earned him another scowl. "When I have something to say, I say it. When I don't, I don't."

She stared at him for a long time. He held her gaze as long as he could without endangering his driving.

"Can I ask you something?" she asked.

"Shoot."

She twisted so she was facing him in her seat. "Does anything ever faze you?"

The question caught him so off guard, he glanced over with arched brows. A surge of pleasure hit him smack in the chest. Yes, sir, he really did like how she spoke her mind.

She spoke plainly and honestly, even when it might offend.

And that, he knew, was a gift. Even if it did tend to annoy people.

And because she asked so forthrightly, he gave the question the thought it deserved.

But of course, she couldn't stay silent long enough for him to formulate an answer. "Seriously. You're always so unflappable and calm. Doesn't anything ever make you feel off-kilter?"

He glanced over again, and when her gaze met his, one word popped into his head. *You.*

He bit it back before he could say it aloud, because… that wasn't the truth, was it?

He frowned. Was it?

She was intriguing, yes. And it was awfully fun trying to get past her prickly defenses. But that was where his interests began and ended. Right?

"Well?" she said.

The exit for the airport came into view, and he took the chance to avoid the question entirely. "This is our exit."

3

D ahlia stared at the pale blonde behind the ticket counter until the airline employee's bright smile began to falter.

"What do you mean *canceled*?" she repeated.

"I'm sorry for the inconvenience, ma'am." The woman winced.

Inconvenience? Dahlia stopped herself just in time, before she could once again repeat the woman's words back to her.

It was starting to sound like she didn't understand English. She did, it was just that she was having a heck of a time believing it.

This could not be happening.

Dahlia's stomach pitched toward the ground as she imagined her bosses' response if she wasn't in the office tomorrow. They hadn't minded her first trip over the holidays, since the office had technically been closed, but this last one…

The timing hadn't been great. Work was busier than

ever, and even though she'd handled it all remotely, they'd been frustrated when she wasn't at their beck and call.

She pinched the bridge of her nose and forced herself to take a deep breath so she didn't lose her cool at the friendly airline worker.

It's not her fault. It's not her fault. It's not her—

"I can try and get you on the next flight," the woman was saying, the sound of typing interrupting Dahlia's mantra.

Her head snapped up. "Yes. Please."

"It's not for another two hours," the woman said. "And there's a layover in Salt Lake City." She glanced up from the computer and cringed. "The weather there isn't the best today, but—"

"I'll take it," Dahlia cut in.

I don't care how you do it, just get me on a flight that will take me home!

She hadn't meant to sound so intense. It was eagerness at play, but unfortunately it came out sounding...harsh. Like she was snapping at the woman and not simply leaping on the offer.

The blonde behind the counter flinched.

A familiar, low voice behind her made Dahlia jolt as well, but for an entirely different reason.

"Thank you kindly for the assistance..." JJ's arm brushed Dahlia's as he joined her at the counter, leaning forward to read the blonde's name tag. "Susan. That's a nice name. We sure do appreciate your help today."

She beamed at the mountain man with his easy smile and Southern drawl.

Dahlia speared him with a sidelong glance, just long enough to see that yes, he was in fact wearing his grin, the one that made her belly do death-defying flips.

So annoying.

"Why are you still here?" she asked in a tight voice, her gaze fixed on Susan. More precisely Susan's fingers, which were flying over the keyboard.

JJ had insisted on helping her with her luggage. Totally unnecessary, but fine. Whatever. She'd said a quick goodbye and had assumed he'd taken off. Back to Aspire, or the ranch, or wherever it was he stayed when he wasn't hanging around the O'Sullivan property.

"Wanted to make sure you made your flight," he murmured.

He was rewarded with another beaming smile from super-sweet Susan.

"We'll get you home eventually, don't you worry," the woman assured her.

Dahlia tried to smile, but it felt more like a grimace.

"Eventually" wouldn't cut it. She could only imagine calling in to her office and explaining that they shouldn't worry because *eventually* she'd be back to work. New Yorkers weren't quite as easygoing as these Montanans.

"Let's just say a prayer that this next flight isn't canceled," Susan said in a conspiratorial whisper, like she and God were hatching a plan together.

She handed over the new boarding pass, and Dahlia took it with what she hoped was a smile. But she was too tense, and whatever expression she was throwing this sweet lady behind the counter must have been something quite hideous, because the woman kind of frowned and looked like she wanted Dahlia to walk away quick-smart.

"Thank you, Susan." JJ put a hand on Dahlia's arm and started to steer her toward the waiting area.

"Two hours," Dahlia muttered. A long line was

forming behind her, and no amount of pestering Susan was going to make her flight un-canceled.

She shrugged JJ's hand off her arm. She didn't need to be led away like a child.

With her luggage in one hand and her carry-on in the other, she wandered over to a handful of empty chairs near a coffee kiosk. She fell into one with a sigh, frowning when JJ took the empty seat beside her.

"You don't have to stick around, you know."

"I know." He nestled back in his seat and threaded his fingers together, resting them on his stomach and getting all comfy like they were about to start watching a movie.

His easygoing manner made her feel even more churlish.

She pressed her lips together and made a point of staring at her phone, even though the airline app had no more information other than what Susan had already told her. The weather was terrible all along the East Coast, especially in New York City. Flights were being canceled or rerouted...

And Dahlia was out of luck.

JJ leaned back in his seat beside her, his long legs thrust out in front of him with his dark, worn boots crossed at the ankles. He had his head tipped back slightly, and without the baseball caps or cowboy hats he typically wore, his shaggy dark hair curled over the collar of his winter coat.

Her hands twitched as she eyed him, and for one moment of insanity, she had an image of reaching out to touch that hair. To see how it felt and to tease him about how many years it'd been since he'd gotten it cut.

She turned away abruptly.

"Sorry 'bout your flight." His voice was a low rumble beside her. "But two hours ain't so bad."

She scoffed as she looked around the small airport. "It is when you're in a hurry to get home. And you're stuck in the middle of literally nowhere. There's not even a bookstore around here."

"Then I guess you'll just have to chat with me."

She turned to find him smiling at her. That smile...

How did he do that? How did he manage to look all gruff and masculine, yet so friendly and at ease at the same time?

Her withering glare, which usually made people squirm, had zero effect on him. If anything, it only made his smile bigger.

"You don't have to stay." She shuffled in her seat, crossing her legs so she was angled away from him.

"I don't mind."

Why did he always stare at her like this? Like she was so very entertaining. She'd nearly terrified the airline employee—not intentionally, but still, she'd seen the woman's pinched expression. And even her own sister got all wary around her when she was tense.

So why on earth did this guy stare at her like she was being funny or...or *cute*?

"Yeah, well..." *I mind.* That was what she meant to say, but another glance in his direction had her swallowing the words.

He'd been nice enough to drive her all this way, and if he left and her flight was canceled, he likely knew he'd have to turn right back around.

She sank back in her seat with a sigh. "I hate waiting."

His chuckle was a low, gravelly rumble. "You don't say."

Her lips twitched at his dry tone. She found herself fidgeting again, her gaze darting between the screen that announced delays and cancellations and the phone in her lap, which was unusually quiet.

Of course, it *was* a Sunday, and even her bosses respected her right to have Sundays off.

"What are you itching to get back to?" he asked.

"Work," she said. "Obviously."

"Obviously," he repeated in that same dry tone. His lips quirked up again, and his eyes…oh heck, they freakin' sparkled. With the beard and his build, and the fact that he voluntarily spent his days riding a range and doing all the manly things, he shouldn't have sparkling eyes. And he certainly shouldn't have such a nice smile. Even through the beard she could see a hint of dimples as his eyes crinkled.

"Did I say something funny?" Ugh. She sounded like a shrew, but she couldn't help it. She was on edge, couldn't he see that? This was so not the time to be teasing her.

"No, ma'am." He was obviously fighting a grin. "You didn't say anything funny."

The way he stressed "say" had her narrowing her eyes. "Am I acting funny, then?"

"I didn't say that."

A sound escaped her that was annoyingly like a harrumph.

His grin widened.

"You didn't *not* say it either." She rolled her eyes.

"Are you always such a stickler with words?"

"I'm a stickler for everything," she shot back. "It's part of my job description."

He leaned in toward her and lowered his voice as if they were sharing a secret. "Why, Ms. O'Sullivan, was that a joke?"

Her stupid lips twitched. "No. It's the truth."

"What is it you do back there in the big city?" His drawl made him sound more country than ever.

Suspicion had her eyeing him for a long moment. But he stared right back, and there was nothing but genuine curiosity in his gaze.

She shifted again, unable to stop fidgeting when he watched her like this.

"I'm an executive assistant at a marketing firm."

"And what does that entail?"

Again, so serious. Like he actually cared to hear her answer.

She lifted a shoulder, glancing away. "Nothing all that interesting."

"I doubt that." His eyebrows rose.

She blinked in surprise and looked back at him. A surge of pride made her chin lift just a touch. "Fine. I find it interesting, but it's just not that exciting to hear about."

"Try me."

She looked away again. He was serious. She tried to think of how to sum up her job in a way that wouldn't bore a man to tears. "I basically keep the place running."

He arched his brows again. "That's impressive."

She shrugged. "I think so."

Her bosses...not so much.

"I'm good at what I do," she continued. "I like organization and schedules and spreadsheets." She felt a surge of ridiculous heat in her cheeks.

Seriously, *why* had her body decided that now she was someone who blushed? And only around this man?

It was stupid.

She forced a smirk as she shot him a sidelong glance. "See? Told you it's not exciting."

He shrugged. "A job doesn't have to be exciting to be interesting."

She blinked at him. How did he do that? How did he always have something to say that made her feel better?

"What matters is that you like it," he added.

"I do." Her tone sounded too defensive. She frowned. "I mean, I like what I do. But the people I work for...the place..." She drew in a deep breath, her belly coiling into knots again as she worried over what they'd do if she wasn't in the office first thing tomorrow. "It can be stressful."

He made a sort of humming noise, as if he understood.

A long silence followed, and she was acutely aware of each passing second.

"Seriously, JJ, you don't have to wait with me."

"Two hours is nothing." He shifted in his seat, angling his body to face her. "You know, once I was stuck in an airport in Germany for twenty-four hours."

Her eyes widened, and then she blinked. So many aspects of that statement shocked her. He'd been to Germany? Why on earth would he be stuck in an airport for so long?

But also, she'd come to think of this man as so very quiet. Was he really about to tell her a story?

"You were?"

He nodded. "The first flight was canceled. And at that point, I'd been traveling nonstop for several days, so I was exhausted."

She gaped at him as he settled in, amusement making his eyes gleam again. "So the second flight they put me on..." His wince was comically self-deprecating. "Well, I slept right through the boarding call."

"No!" She surprised herself with the outburst, and

when he chuckled, she found herself smiling as well. "What did you do?"

He shrugged. "What could I do? I waited for the next flight. But then…"

He shot her an arched look, and she just barely smothered an embarrassingly girly giggle. "Oh no…" she murmured.

"Oh yes," he said. "The next flight was on this little prop plane. I took one look at it and turned green."

"Just from looking at it?"

His answer was a chuckle that had her sinking back into the seat, more curious than she cared to admit. "So? Then what happened?"

4

Nearly two hours later, JJ wondered if Dahlia had any idea how cute she looked when she was engrossed in a story.

Probably not.

Actually, she'd probably smack anyone who had the nerve to say so.

Still, she was awfully adorable when she was trying not to laugh. Even cuter when she was pretending like she wasn't engaged in the tale.

And then there were moments like this one, when she seemed to forget her quest to stay aloof and defensive, and he caught a hint of the girl she must have been.

Her eyes flashed with amusement as she took in his latest revelation.

He wished he could pull out a camera and take a picture of her looking like this. Eyes wide, lips parted, a reluctant, hard-to-earn smile softening her model-sharp features.

This was one of very few outright smiles he'd gotten from her as he'd regaled her with stories from his traveling days, and every glimpse of her gorgeous smile had him itching to see more.

The fact that she didn't dole them out easily made them that much more satisfying when she let one slip like she had just now.

"So wait... you actually *ran* with the bulls?" she asked with wide eyes.

He grinned.

Yeah. She was cute as a button, all right.

"Are you saying you haven't?" He pulled a swig of water from the bottle she handed him.

They'd sought out some snacks and drinks a little while ago, more of an excuse to stretch their legs than anything. Then they'd found new seats, as they watched Dahlia's flight get pushed back, and then back again.

She fidgeted in her seat, her gaze torn between him and the screen overhead where the flashing "delayed" sign next to her flight glared down at them.

"I've never been to Spain," she murmured.

"But if you'd gone..."

Her sidelong smirk made him chuckle. "Oh, I'd have run with those bulls."

"I have no doubt."

She tucked her hands in her pockets and glanced at the board again. "Do you think it's gonna be canceled?"

I hope so.

He swallowed the words and shook off the thought. "Maybe. Maybe not."

She sighed.

"There's nothing you can do about it either way."

She frowned. "I know, which makes it all the more frustrating."

He tilted his head to the side, watching her profile as he thought that over.

She must have felt his gaze because she shot him a quick glance, fidgeting again like she did when he was watching her too closely. "What?"

"What, what?" he teased.

She rolled her eyes. "What words of wisdom did you wish to impart, Yoda?"

His head fell back with a laugh that shook his whole frame. He clapped a hand to his chest, glancing over to see her watching him with a funny, if slightly wary little grin.

"Yoda, huh?"

She shrugged. "You're all one-with-nature or whatever. And you have this way of talking that makes everything sound so philosophical."

He kept his head tipped back as he rolled her words over in his mind. Finally he nodded. "I've been called worse."

He caught her smile before she flattened it.

What had caused this woman to be so grudging with her smiles? No one was born defensive, and from what little he knew of her sisters and their family, he suspected it was her upbringing that had her so guarded. And that he could understand.

His relationship with his own family had shaped the man he'd become. And he supposed that was why he felt a certain obligation to this woman. Sure, he liked her company, but he felt sorry for her, that was all.

"So?" she said. "What were you going to say when you were giving me the Yoda look?"

He snickered. "I'd just been thinking that what you find frustrating, I find relaxing."

Her head snapped to the side, her brows furrowed.

"That makes no sense. Are you saying you enjoy it when your plans fall apart?"

He shrugged. "It depends. Getting stuck in southern Spain because of a strike led to one of the best weekends of my life."

"Yeah, well..." She glanced around the small airport with its stuffed deer heads and moose statues. "This isn't exactly Spain, now is it?"

He grinned. "Some might say it's better."

Her scoff made it clear she was not one of those people. "I bet you're one of those guys who hates big cities, right? You probably think I'm nuts for wanting to get back to New York."

He tipped his head from side to side. "They have their advantages. But I prefer wide-open skies."

She gave another disdainful huff, scuffing her boot heel against the carpet at her feet. "That's just a nice way of saying you don't like city life."

He smiled. He wasn't about to argue.

She turned to him with a scowl. "Are you trying to tell me that if you were stuck at JFK and couldn't get back to the ranch, you wouldn't be irritated?"

"I might not be happy being stuck, but if there was nothin' I could do about it, well, then... there's nothin' to do but relax, right?"

Her eyes narrowed in a confused frown like she was trying to decipher some hidden meaning in his words. "Relax?"

"Yes."

She turned to face straight ahead, shaking her head as if she didn't know what to do with him. "How'd you end up traveling so much anyway? Were you in the military or something?"

"Nope."

She glanced over when he didn't offer anything else. He scratched the back of his neck and looked up at the screen, flinching when the flashing "delayed" sign turned red.

Dahlia's head whipped around to follow his line of sight, her shoulders sagging only moments later.

"Canceled?" she whispered.

The sheer horror in her tone had him biting back any teasing, glib remarks. He might not understand why she was so anxious to get back to a job that stressed her out, but it wasn't for him to judge.

She shot out of her seat, and from the set of her chin and the bulldog expression on her face, he felt a stab of pity for whoever would be stuck dealing with her.

He watched her interacting with an airline employee, but it wasn't until he saw her shoulders sag again and her rigid posture slump that he hopped up to join her.

"Is that the only option?" she was asking.

She wasn't being rude, but her disappointment was palpable. Even the airline employee looked sympathetic.

"I'm afraid so. The closest airport we could get you into tonight would be Philadelphia. You'd have to rent a car from there, or…" She glanced down. "Or we could try rerouting you through in the morning, or—"

"No." Dahlia sighed, scrubbing a hand over her eyes. "No, I'll just…" Her voice faltered, and JJ felt his heart falter along with it.

"Come back with me," he murmured.

She shot him a glare.

Granted, it had come out as a command rather than a request. But what other option did she have?

He tugged on her arm, pulling her away from the

counter. "Come back to the ranch. Enjoy some more time with your sisters. They'd all love to have you there."

She let out a sharp exhale, rolling her eyes like he'd just suggested that Aspire was a thriving metropolis and Dr. Dex was secretly a villain.

He ignored that, even though he ached a bit on her behalf.

But it wasn't his right to do that. He could feel sorry for her, but her issues were hers, not his.

"We can try again in a couple days," he coaxed when her silence went too long.

She sighed. "I guess I'll have to."

He picked up her luggage, and he knew she was really down when she made no attempt to argue with him about carrying her own bag.

"I'll have to convince them I can work remotely," she muttered. She seemed to be talking more to herself than to him.

Still, he hated seeing her so down. So, even though he'd never once adopted a Yoda voice before, he gave it a shot now. "Mmm. Convince them, you will."

She stopped short just outside the sliding glass doors to the outside. Flurries came down and caught in her dark hair as she gaped up at him. "Did you… you…" she sputtered. "Did you just…"

He shot her a grin before walking on. He heard her hurrying to catch up behind him and was pleased to see a little smile on her face when she climbed into the passenger side of the truck.

When the heat was on and her luggage stowed, he maneuvered them out of the snow-covered parking lot.

Dahlia was largely silent, her gaze distant and her

brows drawn together. He'd bet his cabin that she was fretting over what work would say.

"Want some music?" he asked.

She shook her head. And then, after a second, she turned to face him. "Thank you."

The words came out so stilted and forced, he had to fight back a laugh.

She cleared her throat. "You didn't have to wait with me, but... but I'm glad you did. I would have been trapped there all night and—"

"Don't mention it." He grinned. "I had fun."

He felt her gawking stare. She was trying to suss out the teasing or the sarcasm in that statement, but she wouldn't find any. Because he did have fun.

Odd as that might be.

Over the next few minutes, the silence was only broken by the occasional sigh from the passenger beside him.

"You all right?" he finally asked.

She sighed louder. "Just thinking of all the meetings I'll have to rearrange. The excuses I'll have to give."

He arched his brows as he glanced over. "You don't control the weather, Dahlia. They've got to understand that."

Her answering look was baleful. "You try telling them."

He chuckled. "Give me your phone and I will. I'm not afraid."

One side of her mouth curved up in a rueful smile. "That's because you haven't met them."

Another silence followed. He ought to just give her space. She'd be back to dealing with family drama soon enough, and it was clear she didn't want to talk about any of it. But even as he told himself it was none of his business, he heard himself say, "Is that all that's bothering you about being stuck here? The work thing?"

She was silent for a moment too long.

He'd like to think she was debating opening up to him —about how hard it was for her to let Rose grow up. How difficult it was to let new people into what had always been their small family.

That was what he'd seen, at least. When everyone else thought she was acting like a grumpy bossy-pants, all he'd seen was how much she was hurting.

In the end, she didn't open up to him. Not surprising. Instead, she mumbled something about a game that he was sure he'd misheard.

He glanced over. "What was that?"

She drew in a deep breath and shook her head. "I'm going to miss a game I wanted to see, that's all. Nash and Emma don't have cable, so…"

His jaw dropped. "What game?"

She glanced over and shook her head. "Forget it. It's not a big deal. What really matters is my job and—"

"Dahlia," he interrupted. "What game?"

She huffed. "The Rangers."

"Hockey?" He couldn't have been more shocked if she'd said she wanted to watch him rope cattle.

She let out a short laugh at his expression. "I know, I know. I don't seem the type. And like I said, it doesn't really matter."

But her voice said otherwise. She sounded outright dejected, and no, it likely wasn't much to do with the game she'd be missing—but missing the game was one thing he could fix.

He caught the exit for Wellspring, a town about a tenth the size of Aspire, with a main thoroughfare that ran a whopping two blocks. But it had a bar. And more importantly, it was a sports bar.

He took the exit without giving it a second thought.

"Where are we going?"

"What time's the game?" he answered.

"Um…" She looked at the dashboard, and then she sighed. "It's about to start."

He grinned over at her. "Then we should make it just in time."

5

D ahlia thought record-scratching silence only happened in movies.

She was wrong.

JJ held the bar's front door open for her—because of course he did—and when she stepped through, the entire place went silent. The only sound was a clink of glasses and the soft lilt of a country song coming from a radio in the back.

Blinking as her eyes adjusted to the dim light, she found herself center stage as the patrons at the bar and tables stared her down.

She stared right back.

But then JJ followed her in, and the change in the crowd was instant.

"Hey, man," one of the guys at a crowded table shouted.

The bartender nodded at him in acknowledgment.

"Hi, JJ!" The girl waiting tables beamed at him, while a few of the customers sitting at the bar called out greetings.

JJ nodded in return, and when his large hand came to her lower back, Dahlia gave an embarrassing start.

She wasn't used to people touching her, that was all. Especially not men. Definitely not big, burly mountain men like JJ.

He steered her toward a table by the far wall. "Hey, Mack, can you turn this TV to the Rangers game?"

The bartender nodded. "Sure thing, JJ."

Dahlia couldn't even begin to hide her excitement as she gazed up at the screen. The table was sticky, the laughter around her too loud, and the TV straight out of the eighties.

And. This. Was. Heaven.

Or close to it, at least.

"Yes!" She clapped her hands. "Good play. Good play." She watched her team in their red, white, and blue uniforms fly across the ice, putting pressure on the Pittsburgh Penguins. She was confident of a win, although the Penguins had a way of pulling it out of the hat in the third period. She wouldn't be able to relax until the Rangers were up by at least two or three goals.

Her eyes tracked the puck, her body moving with the players. She was vaguely aware of JJ studying her, but she didn't even care. She remembered the first time her ex, Brady, realized she was actually into sports. He'd given her this same look, like he was only just seeing her for the first time.

That was how JJ was watching her now... and maybe there was some truth to it.

Right here and right now, she felt like herself for the first time in a long while.

She hadn't been in Montana more than a few days on this trip—she couldn't get more time off work—but that house where she wasn't wanted, trying to be the sister Rose needed and failing at every turn...

Being in this sports bar was a sweet relief, the sounds from the TV and the background noise around her a strange sort of balm for her tension. It'd always been this way. Well, ever since she'd discovered her love of sports in junior high.

"How'd you get into hockey?" JJ asked when a commercial came on and she sank back into her seat, taking a sip of the beer JJ had bought for her.

"A friend of mine got me into it a long time ago," she said.

He arched a brow. "A male friend?"

She rolled her eyes, which inexplicably made him grin. "No, not a male friend. Her name was Becky, and she was my BFF in junior high."

He sat and waited. There was something so refreshing about that.

She now knew that he could speak—heck, he could tell stories better than anyone she'd ever met. But he didn't feel the need to fill every silence, and that eased her tension almost as much as the soothing background noise of the sports announcers.

"I used to spend whatever time I could at Becky's." She ran her thumb down the side of her beer bottle, marking a trail through the condensation. "I liked hanging out with her family."

Because it meant I didn't have to hang out with mine.

She took a long swig of her drink. "They were big on sports, and they taught me a ton about hockey, football, baseball, you name it."

"So you like 'em all?"

She shook her head. "I don't follow them all fanatically.

Just hockey and football. But…" *Why are you still talking? Stop talking. Watch the game!*

Maybe it was the beer, or his easy smile, but the words kept coming.

"But I love watching pretty much any sport live. I go see the Yankees or the Mets every chance I get—"

"Both?" His brows flew up.

She laughed. "Like I said, I'm not fanatical about all sports, and baseball I just watch for fun."

And for one silly moment she found herself wanting to tell him all she loved about watching a Yankees game in the summer with a hot dog in one hand and a roaring, wild crowd surrounding her. She had this urge to explain to him so he'd understand the joy that came with losing yourself in the crowd's enthusiasm. Or even the rush that came with following your team on TV and knowing all the ins and outs that made them *yours*.

She looked back at the screen, getting caught up in a play. "What are you doing?" She spoke to the TV. "Pass it! Look left!" She was pointing in the air, yelling at players who couldn't even hear her. "The other left!" She flicked her hand in the air and fell back into her chair, only then becoming aware of JJ's chuckle. She glanced at him sideways and muttered, "Shut up."

"Not saying a word." He raised both his hands, and she couldn't resist the look on his face.

He was way too cute for his own good.

Cute and handsome. It was a slightly terrifying combination. At least the way her insides were jittering warned her that it was.

JJ was too easy on the eyes… and too easy to talk to. Dangerously so.

She forced her gaze back to the screen, relieved that the

Rangers had gotten possession back after stupidly losing it and were now careening toward the goal.

"Go, go, go. Shoot it!" The puck flew into the goal, and she raised her hands with a whoop! "That's my boys!"

JJ was laughing again. She ignored his grin and finished her bottle of beer in two large gulps before slapping it down on the table.

"I'll go get us another," he said, already scooting his chair back.

"Oh no," she intervened. "This one's on me. You got the last one."

His jaw moved, and she could practically feel him wanting to argue. He was old-fashioned like that, this much was clear. She set her hands on the table and leaned over with a mock glare. "I pay my own way, Yoda. That's just the way it is."

He gave a huff of laughter as he held his palms up in surrender once again. "Fair enough."

She grinned in triumph before heading to the bar. "Two more, please." She held up two fingers to the bartender.

He grinned at her and turned for the fridge behind him.

Dahlia was still wearing a goofy smile. She spotted it with some surprise when she glanced in the mirror over the bar. She tipped her chin down, shaking her head with a rueful snicker.

Man, she'd needed this. A night of hockey and easy company and—

"Hey there, beautiful." A man with a nasally pitch was standing too close to her. He smelled like tobacco and whiskey, and the first thing Dahlia noticed was the fact that his fingernails needed a trim. His hands were big and broad. They were a working man's hands.

She moved back, not bothering to look up and check out his face. She didn't want to encourage him.

But the dope didn't seem to need encouragement. He just moved with her like they were doing some sort of bar room dance.

"What brings a pretty girl like you here?"

She glanced up, her smile too tight to be polite. If he could read facial expressions, he'd immediately know she wasn't interested, but the man seemed oblivious.

He wasn't unattractive, with a dusting of dark stubble and a square-cut chin, but his eyes were vacant, his smile too... well, dopey. Not clueless-dopey, drunk-dopey.

When he leaned in closer, the stench of his breath only confirmed it. "You want to join me for a drink?"

"No." She kept it simple, not bothering with a "thank you" that he wouldn't even appreciate.

She'd endured more than enough men like this one to know better. Any politeness would only be construed as encouragement.

The stranger ignored her "no" and threw an arm around her shoulders as he called to the bartender, "Mack, get this beautiful lady a drink on me."

She shrugged him off, spinning around to face him. "I said no." She spit the words this time, since he obviously needed a stronger message.

It wasn't fear that had her pulse racing but anger. She couldn't stand men who didn't listen, who assumed they could read a woman's mind.

"Now, now," he said in a drunken drawl. He leaned in close and grabbed her arms. "No need to be rude."

"Let me go." She started to shake him off, but before she could, he stumbled away from her.

No, wait...

She blinked in surprise. He was *thrown* away from her.

He bumped into the bar and made the stool behind him squeak against the floorboards as it slid under his weight. He gaped up at JJ, who towered over him with a look Dahlia had never seen before.

It was primal.

It was… It was…

Much to her annoyance, Dahlia's thoughts derailed.

"Are you kidding me, Bobby?" JJ's tone was glacial, yet his glare could melt titanium.

Dahlia's mouth went dry as she stared at him, gawking just as much as Bobby.

"This lady said no." JJ's tone was unyielding, and Dahlia struggled to swallow.

She should be annoyed. She should intervene. This wasn't his fight! He had no right to go all Neanderthal on her like this. She wasn't his to protect.

But while her mind rattled off this information, her body went into full-blown revolt.

Something warm and sweet slid through her veins, spreading further with each thud of her heart.

"Come on, man," Bobby whined. "I'm just having fun. She's into it, right?"

Dahlia pulled herself together long enough to give the man a withering glare. "No. She's not."

He gave her a sloppy smile, then reached for her again. JJ grabbed his collar, shoving him back against the bar. "You're drunk, Bobby. Now, I don't want to hurt you, but I will."

JJ stayed put, his pointed look sending a message that even the most inebriated person could figure out, before letting go of Bobby's collar.

The drunken fool stumbled away. "All right, fine. Geez,

JJ," he muttered with a childish pout as he turned away to head back to his friends. "Just having a little fun, is all."

"Well, go have it somewhere else," JJ growled. "And keep your hands to yourself from now on, you hear?"

Gone was the carefree mountain man. He was miles away from the Yoda she'd accused him of being. Right now he was all emotion, and she could have sworn she felt it coming off him in waves as he turned to face her.

Anger, yes, but it was on her behalf, and it was... more. There was a possessive heat in his eyes that did nothing to help her body's absurdly primitive response. The fire in his gaze and the way it raked over her face, lingering on her lips, colliding with her eyes...

She couldn't swallow.

She could barely even breathe!

His brows drew down, and the heat melted into something nearly as fatal. Concern. Protectiveness. Affection.

"Are you all right?" His voice was soft and husky.

She had to draw in a deep, long inhale, and even then her pulse still roared out of control.

"I'm fine," she breathed. "Totally fine."

His lips quirked a bit. "Totally fine, huh?"

She nodded, her tongue coming out to wet her lips. This was just ridiculous. She was not some spineless nitwit who went all weak at the knees when a guy turned caveman over her.

Nope. No, sir. Not her.

She swallowed hard.

Now if someone would just tell her knees that...

The bartender set the two beers down with a clink. "On the house," he grumbled. When Dahlia gave him a startled look, he winced. "Sorry about that."

She shook her head. "Totally fine."

She grabbed her beer and turned to her table, ignoring JJ's teasing echo behind her. "Totally."

She sank into her seat and tried to focus on the TV. The hockey game was still in full swing, and she'd usually be fully absorbed, her eyes chasing that torpedo puck as it shot across the ice. But after a second of unbearable silence, she couldn't take JJ's watchful stare a second longer. She had the most unnerving sensation that he was seeing too much—that he was seeing straight through her —so she turned and caught his stare.

"I don't need you to defend my honor, you know." She was trying her best to sound strong despite the fact that her insides were butter in a frying pan. "I can fight my own battles."

He studied her for a long beat, then leaned forward until he was resting on his elbows, which put him far too close. "I wasn't defending you." He shook his head, but then gave away his lie with a lopsided smile that made her belly do a backflip. "I was actually doing it for Bobby's sake. I knew if he didn't back off, you'd scratch his eyes out, so you know... I was really saving *him*."

"Oh really?"

"Uh-huh. For sure."

She tried to keep a straight face.

Oh, did she try.

But his bobbing head, his barely contained grin as he peeled at the label on his beer bottle... she lost it.

She burst out in a laugh so loud and carefree it shocked not only him but herself as well. Clapping a hand over her mouth, she met his smiling gaze, trying to rein in the giggles tickling her belly. It shook and fought her until she managed to clear her throat and settle on a controlled smile.

With a demure eyebrow raise, she turned her attention back to the screen but couldn't help muttering, "You're ridiculous."

His voice held a world of amusement. "Whatever you say, ma'am."

6

JJ was officially having too much fun.

He dipped his head to hide a smile when Dahlia shot up out of her seat to celebrate a score.

"That's my guy," she shouted, her voice louder than he'd ever heard it, and without a hint of that closed-off armor she hid behind.

She turned to him with a brilliant grin, and just like that, his blood started to burn.

She was attractive all the time—there was no denying that. But here, tonight, watching her watch the game... the transformation right in front of his eyes was irresistible.

Without that scowl and the standard suspicious glare that always accompanied it, she seemed years younger— no, scratch that. She seemed her age, which was probably around the same as his. Twenty-eight. But she carried herself like she was so much older most of the time.

Her smile faded a bit when she sank back into her seat. "What?" she asked. "What are you looking at me like that for?"

Because you're beautiful.

Because I can't tear my eyes off you.

"You look good without the weight of the world on your shoulders." He settled for that. It was the truth, after all.

No need to make things stilted between them when she had one foot out the door, right?

But his comment earned him a wary side-eye, like she wasn't sure how to take that compliment.

And it *was* a compliment.

"I'm not picking on you," he added as he reached for a fry from the basket they'd ordered to tide them over. "Just a fact. Most of the time you seem to be carrying all kinds of responsibilities."

"Yeah, well..." She reached for a fry and popped it in her mouth as well. "I told you, my job is multifaceted."

"Uh-huh." He wasn't talking about her job, and he suspected she knew it.

A big part of him wanted to ask her about her relationship with Rose, and that sister of theirs who'd yet to show. Daisy, that was her name. Not to mention how she felt about discovering she had all these half sisters, or the fact that their father had left them his sole property...

But her gaze was already back on the TV, and he wasn't in a hurry to see her return to Miss Serious mode.

"Third period is almost over," she said, not glancing his way. "We're totally gonna win this one."

He smiled. Did she honestly think he cared about the game? That was cute. He wasn't sure she even realized that while she'd been so entertained by the hockey, he'd been more entertained by her.

But he wasn't thrilled to learn the game was about to end.

He was having more fun than he'd had in…

Ah heck, he didn't know how long it'd been since he'd gone out on the town with a woman whose company he so thoroughly enjoyed.

He wasn't nearly the loner mountain man everyone made him out to be. Sure, he preferred his own company, and the peace and quiet of his cabin was almost always preferable to small talk and meaningless chatter.

But that didn't mean he didn't occasionally crave fun. He enjoyed spending time with people he truly respected, people who didn't speak just to hear themselves talk, and people who gave it to you straight so you weren't forever guessing at their real thoughts and emotions.

People like Dahlia.

He finished the last sip of his beer and went back to watching her.

He knew the game was over when she slumped back in her seat with a satisfied sigh. Her lips toyed with a smile that she flashed him for a moment before looking around the bar with an antsy twitch.

That woman did not know the beauty of being still, but in fairness to her, she was hyped up on beer, fatty foods, and a triumphant win for her team.

He wasn't ready to take her home, to squash that joy she couldn't help but exude.

So he drew it out the only way he could think of. "You wanna play some pool?"

She glanced over in surprise, one brow arching. "Depends. How do you feel about being beaten by a girl?"

He laughed. "I think I'd be just fine with that."

Her smile made his insides go upside down, and when they fell back into place, it was like everything had resettled.

It wasn't a bad feeling, just... dangerous.

He glanced away. "I'll pay the food tab and meet you back there."

She didn't argue about him paying this time, and that was a relief. He respected women's rights just as much as anyone, but he still liked to treat a beautiful lady when he could.

He found he was grinning to himself as he leaned against the bar, waiting to get Mack's attention.

Bobby had long since left, but that had felt sorta good too. He wasn't a violent guy, not by any means, but there was something satisfying about being able to protect Dahlia.

Maybe it was the fact that she was so very capable and terrified so many people that to be her protector meant so much more.

Kinda like her smiles.

He shook his head and set down some cash when Mack handed him the bill.

It was about time he stopped trying to figure out why he enjoyed her company so much and just went with it. She wouldn't be here for long, so there was no danger.

She'd be gone back to New York in the next day or so, and he'd go back to his loner ways. But until then...

He spotted her through the back room's open doorway, chalking her cue stick and eyeing the pool table like a warrior before battle. Something inside him melted at the sight.

Until she left, he'd be her friend, that was all. She might not want to admit it, but she needed a friend here in Aspire. She needed someone who didn't judge and who didn't push. Someone with whom she could play pool and watch the game.

She straightened, her hips moving and her shoulders shimmying as the pop song playing got to the catchy chorus.

He chuckled, letting himself have one more moment to watch her before he went in there and joined her. She'd likely kill him if she knew he'd seen her dancing.

A second later, he walked toward her, acting like he hadn't witnessed a thing. "All right, Ms. O'Sullivan. Let's see if you can put your money where your mouth is."

Her grin was everything.

For a second he forgot to breathe. He was her friend, he had to remind himself. Just her friend.

"You're on. I'll even let you have first break."

He wiggled his eyebrows at her, grabbing a pool cue and lining up that little white ball.

About half an hour later, JJ was out ten dollars and even more impressed by this stunning New Yorker than he thought possible. She'd beaten him three games to none, and he had a feeling she probably could have done that with her eyes closed.

His stomach grumbled as he watched her return their cues with a triumphant grin, and as much as he knew he probably shouldn't, he found another way to extend their time together. "What do you say we grab a proper bite to eat?"

She nodded. "I'm starving."

There were no decent restaurants in this blink-and-you'd-miss-it town, so he drove them into Aspire. Mama's Kitchen was still open, but there was a good chance everyone in town would hear of their having dinner together there, and he had a hunch Dahlia wouldn't relish being the subject of small-town gossip.

"The cafe on the corner has decent pizza," he offered.

She shot him a smirk. "He says to the New Yorker."

He chuckled. "Don't tell me you're picky about your pizza."

"Exceptionally," she said with no hint of remorse.

"How about burritos?"

She blinked over at him. "You people have a Mexican restaurant in this town?"

He fought a smile at her shocked expression. "First of all, no one likes to be referred to as 'you people.'"

She rolled her eyes, but she was smiling. "Yeah, okay, fine."

"And yes. There's a couple in town who make a mean homemade salsa… if you're up for it."

She met his gaze and cocked a brow. "Oh, I'm up for it."

He turned to face the street with a grin. How'd he just known that she wouldn't be able to turn down a challenge?

If a man did want to date her, he'd have a battle on his hands the whole time. There'd be nothing easy about dating Ms. Dahlia O'Sullivan.

But, then again, a man would know precisely where he stood with her. There'd be no guessing her feelings or tiptoeing around any issues, but…

His insides huffed with exasperation as he pulled his truck up along the curb to park.

Why are you even considering what it would be like to date this woman?

Good grief. It was a good thing she wasn't staying here long. He might just forget that he'd given up on the idea of a relationship after his failure of a marriage.

She turned to him with one hand on the door, her

brows drawn together in question. "Where'd you go? I feel like I lost you there for a minute."

He shook his head. "Just hungry, that's all."

She nodded and pushed open her door, leaping down to the sidewalk. He sighed as he followed suit. Of course she wouldn't wait for him to help her. But he did beat her to the door of the tiny hole-in-the-wall burrito shop, and he held it open for her with a triumphant grin.

"After you, my lady," he said.

"Don't push it," she muttered.

He was still chuckling as he joined her at the counter.

They ate in silence for a while, both of them hungry after nothing but snacks all day. When she finished, she set down her napkin with a satisfied sigh. "I have to be honest and admit that wasn't all bad, but you can't beat a slice of Uncle Joey's pepperoni."

"Uncle Joey's, huh?" JJ wiped his mouth with his paper napkin.

"It's the best." She nodded. "You'll have to come—" Her words cut off as if she suddenly realized what she was going to say.

JJ guessed it was an invite to the city, and he couldn't deny the little spark of hope that flared inside him.

His eyebrows wrinkled, silently asking for more, but she just linked her fingers together and looked out the window with a pensive frown. Or maybe it was plain ol' resignation. "I guess we ought to get back to the ranch. I can't put it off much longer."

He stilled, hating the fact that her casual comment had the ability to hit him in the chest like a blow. "You really hate the ranch that much?"

To his surprise, she didn't shoot back right away with

some defensive remark. That was what she'd have done if she were surrounded by her sisters or even with Nash and Kit. But here, with him, after their day together, she gave him a more thoughtful response. "It's not like I have anything against the ranch itself. I'm not a rural person—I don't know the first thing about it, honestly. But I can see how people might find it…"

She paused so long he found himself holding his breath.

"Calming." The word came out in a grudging tone that made him smile.

"Oh no, not *calming*," he teased.

She rolled her eyes, and a smile tugged at her lips at his teasing. "No, I mean… it's peaceful and pretty. I get that."

She came to stand, and he fell into step beside her as they headed out the door, calling their thanks to the owner.

"But?" he prompted.

"But it's not for me." Her tone said that was all she had to say on the matter.

He nodded, beating her to her side of the truck to open the door for her. He considered it a win when she didn't so much as roll her eyes at his act of chivalry.

When he started the truck for the drive back, he was certain that was all she'd say on the topic, and that was fine. He wouldn't push her. But then, when the truck lights dimmed and they were driving the long winding road to the ranch in the dark, she spoke up. "I just wish I didn't have to go back there."

His heart gave a sharp tug. He knew what most would say—what he should say. *But they're your family.*

He didn't say it. Because what kind of hypocrite would that make him?

"I sound like a jerk, don't I?" she asked when he was quiet for too long.

"No," he said quickly. "Not at all. Family can be... complicated."

She gave a little huff of rueful laughter that made him smile as well. "That's one way of putting it."

There were so many things he wished he could say. Even more questions he wanted to ask. But it wasn't his place. They might have a friendship starting here, but that was all. And it was temporary, to boot.

Finally, he sifted through the words spinning in his head and broke the comfortable silence. "I don't know you well, Dahlia, but I get the very strong impression that you're not the type of woman to run from her problems."

She shifted slightly and he felt her gaze on him. She didn't say anything, and that was good. That meant she was listening.

"Maybe you being stuck here a little longer..." He took a deep breath. He didn't know how much she believed in God or fate, but he wanted to make her see that maybe it was okay not to be in control all the time. That maybe there were other plans in play...

"You think it's a good thing I'm going back," she said. It wasn't a question.

He glanced over. "It seemed like maybe you hadn't gotten the answers you needed. Like maybe... maybe there's more that has to be said."

She went quiet again, and for a second, he waited for her to scoff or yell or tell him to mind his own business. But instead, she sank against the passenger door, and her breath fogged up the window as she stared out.

"Maybe you're right," she whispered.

He glanced over in shock. Maybe he was right?

A smile tugged at his lips, and a surge of happiness warmed him all the way through.

"Maybe you're right."

Something told him that when it came to Dahlia, those words were not easy to come by.

7

The next day, Dahlia had a plan.

As she stood and stretched in her half sister April's bedroom, her head felt clearer than it had in days.

Thanks to JJ.

She pursed her lips as she stared out the upper-floor window as if JJ might just happen to be strolling the grounds below.

He wasn't. Of course not. He was probably out on the range, or fixing a fence on some distant part of this vast stretch of land, or...

Or... who cared? What did it matter what he was off doing? He wasn't here, and that was for the best. Because today she was going to settle some family business.

She turned away from the window and went back to her open laptop on the pink desk. She'd stayed in April's old bedroom long enough that she was starting to grow immune to the pinks and purples that made up their youngest sister's childhood room. Even the bunk beds didn't bother her anymore. Though when she'd first shown up, they'd brought up more questions than she could handle.

About their father. About his life after he'd walked away from Dahlia and her family.

Questions that no one but the owner of this room could answer, but since April was stubbornly ignoring Emma's every attempt to get in contact, Dahlia wasn't holding her breath for answers any time soon.

No one had any success getting ahold of Sierra, the eldest of this motley sister crew, either. The woman was apparently a nomad. Maybe she was some sort of hippie who didn't believe in the Internet or something.

Whatever the case, Dahlia was officially done waiting for them. They'd all been in purgatory long enough with this inheritance, and it was time someone made some decisions.

And like always, Dahlia would have to be the one to make the hard choices and take the reins.

She shook off a resentment she'd grown to despise.

"You look good without the weight of the world on your shoulders."

Her frown deepened into a scowl at the memory of JJ's words. She'd felt good last night. But he'd been right when he'd said that she shouldn't leave here without some sort of resolution.

Which was why she'd texted Emma, Rose, and Lizzy after she'd gotten settled back in to request a meeting this afternoon after Emma got home from work.

She could hear their voices coming from downstairs. The laughter and the easy conversation—which would come to an abrupt halt the moment she joined their ranks.

She tapped a few keys to bring her laptop back to life

so she could send her bosses a response to their last email but…ugh.

For the third time that day, the Wi-Fi connection decided to act up. She dropped her chin to her chest with a sharp exhale. This pink bedroom was not conducive to work. The desk was too small, and it was miles away from the modem, probably because no one ever thought the upstairs space would be used for working.

She needed to find a spot that had a better connection, but she also needed peace and quiet in order to concentrate. It wasn't like she could work for more than ten minutes without interruption at the dining room table. She'd just have to find an office downstairs. Surely there was one. The house seemed to have rooms to spare.

With a huff, she crossed her arms and glared at her computer after one more failed attempt to connect to the Internet.

Fine. She'd get back to work later when this meeting was over. And maybe by then the Wi-Fi would be working or she would have tracked down that blasted modem!

She headed downstairs to find her sisters all huddled together in the kitchen. Emma was rubbing at her temples as Rose handed her a mug of tea.

"Sounds like a tough day," Rose murmured with a sympathetic wince.

"I hope you gave that mother a piece of your mind." Lizzy looked all worked up on Emma's behalf.

When Dahlia walked in, their conversation came to an abrupt halt, just like Dahlia knew it would. And aside from Rose's small smile, she found herself facing a wall of wary gazes.

She just barely held back a sigh.

"What's this about?" Lizzy asked with narrowed eyes. "Why do we need a meeting?"

Dahlia took a seat at the table and waited for the others to do the same. "Because I think it's high time we make some decisions about how we're going to move forward with the inheritance."

All three pairs of eyes widened in surprise, and silent conversations began between them. Little looks that Dahlia couldn't miss. She wasn't blind.

And once more I'm the big bad wolf coming in to destroy everything.

She shook off the thought. There'd be time to pout and rail against the injustice of it all later. For now, she needed to end this drama before it could drag out any longer.

"B-but not all the sisters have seen it yet," Emma started.

"And who knows if they ever will?" Dahlia shot back. "Look, I don't know about you, but I don't think it's right that we all have to linger in limbo. It's time to start making decisions."

Lizzy's scowl was one of outright mutiny. "And I suppose you've already made yours."

Dahlia lifted a shoulder. "It's obvious, isn't it? We have to sell the ranch so we can all move forward independently. It's the only fair thing to do."

Emma was clearly horrified, Lizzy indignant, and Rose, of course, didn't say anything.

Not one of their responses was a surprise, but it still left Dahlia feeling exhausted. She didn't want to have this battle any more than they did. But she wasn't delusional. There was no ending for this family in which they all gathered around, baking cookies and singing "Kumbaya."

They weren't really sisters. They weren't one big happy family, and they never would be.

"But this is my home." Emma's voice was soft and strained, a touch of pleading coating each word. "And it has to be a unanimous decision, remember? I don't want to sell."

Dahlia's jaw set. Oh yes, the unanimous factor. The thought of it made her want to punch a wall. Or better yet, a picture of their dearly departed, useless, no-good father.

"It was completely unfair of Frank to put that in the will." Dahlia tried to keep her voice calm, but some of the anger she was feeling toward their father seeped through. "He was a failure as a father when he was alive, and then... what? He thought he could somehow control us from the grave? I don't think so."

"You don't know what he was thinking any more than we do," Lizzy snapped. "Don't pretend like you knew him."

"I'm glad I never did!" Dahlia retorted, a burning sensation making her chest feel raw. "Look, this isn't about Frank O'Sullivan. It's about us."

"Exactly," Lizzy shot back. "*All* of us. Not just you."

"We can't even get in touch with everyone," Dahlia tried to reason with them. "Who knows if we ever will. I, for one, don't want to be tied to this place for the rest of my life."

Rose flinched at the raised voices, but Dahlia's heart was pounding faster and faster with each new argument.

Lizzy shook her head. "The agreement was that we wouldn't make any decision until every sister has seen the place."

"That wasn't in the will! It was a ridiculous rule that Emma implemented," Dahlia argued.

All three of them winced at that, and Dahlia felt a sneer creeping over her face. Oh yes, once again she was the wicked witch picking on innocent, sweet little Emma.

It must be nice to be so perfect all the time.

Dahlia tried to lower her voice and be kind. "We can't even find two of the sisters," she reminded them. "What if we never do?"

Emma just shrugged, her big blue eyes wide and helpless. "Then we just don't sell."

"Which works out great for *you*, doesn't it?" Dahlia pointed around the table. "If we never find Sierra and April, then you just win by default, right? How convenient."

Lizzy leaned forward, her eyes sparking with anger. "Watch it. There's no need to be so mean."

Emma was blinking back tears, and Rose did that wilting thing she'd always done as a child when Dahlia and Daisy fought. Like she could disappear in plain sight.

Dahlia took a deep breath and focused on Lizzy, the only one who wouldn't cry if her tone was a little too harsh. "I don't recall ever agreeing to every sister seeing this place before we made a decision."

Lizzy's eyes narrowed as she crossed her arms over her chest. "You could have made the rules, Dahlia, if you'd bothered to show up here when the lawyer called to let us know Frank had left us the property. But you didn't show. Emma did."

Dahlia was rendered temporarily speechless as emotions clouded her mind. Was Lizzy actually trying to say that she'd been irresponsible? That Dahlia was somehow to blame for not taking charge from the start?

Something bitter and ugly slithered through her veins. What did any of these women know about being responsible? What had any of them done to think they ought to be in charge?

"Not all of us have jobs we can just walk away from for a summer." It was an effort to keep her voice even, and she couldn't quite manage it. Her fuming emotions made the words tremble out of her mouth.

Lizzy waved a dismissive hand, like her accusations weren't shredding Dahlia to the bone. "Fine, whatever. But since Emma *was* the one who stepped up, she's got that right to make the rules about how this plays out."

Emma was just sitting there, quiet as a church mouse with those big pleading eyes.

Dahlia's stomach churned at the sight. Only someone who'd been coddled and protected their whole life wore that look. It was the look of a victim. A helpless child.

Dahlia turned on the sweet saint of a sister with a disdainful glare. "Do you always let Lizzy fight your battles for you?"

Emma's lips parted on a gasp. "I don't... I don't want to have a fight at all."

Useless. Dahlia turned back to Lizzy, but it was Rose who spoke next.

"Dahlia, don't you think it's the right thing to do?" Her voice was a quiet squeak. "I mean, he was our dad. All of ours. We... I think we owe it to him to at least see this place like he wanted."

"We don't owe him *anything*!" Dahlia couldn't control her tone a second longer. She wanted to, but... seriously? Was she the only one who saw Frank for what he was? "Rose, that man doesn't deserve to have any say over where we live or how we earn money. That man didn't care about us when he was alive, so why should we care about him when he's dead?"

"Then maybe he doesn't deserve it," Rose said, her gaze meeting Dahlia's straight on—a dramatic feat given their history. "But maybe we do. Not everyone's like you. We can't just forget he ever existed."

Dahlia swallowed down a wave of hurt she didn't want to address. Was that really how Rose saw her? As someone with no emotions who could just forget that her father abandoned her with a mother who wasn't fit to raise them?

Dahlia gritted her teeth and looked away from Rose before her little sister could see how much those words impacted her.

"What did he ever give us other than his DNA?" she finally spit out.

"Well… he left us this place," Emma retorted softly.

"So he wouldn't have to deal with it." Dahlia threw up her hands. "Or maybe he was trying to make amends so he'd get into heaven. Who knows why he left it to us? That's not the point."

"Then what *is* the point?" Lizzy snapped.

They were all distracted as Nash wandered in, his towering presence making the room feel smaller. He tried to act like he was just heading in to get a glass of water, but the concern on his face and the way he was eyeing Dahlia with that suspicious look made his real motives abundantly clear.

She cleared her throat and kept going, refusing to be put off by the overly protective cowboy. "The point is I refuse to be forced into a family and a home that I want no part of."

Nash gave Dahlia a sharp glare as her sisters fell quiet. As always, she was cast as the villain.

Frustration made the back of her eyes sting with

unshed tears. Why couldn't she ever word things in a way that made people understand? Her insides started to tremble as she clung to her control.

Emma licked her lips, obviously fighting tears. "If we can somehow figure out a way to stay... I'd really like that." She looked up at Nash, who was standing right behind her, lightly squeezing her shoulder. "Can we afford to buy everybody out?"

He winced. "Not without my dad's help, and I doubt he'd agree unless he could attach the Donahue name to this place."

Emma slumped.

Crossing her arms, Dahlia glanced up at Nash. "What's the ranch's financial situation, anyway? Since I've arrived, you two have been very vague about what the profits and losses look like. I want to go over the figures."

Nash shot her a skeptical frown.

What, did he think the financial statements would be too much for her? She clenched her jaw and gritted out, "I'm good with numbers."

He frowned. "I thought you worked for a marketing firm."

"I'm an executive assistant, and I could run circles around our finance department." If only they'd ever give her the chance to. "I can handle looking at the ranch's books."

"She *is* good with numbers," Rose offered quietly.

Dahlia's nostrils flared. She didn't know whether she was grateful for Rose's support or angry that she required it.

"It's just..." He started spinning his hat in his hands. "It's all ranch related. I didn't think you knew about that stuff."

"I'm sure I can learn. All I really want to know is what the turnover is each year and how sustainable this place is."

"We do okay."

She huffed in annoyance. Another vague answer. "Is there room to expand, grow, build profit?"

He nodded but seemed hesitant.

Dahlia sighed. His lack of confidence in his answers was far from inspiring. "As part owner in this ranch, I reserve the right to look over the books myself. But I still think selling is the best answer."

"Only to you," Lizzy snapped. "You're not the only member of this family, and you're not the boss of us! You can't just come in here demanding the result you want."

Dahlia hated how her voice shook. She hated it even more that it was the urge to cry and not a surge of anger that had her trembling. "I came in here trying to start a discussion so we could find a solution and wrap this thing up."

"Which we can't do until we contact every sister! So stop trying to control everything, you big dragon!" Lizzy huffed and slumped back in her seat.

Dahlia glared at her. Oh, she wanted to see fire? Dahlia could burn the little fashion princess to a freakin' crisp!

Rose's hand shot out from under the table, lightly resting on Dahlia's wrist, as if silently telling her to be calm and not embarrass her.

Clenching her jaw, Dahlia jerked away from the table and headed for the door.

"Where are you going?" Emma asked.

Dahlia was facing away so no one saw her eye roll at the kind concern in Emma's tone. As if she was actually worried about Dahlia. *Please.*

"I need some air," she muttered over her shoulder. Reaching for the coatrack, she pulled the first winter jacket she could find off the peg and stuck her feet in some too-big muck boots that were sitting by the door. "After I've reviewed the numbers, we'll talk again."

She heard Lizzy start to sputter something, but Dahlia was done. She needed to clear her head. Her throat was too tight, and the sinking sun with its burnt orange glow seemed to echo how she felt.

Like she was fading. Like she was misplaced.

Like if she didn't get out of this house and this town, she'd lose it completely.

8

Z ion was the first to spot Dahlia.

JJ looked down at his horse, who'd come to a halt. "What's the holdup, mister?"

But then he lifted his head to follow Zion's gaze, and he saw her.

Dahlia.

Her dark hair gave her away, even though she looked like a big cream puff in a big ol' shapeless jacket. She wasn't walking with her usual purposeful strides but rather stomping through the snow in men's boots.

He nudged Zion forward, the snow giving way beneath his hooves with a satisfying crunch as he ambled toward her. She didn't seem to notice him coming, so JJ had plenty of time to watch her as she swiped at her face with impatient movements.

Was she…

Was she *crying*?

His heart took a tumble, and he urged Zion into a canter. She stopped walking and blinked up at him when he slowed to a stop beside her.

Her eyes were a little red around the edges, though her cheeks were dry. He kept his voice as gentle as he could. "Howdy."

She flinched, shying away from the large beast who was doing his best to sniff her hair.

"Stop now, Zion. Come on, boy." He dismounted and walked around, gently pushing the horse's nose away. Though he couldn't blame Zion for being curious. "You okay?"

"I'm fine." Her voice and face said otherwise, and he waited quietly for her to elaborate. After a few moments, she crossed her arms and frowned. "Stop staring at me."

He shrugged. "You're pretty. It's hard not to."

Maybe he shouldn't have said it, but it felt right. This woman was beautiful; there were no two ways about it. And right about now, he suspected she could do with a little kindness.

She narrowed her eyes. "Is that a line?"

He grinned. So defensive. "Nope. Just a fact."

Her brows came down with confusion, and she opened her mouth like she wanted to say something sharp and witty.

But then her lips twitched like she wanted to smile. She clamped down on her bottom lip with her teeth instead.

He idly patted Zion's neck as he studied her. He'd rarely seen her outside the house during her visits. Not surprising since it was bitterly cold this winter. Whatever had her coming out here must have really rattled her.

It was none of his business. He knew that. And yet he couldn't combat that surge of protectiveness—the same one that had swept over him at the bar when Bobby had hit on her. He had an urge to fight her battles again... but it would help if he knew what they were.

"You look like you're having a bad day." He kept his tone mild, almost as if he wasn't interested, yet his ears were on fire for the truth.

She gave a snort of rueful amusement. "Is it that obvious?"

He regarded her with a grin. "You still look pretty, though."

She rolled her eyes, but he could have sworn her cheeks were a little pinker than they had been before.

But then she started to walk away.

He just barely held back a sigh. He'd love nothing more than to fight her battles and slay her dragons, but right about now, he'd settle for her telling him what was wrong.

That alone would be a triumph with this closed-off lady. He took Zion's reins as he followed her, easing into a slow amble to give her some distance.

"Why are you following me?" she asked a minute later.

"You're heading toward the stables," he said. "I'm not following, you're just leading the way."

A puff of steam rose in front of her as she let out a short laugh. Not exactly a guffaw at his teasing, but he'd take it.

She glanced over her shoulder. "I'm not in the mood for company."

"Fair enough," he said easily. "Then I guess Zion and I will just have to keep each other company back here. Isn't that right, boy?"

Zion whinnied in response.

They trudged forward through the snow some more.

"Is that right, Zion?" JJ said softly, his gaze on Dahlia as he spoke loudly enough for her to hear. "You don't say. You had a bad day too? Well, what are the odds?"

Dahlia stuck her hands in jacket pockets and hunched forward.

"Uh-huh." JJ nodded, grinning at his own foolishness. First talking like Yoda and now holding a loud, obvious conversation with his horse?

This woman sure did drive him to do nutty things.

"Well, then, I'm glad you're talking about it," he replied to the silent horse. "I bet it makes you feel better to get that off your chest, huh?"

Dahlia stopped short with a loud, exasperated sigh. When she spun around, her lowered brows said she was peeved... but her twitching lips told him otherwise. "What do you think you're doing?"

"Ask him." JJ nodded toward an oblivious Zion. "I'm just tryin' to walk in peace, and this dang horse won't shut up."

Her lips rolled inward as she tried and failed to squelch a grin.

"Now that he's finally talked his fill..." JJ arched a brow. "Maybe you want to tell me what has you stomping around in the freezing cold."

"I don't want to talk." Her tone was stubborn and childish—and so dang cute it hurt. "Which is why I'm trying to go for a long walk... *alone*."

He tipped his head to the side. "Yeah, well, sometimes being alone is overrated."

She snorted and shook her head, her smile growing. "You don't believe that."

He had to grin, because she was right. He normally did prefer to be alone. And he suspected she did just fine on her own too. But right now...

Aw heck, he could practically feel the pain radiating off her. He could see the hurt in her eyes plain as day.

He shifted his weight, giving Zion some room to wander. "I can leave if you want me to. Or I can stay... and listen."

Sucking in a breath, she shook her head again, crossing her arms with a shiver before stamping her feet in the snow. She was antsy and twitchy again. Struggling to just breathe and be still.

He stayed put. Silently waiting.

A hawk spread its wings above them, soaring across the sky, and JJ watched it turn and swoop. Silently waiting.

Dahlia stomped her feet some more, then uncrossed her arms and gave them a shake before sewing herself up all tight again. She gripped the big jacket sleeves and then let out a trembling sigh.

"I wish I was better at communicating, that's all," she muttered. He had a feeling she didn't even mean to blurt it out, but the silence was eating at her, so she kept going. "I went in there with good intentions, but... all I ever do is repel people and make them see red... or... or make them cry! I can't say what I need to without irritating or offending everyone around me. It's frustrating."

She was downplaying it, that much was clear. He had no doubt she was annoyed with herself, but it wasn't a stretch to guess that someone had said something to her that hit a nerve.

It was the ones with the softest underbellies that grew the hardest shells and the prickliest armor.

He thought over his next words for a long while. Like him, she wouldn't want platitudes for the sake of being nice. She spoke her mind, and she spoke the truth, and she respected the same in turn.

"I can't speak for anyone else," he began, "but personally, I like that you say it how it is. You don't beat around the bush. In my humble opinion, the world needs more of that."

She gave a rueful huff. "If that's true, then you're the only person who believes that."

Looking out to the horizon, she shivered and hunched her shoulders.

"It's only gonna get darker and colder out here." He walked toward her. "You sure I can't coax you back to the house?"

She sniffed and kept her eyes on the mountains in the distance. "I don't think anyone's that interested in seeing me return."

"I doubt that."

Her lips pressed together with another sniff. "I don't want to be where I'm not wanted."

"In that case…" He moved until he was standing right in front of her. Until she was forced to see his face, and his sincerity. "You can come hang out at my place for a bit if you'd like."

She looked up at him, her eyes narrowing with what he could only assume was suspicion.

He snickered. "I tell ya, you're in for a treat. We're talking darts, burnt beans, and the riveting conversation of me and Cody Swanson."

"Kit's brother?" she asked.

She looked intrigued but obviously didn't want to admit it.

He fought another grin. "That's right. He's Kit's younger brother. I'm guessing you've seen him around the ranch."

She nodded.

"If you're real lucky, Boone might even stop by."

She arched a brow. "Who's Boone?"

"Nash's younger cousin. He's got his heart set on becoming a rancher just like his uncle Patrick. He works at the Donahue place but comes and hangs out with the big boys sometimes."

Dahlia's expression relaxed, her lips playing with a little smile. "I don't want to intrude…"

Now it was his turn to scoff. "You really think I'd invite you to our digs if I thought you'd be an imposition?"

She shrugged, and her smile grew ever so slightly. "I guess not."

And that right there was why it paid to be honest and only say what he meant, he thought with a grin. Because when the time came, and he needed to earn a woman's trust, she knew better than to doubt his word.

He nodded toward Zion, who was already halfway to the stables. "Come on, help me settle Zion for the night."

"How do we do that?"

"I'll show you." He glanced over. "If you're interested."

She nodded, her expression lit with curiosity as she picked up her pace to catch up with Zion. "Sure, why not?" But her steps faltered and she turned to look at the ranch house in the distance, a frown fluttering over her expression. "Maybe I should tell Rose…"

"I'll let them know," he said quickly. "I've got to text Nash about work stuff anyway."

He was rewarded by a small, grateful smile before she turned back to the stables.

He fell behind a step, a little rattled by the wave of happiness that filled him at the thought of spending another evening with Dahlia.

He shook his head in exasperation as he pulled out his phone to text Nash.

It wasn't like he had anything against enjoying time with a woman. It was just getting attached he wasn't so fond of.

But it was just one night. And her stay here couldn't last more than a couple more days tops. There was nothing to be nervous about.

He tapped out a message to Nash, letting him know that Dahlia would be having dinner at his place tonight if anyone asked.

Nash replied, *Good luck.*

The response made him frown as he tucked the phone away once more. If that was the sort of attitude even Nash had toward Dahlia, it was no wonder she didn't feel welcome.

9

"All right, gentlemen." Dahlia leaned forward over the thick wood table that took up most of the bunkhouse's main room. Snatching up the darts Boone had tossed down, she brought them up in front of her face and fanned them out like a bouquet as she arched her brows. "Watch and learn."

She strode over to the dartboard as Boone groaned behind her and JJ chuckled. Cody was sitting on a barstool near the dartboard, keeping score on an old chalkboard. He grinned at her. "You got this, Dahlia."

She smiled back at him and gave him a wink. "You just want me to buy you a drink with my winnings, don't you?"

He teasingly clasped a hand to his heart. "You wound me, Miss O'Sullivan."

"It's Ms. to you," she said in her best teacher voice.

All of them were grinning like fools as she took her place. One more bull's-eye and she'd be the winner of the night. Granted, the pot of twenty bucks wasn't going to buy her much, but it was the principle of the matter.

"Ladies and gentlemen, the crowd goes wild," Boone called from behind her in a sports announcer's boom, cupping his hands around his mouth.

She shot him an arched eyebrow, and he grinned.

"Too soon?"

JJ reached over and smacked the youngster upside the head. "Let the lady concentrate."

The lady. She smirked as she eyed the dartboard. Tonight she'd been anything but. All evening she'd been one of the boys. Talking football with Cody, teaching Boone the difference between ales and pilsners. Not to mention all the joking and laughs she'd had with JJ.

She'd been one of the guys, and it had been glorious.

Such a relief after the tension within the house.

She lifted her arm and threw.

"Bull's-eye!" Cody jumped down from the stool, pumping his fists in the air like he'd just won and not her.

He rushed her in a tackle of a hug that swept her off her feet and made her laugh so hard tears welled.

When he set her down, Boone was on top of her as well, his arm tight around her shoulders as he hollered out that they needed to celebrate proper like.

She assumed that meant another round. Or maybe some more burgers on the grill.

"Get your hands off the lady," JJ jokingly growled as he pried the younger man's arm away.

And then JJ was standing in front of her.

For a second, her lungs hitched in anticipation. Would he scoop her up in a bear hug like Cody had? Wrap an arm around her like Boone?

But no. The burly mountain man tousled her hair like she was his kid sister.

She found herself sticking her tongue out at him in return as she mock-glared through her now messy locks.

Was it childish?

Absolutely.

But did they both crack up?

Yep.

Boone rubbed a hand over his T-shirt-covered abs. "Anyone else hungry again?"

"Boy, you're always hungry." JJ rolled his eyes, then winked at Dahlia.

She snickered along with him.

Cody headed outside to the still-burning charcoal grill. "I'd have some more." He looked to Dahlia with arched brows.

She shook her head. "I'm still full, but thanks."

JJ nodded that he'd have some more, and then the two younger ranch hands bundled up and went outside.

Dahlia took a deep breath. For the first time all night, she and JJ were alone.

Not that there was anything of significance to that.

Not that she'd been *hoping* to be alone with him.

She turned with a shake of her head. *Get a grip, Dahlia.* "I should, uh… I should get back to the main house before it gets too late."

She felt him moving behind her, but he didn't say anything.

When she turned, he was closer than she'd realized, and she stumbled a step in surprise. The twitch of his lips told her he'd noticed.

"Thanks." She swallowed. "For tonight. This was… fun."

His smile warmed her all the way through, and she

wished she'd said something different. Once again words had failed her.

But… fun? Really?

Tonight *had* been fun, but that wasn't what she'd meant to say. It wasn't just fun, it was a relief. It was what she'd needed. To not feel like the big bad dragon. To not feel like every word out of her mouth was being picked apart.

"I, uh… I don't get to have nights like this very often," she admitted.

Again, not good enough. But it was closer to what she wanted to say.

He nodded, tucking his hands into the pockets of his jeans as he watched her.

How did he do it? How did he manage to look so attractive while so very unkempt? His beard was a mess, his hair too long and hanging in his face when it wasn't pulled back like it was right now. His clothes seemed like they were purely functional. The gray T-shirt and tattered jeans he was sporting looked like they'd been through battles, but they also had that well-worn comfort to them. Cotton softened and stretched by hours of wearing and multiple washes until it knew the body it clothed all too well. She had the most alarming urge to touch the fabric of his worn tee and press her cheek against it to see what it smelled like.

But then again, she already knew. It would smell like peppermint and leather and whatever else it was that made up that smell that was so uniquely JJ.

"You have nights like this in New York?" His question called her out of her thoughts, and she blinked in surprise.

"New York? Uh… no. At least, not often. I'm usually too busy with work or work-related events…" She trailed off as she realized how pathetic that must sound to a guy like him. He wouldn't think it admirable and noble that she worked herself to the bone. Some people would— some did—but not this guy.

For better or for worse, most of her free time at home was spent recovering from work in her studio apartment, or checking up on her sisters, or going out with some of her work friends whose interests were more in line with wine bars and cultural events than sports bars and football games.

She looked away from his searching gaze. He wanted to know about her life in the city, but she was reluctant to admit that 99 percent of it was based around her job. Even her social life.

"My ex and I used to go to bars," she blurted. "We'd take turns—music one week, sports the next."

Ugh, the mention of Brady made her feel cold all over. And she couldn't bring herself to look at JJ to see his reaction.

To say Brady hadn't made a good impression on Rose's new family would be an understatement. He'd knocked up the second youngest O'Sullivan sister and left her stranded. There was no excusing that.

And Dahlia had no urge to try. But there was a part of her that itched to explain. To JJ, to Rose—to *someone*. It hadn't all been bad. She wasn't the worst judge of character. Their breakup had been her fault. She'd been the one who couldn't commit.

She'd been so afraid of turning out like their mother—a woman whose life had ended when her husband left to the point that she couldn't even care for her own children.

So no, Brady wasn't a prince, but at least he'd been willing to try when they were a couple. She'd been the one who'd walked away.

She'd been the one to realize that she just wasn't cut out for a long-term relationship.

"You know where we are if you want to hang out again," JJ murmured.

She swallowed down a thick wave of gratitude.

"I like your friends." She pointed a thumb over her shoulder, hearing strains of their laughter reach her from outside.

JJ was grinning when she glanced up. "I'm pretty sure they're both head over heels for you."

She choked on a shocked laugh. "No way."

"Yes way. Poor Boone's definitely infatuated with the city slicker who can give as good as she gets."

She laughed outright at that description. "Yeah, well… he's young."

And adorable. He wasn't a child but not quite a grown man. But with his friendly grin and charming smile, she had no doubt he'd have his pick of ladies.

"He'll get over it," she added.

JJ chuckled, his smile knowing. "What about Cody?"

She rolled her eyes. Now he was just teasing. Cody had treated her like a sister or a friend, nothing more. "I'm sure Cody has plenty of girlfriends. He doesn't need to pine over"—she used air quotes to make him laugh—"the 'city slicker.'"

JJ didn't try to deny it.

Cody was just as good-looking as his older brother Kit but without the cocky swagger. Which, to her mind, made him that much more attractive. Between the two of them and JJ, she had a feeling she'd just spent the evening with the town's most eligible bachelors.

Her smile faltered as JJ moved closer.

"What's with that frown?" he asked.

She shook her head, trying to shake off the thought as well. She didn't care who Cody and Boone hooked up with, but the thought of JJ being sought after by all the pretty young women in this town…

His laugh was low and soothing to her nerves. "You look like you just bit down on a lemon. What's up?"

She shook her head again, and this time she could feel her cheeks burning. What was she doing getting jealous over unknown, faceless women?

She was losing her mind. That was the only answer. Being in this rural Siberia had made her lose all her wits.

"What I wouldn't give to know what you're thinking about right now," JJ teased. His gaze was so intense and so searching, she feared that maybe he did know.

She turned away from him and cleared her throat. "It's getting late, and I've got to work on East Coast time tomorrow. I really need to go."

"I'll walk you," he offered.

She shook her head, already slipping her feet into the work boots and reaching for the oversized coat. "That's really not—"

"Dahlia…" His hand on her shoulder had her stopping short. When she went to turn, she realized he was helping her into her coat. His soft, unhurried gaze met hers, and she felt that jarring jolt like it was the first time they'd ever seen each other.

"I know you don't need me to walk you back to the main house," he said in a voice so low and rumbly she felt it in her belly. "But I'd like to."

She opened her mouth to protest. She should argue. But when he smiled, she clamped her lips shut.

"Yeah, okay." Her voice sounded too breathy, so she turned away to the door. "But only if you want to."

81

10

The sky was still pitch black when JJ left the bunkhouse the next morning. The stars shone bright, and the snow seemed to glow in the moonlight. Winter in Montana had its difficulties—especially for a guy who'd been raised in South Carolina—but it had its perks too. This peace and quiet, and the slower pace on the ranch, it made the bitter cold worth it.

He tucked his hands into work gloves as he strode across the snow-covered land. His feet seemed to have a mind of their own as he wandered in the direction of the main house, where he'd dropped Dahlia off a mere eight hours ago.

So why was he already itching to see her again?

He ran a hand over his mussed hair before tugging a cap over it for warmth.

He just wanted to make sure she was doing all right this morning, that was all.

Best not to overthink it.

He let himself in through the back door, where the warm glow of the kitchen beckoned. He spotted Nash and

Emma at the kitchen table, each lost in their own business, giving him a quick nod before getting back to it.

Emma was nibbling on the edge of her pen as she worked on what looked to be a lesson plan, and Nash was poring over something on his phone. Probably the news.

There were breakfast dishes stacked near the sink, and the warm kitchen smelled of fresh coffee.

He didn't typically come here for coffee in the mornings—he and Cody brewed their own in the bunkhouse. But no one seemed to find it odd that he was here first thing in the morning, so he helped himself to a mug.

He heard a voice coming from the living room, but when he glanced in, he saw a smiling Rose talking all soft and sweet on the phone. No doubt she was chatting with her beau, Dr. Dex.

But there was still no sign of Dahlia.

Maybe she was asleep. He grinned against the lip of his mug as he took a sip.

Probably not. He couldn't imagine Dahlia slept in often, and definitely not on a workday.

He should head out. Get to work.

That was what he told himself as he wandered around the first floor. It was ridiculous to be disappointed at not seeing her this morning. The woman was a friend, that was all. It wasn't like he had to see her every minute of the day.

But even as he thought that, he couldn't bring himself to walk out the door and leisurely drink his coffee on the porch, taking in the sunrise before getting on with his chores. And so he headed outside the extra-long way, down a hall that led to the guest bedrooms where Emma and Rose had set up home.

He honestly couldn't tell anyone what he was up to, but something drew him around that way.

And sure enough, just past Emma's door, in a little office area that held the home's printer, he found her.

Or rather he heard her.

Dahlia was on a call, and he could hear the printer whirring in the background as she spoke, a hint of pleading in her voice that he didn't care for.

"It's not a huge investment," she said. "And it'll save so much time."

"It's outside of the admin budget," the woman on the other end replied, her voice cool yet emphatic even through the tinny sound of the phone's speaker.

"But it takes me twice as long using the current system —" Dahlia started.

A loud, exasperated sigh cut her off. "We've been over this," a male voice clipped. "We know the current software works, and it's not like you're pressed for time right now. You're stuck in Nowheresville, so get to it."

Dahlia was quiet for a moment, and JJ had to fight the urge to go to her. To step in and press End Call. *Let's see how they like being cut off midsentence.*

The woman spoke up again. "We're being lenient in letting you work remotely *again*. But if you can't handle your current responsibilities…" She let the words hang, like she was somehow daring Dahlia to have a problem with it.

"I can handle them just fine." Dahlia's words were tight, no doubt gritted out between clenched teeth.

JJ felt a surge of pride. He far preferred Dahlia's tough city-slicker tone to that pleading note she was using before.

A strong woman like her shouldn't be kowtowing to anyone. Least of all these jerks.

"If that's the case, then stop bringing up this software and do the work yourself," the woman snapped.

Dahlia's exasperated huff was soft enough that he suspected the people on the other end didn't hear it. But he did, and he felt a wave of exhaustion on her behalf.

"Fine." Her tone was polite but stiff. "You do realize this means I'll be tied to my computer all week. Taking a day off to fly back will put me behind the deadline. I may as well stay here and return after the weekend."

The man's sigh was sharp and churlish. JJ's jaw clenched, and he eyed the partially open door. How much would Dahlia hate him if he stormed in there and gave those people a piece of his mind?

She'd probably never forgive him. He gripped his coffee mug and glared at the door instead.

"Fine, stay until next week," he said. "But don't think this means you can slack off and take another vacation."

"I never slacked—"

"We still expect you to complete your workload."

"Of course," Dahlia said quickly.

"We need the financial department's reports organized and distributed by the end of the day," the woman said.

"Unless you take on my new software proposal, that is an unrealistic expectation. I can have that done by Friday afternoon."

JJ was impressed at the way she was standing up for herself, but the silence that followed her statement was thick with foreboding.

"Fine, but we also need you to proof Darian's analysis report. The client would like it by 8:00 a.m. tomorrow."

There was the slightest of pauses before Dahlia spoke. "That's not usually my job. Is Kelly unable to do that?"

"We have her working on another task. She's having to pick up extra duties in your absence. We figure you can return the favor."

"Yes, but—"

"You will be able to get all that done, won't you?" the woman asked. "We really need you to step up, Dahlia."

There was a challenge in her voice that set JJ on edge.

"Of… of course." Dahlia cleared her throat. "Who needs sleep, right?" she muttered the words under her breath, but the woman didn't seem to notice.

"Wonderful. See you next week, then." Her boss ended the call before Dahlia could reply.

JJ shifted so he could peer through the half-open doorway.

Dahlia slumped against the desk with a heavy sigh, pinching the bridge of her nose and shaking her head. She hadn't heard him, and he just stood there watching her. His chest felt too tight at the sight of strong, fierce Dahlia looking defeated.

For a second he wished he could call Rose, Emma, and Nash in here to take a look for themselves. To see that Dahlia wasn't impervious to their judgments and that she wasn't the enemy here.

She definitely wasn't some dragon. She was human, and flawed, and vulnerable, and complicated, and…

And loving.

She had a sensitive heart beneath that thick armor, and JJ had no doubt that if she ever let her sisters see this side of her—the part that wasn't bullheaded and self-assured all the time—they'd see what he saw.

But she'd hate it if anyone spotted her like this, so defeated and downtrodden.

So, even though he itched to go to her, to give her a hug and tell her those jerks didn't deserve her, he didn't. Instead, he turned to give her some space.

But the floorboards didn't play fair.

They creaked, and her head popped up.

"Is someone there?"

He winced and wondered if he should just walk away. Homesteads like this made funny noises all the time.

But he just couldn't do it.

He opened the door with a grin. "Good morning."

"Oh. Hi." She looked a little confused to see him, but her lips twitched with the onset of a smile before she could catch it.

She looked gorgeous. Her hair was pulled up in a ponytail, and she wasn't nearly as put together as he was used to seeing her. She was wearing yoga pants and a T-shirt instead of her usual chic attire. Plus, she had no makeup on. There were shadows under eyes that said she hadn't gotten enough sleep, but still...

She was gorgeous.

More gorgeous than ever, actually.

For a second, he forgot how to breathe.

"What are you doing here? Did you need to see me?"

"Uh." He scrambled for a decent excuse, figuring *I just wanted to see your pretty face* wouldn't fly. Glimpsing the mug in his hand, he took it as inspiration and held it out to her. "Brought you a morning pick-me-up."

"Thanks." She took the mug and blinked with surprise. "How'd you know I like my coffee black?"

A ray of sunlight burst through him.

It was silly. Knowing they drank their coffee the same way should not have made him feel this giddy.

He fought a grin and shrugged. "That's how all the cool people drink it."

Her soft chuckle made the sun inside him burn a little brighter.

He dipped his head with a rueful grin.

"I'll see you around, Dahlia."

"Yeah. And… thanks." She held up the mug and smiled at him.

He smiled back and was still grinning like a fool when he walked outside and spotted the sun rising in the east.

11

D ahlia pinched the bridge of her nose as she squinted and stared at the spreadsheet on her screen.

Nope. No good. The numbers still blurred together.

With a sigh, she sank back in her chair and shut her gritty eyes. Her head had been pounding for the past hour, her eyes feeling the strain of so much tedious data entry and analysis.

She peeked over at the clock and groaned.

No wonder her eyes and fingers were giving out on her. She hadn't come up for air since she got out of bed. The workday was coming to an end, and the only interruption had been JJ's unexpected visit early this morning.

Her stomach growled, and her head throbbed.

She should probably grab a late lunch. That would help.

But she'd heard Emma's and Lizzy's voices coming from the kitchen, and she couldn't bring herself to go in there and face them. She wasn't up for awkward tension or another argument, and somehow that was all she seemed capable of with those two.

Not that she had such a great relationship with Rose or Daisy either. But at least with them there was history and the comfort that came with familiarity.

She let her head fall back against the desk chair with a thud as she gave her eyes and her brain a much-needed rest. The second she stopped focusing on work, though, her mind went rogue.

Next thing she knew she was mentally replaying every moment from her walk back to the main house with JJ the night before, and then the way he'd smiled at her when he'd brought her a coffee.

Her eyes snapped open, and she frowned up at the ceiling.

He'd brought her coffee.

Why had he done that?

She sat up and gave her head a shake. Didn't matter. It didn't mean anything, just like their time together last night hadn't meant anything.

It couldn't mean anything because her time here was limited.

One week and then she'd be gone. Back to her real life. And these moments with JJ would just be a memory.

She straightened in her chair, finally feeling like she was getting her head on straight. What mattered now was that she put her time here to good use.

Lizzy's laughter floated back to the office Dahlia had imprisoned herself in, and far softer was Rose's giggle.

So Rose was with them too.

Her throat grew too tight, and that was followed swiftly by a rush of annoyance. The sooner she cut ties with this place the better.

But with Emma and Lizzy so insistent on this rule that they wouldn't make a decision on selling until every sister saw the place, Dahlia's hands were tied.

She tapped a finger against her lips as she mulled it over. Take the emotions out of it—that was a lesson she'd learned as a kid. Whenever a problem came along, it was so much easier to deal with when you took the emotions away and thought logically.

She'd become an expert at it.

"Not everyone's like you. We can't just forget he ever existed."

Rose's words echoed and stung. Maybe she'd gotten too good at it. But then again, it wasn't Rose who'd had to step up and take over as mom when their own mother lost all interest in the job.

No, that wasn't fair. She knew enough about mental health issues now to realize it wasn't her mother's fault. In hindsight, Dahlia could see clearly that her mother had always suffered. She suspected their mom was bipolar, from what Dahlia read on the topic. And then after Rose had been born, she'd clearly suffered from postpartum depression.

It was all so obvious in hindsight. But at the time…

Well, she'd been a kid. A kid with two sisters who needed to be taken care of. So she'd stepped up. And she'd been stepping up ever since.

Lizzy's comment about how she hadn't been the one to take responsibility after their father died still rankled even now.

She ought to get over it. But Lizzy hadn't just found a nerve, she'd touched it with a live wire.

Dahlia shot up out of her seat and paced the room. One time. The one time in her life that she didn't leap to take charge of a family crisis, and this was how she was punished. Now she was at the whim of Saint Emma and her loyal guard dog Lizzy who wanted some dream life here at the ranch like they really were one big happy family.

"Impossible," she mumbled.

But it was two against one, and they were stuck at a standstill until the other sisters showed.

Dahlia stopped short. This she could do. She wasn't sure she'd have any more luck than Emma tracking down the mysterious Sierra or the reclusive April, but she could darn well get her own full-blooded sister here.

Snatching her phone from the desk, she brought up Daisy's contact info and hit Call before she could overthink it.

If she did, she'd psych herself right out of doing what had to be done.

Dahlia rubbed at her throbbing temple. It probably didn't matter anyway. Daisy likely wouldn't even pick up—

"Dahlia?" Daisy's voice surprised her more than she cared to admit.

It wasn't like she'd been hoping Daisy wouldn't answer, but…

Yeah, okay, fine. She'd been hoping to get voice mail.

Dahlia cleared her throat. "Hey, Daisy."

Silence.

Dahlia could just imagine Daisy's pretty features screwed up in confusion at the unscheduled call. They had regular check-in calls every other weekend—a system Dahlia put in place to ensure that she and her flaky twin sister didn't go months without speaking.

"Is Rose okay?" Daisy asked, concern twinging her

voice, which sounded melodic and sweet even when she was just talking. "Is something wrong?"

"Yeah. She's fine. Nothing's wrong. I just wanted to talk to you about this ranch business—"

Daisy cut her off with a sigh. "Not now, D, okay? I'm too busy with the band at the moment. I can't even think about the inheritance right now."

"*No one* wants to be dealing with this right now," Dahlia snapped, her tone already getting too harsh, but there was little she could do to stop it.

No matter how much she wanted things to be different between them, the moment they interacted it was like they reverted back to being twelve years old. They were trapped in their roles—all the time, really, but whenever Dahlia talked to Daisy she felt it more than ever. Her role in the family that she couldn't seem to escape.

"So stop trying to control everything, you big dragon!"

Lizzy had nailed it. Dahlia couldn't even escape her family role with her newfound sisters.

She scrubbed a hand over her eyes. It was pointless to even try.

After all, someone had to take charge, right?

But why does it always have to be me?

She'd been so caught up in her own thoughts, she hadn't even realized that Daisy had totally ignored her comment and was babbling on about the tour she'd just finished.

Dahlia pinched her lips together. Daisy was a master at avoiding topics she didn't want to discuss. She was equally adept at ignoring problems she didn't want to see, or handling responsibilities she didn't want to face...

And why should she have to when Dahlia was always there to handle those responsibilities for her?

But not this time.

"Daisy… Daisy!" she interrupted. "This isn't going to just go away. At some point we have to deal with the fact that there are sisters in the world we didn't know about and our father left us an inheritance."

Daisy was quiet for a second. "I really don't have time for this right now, D—"

Dahlia heard someone shouting in the background.

Daisy's answering laughter was high and sweet. "I'll be right there!" Her hand over the speaker muffled her voice, but it was still there in her tone. The fun, lovable, flaky-as-a-pastry Daisy. Same as ever.

"Daisy, are you listening? You don't have to stay long, but I need you to get to Montana to see this ranch."

"No can do," Daisy chirped. "We're about to start recording an album in LA! Can you believe that? So I'm gonna be busy with that for a few months."

A few months?

Dahlia winced at the thought of this inheritance issue hanging over her for months to come. The sooner she got this place and her newfound sisters out of her life, the better.

"This is important," she huffed. "You can't just get one day off?"

"Come on, I'm not going to make such a big trip for one day. I'll get there when I'm ready." Daisy's tone was a sweet as ever, but Dahlia heard the edge to it. She was the only one Daisy talked to like this. Like they were enemies.

The thought made her heart hurt. They were twins. It shouldn't be like this. How different would their lives have been if they'd gotten along? If they'd been on the same team rather than in two separate worlds?

How nice would it have been if Dahlia hadn't been so freakin' alone all the time?

Oh, Daisy had been there physically, but she'd chosen to ignore anything that wasn't sunshine and roses.

And right now… well, right now Dahlia felt like a kid all over again.

She heard the laughter coming from the kitchen. Rose had found the sort of caring, doting sisters she'd always deserved. And Dahlia was alone. Again.

"Daisy, please…" She squeezed her eyes shut and hardened her tone so her sister wouldn't hear her pathetic, childish hurts. "You're holding everything up right now."

Daisy sighed, and Dahlia knew she'd taken the wrong approach. She couldn't argue Daisy into coming. The more she pushed, the more Daisy would run in the opposite direction.

"Look, Daisy…" Dahlia made an effort to soften her voice. To find some sort of middle ground that wouldn't stir up another fight. Rose. This baby. That was something she and Daisy could come together around.

Besides, Rose was the one person Daisy might actually want to see.

"You really should see Rose. She's beautiful with her baby belly, and I know she wants you here."

"Stop speaking on her behalf," Daisy snapped. "You always do that."

Dahlia let out a surprised huff. "I'm only telling you the truth."

"Rose is fine. I talked to her the other day. And I'm not giving up this awesome opportunity just so I can do what *you* want me to, Your Highness."

Dahlia clamped her lips together. *Great, now I'm a*

dragon and *royalty.* Her throat burned, but she kept her voice even. "Well, when can you get here, then?"

"After the album is finished. Like I said, a month or two... or three."

Dahlia snapped her eyes shut and fought the urge to yell into her phone. Taking a silent breath, she gritted out, "Well, I guess we'll look forward to seeing you then."

End the call now. Take the higher road.

But even as she thought it, she felt her mouth opening as an age-old bitterness surged up inside her. "Unless, of course, you come up with another excuse to avoid your family by then."

Dahlia hung up before Daisy could respond. Her hands were shaking, and she balled them into fists.

She shouldn't have said that. She shouldn't have ended it that way.

She dropped her head into her hands with a groan. Why was it that the more she tried to make things right, the worse things seemed to get?

When had she become her own worst enemy?

J J tipped his hat as old Mrs. Fogerty called out a good afternoon from the library steps.

"Have a good weekend, ma'am," he called back.

Everyone he passed on Main Street seemed to be in good spirits this afternoon. Probably because it was a Friday and the sun was shining bright.

JJ shifted the sack of groceries from one arm to the other.

It was a good day for a trip into town. His gaze caught on the sign for Mama's Kitchen. It was an even better day for one of Mama's famous burgers.

He headed in, the bell above the door clanging as it opened.

The diner was full for the midafternoon, and he spotted familiar faces straight away.

"JJ!" Lizzy called as she waved. Rose gave him a welcoming smile, and Lizzy's step-twins, Chloe and Corbin, nearly knocked over their water glasses in their eagerness to say hello.

"Want to join us?" Lizzy laughed as she mopped up water droplets and smiled at him.

JJ snagged a menu off the counter before heading their way. "Aw, I don't want to disturb you guys."

"You're not disturbing anything," Rose said quickly, her eyes all wide and earnest. "I just ran into Lizzy and the twins while waiting for Dex to finish up with a patient."

Lizzy smiled. "And the twins and I are just enjoying a quick snack before we head to a playdate."

"You should join us, JJ," Corbin said. In what JJ had to assume was an attempt at a whisper, Corbin added, "They're talking about you."

Chloe nodded in affirmation when JJ arched his brows.

"Corbin." Lizzy gave him a sharp look, but he ignored it, going back to his coloring with a grin.

Chloe giggled. "They want you to take the dragon out for Aunt Emma's auction date."

"If you two don't quit tattling, I'm gonna stop treating you to after-school snacks at Mama's," Lizzy warned. But her indulgent smile made it impossible to take her seriously.

"It's not tattling. It's the truth," Chloe argued.

Rose dipped her head with a snicker. "I think maybe Emma needs to add 'tattling' to their vocabulary list."

JJ was too caught up on another word Chloe had used to pay any mind to their banter. "The dragon?"

Chloe nodded happily, clearly not understanding that "the dragon" was not a term of endearment.

JJ looked to Rose, who blushed as she dipped her head again, avoiding his gaze.

Lizzy just grinned. "A Ms. Dahlia O'Sullivan." She'd adopted a snotty tone when she said it, as if Dahlia was some snooty, standoffish witch and not her own blood who felt more out of place in this town than any of them could imagine.

JJ's insides rebelled against the insult. Did no one in this family see her for who she truly was? She was a woman who desperately cared. Maybe she went about showing it all wrong, but it annoyed him more than he cared to admit that no one else seemed to notice.

They were having too much fun making her out to be the bad guy.

He slid into the booth beside Chloe, placing his grocery bag under the table and hiding his displeasure behind a neutral expression. "Why are you calling her the dragon?"

Lizzy scoffed. "Do you seriously have to ask that?"

"I suppose I do." The Southern drawl that had faded over the years came back when he was riled, and right now it sounded more pronounced than ever.

Lizzy gave him an exasperated look, like he was being purposefully obtuse. "You must have seen how she acts. And the way she's always snapping at people and trying to boss Rose around…"

He glanced over at Rose. She was rubbing her baby bump and not meeting his gaze. But to Lizzy, she said, "She's been better about that since I stood up to her."

"Well, that's something," Lizzy murmured, giving Rose an encouraging little grin.

JJ's head fell with a huff of rueful amusement. Lizzy was a good woman, kind and loyal and generous, but at first glance some people in this town had gotten the wrong impression, taking her for a spoiled brat just because she was in a bad spot and didn't know where she belonged.

Now here she was judging Dahlia harsher than anyone. It would have been amusing if it wasn't so irritating.

But then again, maybe that was the issue. Maybe it was the fact that they did share similarities that bothered Lizzy.

"What are you laughing about?" Lizzy narrowed her eyes at him.

He shook his head. "Just wondering what Chloe meant about me taking Dahlia out."

He arched a brow, and Rose blushed again.

"Oh, well, um…" Rose started.

"You know how Emma won a date with you in the bachelor auction," Lizzy began.

He grinned. He'd been teasing Emma and Nash about it for months now. "Yeah, I remember."

"Well, what about taking Dahlia out instead?" Rose finished.

His heart skipped a beat, his pulse picking up its pace. "You want me to take Dahlia on a date?"

Both women nodded, and the twins grinned, all mischief and enthusiasm.

"When's she flying back to New York?" he asked.

"Monday," Rose said. "She figured she may as well spend the weekend with me before heading back."

"But instead you want her to spend it with me?"

She blushed. "Just one date. Maybe Saturday?"

It was disorienting how much he loved this idea. He hadn't seen her much this week, and when he had, everyone else was around as well. One more one-on-one outing with Dahlia sounded perfect. But he pretended to mull it over. "I'm not sure Emma will just want to give our date away so easily."

His mischievous grin made the women laugh, and the kids joined in too, though he suspected they didn't know what they were laughing about. JJ mussed up the kids' hair and picked up a crayon, getting to work on Chloe's picture.

She gave him an adoring grin and tapped the paper. "You do the grass."

"Should we make it rainbow grass?" He wiggled his eyebrows, and she beamed.

"Yes, please!"

A waitress came over to take JJ's order, and he handed her the menu, not even sure why he'd grabbed it in the first place.

"The usual?" she asked.

"Yep, but hold the fries. I'm only here for a snack."

The waitress cracked up laughing as she walked away from the table. "One monster burger for a snack. Gotcha."

"And don't forget my vanilla milkshake!" he called after her.

She was still laughing as she wandered around the counter to deliver his order.

"Mmm, milkshake," Rose murmured.

He winked. "I'll let you have some, baby mama."

Rose grinned, and Lizzy lightly slapped the table to get their attention. "Come on, JJ, say you'll do it."

He shrugged. "I have no problem spending time with Dahlia. I enjoy her company."

Lizzy narrowed her eyes like she suspected he was lying.

She turned to Rose. "I don't know her as well as you, Rosie, but do you think Dahlia will go for it with JJ?"

"On a date?" Rose shook her head. "No way."

He kept his gaze on the rainbow grass, hoping no one caught his flinch.

For a second there, he'd thought Rose wanted him to take her out because...

Aw heck, because she'd expressed some sort of interest in him.

But clearly that wasn't the case. He shook off the wave of disappointment. So, Rose thought Dahlia wouldn't want to go on a date with him. So what? She was likely right. He was probably nothing like the sort of men she met in New York.

"So, why are we doing it, then?" JJ picked up an orange crayon and glanced up at Rose. "If she doesn't want to, I mean?"

"To get her out of the house," Lizzy muttered.

He and Rose ignored that. Rose leaned forward, her expression pleading. "I just think it'd be good for her to get out and have some fun."

He couldn't argue with her. Dahlia had seemed more tightlipped and miserable each time he'd seen her throughout the week.

"She's technically come to Aspire and seen the ranch," Rose continued. "But her first visit was all about trying to take care of me and the baby and that whole situation with… ugh." She stuck out her tongue, obviously referring to the baby daddy who had turned out to be nothing more than a sperm donor. "And on this trip, she's either been working or driving me miles for the baby scan." She rubbed her belly, a dreamy smile taking over her face. She was having a girl, and Dahlia had specially flown over to be there for that moment when Rose found out.

How could she ever think that Dahlia didn't love her with everything she had?

Lizzy gave him a rueful smile. "I think we're all hoping that if Dahlia can find some way to enjoy it here, she'll get off her high horse about selling the ranch."

His brows arched again. "That's asking a lot of one date."

Rose giggled.

"I mean, I know I can be quite the charmer, but—"

Lizzy laughingly slapped his forearm. "Come on, JJ. Do us a favor. Take Dahlia out."

He focused on his coloring, trying to stay within the lines, because he knew that was what Chloe wanted. His mind was already racing ahead of him, thinking about a date with Dahlia. "I guess I could take her fishing with me."

"You're going fishing? How?" Rose's nose wrinkled. "Everything's frozen over."

He chuckled. "That's why it's called ice fishing."

Lizzy's laughter held a hint of evil. "Oh, I'm sure the dragon will just love that."

She was being sarcastic, but he could imagine Dahlia having the time of her life out in the wild. If his brief time with her had taught him anything, it was that she was a tomboy at heart.

And he freakin' loved that.

He looked to Rose. Surely she knew that about her sister. But she looked unconvinced. "I don't know. I can't really picture it…"

He swallowed a sigh of frustration, and for a second, he wasn't sure if it was toward Dahlia's sisters for not seeing the woman he saw or with Dahlia herself for not letting herself be seen.

Lizzy wrinkled her nose. "It's not exactly… romantic."

He laughed. "What would you do?"

Lizzy's expression turned dreamy. "Candlelit dinner, classy food, maybe a little dancing?"

"Do you honestly think Dahlia would be into that?"

His frown was skeptical. "She doesn't want some textbook date. That's boring. She needs excitement, adventure. If I do agree to this, I am most definitely not doing some carbon-copy date from a romance movie."

Both sisters stared at him in surprise. He supposed he had gotten a little passionate on the topic.

He shrugged, flashing them a mischievous wink. "Emma paid for this service fair and square, and I'm gonna deliver."

"But... ice fishing?" Lizzy bulged her eyes at Rose. "I know Dahlia's annoying, but do we really want to put her through that?"

Rose giggled. JJ feigned insult, but then his food arrived, and he was so hungry, he started devouring his burger.

He was just wiping his mouth with a napkin when Emma bustled into Mama's Kitchen with a scowl.

"Emma! I thought you were going straight home after work." Lizzy blinked in surprise as her sister took off her scarf and slid into the booth beside Corbin.

"I was, but I just got off the phone with Dahlia, and she's in a foul mood and I need to delay." She gave Rose an apologetic wince. "Sorry. I don't mean to talk badly about your sister, but I'm just a little tired after a big week."

Rose smiled. "That's okay. I get it."

JJ frowned, hating the way they were all talking about Dahlia like she was some beast.

"I'll do it." He finished off his shared milkshake with a loud slurp. "I'll take Dahlia out tomorrow."

"Seriously?" Lizzy gasped, then started clapping with glee.

Emma looked a little confused, but she was laughing as

she clapped along with the twins, who'd cheered at his announcement.

The crowded tables around them turned to stare at the kids' loud celebration.

JJ could already imagine how quickly word would spread that he was dating one of the O'Sullivan sisters. He pointed at the twins with a stern expression. "This is top secret information, and you are not to breathe a word to anyone. Got that?"

"Sir, yes, sir!" They both saluted him, and he saluted back, energy coursing through him as he went to pay for his meal… and start planning for a date that Dahlia would never forget.

13

Dahlia dallied in her bedroom the next morning. She'd been up and dressed for ages, but she couldn't stop this nagging sense of dread every time she thought of going downstairs to join the others.

It was ridiculous, obviously. It wasn't like she was afraid of these people. Besides, this was her house too… technically. But it was a Saturday, which meant no one had anywhere to be.

She'd smelled bacon cooking earlier and had heard the lively chatter and laughter as she sat up here alone in her room.

She met her gaze in the bedroom mirror and gave herself a hard glare.

It was just plain cowardly to hide away up here, and she was no coward. She held her phone up, the screen still on the airline's flights for later today.

It wouldn't cost much to change her departure flight. A pang of guilt made her frown. She'd planned to stay through the weekend for Rose's sake, since her week had been eaten up by work. But would Rose even care if she left early?

She might even be relieved.

With a deep breath, she reached for the doorknob. There was only one way to find out what Rose was thinking, so she couldn't put this off any longer.

There were few sounds coming from the kitchen, and Dahlia let out a sigh of relief. If she could avoid a run-in with Lizzy or Emma this morning, all the better. That wasn't cowardice, just self-preservation.

She wasn't sure how much more awkward politeness she could stand from Emma. And if Lizzy called her a dragon one more time... Dahlia huffed as she hit the bottom floor... well, she wouldn't be held responsible for her actions.

But fortunately, when she came into the kitchen, she found Rose alone cleaning up after breakfast.

"What are you doing scrubbing dishes?" Dahlia scolded. "You should be resting."

Rose smiled over at her, the smile so sweet and innocent that Dahlia felt another stab of guilt alongside a crushing wave of affection.

Part of her wondered if there would ever be a day when Rose's smile didn't have this bittersweet effect on her. To say their relationship was complicated was an understatement—for Dahlia, at least.

Rose would probably just say she had an overbearing bully for a sister. But for Dahlia...

She rested her hands on Rose's shoulders and steered her away from the sink.

"What are you doing?" Rose asked, a dirty dish scrubber still hovering in her hand.

"I'll get the dishes," Dahlia said. "You sit."

Rose sighed, but she sank down into one of the kitchen chairs with an indulgent smile. "Between Emma cooking for me all the time, Lizzy buying me maternity clothes, and you not letting me do any housework around here, I'm getting too spoiled."

Dahlia forced a smile, hoping Rose couldn't see her flinch at being thrown in with Emma and Lizzy.

"None of us are as bad as Dex." She tried to sound light and playful, glancing back at Rose in time to catch her blush.

Rose rubbed a hand over her belly with a dreamy sigh. "You're right. Dex spoils me most of all."

Dahlia turned back to the dishes, blinking rapidly against a sudden and silly urge to cry. She scrubbed the pot in her hand that much harder.

Honestly, what was wrong with her this week? She was happy for Rose, that was all. If anyone deserved a prince charming like Dex, it was her sweet little sister.

She scrubbed at a burnt spot like her life depended on it as she tried to get a grip on her wayward emotions.

It was just all this enforced family time. Who wouldn't be rattled by living in their estranged father's house? In using a bedroom he'd painted for another daughter… a daughter she hadn't even known about?

"Are you, um… are you okay, Dahlia?" Rose asked from behind her.

Dahlia stopped scrubbing. The pot was as clean as it could get.

She rinsed it and put it to the side.

"I'm fine." She took a deep breath and turned to face her baby sister. "Actually, I wanted to run something past you… about this weekend."

Rose brightened. "I wanted to talk to you about plans for the weekend too."

"Oh." Dahlia blinked in surprise. "You did?"

It wasn't that she thought Rose wouldn't want to spend any time with her—they'd both been making an effort to have a better relationship. But Rose was also so preoccupied with Dex and her newly discovered sisters that...

Dahlia looked down at the ground with a rueful shake of her head.

Okay, yes. Fine. Maybe she was a little jealous. Not of Dex but of Emma and Lizzy. It was so silly, but ignoring issues was never her style.

"I'm really glad you decided to stay a little longer," Rose was saying. "I know you didn't want to, and it must have been hard working remotely and—"

"Rose."

Rose glanced up with arched brows.

Dahlia smiled. "I'm glad I'll get to spend some actual quality time with you before I go."

Rose's smile was blinding. "Me too. And I hope... that is, I know things are a little strained right now, but... I'm glad you're getting to know Emma and Lizzy better too."

Dahlia's jaw grew tight, but she managed another smile and a nod for Rose's sake. "So, what did you have planned for the weekend?"

"Oh, well, actually..." Rose turned beet red.

Dahlia's eyes narrowed as her little sister squirmed in her seat.

"I, um, I thought... I thought maybe..."

Dahlia cocked a hip, amusement warring with suspicion. She'd only seen Rose act like this a handful of times in her life, and it was always when she'd been up to no good. "Rose, what are you up to?"

Rose stopped squirming and widened her eyes. "Nothing."

She was the picture of innocence, but Dahlia had seen that look on Daisy enough times to know when she was being fed a lie. All she had to do was arch a brow and Rose's shoulders slumped in defeat.

"Okay, fine," Rose huffed. "I was wondering if I could sweet-talk you into spending the day with JJ."

The sound of his name had her blinking in surprise. And then what Rose was suggesting registered.

A day with JJ.

The idea sent a thrill racing through her, but she willed herself to cover it. "Why?" It came out too snippy.

"Well, he's been trying to get everyone to go ice fishing with him, and no one really wants to, and I feel bad for the guy. But I'm not about to go, and I was just wondering..." Rose's eyes widened again, taking on a puppy dog look that she'd spent most of her childhood perfecting.

Dahlia frowned. "He seems like the kind of guy who enjoys his own company. I think he'll be fine."

"You should have seen his face," Rose kept going. "And if he's asking me, then you know he's desperate. Right?" Her brow wrinkled, puppy dog eyes now tinged with an extra shot of pleading. "Come on, please?"

Dahlia sighed. She'd never been able to resist Rose's cute face.

And yeah, fine, maybe she didn't like the idea of JJ being lonely or rejected. Her lips hitched to the side. Did he really need company?

The back door opened, and JJ sauntered in. His gorgeous smile when he spotted her made her belly flutter in a way that went beyond disconcerting.

It was annoying the first time it happened. But every single time he smiled?

So he has a nice smile. Get over it already.

"You ready to go?" His husky voice made the tingle spread down the back of her legs, and she had to turn away so he wouldn't see the effect he always had on her.

She gave Rose a pointed look. "You told him yes from me already?"

Rose winced. "You're really good at not letting people down, so I just assumed…"

When she turned back, JJ was grinning at her, and she knew there was no way she could say no. Instead, she said, "Ice fishing, huh?"

"Yes, ma'am," he said, crossing his arms as he leaned against the counter. "Ever been?"

She scoffed. He was kidding, right?

His chuckle said yes, he was.

"Don't I need, like, equipment or gear or something?"

He shook his head. "I've got everything you'll need. You just have to put on your warmest sweater and your comfiest winter boots."

"Won't I freeze out there?"

JJ tilted his head to the side and shifted slightly until he was close enough that she could smell that heady scent of his. Woodsy and masculine, it wrapped around her and warmed her through.

"Now, Dahlia, don't you trust me to take care of you?"

I don't trust anyone to take care of me. She swallowed the words, but the truth of it was hard to ignore.

No one looked after her. She'd always been the one taking care of everybody else. She'd even felt like a nagging mother with her ex, Brady.

His gaze softened, along with his voice. "I promise I won't let you freeze or go hungry today."

Her heart gave a sharp kick to her ribs.

"What's more..." He winked. "I promise you'll have fun if you give it half a chance."

She laughed at that. "You sound awfully certain of that."

He shrugged. "I think I know you well enough to keep that promise."

She blinked in surprise, and a quick glance over at Rose had her swallowing another laugh.

Her sister was gaping at them like she'd never met either of them before.

Dahlia turned back to JJ—anything to avoid the questioning gaze. "All right, fine. You're on."

14

―――――――

"*You're on.*"

JJ was still grinning over Dahlia's challenging tone as they piled into his truck a little while later.

"Where are we heading?" she asked as he put the truck in Drive.

"You'll see." He shot her a grin in lieu of an answer. He typically went to a lake near his cabin, but after thinking over what Rose had said about Dahlia not having a good introduction to this town or her family's ranch, he'd changed his plan.

She glanced over in confusion when he drove them onto a narrow dirt road that led farther into the O'Sullivans' property rather than off it.

She gripped the door handle as the truck rocked and jostled over the rough route that led away from the flat, sprawling meadows surrounding the house and into the rocky foothills and valleys that led to the heart of the property.

This land spread far beyond the reach of the main roads, where the world was still untouched. It was back in these parts that the real magic of Montana resided, as far as he was concerned. The small towns were quaint and the national parks were majestic, but every time he rode back into this pristine stretch of nature, he knew he'd been blessed to work here.

"Is this lake…" Dahlia turned in her seat, trying and no doubt failing to take it all in as he rounded another turn and another sweeping valley came into view. "Is the lake on my sisters' property?"

He smiled. "It's on O'Sullivan property."

Your property.

"This is…" She shook her head. She didn't have the words, and he couldn't blame her. There were no words for the sight before them.

Hawks swept overhead, and a white-tipped mountain range ran along the horizon. White clouds dotted a bright blue sky, and the snow-covered meadows around them spread out as far as the eye could see.

"Wow," she whispered.

JJ considered himself a spiritual man, but he'd stopped attending church once he'd arrived here in Montana. This land was holier than any building he could ever walk into.

He knew Nash had taken Emma on a tour of the property when she'd first arrived. But with the onset of winter and the wicked snowstorms they'd had, he suspected Dahlia hadn't seen much beyond what was in view from the house.

Turned out he was right.

"I didn't know this was all back here," she whispered.

He didn't say much, just let her take it in.

They followed a creek through a narrow canyon, and he laughed at Dahlia's gasp of delight when she spotted a moose running along on the other side of the creek.

To his surprise, she laughed too, the sound more youthful and sweet than anything he'd ever heard from her before.

He glanced over in time to catch her wide smile as she leaned into the window for a better view.

"They're not exactly graceful creatures, are they?" she mused.

He chuckled. "No, ma'am. They're gangly and awkward, at best."

She giggled. A straight-up *giggle* as she watched the moose lumbering along, long-limbed and stumbling in the snow.

He clamped his own mouth shut to keep from laughing. It wouldn't do if she thought he was laughing at her. And he wasn't. It was just too stinkin' cute to watch this hardened city chick go all soft and silly over a moose.

When at last he found the snow-packed path to the lake, he stopped the truck. "We'll have to walk in from here," he said, "or risk getting the truck stuck in a snowbank."

She nodded, not even hesitating before hopping out. She followed him to the back, where he pulled out some supplies.

"What can I take?" she asked.

"I brought most everything we'll need out here earlier." He gestured to the box in his hands. "This is the last of it."

"You came out here already this morning?" Her brows drew together in confusion.

"I want your first time ice fishing to be fun." He grinned. "So I did some of the prep work."

"Oh. Thanks." She fell into step beside him, using the path he'd forged earlier to make their way through the snow.

When they reached the lake, she stopped to stare. He couldn't decide which was better—the view, which was spectacular, or Dahlia's face as she took in that spectacular view.

"Wow," she whispered again. Her breath plumed before her in the cold air.

"Yeah," he agreed. Because really, what else was there to say? There were no words for this.

The lake wasn't large by most standards, but it was still plenty big, and what lay beyond it was a picture-perfect view of one of the tallest peaks in the Tobacco Root range. White-peaked and awe-inspiring, it loomed over the lake like a shrine to all that's holy.

He set the box down and reached for her hand. "I pitched the tent on the ice already." He called her attention away from the view to the small, makeshift structure they'd use to keep warm. "Let me help you over there." He could see her about to argue, so he added, "Walking on ice takes some getting used to."

She clamped her lips shut and thrust her hand into his. He steadied her as she stepped onto the ice and immediately began to wobble. Like a newborn foal, she struggled to find her feet, but she never once fell. He held her tight and helped her to the tent, grinning like a fool the entire way.

"Do you always use a tent?" she asked. "Or is this for my benefit?"

He laughed. "Actually, I typically go to a lake out by my cabin, and out there I have a little shed that I keep up all winter."

She stopped short to glance at him. "So why are we going here instead?"

He shrugged. "I thought you might like to see your own land while you're here."

Her expression was funny—partly irritated, partly awed, and almost entirely baffled.

"It's not *mine*," she murmured.

He didn't protest. Instead, he tugged her along until they got to the tent. He found the too-large, but incredibly warm, overcoat he'd brought for her and draped it around her shoulders, helping to secure all the fastenings and zippers despite her muttering about how she wasn't a child.

"Not a child," he murmured, "but we all need help now and again."

She took the snow pants from him with a raised brow that was tempered by a small smile. "I don't need help putting my pants on."

He held his hands up in mock surrender. But while she was working on the fastening of her pants, he snagged a fur-trimmed hat and stuck it on her head.

She pouted, and he…

Well, he laughed. He couldn't help it.

She planted her hands on her hips, which only made him laugh harder.

Gradually, her lips started to twitch too. "I look stupid."

"No," he said quickly, tugging at the ear flaps to adjust the cap. "You look adorable."

And she did.

Everything was too big on her, and she was all but drowning in the snow pants. Even the hat was too big. "You look like a kid playing dress-up."

She snickered. "That was more Daisy's thing."

"What was your thing as a kid?"

Her gaze darted away, and once again he was reminded of a spooked colt. He gentled his touch as he adjusted her collar, covering every inch of her that she didn't need for breathing or seeing.

"Personally, I was always outdoors as a kid," he said.

"Shocker."

"My mama would be hollering for me on the porch steps long after the sun went down."

Her smile was small and sweet and... just a little sad.

"What about you?" he asked.

"What about me?"

He narrowed his eyes like he was thinking it over. "I bet you were a tomboy. Am I right?"

Her chuckle was rueful. "I probably would have been, but..." She shrugged. "I didn't have that luxury."

His chest constricted at the flicker of emotion in her eyes before she looked away. *What does that mean?* He stopped the words before they could tumble out.

She'd talk in time... if she wanted to.

"So, how do we do this?" She eyed the gear next to the tent, obviously keen to stop talking and just do. He understood—action was easier than words.

"Ever been fishin'?"

She shook her head.

"Then I guess we'll start with the basics, city girl."

"Don't worry. I catch on quick." She mocked his accent with a playful grin.

"I have no doubt." He held up the box of maggots and wigglers. "Does that mean you want to bait your own hook?"

She wrinkled her nose. "Um, how about I watch you this first time."

He chuckled. "Fair enough."

He led her over to the hole he'd drilled in the ice and situated a seat for her nearby.

"You really thought of everything," she murmured.

"Yeah, well, I promised your sisters I'd take you out on a proper date, and where I come from, that means making sure a girl is comfortable." He held up the box again. "So, I'm baiting your hook like a true gentleman."

He'd meant to make her laugh. He'd been hoping for another smile. But instead he got a wide-eyed stare. "You... you promised my sisters you'd take me on a date?"

Oh.

Oh shoot.

That look on her face is not a good sign.

"Yeah, well, uh..." He adjusted the beanie on his head. "Isn't that why you agreed to come with me today?"

Her lips grew pinched as she glanced away. "Rose said you were looking for company."

"Yeah, well, that's true." He stepped closer, angling his head, trying to get her to meet his gaze. "I was hoping for *your* company, in particular."

She shot him a sidelong glance. There was that suspicion again, the wariness that made his insides tighten.

What he wouldn't give to rid her of those emotions once and for all.

But he knew better than anyone that trust was earned, and it meant the most coming from those who didn't give it easily.

That was why he opted for honesty. A straight shooter like Dahlia would appreciate the truth more than pretty words. "You see, your sister Emma—"

"Half sister," she clipped.

"Right. Your half sister Emma won a date with me

during a bachelor auction. We were raising money for the fire station, you see…"

She pursed her lips. "Okay. What does that have to do with me?"

"Well, as hard as this is to believe…" He gave a rueful grimace. "Miss Emma lost all interest in our date once Nash proposed."

Dahlia's lips twitched ever so slightly. "That's not so hard to believe."

He chuckled. "I've been having fun teasing Emma about it, so she and the others decided you should go on that date instead."

She looked away, but not before he caught her flinch. "So this was just… what? A joke? A prank?"

"No, ma'am." He crouched down on the ice in front of her chair so his head was level with hers. "This here is a date."

Her gaze darted over to meet his, and he felt it like a collision. He swallowed hard but didn't look away. He needed her to know he was sincere.

She didn't speak for the longest minute, and he couldn't help saying something.

"Well?"

She arched a brow, and he was gratified to see her pinched lips soften. "Well, what?" she snipped, her tone saucy and cute. "I'm just waiting for you to bait that hook so I can catch myself a fish."

He dropped his head with a chuckle and set about the task at hand. "Yes, ma'am."

15

Dahlia lost all track of time out there on the lake. She wasn't sure how long they'd been sitting there, quietly talking, or sometimes just sitting in silence, when it happened.

She felt a tug on her rod.

Leaping up with a start, she turned to JJ. "I got one."

He stood too, coming to her side, one arm around her waist as he helped her to keep hold of the wiggling rod while she used her free hand to reel it in.

"That's it. Nice and easy," JJ coached her, his arm still around her waist, his other hand touching her forearm as she pulled and fought with the fish.

With a little grunt, she wound the reel a little tighter and caught her first glimpse of the flailing fish.

"There it is!" she practically squealed, sounding more like a five-year-old than a woman in her late twenties.

JJ laughed. "Good job. Pull!"

The icy water splashed, and her feet nearly gave out on the slippery surface, but JJ held her tight, and she was soon holding the fish in the air and grinning like it was a golden trophy.

"I did it!"

He was beaming back at her. "You certainly did. That was well done."

She watched with fascination as he took the hook out and dealt with the fish, still reveling in her triumph.

He was chuckling as he showed her how to add more bait and answered all her questions about the kinds of fish in this lake and the different styles of fishing.

Despite the fact that it was freezing out and they were sitting on ice, Dahlia was having a blast. She wasn't even all that cold. How could she be when every time she started to feel the chill, JJ would take her into the tent to warm up by a fire or he would pour her some steaming hot cocoa from a thermos?

He hadn't been exaggerating about making sure she was comfortable.

She hadn't been this pampered since... well, ever. She wasn't sure anyone had ever fussed over her like JJ was doing.

The sun was starting to sink in the sky when JJ declared it was time to take their catches home and fry 'em up. Despite his protests, she helped him pack up all the gear and load it into the truck.

"How does fish sound for dinner?" he asked.

They were dirty, tired, and smelly in the warm truck, and she wondered if she should be opting for a hot shower. What man in their right mind would want to spend more time with her looking and smelling this way?

He turned to face her with a sudden seriousness that took her aback. "You do like fish, right? I mean... to eat?"

She laughed and was a little appalled at how girly it sounded. "Yeah, I eat fish."

He grinned. "Good. Because those two you caught are gonna be awfully tasty."

She half expected him to take her back to the main house so they could share the feast with the others, but he turned and parked by the bunkhouse instead.

Her idea of a shower was slowly losing its appeal. JJ didn't seem to mind her fishy stench, and she couldn't quite bring herself to end this unexpected date.

"Should we unload the gear?" she asked as he helped her down.

"Nope. I can do all that later. I told Cody to clear out so I could make you a nice dinner. All you need to do is go clean up and find your way out of that mountain of clothing."

She nodded, a silly grin still on her face. "If you insist…"

By the time she came out of the bathroom, her hands no longer smelling of fish and her hair somewhat tamed into a ponytail, JJ was already hard at work in the kitchen.

"Can I help?" she asked.

"Nope. But you can keep me company."

She smiled and nodded. "I can do that."

He lifted his chin toward the living area right off the kitchen. "I got a fire going. Why don't you make yourself comfortable?"

She padded over to the fire and sank into a leather armchair. From where she sat she could watch him work. "You seem comfortable in the kitchen."

He shot her a smirk. "Surprised?"

She shrugged. "A mountain man who can catch his own dinner *and* cook it? You're a talented man."

"Correction: you caught this dinner." He winked as she rolled her eyes.

She'd caught two fish, yes. But he'd caught even more than that, and she'd needed his help to reel hers in. "We'll both take the credit."

He chuckled. "Sounds fair."

After a while she leapt up again. "I'm not very good at sitting still while other people work," she explained as she reached his side.

"You don't say," he teased.

"Show me what you're doing?"

He turned his body slightly and showed her what he was up to. "Gutting fish was not exactly on the agenda for our date."

She grinned. "What? Gutting fish isn't romantic?"

"Some people don't think so." He feigned confusion. "Can you believe that Lizzy didn't think ice fishing was romantic?"

She gasped. "She didn't?"

They shared a laughing smile before he held up his knife for her perusal. "First lesson. You need the right tools for a job like this."

She nodded, resting her hip against the counter as he continued, walking her through every step of the process, including the equipment and the unfamiliar terms.

"You must have done a lot of fishing growing up," she said. "You're a pro."

"Fishing, yes. Ice fishing, that's been a new endeavor."

She tilted her head to the side as she studied him. "Where did you grow up?"

"South Carolina."

That was it. She waited a second for him to fill the silence with more. Most people would say where in South

Carolina, or make a mention of the family that was still there.

But he didn't, and Dahlia knew better than to pry. She hated it when people asked her about her upbringing. Even JJ's mention earlier of his mother shouting from the porch steps had made her uneasy as she'd waited for it. Those well-intentioned questions that people thought were small talk.

What are your parents like? Where do they live?

All should have been easy questions... but they weren't for Dahlia. They never had been.

She couldn't say if she was just projecting her own dislike for those sorts of topics or was picking up on something from him, but either way she shelved the questions that popped up as she watched him work.

Who taught you how to cook? Why did you leave South Carolina?

Instead, she kept her questions to the task at hand. And when it was time to sit and eat, she laughed as he told her stories of his first failed attempts at catching his own dinner.

"That was amazing," she said with a sigh when her plate was empty.

His eyes were glittering with what looked like joy as he leaned forward on his elbows. "You were amazing."

She arched her brows, ready to laugh at the teasing. But he grew earnest. "Honestly, Dahlia, I'm not sure when I last enjoyed a fishing trip so much."

Her smile wobbled, and her insides seemed to shake.

She wasn't used to this sort of sincerity, and she couldn't quite meet his gaze. "I had fun too," she murmured, her voice made soft by the unexpected nerves jittering through her.

Truthfully, she didn't want the date to end. There was a big part of her that wanted to stick around even after she finished helping him with the dishes. A part of her that was so much more comfortable here in this little bunkhouse with him than with her own flesh and blood at the main house. Or… anywhere, really.

Even back home in New York she couldn't recall many occasions like this, where she didn't feel like she was putting on an act or had to impress someone.

But that was all the more reason she ought to go. The voice of reason was nagging at her to leave before she got any more attached to this man or the way she felt here in his home.

It was his home, not hers.

And the main house was Rose's home… and Emma's and Lizzy's. But not hers.

"I should get back." She picked up her jacket by the door, then slid her feet into her boots.

"I'll walk you," he said.

She knew better than to argue. He'd walk her back no matter what.

The chill hit her as soon as she stepped out of the bunkhouse, and she buried her hands in her pockets and hunched her shoulders, hiding her mouth behind the tall collar of her jacket.

They walked most of the way in silence, and Dahlia was enchanted by the way the full moon lit the snow.

"Looks like it's glowing."

"Mmm," he murmured.

She tipped her head back to take in the bright, clear sky, the stars twinkling overhead. "I'm not sure I've ever seen anything so pretty."

"Neither have I."

His voice was so low she almost missed it, and when she glanced over, his gaze was fixed on her, not the sky.

She dipped her head, grateful that he likely couldn't see her blush in this dim light. As they drew close to the main house's back door, she found her footsteps slowing.

"Well," she said, coming to a stop at the edge of the back porch, "I guess this is good night."

She nearly rolled her eyes at how silly she sounded. She'd never once gotten nervous at the end of a date, so why was she acting like a total girly girl right now? She cleared her throat as she turned to face him.

"Thank you for a lovely day," she added.

Oh heck. Now she sounded like a prissy schoolmarm.

His lips hitched up on one side, and she felt the warmth of his smile like a bolt of lightning.

"I'm the one who should be thanking you." He inched a little closer. "Ice fishing has never been so fun."

She smiled and edged toward the door.

"Now hang on one second." He smiled as he spoke, and that Southern drawl of his had never been so prominent.

She arched a brow as he moved in closer again.

"Isn't it customary to end a date with a kiss?"

Heat rushed through her at the mischievous glint in his eyes. And then his gaze dipped to her lips.

Her mouth went dry, and her knees felt suspiciously weak as she tripped over her words. "Oh, um, I don't... I don't think that's a good idea."

A hysterical laugh nearly exploded out of her at that understatement. Her lips tingled with the urge to lean forward and touch his. She had to clench her hands into fists to keep from reaching for him.

Goodness, what had come over her?

She stumbled back a step.

Not a good idea? Letting him kiss her would be a terrible idea. She was already too drawn to him, already oddly attached.

She backed up even farther, and his smile softened, his eyes warm with understanding. "How about a handshake, then?"

No! She bit her lip to hold back the panicked response. *Don't be silly. A handshake never hurt anyone.*

She stuck her hand out, and when his large, calloused hand wrapped around hers, she knew she'd made a mistake.

His fingers were warm, and her hand was swallowed up. His thumb brushed over hers, and the touch felt more intimate than any kiss she'd ever shared with her ex. And then he brought her hand to his mouth, lightly pressing his lips to her knuckles the way a true Southern gentleman would.

Her wild heart could barely contain its beat.

She swallowed hard before tugging her hand from his. "Um… good night. And thanks again for the day."

"My pleasure." His drawl was warm and liquid like molasses.

She turned away with a silly smile because… he meant it. She heard it in his voice. He'd enjoyed their day just as much as she had.

It took everything in her not to lean against the door and swoon after she closed it, but the joy bubbling through her veins fell flat when she heard her sisters' laughter. They were in the kitchen, mugs of hot chocolate in their hands and what looked like wedding invitations strewn all over the table.

All at once it came back to her. They'd tricked her into

this outing today. She should be furious with them. The thought had her scowling as she walked into the room.

As soon as they saw her, the three of them stopped talking, their laughter cut short as they exchanged wary glances.

That's right, be afraid. The fire-breathing dragon is back, and she's angry.

Rose's cheeks were pink when Dahlia looked her way, but her eyes were wide and sweet. "How was it?"

Before Dahlia could respond, Lizzy choked on a laugh as she added, "Yeah, did you enjoy… ice fishing?"

Lizzy nearly lost the battle with laughter on that last part, and even saintly Emma looked like she was having a hard time holding back a giggle at Dahlia's expense.

"Actually…" Dahlia cleared her throat, lifting her chin a little. "I caught two fish, so—"

"No way!" Rose looked delighted.

"You caught something?" Emma's voice pitched with excitement. She and Lizzy applauded loudly, making Rose giggle, and Dahlia…

Well, Dahlia felt a smile tug at her lips. She didn't appreciate how they went about it, but she'd had the best day she could remember thanks to their meddling. And it was hard to be too mad about that.

Rose leaned forward, so eager it hurt Dahlia's heart. "So you had fun?"

Dahlia glanced at the others but couldn't lie to Rose. "Yeah," she said. "I had a blast."

Rose beamed. And when she glanced over, she saw that Emma and Lizzy were genuinely smiling at her.

Not laughing at her, but actually happy that she'd had fun.

She glanced down at the table, uncertain of what she

was supposed to say or do without the ever-present tension between them.

"What have you been up to?" She pulled out one of the dining chairs and took a seat.

"Helping Emma with the invites for her wedding." Lizzy held up an embossed envelope.

Emma winced. "There are so many. It's a little overwhelming."

Dahlia reached for a stack of envelopes that still needed to be stuffed. "I can help."

This earned her a wide-eyed look of surprise from Emma and Lizzy, but they got over it quickly enough.

"Thanks." Emma grinned. "I feel like maybe I've bitten off more than I can chew with such a big wedding."

"You've got me to help you." Lizzy patted her arm.

"And me." Rose smiled.

Dahlia only hesitated for a second. "And me."

All three of them turned to face her, but Rose's huge smile had Dahlia smiling back at her. "I'm really good with organizing stuff, you know."

Rose nodded, turning to Lizzy and Emma with excitement. "She's the best at planning."

"Well, then…" Emma and Lizzy exchanged a quick look, but then they were both wearing genuine smiles when they turned to her. "Welcome aboard the wedding crew."

Lizzy leaned over and adopted a stage whisper. "You might regret it."

A surprise laugh slipped out of Dahlia.

But then Rose's hand covered hers, giving it a little squeeze.

Dahlia might regret the offer… but she doubted it.

There was nothing better on a Sunday morning than a gorgeous sunrise and a walk in the wild. It was the best way to spend a little time appreciating the true blessing of all God had given him. He'd walk and pray, meandering through forests and fields, refueling his soul for the week ahead.

JJ stopped at the creek. He'd normally hike much farther, but the snow was thick after the last storm, and it was tough going.

He paused where he was, breathing in the crisp air and pulling a water bottle from his backpack.

Sunday mornings were normally a time for him to get the silence and peace he craved. He loved the ranch, but between living with Cody and having coworkers around him throughout the day, he still valued his alone time.

These walks in nature were a big part of that. His little cabin in the woods was where he went when he had more than a morning to himself.

He turned in place to take in the view and felt a smile

forming at the memory of Dahlia's reaction to this sight the day before.

The sun had risen high already—he ought to start heading back soon so he could be in town for the kids' art expo down at the school. The twins had taken part, and he'd promised Chloe and Corbin he'd be by to check it out.

But he had a few minutes, at least, to bask in the sunshine and revel in the view. Nearly everyone else was at church right now.

Was Dahlia there?

He ran a hand over his chest, as if he could actually touch the pang he felt whenever he'd thought about her this morning.

Was this what it meant to miss someone?

He shook his head with a huff that startled some birds in the nearby shrubbery.

He couldn't *miss* Dahlia. He'd just seen her the night before. And he'd no doubt see her again tonight, before she left for New York tomorrow.

JJ winced at the thought. There really was no use denying it. He missed her even though she was still in town.

That did not bode well for how he'd feel after she got on that plane.

He took a deep breath and let it out in a cloud of steam.

That was why it was for the best that she was leaving. Better she go now before whatever he was starting to feel developed into something even harder to get over.

With one more deep, fortifying breath, he turned back the way he'd come. He'd need to take a shower and eat some breakfast before heading into town. And then, of course, there was his obligatory Sunday call.

Every other Sunday, he called his mother. He timed it

so that he called when she and his father and his younger sisters had returned home after church for their weekly lunch together, so he could say hello to them all at once. The call was brief, and not exactly warm, but it let everyone know he was alive and well and made him feel like he was doing his due diligence as a son.

Of course, it was too little too late for that as far as his parents were concerned. He'd already proven to be a disappointment.

He shoved those thoughts to the side. These Sunday morning hikes were to clear his head of the past. To cut off any worries about the future.

These Sunday hikes were to feel close to God and to find peace in the present moment.

And at this particular present moment, he had a lot to give thanks for. As he made the slow hike back to his lodgings, he listed them out. He loved his job. Loved his friends. Loved this town and the community that had embraced him.

Before he knew it, his thoughts had drifted back to Dahlia again.

He was thankful for the day he'd spent with her, that much was certain.

He wished he'd thought to ask her if she had any plans for today. But she probably did. It was her last day in Aspire. She'd want to spend it with Rose.

And he wouldn't try to seek her out, he told himself.

He'd just let things lie, because there was no use trying to get close to a woman who had one foot out the door.

He'd decided he wouldn't take another shot at a long-term relationship when his marriage had fallen apart, and he wasn't going to rethink that decision now just because some stunning brunette had made his heart pound and his blood run hot.

Still, when he got out of the shower a little while later and was getting changed to head into town, he found himself wondering if he'd run into her.

And there was no denying that it was hope he felt when he thought it.

Right or wrong, he sure hoped he could see Dahlia one more time before she left.

M aybe Dahlia was getting sick. That would explain it.

She sniffled once more. and Rose glanced over at her with a concerned frown before passing her a packet of tissues.

"Let he who is without sin cast the first stone..." The minister's voice carried throughout the small church as he went on about the redemptive power of love. About forgiveness and healing.

Dahlia tugged out a tissue and dabbed at her nose.

She wasn't crying. She never cried, and definitely not over a sermon, no matter how well-spoken it might have been.

Rose reached for her hand and squeezed. Dahlia squeezed back.

Maybe it was allergies.

The minister had started by talking about a woman caught in adultery, and Dahlia had worked herself into a fine fury over the way the woman had been treated while the man she'd been sleeping with had walked away scot-free. These religious men wanted to stone her to death. And then Jesus stepped in.

The minister then started down this path about love and forgiveness and—

"Are you all right?" Rose whispered.

Dahlia nodded quickly. "Of course. It's just allergies."

Rose arched a brow in disbelief.

Probably because it was late January—not exactly a high time for allergies. And also, Dahlia had never really been prone to hay fever in the past.

She ignored Rose's searching gaze.

She was totally fine. This week was just taking a toll on her, that was all. She needed to get back to normal. The sooner the better.

The thought of the mountain of work that would await her when she returned was enough to distract her. She was feeling more like herself again when she tuned back in to what the minister was saying.

"… And that, my dear friends, is the true healing power of love."

She swallowed down a scoff.

"The healing power of love"?

Please.

She crossed her arms with a huff.

Had she honestly gotten emotional over this topic?

Love was many things, but healing? Hardly.

Sure, maybe when it came to God and Jesus, but in everyday life with ordinary people?

Nope. No, sir. When it came to mere mortals, love didn't heal. It destroyed and burned and bruised.

By the time the service ended, Dahlia had wound herself back to her usual state of unrest. There was an odd comfort to the norm, and she found herself itching to get on that plane the next day.

She followed Rose as she shuffled out of the pew and into the aisle.

Maybe it wasn't traditional allergies she was suffering from, but she was definitely starting to think she might be allergic to this town and its inhabitants. There was nothing for her here other than Rose.

"Oh my, you've gotten so much bigger," an older woman was saying to Rose.

Another woman reached out and touched Rose's belly. As if she had any right.

Dahlia would have slapped the woman's hand away if it were her, but of course, Rose was too nice for that.

"This baby can't come soon enough." She smiled sweetly, as though she honestly didn't mind the probing questions.

"Dr. Dex was telling us that you're working on choosing the perfect name for this little one." The older woman's face begged to be let in on the secret.

As if!

Rose hadn't even told Dahlia what she was thinking of naming her daughter. She wasn't about to tell some strange old lady.

"Have you and the doctor set a date?" another woman piped up.

Rose smiled, her cheeks flushing red, and Dahlia felt all her mama bear instincts kicking in. "Will you excuse us?" She snagged Rose by the elbow and, with a polite smile, started walking for the exit. "I think our sister Lizzy is waiting."

Rose giggled. "Lizzy's waiting, huh? You know, you really shouldn't lie in church."

"How do you put up with all these small-town busy-bodies?" Dahlia muttered when they were out of earshot.

"You get used to it," Rose said with a good-natured shrug. "Besides, there are good things about living in a small town too. It's not all about the gossip."

Just then, they overheard a group of older men beside them. "Well, I heard they still can't find April. I wonder whatever became of that girl."

Dahlia arched her brows at Rose meaningfully, but Rose just burst out laughing. "Oh, that's just Norman and Chicken Joe for you. You'd like them."

"Chicken who?"

"You want me to introduce you?" Rose started to turn toward the old men, but Dahlia put a hand on her arm. "Maybe another time."

Rose grinned. "Okay. But I think you'd really like them."

"I'll take your word for it. Besides, I leave tomorrow, remember?"

"Yes, but you'll be back." Rose patted her belly with a knowing smile. "You have a little niece who'll be excited to meet you, remember?"

Dahlia smiled and… oh crap. There were those dang allergies again.

"There you are!" Lizzy joined them, her husband, Kit, right behind her. "The twins are already at the school, and they're waiting for their aunties to ooh and ahh. Come on, Rose…" She wrapped an arm around Rose's shoulder, and Dahlia was left to stand there alone, frustrated that she wasn't even being given a chance to say goodbye.

And how the heck was Rose getting back to the ranch? Were they going to drop her, or were they just expecting Dahlia to come back and pick her up?

All these questions were so busy buzzing around her brain that she nearly missed the fact that Lizzy had stopped walking and was staring at her.

"Dahlia? Aren't you coming?"

Dahlia blinked in surprise. She'd met the twins, of course, but... She pointed at herself. "I'm one of the aunties?"

Lizzy rolled her eyes. "Of course you are."

Kit winked at Dahlia as Lizzy steered Rose toward the parking lot. The handsome cowboy fell into step beside her. "Before we get there, I should probably fill you in on who's who in Corbin's family portrait."

Dahlia arched her brows. "And why's that?"

"It's a little hard to tell," Lizzy said over her shoulder. "And he gets awfully insulted if you can't instantly point out who's who."

"I saw it the other day." Rose laughed. "I was easy to pick out. He made my belly bigger than Emma's entire body."

"You're in there too, you know," Kit informed her.

"Let me guess," Dahlia deadpanned. "I'm the dragon."

Lizzy laughed so hard she had to stop walking and bend over.

Dahlia tried to act annoyed but found herself shaking her head with a rueful grin as Lizzy tried to get herself under control. "No," she wheezed. "But wouldn't that be hilarious?"

Kit chuckled. "Chloe's picture is easier to decipher." He turned to Dahlia. "Her picture is of flowers. Don't guess anything else if you don't want a wailing child on your hands."

Dahlia nodded. "Flowers. Got it."

They were part of a large crowd heading toward the

school after the service, but they stuck together. And when Emma spotted them, she waved them over. Nash was at her side, handing out flyers to the parents and guests.

The moment they entered the school building, the crowd turned raucous. All the quiet and humility of church faded fast in the face of proud parents.

"Look, John, there's Monica's piece!" a mother shouted, nearly pushing Kit out of the way in her hurry.

"The annual art show is a big deal in these parts." Kit grinned.

"I can see that."

"For the little ones, it's a chance to show off some of their coloring," he went on. "But the older ones get to choose whatever sort of art they want. Some do theatrical pieces, other students choose to sing or dance, there's sculpture and painting and…"

"What did you do when you were a kid?" Lizzy turned with bright, eager eyes.

He gave them a grin. "I showed off my roping skills."

Dahlia barked out a laugh before clapping a hand over her mouth.

"You did not." Lizzy giggled.

"What?" he said. "Roping is an art."

Rose's laughter was cut short when she spotted Dr. Dex. "There he is! Dex!"

He came over, wrapping his arms around Rose as he kissed her cheek. "How are my two favorite girls?" He rubbed her belly like it was a magic lamp.

"Better now," Rose murmured with a dreamy smile.

Lizzy raised an eyebrow at Dahlia. "They're nauseating sometimes, amiright?"

Dahlia silently laughed as Rose turned on Lizzy with a fake scowl. "Like you and Kit are any better."

Chloe and Corbin spotted them at that moment and came rushing over. "Come on, Daddy!" Chloe grabbed his hand.

With the twins leading the way, they fought through the crowd to get to Emma's classroom, where their work was displayed.

Dahlia let the others go first, happy to fall behind and watch them interact. It was nice that Lizzy and Emma were making an effort. Last night and this morning, they'd both gone out of their way to make her feel included. And she appreciated that—she really did.

But she had a hunch it was more for Rose's benefit, and she wasn't about to mistake their kindness for some family bond.

But for Rose's sake, she'd do her best to be nice in return. Rose deserved that much. Just like Rose deserved a husband like Dex.

She smiled as she watched them together now. He was so good with her. Gentle and understanding, but also encouraging. He didn't fight her battles on her behalf but rather stood at her side and helped her to be a stronger version of herself.

It was something Dahlia had never been able to do. She was always so busy taking charge. She winced and rubbed her forehead.

Dex was the perfect man for Rose, and that was a relief.

If anyone in their family deserved a happy home life, it was her baby sister. Daisy would likely never settle down long enough to have a family, and Dahlia...

Well, she had no desire to.

She'd already raised Rose, in many ways. Daisy too, in some regards. The last thing she needed was to have that responsibility thrust on her again. And besides, she wasn't cut out for love.

It hadn't taken her failed relationship with Brady to prove as much. She'd always known she didn't have what it took to give of herself like that.

Or…

No, that wasn't it.

It was that she'd seen too clearly what happened when you gave of yourself and the other person didn't appreciate it. Her mother hadn't been stable at the best of times, but Dahlia couldn't help thinking things might have been different if the man her mother had loved hadn't walked away.

If he hadn't left her with three kids and a broken heart.

Dahlia wrapped her arms around herself, suddenly cold as she took in the warm family scene before her. Nash was whispering something in Emma's ear that made her smile. Kit and Lizzy were making a fuss over the twins' artwork. Rose and Dex were laughing about something right behind them.

It was so very perfect… for Rose.

But for Dahlia?

For Dahlia, it was way past time she got back to reality. If she stuck around much longer, she might just forget that this wasn't her future.

That this wasn't her home.

18

Aspire's school was bursting at the seams by the time JJ arrived.

The hallways were filled with children, the classrooms packed with families, and there was no tough brunette anywhere to be seen.

JJ leaned against one of the walls in the school's main lobby as he eyed the crowd. It wasn't like he'd come here to see Dahlia, but he couldn't seem to stop himself from seeking her out.

"Hey, JJ!" one of Cody's friends called out to him.

He lifted a hand before losing the woman in the crowd again.

"Hey, buddy." This came from Ethan, who was impossible to miss even in all the people. Tall and broad, the firefighter probably didn't even realize how many women were looking his way as he cut through the crowd.

"Ethan." JJ shook the other man's hand. "You trying to find a place where you won't be trampled too?"

Ethan chuckled as he leaned against the wall beside JJ.

"It never ceases to amaze me how the people of this town come together for events like this one."

JJ murmured his agreement. It was one of the things he liked best about this place. He'd overheard some tourists talk about Aspire like it was just another quaint small town, but he knew better.

There were lots of quaint little towns around where he'd grown up, but none of them had ever felt like this. Like a true community.

Like home.

He supposed if one had, he might not have wandered all over the world trying to find it.

"Have you seen Levi?" Ethan asked.

Levi was one of Ethan's closest friends, and the town's sheriff. His two young sons went to this school, so he was bound to be around here somewhere. "Not yet."

"How're things going up on the ranch?" Ethan asked. "Dex says the mean O'Sullivan sister is back in town for a few extra days." His grin was filled with mischief, but it quickly died. No doubt hustled away by JJ's scowl.

"She's not mean," he muttered.

"Sorry. I was only teasing." Ethan cleared his throat, looking slightly uncomfortable and so obviously trying to amend his faux pas. "I haven't officially met her yet, but I caught a glimpse of her in town a couple weeks back. She's as pretty as the others, don't you think?"

Prettier.

JJ shrugged, keeping his mouth shut. But there was a flicker of something dark and green in his gut at Ethan's mention of Dahlia.

Nope. Not pretty at all, he wanted to say. It would be a lie, of course, but some part of him had a hankering to keep her to himself.

148

All the ladies seemed to love the tall, dark, and handsome firefighter. And the thought of Dahlia giving Ethan one of her hard-to-earn smiles had him frowning.

He looked away with a huff of amusement at his own idiocy. Yes, sir, it was a darn good thing she'd be leaving the next day.

Even as he thought it, fate called him out as a liar.

Dahlia came into view, shuffling along in the crowd behind Rose, Dex, Lizzy, and Kit. He only caught a glimpse of her before she was swallowed up by the crowd again, but that glimpse was enough. A surge of happiness hit him hard at the sight of her, and when she didn't see him and kept walking…

Well, this falling sensation could only be called disappointment.

But you're glad she's leaving, huh?

He shook off the thought, focusing on Ethan instead. "We still on for the pancake fundraiser next month?"

Ethan nodded. "If you're up for it."

JJ cracked his knuckles and adopted a fierce scowl. "No one makes pancakes like I make pancakes."

Ethan chuckled. "That's the spirit."

They were both laughing by the time Levi showed up, only one of his kids in tow.

"Howdy, Mikayla." JJ nodded to the thirteen-year-old, who looked like she was sucking on a lemon.

"Hi," she grumbled.

JJ arched a brow at Levi, who had a harried air about him—not uncommon for the single father.

Levi rested his hands on his hips, giving his daughter a sideways glare. "She wants to go off with her friends, but I won't let her," he explained to Ethan and JJ.

"Everyone else is allowed to go off on their own," she complained.

"Yeah, well, if everyone else jumped off a cliff, would you?" he retorted.

Ethan shot JJ a wince. It was no secret that Levi had been struggling to raise three kids on his own after his wife died a few years back. But at times like this, JJ wondered how much the kids were struggling too.

Everyone knew Levi was strict—maybe it came with the territory, being sheriff and all—but as a child of strict parents, JJ found himself watching a disgruntled Mikayla with sympathy.

He felt even more sympathy when he looked back to Levi. He didn't seem angry. Not even frustrated. Just... lost. Tired.

JJ clapped a hand on his shoulder. "What if I was to take Mikayla around, see if maybe we can find some of her friends while you go check out your boys' artwork?"

Mikayla's eyes widened with hope, and Levi shot him a wary look. "You don't mind?"

"Nah, I'm getting tired of just standing around," JJ said. "I could use a stretch of my legs."

Mikayla beamed at him, and he shot her a wink in return.

"All right," Levi said slowly. "If you don't mind... Thanks, JJ."

"Not at all." He and Mikayla were already starting to join the crowd heading toward the cafeteria.

"So, where are these friends of yours hanging out?" he asked.

She was all smiles now as she craned her neck to look for them. "Tamara and Lindsay were going to check out the music in the auditorium." She looked up at him with wide eyes. "Can we go?"

"I don't see why not." He earned himself another beaming grin.

"Thanks, JJ," she said. "If it was up to my dad, I'd be on a leash all day and all night."

He chuckled. "Now, I'd say that might be a bit of an exaggeration."

She arched one brow, and the cynical look made her look ten years older than she was.

"He only wants to keep you safe. But," he added slowly, "my parents were strict as well, so I get where you're coming from."

"You do?"

He nodded. He rarely talked about his family, and he wasn't about to start now. But apparently what he'd said was enough. "I'm glad somebody understands," she sighed.

Mikayla found her friends right away, and JJ gave them some space, staying close enough to make sure she didn't wander off but not so close that she couldn't have some privacy with her friends.

He was content to stand on the sidelines and babysit, but after about ten minutes, he was distracted by the sight of Dahlia. She was standing next to Dex and Rose, watching one of the young musicians.

A little smile curved her lips, and when Rose whispered something to her, that little smile grew into something so beautiful it stole his breath.

He waited for her to notice him. But when she did, his insides gave another jolt of disappointment. She spotted him, all right—but she looked away just as quickly.

For the next twenty minutes he couldn't shake the feeling that Dahlia was looking everywhere but at him.

"My friends are heading out." Mikayla joined him by the wall. "Want to go find my dad and brothers?"

He nodded. "Sure."

As he walked away, he couldn't say for certain, but he was pretty sure Dahlia was pointedly ignoring him.

So... good.

That was fine. She'd been tricked into their date, anyhow. And he'd been coerced.

Yup. It was probably all for the best that she was leaving that next morning.

19

Dahlia's bag was packed and waiting by the door when she strode into the kitchen to say her goodbyes.

Again.

Emma was poring over papers at the table as Nash made himself a cup of coffee.

"Don't think you're getting off easy with the wedding planning just because you're leaving town," Emma teased when Dahlia started to say her goodbyes.

Dahlia smiled. "Don't worry, I can plan just as well over the phone as I can in person."

Emma narrowed her eyes. "I'll hold you to that."

"And I'll send you those financials you were asking for," Nash said. "Sorry, it's been so hectic lately, and—"

"No rush." Dahlia brushed her hand through the air.

Emma and Nash both paused what they were doing to stare at her. Dahlia looked away quickly. She'd honestly surprised herself with that reaction. Maybe she knew that fighting for the sale right now was a fruitless endeavor.

She just had to accept that this inheritance hoopla would stretch out for longer than she'd like.

The important thing was to get back to her life the way it was.

Normality. She was craving it.

Nash cleared his throat. "Have you checked on your flights this morning?"

She blinked in surprise; something about his tone put her on high alert. "I did when I first woke up…" Fear had her belly twisting into a knot. "Why?"

Nash grimaced. "There's a weather advisory in effect, so… just wanted to make sure."

"What are they saying?" Dahlia scrambled for her phone so she could check for herself.

He shook his head. "Another big storm's coming through, but it's not supposed to hit here until later this afternoon."

Dahlia tensed. "Please don't say they're canceling flights again."

"Probably not," he murmured. But his furrowed brow and the "probably" were not exactly heartening.

She nibbled on her lip, her fingers clenching and unclenching the phone. She checked the app and saw her flight was still scheduled to go.

Thank goodness!

Her bosses would kill her if she didn't show up first thing tomorrow morning. Well, maybe not kill. But firing? That could definitely be a possibility.

If she had to push this trip back *again*?

She didn't even want to think about it.

Rose came into the kitchen behind Dahlia, moving slowly as she headed toward the table and sank down into a seat.

"Are you okay?" Dahlia's instant worry replaced her own fears as she took in Rose's pale complexion. She was white as a ghost.

Rose rubbed her temple, her expression pinched. "I just had a really bad night. Couldn't sleep. Couldn't get comfortable, and now I've got a killer headache."

Dahlia hurried over to her. "Can I get you anything? Do you need me to call Dex?"

"I've already spoken to him. He told me to drink plenty of fluids and put my feet up." Rose rested her head in her palms. "He's going to swing by later and pick me up so I can spend the afternoon at his place. After I take you to the airport, I mean."

Dahlia frowned. "I don't think you should be driving me."

"I'm with Dahlia on this one," Emma said. "You shouldn't drive if you feel this bad."

Nash joined them at the table. "I'll see if JJ can do it."

Dahlia stiffened at the mention of his name. She had to physically force herself to relax as Nash continued.

"He was asking if he could take the morning off to go check on his cabin before the storm hits." Nash glanced her way. "It's on the way to the airport, so if you don't mind swinging past there first…"

The anxiety that twisted her insides wanted to protest. She didn't have time for detours!

But she did, and they all knew it.

She'd allotted plenty of time to get to the airport, and if the cabin was on the way, how could she say no?

"Sure. As long as I don't miss my flight." Dahlia had to force a smile.

"Great, then I'll give him a call," Nash said.

Emma beamed at her like she'd just offered to donate a kidney or something.

Dahlia's smile faltered. Why hadn't she argued? Or seen if someone else could drive her?

She crossed her arms as she listened to Nash talking on the phone to JJ.

This was... not ideal. And not just because she didn't want to make a detour. She'd done a stellar job of avoiding JJ all day yesterday. She didn't want to see him again, let alone have another long drive together.

Her feelings when he was around were too... fuzzy and confusing. Too *messy*.

She didn't do messy. Especially not when she was about to get on a plane for the East Coast and had no intention of coming back until just before the baby was due, which wasn't until June.

Her eyes darted to Emma as she thought about being on the wedding crew. But she could still help with planning an event she had no intention of attending, right? They'd all understand if she didn't come. It wasn't like New York was the next state over, and she couldn't keep flying back and forth for every little thing.

A wedding is not just a little thing!

She winced at the thought but cleared her expression when Nash turned to smile at her.

She'd only half heard his end of the conversation, but it was clear that JJ agreed to this new plan.

So good. Awesome. Now she and JJ could have another road trip.

Nash leaned over to kiss Emma goodbye. "Be careful on those roads, all right?"

"I'm always careful," she shot back with a grin.

"I know, but if the storm hits while you're at school..."

He frowned in concern. "I'll come pick you up. Your car can always stay at the school overnight. I just want to make sure you're safe."

Emma gave him such a sweet, loving look that Dahlia had to glance away, her heart giving a little ache.

This time she wasn't forced to wait around for JJ. He showed up right after Nash walked out the door. His gaze collided with hers the second he appeared, and she couldn't look away.

Not even when he smiled. And that smile...

She swallowed hard. What was it about that smile that made her feel like her insides were unraveling?

It wasn't fair.

"Morning," she mumbled after Rose and Emma had already greeted him and thanked him for taking over as Dahlia's chauffeur.

This time Dahlia didn't dally over her goodbyes with Rose. She didn't quite trust herself to hold it together if she did. She squeezed her little sister tight and whispered in her ear. "I'll be back."

"I know you will," Rose whispered. "Love you, sis."

Love you too.

She couldn't get the words out past the lump in her throat. So instead she kissed Rose's cheek and let her go, turning abruptly to follow JJ out the door.

She stopped beside the front door, but her luggage was already gone. JJ had taken it for her.

She sighed as she shut the door behind her.

Of course he had.

20

JJ wasn't sure if he should be offended or delighted by Dahlia's behavior as they headed toward the cabin.

He cast a quick sidelong glance her way. Yup. Sure enough, she was still fidgeting with the handle of her bag, crossing and uncrossing her legs like she couldn't get comfortable.

And her silence? It was a doozy.

She hadn't met his eyes once since she'd climbed into his truck. And her contributions to small talk had been awkward at best.

He felt a grin tugging at his lips. Another man might think she was being rude, but he knew better. If she were truly unhappy with him or to be in his company, he'd know it.

The way Dahlia was so upfront with her emotions and said precisely what she was thinking, that was one of his favorite things about her. If she was mad about something, she'd have told him.

So no, this anxious tension was something else altogether. And by the way she wouldn't quite meet his gaze, the way her breathing had grown erratic and her lips parted for air when he'd leaned over her to grab his phone out of the cup holder where he'd stashed it....

Well, that was all the confirmation he needed that she felt it too, that strange but undeniable connection whenever they were close. The way a simple glance could make a room feel charged like lightning was about to strike.

He shifted his hands on the wheel and glanced over once more. Her posture was so rigid, it looked like she was trying to balance a book on top of her head.

He fought another inappropriate chuckle at the sight of her pinched lips.

She might be tense, and no doubt on edge about making her flight, but she was just as beautiful as ever.

Her hair was all perfect and straight, shiny like silk. She was wearing a little makeup, and her city style was back on full display with the perfectly fitted tight jeans and the leather jacket.

It was like she'd donned her armor to head back home, and while he preferred to see her relaxed and casual, there was no denying how beautiful she looked.

Untouchable, but beautiful.

The thought had his hands fidgeting again like they were just itching to touch her. To mess up that perfect hair, to kiss those red lips until her gaze was dazed and that tension gone.

He took a deep breath and forced his eyes back to the road.

"Thank you," she said suddenly, breaking the silence. She cleared her throat. "For driving me. Again." She cast him a quick rueful grin. "I'm sure you have better things to do with your time."

"I can't think of anything," he said. "In fact, there's nothing I'd rather do more than hang out with you right now."

Her cheeks grew pink, and he had to swallow hard to hold back a laugh. Not at her expense, of course. She was just too adorable when she was flustered.

And besides, he just couldn't help these waves of happiness whenever he got past that armor of hers. A blush from Dahlia was basically the equivalent of an emotional outpour from anyone else.

"You're just being nice," she muttered as she looked out the window.

"Yeah, that's me," he said, not trying to hide his amusement. "Mr. Nice Guy. Always blowing smoke, trying to make people feel good."

She made a choking sound that sounded suspiciously like a laugh. "That's not what I meant."

"No, you're right," he continued. "Everyone knows I'm a charmer. Slick and savvy, that's me—"

"Is that so?" She shot him a funny, narrow-eyed look as he continued.

"JJ the silver-tongued sweetheart, that's what they call me," he drawled.

She snickered, and he grinned over at her.

"It's true," he continued, loving the way her lips were fighting the battle with a smile. "I'm just a shameless flirt."

"Uh-huh."

"It's nothing to do with you personally." He grinned, giving away his outrageous lie.

Her cheeks were bright red now as she rolled her lips between her teeth, her eyes dancing with laughter. "Not personal, huh?"

"No, ma'am." He let his Southern accent come out to play. "I take every beautiful woman I meet out ice fishin'."

She laughed then, and the sound was so sweet and girly, he felt a burst of affection so intense it made his heart swollen and achy.

"I hope you didn't get the wrong idea," he continued, shooting her a lopsided smile. "You're about the tenth gorgeous woman this month who I've brought back to the bunkhouse for a home-cooked fish dinner."

"Uh-huh." Her voice was light with laughter. "I see how it is. You lure in all the ladies by gutting fish, huh?"

His head fell back with a laugh. "That's right." He shot her a quick glance. "But you're the first I've walked home after."

She arched her brows, her eyes still filled with amusement. "Is that right?"

"And I can safely say you're the only ice fishing partner I've ever asked if I could kiss good night."

Her grin was magic. "I guess I'm a lucky lady, then."

He feigned humility with a shrug. "Some might say that."

For a heartbeat, she held his gaze, and he felt that connection as surely as if she'd struck him with a cattle prod. Then she looked away, staring out the window. But her posture was a little more at ease.

"So, Nash said we're stopping by your cabin first?"

"If you don't mind." He nodded. "My cabin is old, and while she's withstood more than her fair share of winter storms, I'd still like to make sure it's ready for all the snow coming our way."

He felt her stare as he kept his gaze on the road. Part of him tensed as her silence drew out.

It would only be natural to ask questions about his

cabin, and he typically avoided all talk of how he came to own this land… and why.

But this tension was different. It wasn't that he didn't want to tell her, just… he wasn't sure how. Or where to start.

But he had a weird urge to talk about it. A first since he'd come to this state.

"How old is it?" she asked.

"It was built at the turn of the century. The exact date isn't clear, but it goes back to at least the late 1800s."

"Wow." She shifted so she was facing him. "How'd you come to own it? Was it in your family or something? I mean, I know you grew up in South Carolina, but…"

She trailed off with a shrug, and when he glanced over, he saw the curiosity in her eyes.

"No. I have no family in these parts. My entire extended family is back in South Carolina. They've been there since this country was founded, and so far as I know, I'm the first to leave."

The silence filled the truck's cab. For his part, his heart was pounding. It wasn't like he'd spilled some deep, dark secret, but…

That was the first time he'd spoken of his family at all since he'd left.

The realization was jarring.

"Why did you leave?" He tensed for the question, but it never came. Instead, she asked, "Do you ever miss the East Coast?"

He felt a smile tug at his lips. "Not really."

She nodded and sank back in her seat as he turned off for the long, winding road that led to the cabin. She seemed content to let the conversation end there. He should be grateful that she didn't pry and let it drop.

But to his surprise, he found himself talking as the truck rattled over the dirt road. "I miss my family sometimes," he murmured. "But..."

She said nothing as he searched for the right words to explain his complex family relationships. He felt her gaze on him, but she kept quiet.

"But I left for a reason," he said slowly. There was that drawl again. It always became more pronounced when emotions reared up. "I didn't fit in, I guess. I wasn't the son or the grandson or the nephew that everyone wanted me to be." He shot her a rueful smile. "I guess I've always been a bit of a loner. Always preferred marching to the beat of my own drum."

She nodded, and while there wasn't even a hint of pity in her expression, he saw understanding in her eyes.

"So you struck out on your own?" she said.

He tipped his head from side to side. "It was a little more complicated than all that. But long story short, yes. I made my way west, working odd jobs. I've always been good with my hands and never minded physical labor." He shrugged. "I ended up working for Patrick Donahue." He glanced over. "You've met Nash's father?"

She nodded.

"Well, when Nash was hired on by Frank O'Sullivan to run his property, he asked me and Kit to come along and help. Cody joined shortly after."

"And the cabin?" she asked.

He shifted in his seat. Explaining where the money came from to buy the cabin only led to topics he didn't want to dwell on. "I had some money to my name." He glanced over. "An inheritance from my grandpa. Once I realized Aspire was the place I wanted to call home, I got an urge to make it official, you know? Put down some roots."

"And so you bought a cabin," she said.

And a whole lot of the surrounding land. But he didn't offer that part up. It was enough that she knew about the cabin.

"It must be nice to have a place that's all yours." Her voice seemed wistful. "A place you know will be there for you no matter what."

He nodded, his chest tight with emotion. That was it exactly. For him, the cabin was home even if he didn't stay there all the time. It was the one place in this world where he belonged.

"That must be nice," she murmured. And for once there was no sarcasm in her voice, and no judgment either.

No judgment and no pity. Maybe that was why he found her so easy to talk to. Well, that and the fact that he could count on her to give it to him straight.

He had a feeling she and everyone else in her life took her unbridled honesty for granted.

"Almost there," he said as the dirt road turned steep and narrow.

She glanced at her phone. "We won't be late, right?"

"No, ma'am. It shouldn't take long to make sure all the doors and windows are secured. Plus I want to check the pipes and make sure a little water is dripping into them. Stops them from freezing over. It should be quick, and then we'll get back on the road and have you at the airport well in time for your flight."

His insides fell at the reminder of where they were ultimately headed.

He was going to miss her, which was... unexpected. But that was why it was for the best that she left now. The more he got to know her, and the more time they spent together, the more disappointed he'd be when she left.

She nodded and turned to look out at the view as they rounded the next bend in the road.

"Wow," she whispered as the trees opened up to reveal the snowy valley below. "So beautiful."

His gaze caught on her profile, and he murmured his agreement. "So beautiful."

21

D ahlia wasn't sure what she expected to find at a rustic cabin, but it wasn't this.

She stopped breathing the moment the trees gave way to the clearing. The small, snow-covered log cabin sat in the center of a clearing—a little plateau in the midst of the mountainside.

Her breath came out in a long sigh as she opened the truck door and slid down.

The cabin looked ancient, the trees and shrubbery over-grown and unmanicured. It looked wild and free. Even with snow covering the trees, the dark green was visible, and the smell of evergreens filled her veins with a fizzy sensation like she might float away. Blue sky could be seen through the clearing overhead, and the treetops swayed gently with the breeze.

There was nothing fancy about the rustic cabin or the setting, but all together it was… perfect.

It was so utterly perfect despite its imperfections—or maybe because of them—that she couldn't seem to breathe properly. It was as if some part of her was afraid if she moved too quickly, she'd wake up from this dream.

And the best part of the dream?

JJ.

She swallowed hard as he moved toward her. He looked exactly the same as he had when he'd strode through the ranch house's back door not even an hour earlier. But in this setting, with the trees overhead and the cabin at his back…

Dahlia tried to swallow again and ended up choking on her own saliva.

This was JJ in his natural habitat. He belonged here in this setting in a way she could never explain but that was so clear.

She imagined it was what one would feel seeing a lion in the plains of Africa after only ever seeing the creature in a zoo.

This was JJ in his element, and the sight was… stunning. He wasn't any more handsome than usual, but she'd also never been so painfully aware of his masculinity.

As he strode toward her now, her belly fluttered, and her blood turned to lava.

She had to force an exhale.

One corner of his mouth tugged up, and she wondered if he could see the effect he had on her.

Goodness, she hoped not. Her palms were clammy as she tucked them into her pockets, but she couldn't stop her imagination from running wild. She pictured JJ heading off to hunt for his dinner, JJ felling a tree with an ax, JJ making a fire…

She wet her lips. Oh dear. Her imagination had never been so vivid in all her life.

"This won't take long." JJ reached for her hand. "It's a

little warmer inside, or you can stay in the truck if you want."

She shook her head. "I'd love to see your cabin, if you don't mind."

His smile warmed her better than any fire. "'Course not. Come on in." He paused and took her hand, helping her through the thick snow. "I should warn you, there's nothing pretty about it."

"It's a cabin," she said. "It's not supposed to be pretty, is it?"

He chuckled. "A woman after my own heart."

Her heart did a wild flip in her chest, and she looked up to the heavens, exasperated by her body's foolish reactions. She'd managed to go her whole life immune from the giggly, inane stupidity that had afflicted her sisters and their friends when they developed crushes. She wasn't about to start now.

He unlocked the door and threw it open. "Here it is. Home sweet home."

She walked in first, and she had to bite her lip to hold back another goofy grin.

She loved it.

It was even more rustic than she'd imagined, but that was its charm. It was all wood inside, from the floors, to the walls, to the ceiling. And it felt homemade, with all the rough edges and the bare-bones attempt at architectural style. There were no flourishes, aside from some antlers over the fireplace, but at the same time, everything looked as though it had been handcrafted.

It was sparsely furnished, with a sofa and coffee table on one side of the room and a bed on the other. A little kitchenette with a small table took up the far corner, and an open door showed a tiny bathroom. "You have plumbing?"

"Mmm, and electricity, though I usually shut it off for the worst of the winter."

There was a closed door on the far side of the cabin, and Dahlia glanced back at JJ. "Another room?"

He scratched the back of his head with a rueful wince. "Sorta?" He led the way and opened it to reveal a small screened-in porch. There was another bed out there, along with a rocking chair and a heaping stack of books. "I sleep out here in the summer."

Dahlia nodded. She couldn't have spoken if she tried because all at once her throat was tight with a sense of… yearning? Was that what this was?

It was like feeling nostalgic but for something she'd never experienced.

She gave her head a shake and turned away as JJ shut the door against a strong wind.

"Make yourself comfortable." He pointed at the couch. "I just need to make sure this place is secure."

JJ moved around the cabin with a sense of purpose that made her even more acutely aware of the fact that she was standing there doing nothing.

"What needs to get done?" she asked.

"If a blizzard comes through, this place could get a hammering, and I don't want to come back and find a window blown in and snow covering the floor."

"Then let me help."

He paused, glancing at her with surprise.

She arched her brows. "Do I seem like the type who'd prefer to sit back and relax while you do all the work?"

He chuckled, dipping his head.

"Besides," she continued, "the sooner we get this done, the sooner we get back on the road."

His chuckle faded. "You're right. Here's what we need to do…"

It didn't take long with two of them working, and within ten minutes he was clapping his hands together with a satisfied sigh. "Right, all done."

She peeked at the time on her phone. Thank goodness, they still had over two hours to get to the airport. She was annoyed with herself for being so uptight about it, but a lifetime of being "the responsible one" was hard to shake.

She glanced up to see JJ scanning the place with a smile that made her heart flutter again.

This little cabin was obviously important to him. And being here with him… she could feel it. His connection to this home was palpable, and she felt the echo of it. Like if she was here with him, then she belonged here too.

They shared a smile that was almost intimate, and it unnerved her, so she quickly looked to the floor.

She was being silly and fanciful and… ugh. This was so not like her.

But it was yet another sign that she needed to leave. "If that's everything…" She headed for the door. "Let's get to the airport, then."

"Right." He followed behind her. "Wouldn't want you to be late."

JJ walked to her side first, opening the door for her. He went to help her in, but she beat him to it.

He paused for a second, and she felt her insides tighten with anxiety as the seconds to her flight ticked down. Her arrival home felt like it was looming, and not in a good way.

"Thanks, Dahlia," he said, nodding toward the cabin. "Your help made it go much faster than usual."

She smiled. "Anytime."

He grinned and shut the door, and she... rolled her eyes.

"Anytime?" she muttered to herself. What a stupid comment.

She was nearly gone and wouldn't be back for months. How would she help him "anytime"?

When he climbed into his seat, he shot her a lazy smile. "Don't worry, Ms. O'Sullivan. I'll have you at that airport with time to spare."

She opened her mouth to make a flippant retort, but the words died in her throat as the engine sputtered when he turned the key.

Her panicked gaze went from his hand to his face, searching out a reassuring look as he tried again.

But his smile melted into a frown when he turned the key for the third time and... nothing. The engine didn't even sound like it was trying to turn over. All they heard was a grinding complaint.

Dahlia didn't know much about vehicles, but that noise?

"That doesn't sound good."

2 2

JJ stared under the hood with a frown. He tucked his hands in his pockets to warm fingers that were getting numb from the cold. His brow furrowed. It didn't make sense that it'd be the battery, as that was replaced relatively recently.

He was no mechanic, but he knew enough. He'd systematically gone through every issue he could think of, but it wasn't anything obvious. At least, nothing that could be fixed in a jiffy.

Which meant…

The truck door slammed, and JJ winced. Guilt nagged at him. He supposed there was no denying it any longer. Dahlia came to stand beside him, crossing her arms and shivering against the cold as she frowned down at his engine. "What's the problem?"

"I'm not sure yet." But he had a suspicion. And it wasn't a good one. "Why don't you wait in the truck? It's warmer in there."

She gave a huff of laughter. "Not by much."

He flinched.

"Can I help at all?" she asked.

There was impatience in her tone, but the offer was genuine, and it did nothing to ease his guilt.

If his suspicion was correct, they weren't getting off this mountain anytime soon. At least, not soon enough to make her flight.

Five minutes later, he pulled back from where he'd been leaning over the engine and scrubbed a hand over his face. "I think the starter motor's shot."

Dahlia was quiet for a second, her pointed look silently asking if this was going to be a big problem.

He winced, and she huffed. "Please tell me you can fix it."

He shook his head. "Not without a replacement."

"What? How long will that take?"

He glanced out at the sky. His gut grew heavy at the sight of the dark clouds looming. They were closer and more ominous than the last time he'd checked. "I'll need to give the guys a call."

He pulled out his phone and saw Dahlia pinch the bridge of her nose. "I'm not going to make my flight, am I?"

She sounded so dejected, it made his insides tighten. He wished more than anything he could reassure her and tell her he'd have her there in time.

But while he prided himself on being reliable, not to mention handy, he wasn't a magician. He couldn't magically summon the supplies he'd need.

Pulling out his phone, he trudged away from the cabin. Reception was very unpredictable up here, and normally that was something he liked best about this place. It was nice to feel like he was totally off the grid.

Most of the time.

Right now? Not so much.

"Where are you going?" Her voice had a hint of alarm, and it made him stop short.

He'd seen many sides of Ms. Dahlia O'Sullivan, but he'd never seen her scared... and in that moment, he knew he'd never be able to stand it. "I'll be right back." He pointed behind him. "Reception is bad around here. There's a spot about a half mile from the cabin, up that hill."

She stared at him like he was a lunatic. "You have to take a hike to make a phone call?"

"Why don't you go back inside the truck and keep warm? I'll make this call and be back in a few."

She turned from him to the truck with a sigh, muttering under her breath. "I'm gonna be fired, I just know it."

Guilt rippled through him again even as he told himself it was unwarranted. It wasn't like he'd intended to have his truck break down. Still... He hurried as fast as he could to the clearing where he got the best reception.

Nash didn't answer, so he tried Cody.

JJ sketched out what had happened in a few short sentences, and Cody groaned. "That's some bad luck, man."

"Tell me about it," he grunted.

"Look, I'm happy to help you, but I don't see what you need in the ranch's garage. I'm gonna have to head into town to get it."

JJ cursed under his breath, tipping his head back to look up at the rapidly encroaching clouds. Downtown Aspire was the opposite direction of his cabin. By the time Cody got into town, bought the supplies, and headed out here...

175

"If I leave right now, I might make it."

JJ sighed, his stomach sinking as he realized the inevitable. "Yeah, and then you'll get stuck up here to ride out the storm."

Cody's voice was uncharacteristically serious. "How's it looking where you are?"

"Honestly? Not good." JJ stared at the horizon. He had a better view of the valley from here. "My gut tells me the roads are gonna be too dangerous within an hour or so. The wind has picked up a lot in the last ten minutes, and the sky isn't looking great."

"You better hunker down, then. You got enough to see you through?"

"Yeah. I always keep this place well stocked." He scrubbed at his eyes, already dreading the conversation to come. "Can you, uh… pass the message along? I don't want anyone to worry about us."

"Will do. And good luck, man. I can't imagine Dahlia taking this very well."

"Oh, no, she definitely won't." And he couldn't say he'd blame her. Her plans were about to be blown to pieces for the second time this week.

Trudging back to the cabin, he tried to work out the best way to word things, then quickly came to the conclusion that direct would work best.

She'd hate him to sugarcoat it.

She'd gotten out of the truck and was pacing in front of the cabin, blowing into her hands to keep them warm. "Well?" she said as soon as she spotted him. "What's the outcome?"

"I spoke to Cody, and he's happy to help us out, but he can't do anything until after this storm passes through."

"But… but it's not even snowing."

"The wind is picking up real fast. It's coming, and I don't want him getting stuck in his car overnight. We're just gonna have to wait it out."

"And my flight?" she clipped. Her mouth was pinched, her brows drawn together. She already knew the answer.

He let out a sigh. "I'm sorry, but you're not gonna make it."

She swallowed visibly. "I'm supposed to be back in the office tomorrow morning."

He remembered the way her bosses had spoken to her. Some part of him wanted to tell her she shouldn't care so much what they thought. That she should worry more about her own safety than what those jerks demanded of her.

But he'd never been one to judge someone else's way of living before, and he wasn't about to start now. She had her priorities, and his broken-down truck was messing with them.

"You're not gonna be there, Dahlia." He said it as gently as he could while still being firm. "I'm not gonna ask Cody to put himself in danger so you can get to work on time."

She looked away, but not before he caught a flicker of guilt in her eyes.

"Even if he got here before the storm hit, I wouldn't take the risk of driving you to the airport in a blizzard."

She pressed her lips together, but then she nodded.

"I told Cody to let your sisters know where you are so no one's worried."

He got nervous when she didn't speak. He'd prefer a caustic, irritated Dahlia to this quiet, unreadable silence.

He liked knowing what she was thinking, but right

now he couldn't say. "Do you, uh… do you want me to walk you up the hill so you can call someone?"

She closed her eyes and pinched the bridge of her nose. "So, we're going to be stuck in the cabin together for… how long?"

"Until the storm blows through. It usually only takes a day or two."

"A day or two?" Her eyes widened, and he could have sworn he caught a hint of panic.

It was at that moment that he suddenly remembered there was only one bed in the cabin.

One.

Sure, there was a couch too, but it was a one-room cabin.

Was that why she looked so scared?

Ah heck.

"I'll get your stuff." He moved to the truck and took his time gathering her things and bringing them into the cabin.

She'd need some time to adjust to this new plan, and he meant to give it to her. Besides, there was plenty to do to make the cabin habitable and somewhat comfortable for their unplanned stay.

He let them both into the small space and set her luggage down beside the bed. "Feel free to change and get comfortable. I'd suggest wearing all the layers you've got."

He headed for the door as she stared at him with a frown. "Where are you going?"

"Oh, well…" He fished some work gloves out of one of the drawers. "I need to turn on the electricity so we can use the bathroom and the stove. Then I was going to chop some firewood and find some kindling."

She moved toward him as he spoke.

"There's some food, but it's mostly frozen or canned, so—"

"I'm coming with you."

He blinked in surprise. She'd stopped short so close he could see the flecks of gold in her eyes. "You're… what?"

She huffed, her shoulders going back, her chin jutting out, and her voice all no-nonsense. "I'm not just going to sit around and let you take care of everything all by yourself. Now tell me how I can help."

He laughed. He couldn't help it. She was adorable when she was all temperamental and irritable. But moments like this one, when she was all practical and tenacious, and ready to get her hands dirty to help out…

That was just plain sexy.

23

One thing was instantly clear as Dahlia followed JJ into the small shed tucked in the woods directly behind the cabin.

She'd worn the wrong shoes.

Her ankle booties slid in the snow for the fifth time as she stopped in the doorway. She wanted to help, but maybe JJ had a point when he'd suggested she get changed into something more appropriate.

At least she wasn't wearing her work clothes—she would have arrived back in New York too late to make it to the office today. But she was dressed in her normal New York clothes, and while these booties worked well enough for the occasional trek to the subway, they were definitely not meant to be trudging through several feet of snow.

"Why don't you start hauling this stack into the cabin?" JJ said as he reached for some rough logs piled high in the corner. "I'll chop some more just in case."

In case… what? They had to stay here even longer than two days? She wasn't sure she wanted to know. It was taking all her willpower not to give in to the urge to cry.

She was not a crier, so she wouldn't cave. But she was seriously starting to wonder if she'd done something to offend this state. She didn't exactly consider herself a lucky person to begin with, but being trapped *here*? With *him*? In *this*?

She glanced around her as JJ stacked some logs in her outstretched arms.

All right, fine, so *this* was actually really kind of incredible. Not even an impending storm could take away from the natural beauty everywhere she turned.

But even so, she had places to be. And a cabin in the middle of nowhere was not one of them.

She brought in the stack and took a minute to change into better boots. When she headed back to the shed for another load, she caught sight of JJ. The way she tripped and stumbled had nothing to do with the boots and everything to do with the fact that JJ was chopping wood.

JJ. Chopping wood.

Her brain came to a screeching halt at the sight. His hair was being held out of his face with a cap, and the way he moved was all natural athleticism. She'd only ever seen him wearing heavy jackets or flannel shirts, like he was now. But if there'd ever been any doubt before that what lay beneath was all muscle, it was gone. Men who moved the way JJ was right now had six-packs and rippled torsos. Dahlia was convinced of this... and she couldn't help picturing what JJ's body looked like beneath his layers.

She clamped her mouth shut when it started to water.

Giving her head a shake, she tipped her chin back, watching as the clouds rolled in overhead.

She would be staying at this cabin alone. With JJ. She shook her head again as she addressed God directly. "Is this punishment? Am I being punished?"

"Dahlia?" JJ's voice had her straightening. He'd paused in chopping and was watching her with a curious frown. "You all right?"

"Oh, uh..." She started walking toward the shed quickly. "Fine. I'm fine."

She was not fine.

It would be awkward enough spending a night alone with JJ in a one-room cabin. If she couldn't get over this ridiculous attraction, it would only be a hundred times more awkward.

"Just stop thinking about him," she whispered in a scolding tone as she gathered another armful of wood. "You are not a teenager," she reminded herself as she took another load inside and stacked it. "You know better."

She continued her pep talk through the next couple trips back and forth to the shed, each time studiously ignoring JJ and his ax skills as she passed.

"He's not even your type," she grumbled as she finished stacking the last of her load.

"What was that?"

With a squeak of surprise, Dahlia spun around to see JJ shaking snow off his boots as he came inside.

"Nothing," she said a little too quickly. Standing, she brushed some dirt off her hands. "What's next? Want me to take inventory in the kitchen? Or—"

"Actually," he cut in, "it looks like the snow will be on us any minute now. If there's anyone you want to call, now's the time."

She nodded. "Right. Good thinking."

Was her dread obvious? It felt like it was seeping out of her skin like sweat. Her insides kept twisting and churning as she mentally rehearsed what she'd say. All the while, JJ was bundling her up for the walk. "Are those the only boots you have?"

She shrugged. "They're the best I've got."

He grumbled something about buying her boots for her next visit, and she only just stopped herself from pointing out that her next visit wouldn't be until June, when the baby came. She hoped she wouldn't be needing snow boots in June.

"Here." He tugged his own cap off and settled it over her hair with a rough pull. Next came a pair of thick leather gloves and a scarf that he wrapped around her head three times until only her eyes showed.

For a second, when he was done, he just stared down at her. A glint of amusement lit his gaze. "Can you breathe?"

She tried to nod but only managed to knock the cap into her eyes, making them both chuckle.

"Better get this over with," she mumbled.

"Follow me." He reached for her hand and tugged her along as he made his way up through the trees, over some fallen branches, and through thick layers of snow. He seemed to be trying to follow his own tracks from earlier, but it was still slow going.

She wished she could tug her hand from his and say, "I got it," but the truth was he'd helped her keep her balance more than once. And his legs were longer than hers, so while he made climbing over fallen trunks look like a breeze, she was far less graceful.

Finally, when she was out of breath from the climb, he came to a stop. "This is it," he said. "Your best bet for a couple bars."

She tugged off the thick leather gloves and instantly regretted the lack of warmth as her fingers turned to ice.

184

She fumbled with her phone, but soon enough, she'd brought up Jason's number and hit the green Call button.

After a brief explanation, he included Marian in on the call. You know, just so he could torture her a little bit more. Her matter-of-fact story about a broken-down truck and a snowstorm was not going over too well.

"You're... what?" Marian's voice was so shrill, Dahlia flinched.

Turning her back on a silent, frowning JJ, she cleared her throat. "I'm afraid it couldn't be helped—"

"I can't believe this," Jason muttered under his breath... but loudly enough for her to hear.

"I'm sorry for the inconvenience," she said. Her voice was getting all stilted and cold, but she couldn't do anything about it.

She hated apologizing. But she hated it the most when she knew she wasn't in the wrong. And right now? She was the one who should be pitied. She was trapped in a storm. Shouldn't they be more concerned about her welfare?

"When *will* you be back, then?" Marian asked.

"Well, um... I need to call the airline and—"

Jason's sigh cut her off. "Let me guess. You won't be able to work from this cabin in the woods?"

She blinked in surprise. It almost sounded like... like he didn't believe her.

Dahlia heard JJ shift behind her, and she couldn't bring herself to face him. Out here in the quiet forest, with only the sound of wind, birds, and the occasional snapping twig to break the silence, the voices coming over the phone sounded like she had them on speaker even though she didn't.

She took a deep breath and tried to ignore the fact that

185

JJ was standing so close. "I finished the spreadsheets that were due for this week—"

"So you think you can just take off, then, or—"

"No!" she cut in quickly, interrupting Marian before she could go off on a tirade. "I just meant that all the urgent, time-sensitive work is done, so while I may fall a little behind by not being back tomorrow, I should be able to catch up quickly when I return."

"You should? Hardly encouraging," Jason muttered.

He was always muttering. Dahlia clenched her fists, her fingers aching with the cold. She far preferred Marian's shrill anger to Jason's muttering. She couldn't argue when he wasn't addressing her directly.

Coward.

She squeezed her eyes shut as Marian launched into a lecture about how she'd used up her vacation time.

Her company didn't roll over unused time off, but for years she'd never taken a single day. It was only this year that she'd needed to travel, thanks to Rose suddenly fleeing out west.

She supposed she'd thought all those years of never taking a day off would be remembered. That all the years of coming in early and staying late would add up to something.

But that wasn't the case. Clearly.

And maybe it had been stupid of her to hope for it.

A few minutes later, Dahlia had promised to call just as soon as the storm passed with an update on when she would be back in the office.

The silence after she hung up felt weighted… but nice. She took a second to revel in the sound of wind moving through the trees overhead before turning to face JJ.

When she did, she jerked back in surprise at the glare he wore.

She blinked, temporarily speechless. She'd never seen JJ looking angry before, and for a second, her insides went into turmoil trying to figure out what she'd done wrong.

What had she said to faze the seemingly unflappable mountain man?

"We should get back." He nodded toward the cabin.

She fell in step beside him, still mystified by his behavior. She should just ask but wasn't sure she wanted the answer. JJ was the one person in Montana who she didn't seem to irritate. She didn't want to lose that.

But then he reached for her hand and gripped it, steadying her through the uneven snow. If he was really mad, he wouldn't help her, would he?

Maybe his frustration wasn't about her.

She told herself that had to be the case, and her steps felt lighter on the way back. Maybe because it was mostly downhill. Or maybe because she'd gotten that dreaded call over and done with.

But the second the cabin loomed into view, that light feeling evaporated.

There was no avoiding that small space any longer. The sun hadn't even started to set yet, but the sky was already dark with heavy storm clouds.

And Dahlia had a feeling that this was going to be the longest night of her life.

24

J J was so riled, he didn't even notice the first few snowflakes that fell, even when they landed on his face.

It was only the fact that he was holding Dahlia's hand that kept him from flying off into a royal rage. But when she stumbled over a tree branch, he came to a stop to steady her, and he took a deep, calming breath.

When he glanced over, he saw Dahlia staring up at him with blatant curiosity.

He tried to ease some of the tension from his features. A smile wasn't happening, but he didn't want to scare Dahlia with his temper.

"You okay?" she asked.

Her voice was quiet, but there was genuine concern in her eyes. He looked away, expelling a sharp exhale as if that might help rid him of this roiling fury.

He wasn't quick to anger. In fact, his younger sisters used to tease him that he had the patience of a saint. But when someone did light his fuse, look out.

His temper only came out when he was feeling protective. Like when he'd caught Bobby getting too handsy with Dahlia, for instance. Or just now, when he'd heard those vile city folk talking to Dahlia like she was beneath them somehow.

"I'm fine," he muttered. But when she cocked an eyebrow in clear disbelief, he gave a huff of rueful amusement. "All right, maybe not fine. I just…" He turned to face her. "Why do you put up with those fools?"

Her eyes widened, her lips parted, and… oh heck. Did she have any idea how kissable she looked right now?

The woman was temptation itself. With snow falling around her and flakes catching in the dark hair that fell over her scarf. With her delicate features all flushed and pink from the cold…

He cleared his throat and looked away before he could do something to make their situation even more awkward than it already was.

"You… You're angry because of my bosses?" Her voice was soft and uncharacteristically high.

He glanced back down, amused and irritated by the confusion written plainly across her features.

Hadn't anyone ever gotten mad on her behalf before? And also, why wasn't *she* angry? Didn't she realize she deserved to be treated better?

She turned away from him, heading toward the cabin, and when he saw her shiver, guilt spurred him on beside her.

"Let's get you warm in front of a fire." He reached for her hand.

He loved that she gave it to him so trustingly. He suspected this was not a woman who'd let just anyone help her, even if it was just to step over some fallen branches.

It wasn't until they were back in the cabin and he was bent over the fireplace getting the kindling ready that the topic came up again.

"Did you really just get angry because of my bosses?"

The confusion in her voice had him glancing over his shoulder to face her.

"I don't like the way they talk to you."

She gave him a funny little smirk. "Yeah, well, they're my bosses. They're allowed to talk to me however they want."

He turned back to the kindling with a scowl, snapping his jaw shut to keep from saying something he'd regret. The anger he'd felt earlier came back in a rush. "I guess I just don't see it that way. No one deserves to be treated like that, least of all you."

"Why least of all me?" Her voice snapped with irritation, but he knew better than to take it personally.

He kept his gaze on the task at hand as he thought over how to respond.

Or, really, he sifted out what he couldn't say.

What he *shouldn't* say.

Because what he wanted to say was inappropriate. *You deserve better. Don't go back to a place where you're not wanted. Don't leave the people who love you.*

He shook his head with a grunt of annoyance at his own wayward thoughts.

Who was he to tell her that? No one. He had no place in her life, so he surely had no say in how she lived it.

But she was waiting quietly behind him, her feet shuffling against the hardwood floor every once in a while as she tried to stay warm.

He held a match to the kindling as he responded. "I

don't need to see you at your job to know you're a good worker, Dahlia."

She shifted again but stayed quiet.

"I've gotten to know you well enough to see you have a strong work ethic, not to mention a sense of duty to others..." He trailed off with a shake of his head. "I might not know much about your career or how things work in a New York City office, but I'd bet everything I have that you deserve more respect than what you're gettin'."

The kindling caught and spread quickly as he shifted the logs to help it along. All the while he cursed inwardly in frustration as Dahlia's silence stretched behind him.

He'd sounded like a freakin' guidance counselor. His words were too stilted, because he wasn't sure he trusted himself not to say the words that threatened.

You don't belong there with them. You belong here.

With me.

He froze in the act of tending the fire.

Stay here with me.

The words died on his tongue, but they burned his throat and made his lungs feel like they'd caught fire along with the logs. He couldn't say that. He didn't mean it...

Did he?

He fell back, resting on his haunches. The fire was done, but it took him a minute to turn and face Dahlia.

When he did, his heart squeezed in his chest.

In the flickering glow of the flames, still bundled up in his scarf and hat... he'd never seen her looking more vulnerable. And every part of him wanted to take care of her.

He stood up abruptly and turned away, heading toward the chest of drawers and trunk near the bed. He made quick work of sorting through the contents as his mind went to war with his heart.

He'd tried that once before, hadn't he? He hadn't wanted to let his ex go, so he'd made a commitment he wasn't ready for. A lifelong commitment that neither of them could keep.

Was that what this was?

Did he just want Dahlia to stay because he didn't want to see her leave? Not wanting to see Dahlia walk out of his life was not the same as wanting her to stay here for him. With him. He'd learned that lesson, and he wasn't about to repeat it.

He stacked some clothes together in a pile and snagged a pair of UGG boots he found tucked behind the trunk as his mind continued to race, trying to sort through the confusing chaos of the past versus the present.

But like trying to pin down a cloud, the more he tried to figure out what he was feeling, what emotions had made him want to ask her to stay, the more confused he felt.

Meanwhile, Dahlia had been quiet for too long, and when he turned back to her, his arms full of clothes, he found her frowning down at the fire, lost in thought.

"I found some warm clothes for you," he said, handing them over. He picked up the boots he'd found and held them out to Dahlia. "Looks like Lizzy left these behind when she and Kit honeymooned here. Want to try them on and see if they fit?"

Dahlia snagged the boots, a funny smile tugging at her lips. "They honeymooned here?" She glanced around at the admittedly rustic, not-at-all luxurious accommodations. "I have a hard time picturing Lizzy here on her honeymoon. I would have taken her for a Bahamas kinda gal."

JJ chuckled as he moved toward her to hand over the boots. "Yeah, well, I guess when it comes to honeymoons, they decided as long as they had privacy, they were happy."

Her gaze flitted past him to the bed, and he felt a surge of heat when her cheeks turned pink.

She cleared her throat and turned away, tugging on one of the thick wool sweaters he'd found and sliding her feet into the fur-lined boots.

"They fit." She glanced up with a grin that spread the heat in his veins to his chest so quickly he could hardly catch his breath. "Would you look at that? We're the exact same size." She turned her foot left and right to show them off. "I guess Lizzy and I have something in common after all."

He chuckled, and her small smile was sweet as she added quietly, "I'm only kidding. I know we have more in common than that."

"You're both strong," he agreed. "You're both smart. And you both have the mistaken belief that cities are where it's at."

She laughed at his teasing. "Spoken like a true mountain man."

He chuckled as she put on the other boot and headed toward the kitchen area. "We should probably tackle the food situation next, huh?"

He nodded, following in her wake. "Might be good to get an idea of what we have. There should be plenty to tide us over."

She shivered and rubbed her hands together. The fire was starting to warm the place, and a little electric heater was chugging away in the corner, but they could still see their breath when they exhaled.

"How about a hot cup of coffee first?" he said.

She nodded. "That sounds great. We don't have any milk, though, if that's how you take it."

He grinned, remembering that morning when he'd surprised her in the downstairs office. "I told you. Black is how all the cool kids drink it."

Her face split with a grin that knocked the wind straight out of him. And all those battling thoughts he'd been stewing over, about why he wanted her stay and what that meant…

For a second they scattered like the wind in the face of that smile.

He wanted her to stay all right. He couldn't say why or for how long or what it all meant, but there was no denying the fact that if he had his way…

Dahlia O'Sullivan wouldn't be going back to NYC.

25

D ahlia knew it was incredibly stupid to feel this giddy.

She was trapped, for heaven's sake. She was snow-bound on a mountain with a man she hardly knew.

She should not be giddy.

But as she accepted the steaming mug of black coffee from JJ, there was no denying the flickering glow of happiness in her chest. *And all because of a silly cup of coffee.* She shook her head in exasperation.

But it wasn't just this cup of coffee—it was the fact that suddenly she got it. That morning when he'd come to her office, he'd given her *his* coffee. Such a simple gesture. Not exactly a lavish gift by anyone's standards. But something about it felt... intimate.

Like something a husband would do for his wife. Or a boyfriend for his girlfriend...

She turned toward the fire with a huff. *Get a grip, Dahlia.*

He was not her boyfriend, and he definitely was not her husband. Her gaze flickered over to the bed for what

197

had to be the hundredth time. Most importantly, this was no honeymoon.

This cabin might have been a romantic getaway for Lizzy—and truthfully, Dahlia had no trouble picturing it. How cozy and romantic this little hut could be if you were here with the man you loved.

But this was not that.

She strode toward the windows and looked out, temporarily distracted from thoughts of beds and coffee and handsome mountain men, when she caught sight of just how much snow had already fallen.

"My goodness, that was quick," she murmured.

The truck was already thoroughly coated in the thick snow that now blanketed every bit of green on the trees, and every fallen branch and brown, leafless shrubbery.

In no time at all, the world outside this window would be nothing more than a thick, white carpet. Watching it happen right before her eyes was equally mesmerizing and alarming. She was watching the world be reset.

A blank slate. A fresh start.

The thought made her ribs feel too tight and her lungs too shallow. The words JJ had said to her earlier came back and echoed through her mind.

"No one deserves to be treated like that, least of all you."

Even now, those words made her throat tighten with emotions she wasn't sure she knew how to name. It wasn't gratitude. It wasn't relief. But it was something like that.

It was the feeling of being seen. Appreciated. Of having someone tell her she deserved more than the hand she'd been dealt.

She leaned forward until her forehead rested against the cold glass and her breath fogged the window.

It was a feeling she hadn't even known she'd needed.

"I'd bet everything I have that you deserve more respect than what you're getting."

Her breath hitched and her gaze caught on a single black bird that soared overhead, fighting against the strong wind.

Respect. Validation. To be seen and appreciated for her work. Wasn't that all she'd ever wanted from her job?

Dahlia swallowed hard as age-old memories stirred. No, not just from her job. It was all she'd ever wanted, period. Growing up, that was all she'd needed. To have her mother, or teacher, or... or *anyone*, for that matter, recognize all she was doing. To say "thank you" or "good job" or just the odd "hey, well done, you" when she put aside her own childish wants to make sure Daisy passed her history test and that Rose ate her vegetables at dinner.

But no one ever did acknowledge what she'd done. What she'd given up. Instead, boys would marvel over Daisy's beauty and charm, while teachers oohed and aahed over sweet Rose's angelic nature.

Dahlia pulled back from the window with a rough exhale. Tears were stinging the backs of her eyes, but they made no sense. She was much too old to be dwelling on childhood woes, and she didn't believe in wallowing in self-pity.

She turned away from the window to pace in front of the fire.

And besides, the issues she had with her boss weren't at all the same. She didn't even know why her thoughts had gone there. She wasn't a child anymore. And she didn't need validation from anyone—least of all some stranger she barely knew.

She took a sip of the coffee before remembering how hot it still was. She muttered a curse as it burned her tongue. The pain helped her to focus on the present. And the present was a disaster.

She cringed as she thought over what her bosses had said. They had been a little harsher than usual, but could she blame them?

She'd only just returned to the office when Rose had told her about the upcoming scan and invited her to be part of the gender reveal. How could Dahlia pass that up? So she'd been off only nine days later to be there for her sister and then got stuck for the week. And now she was stuck again.

But neither time had been her fault. She didn't control the weather!

While typically she could justify her employers' rudeness, or even reclassify it as urgency or stress, right now she couldn't help but hear how they must have sounded to JJ. And then, as if that wasn't bad enough, her mind chose that moment to call up every promotion she'd been passed over for, every proposal she'd put forward that'd been shot down.

The more she stewed, the more unsettled she felt.

"Are you still worrying over your job?" JJ's voice came from the kitchen area, and when she glanced over, she saw him leaning against the counter.

He was watching her with a quirk to his lips and amusement in his eyes. "I assume it's work that has you wearing a hole in my floors."

She stopped pacing, but her nervous energy wasn't going anywhere. "I know you think I should just quit, but it's not that simple. You don't understand."

She nearly flinched at the sharpness of her voice, but he only shrugged. "Then explain it to me."

She opened her mouth and then clamped it shut.

Where to even begin? "They weren't always in charge," she said. "The woman who owns the company—the one who hired me straight out of school—she's mostly retired now."

He eyed her evenly, his gaze fixed like she had his full attention.

"But she gave me a chance when I had no skills to speak of." Her lips curled with a little smile, but she could feel how sad it was. Why was she telling him this stuff? Her voice got small. "I didn't even have the right degree because we didn't have the money."

More like because she'd earmarked the money for Rose's education. But that wasn't what mattered.

"I owe that company a lot."

"The company, huh?" He tilted his head to the side. "And does this company show you the same loyalty?"

"Yes," she said quickly. Maybe too quickly. "It's been steady work. It's been reliable and… and…"

And how did she explain how much that meant to her? How did she tell someone who didn't know her life that when she'd first graduated high school, there'd been nothing she'd wanted more than steady and safe?

And this company was that. She winced as she recalled how much she'd been worrying about losing her job lately.

Okay, fine. It *had been* that.

"You know," JJ said finally, "no one can fault you for being loyal. Definitely not me. I guess I just wonder if you're giving your loyalty to people who deserve it."

She stared at him for a long moment. Part of her wanted to be annoyed. Irritation would be a welcome relief right now. Because what she felt when she looked in his eyes… when she heard what he was saying and how reasonable he sounded…

She glanced away, swallowing hard.

Well, it wasn't annoyance she felt. But that would definitely be preferable.

Her gaze fell on the bed again before she turned away, trying to find something—*anything*—to take her mind off this conversation.

Her gaze fell on the window where the snow fell in heavy clumps. A smile tugged at her lips at a memory of Rose as a child. She was standing out in the snow, her tongue catching flakes while she giggled.

"Do you think Rose is all right?" Her voice caught on the question, and she couldn't even explain why.

"I'm sure she's fine." JJ's even tone left no room for doubt.

"But if she's caught in—"

"Dahlia," he interrupted gently. When she turned to meet his gaze, he smiled. "Rose has plenty of people looking after her. Between her sister and Nash and Kit, not to mention Dex…" He took a step toward her and lowered his voice. "You don't need to be her mother anymore."

Her lips parted, and a sound escaped that was horrifyingly close to a sob.

No one had ever said it like that. She blinked rapidly and turned away. After a long silence, she heard him moving around behind her as she went back to pacing. From the window to the fireplace and back, over and over as her mind dwelled on what she'd do or say when she got back to the office.

Should she ask for more flexibility to work remotely? Push that new software again? Or—

"Dahlia." JJ's voice held that hint of laughter that made it impossible to ignore.

She turned and faced him. He was sitting at the small

table, his booted feet kicked out before him. "Much as I enjoy watching you pace, I promise you that no amount of fretting is going to make this storm come or go any quicker."

She sighed, torn between amusement and annoyance. How could he be so laid-back all the time? Didn't he have places to be and responsibilities to tend to as well?

He kicked the chair out that was sitting across from him. "I hate to be the one to break this to you, but there's nothing you can do to control Mother Nature." He arched his brows. "Your only option is to surrender."

"Surrender?" She drew the word out in disgust, her lip curling in a sneer.

He laughed. "Relax. Kick back. Try to look on the bright side."

She felt a reluctant smile tugging at her lips. "Please do not be Mr. Glass Half Full right now. I don't think I can handle the glare of your sunny attitude."

He tipped his head back with a full belly laugh. "Okay, fine. If you can't find the fun in this situation, you can at least try to distract yourself so you don't drive me nuts with your fretting."

She rolled her eyes but found herself moving toward him like he had some sort of gravitational pull. "Fine. What do you suggest I do, then?"

He held up a stack of cards. "Come play with me."

A laugh bubbled out of her at the boyish grin he wore.

"What do you want to play?"

He seemed to think it over. "Depends. What do you know?"

She smirked as she sank into the seat across from him, a new sort of energy making her toes tap against the floor. She always loved a good competition. "Well, I know gin, rummy, hearts, poker." She leaned forward with a wink. "You name it, I probably know it."

His laugh filled the cabin, and he leaned forward as well, setting the deck down between. "All right, then. Let's go with a classic—Texas Hold'em."

She couldn't have stopped the grin that spread across her face if she'd tried. "You're on."

He narrowed his eyes with mock suspicion as she picked up the deck and started to shuffle.

"Why do I get the feeling that I ought to be scared?"

She laughed, the sound horrifyingly close to a giggle. "Because you probably should be, especially if we're placing bets."

He leaned back in his seat and crossed his arms. The lopsided grin he gave her had an edge to it that set off butterflies in her belly.

There was something wicked about it. Something… sexy.

She turned her gaze to the cards in her hands. Maybe he wasn't the one who ought to be afraid. The way he made her feel?

If she had any sense at all, she'd be running scared.

26

JJ leaned back, keeping his hand close to his chest. "You are truly terrifying when you look at me like that."

Dahlia's expression didn't budge. "This is my poker face."

He grinned, delighted more than he could say by the wicked scowl she had him pinned under. "You know a poker face is supposed to be bland, right? It's supposed to be unreadable."

She arched a brow, but her glare didn't waver. "You think you can read me right now, cowboy?"

He chuckled. "No. I have no idea if you have a good hand or not."

"Exactly," she shot back. "Which means my poker face is working."

He leaned in close with a pleading expression. "But do you have to glare at me like I just kicked your puppy? It's disconcerting."

Her lips twitched ever so slightly. "Which might explain why I'm winning."

"Last I checked we were tied. You've won ten hands, and I've won ten."

"Yes, but I'm about to win this hand." She tilted her head to the side, evil glare firmly in place. "Which makes me the winner."

He laughed as he fell back in his seat. "I never took you for the trash-talking type."

Her lips twitched again, and he could have sworn he felt it in his belly.

Maybe it was the small space, or the fact that they'd been alone together for hours, but his whole body felt attuned to hers, their moods and their thoughts oddly in sync.

"All right, then," he drawled, holding out his cards. "Time to put your jelly beans where your mouth is."

He laid his cards down, and she did the same.

And they both realized it at once.

He grinned. She scowled.

"I guess your poker face isn't so helpful after all, now is it?" he teased, pulling the small pile of jelly beans across the table.

She pursed her lips as she reached for the cards and started to shuffle with far more aggression than it warranted.

"You cannot honestly be put out because you lost." He chuckled out the words, disbelief in his tone.

"Why not?"

"Because it's a game!" He threw his hands up, another laugh slipping out.

This only made her narrow her eyes. "Yeah, well, the point of game is to win it."

"Oh man, I knew you were competitive." He paused,

waiting until her gaze met his. "But I never realized you were a poor loser."

She stopped shuffling, her jaw dropping. "I am not."

He chuckled. "Whatever you say."

"I just don't like losing."

"Uh-huh."

She tapped the edges of the cards against the table to straighten them. "What's the point of playing if you're not going to win?"

"Uh, because it's fun?" he offered.

"No, losing is not fun."

He grinned, leaning across the table and covering her hands with his before he even really knew what he was doing.

She stopped shuffling, locked still by his gaze or maybe his touch. He wasn't sure, but he liked whatever was happening right now.

A smile tugged at the corner of his mouth. "Aw, come on now, Lia, you can't say you don't like—"

"What did you call me?" She tugged her hands from beneath his and went back to shuffling, but her gaze grew wary.

"Lia," he said with a shrug, grabbing a jelly bean and popping it in his mouth. "I don't know. I like nicknames, and there's not much to do with Dahlia, unless I call you Dee—"

He stopped with a laugh when she shook her head vigorously. "No way. I had a teacher named Miss Dee." She pretended to shudder in horror.

"That nice, huh?" he teased. "All right, then, what nicknames do your sisters have for you?"

She arched her brows. "Aside from dragon?"

"Aside from that," he said with a grin.

And all at once he was desperate to know. He wanted to learn more about what this woman was like to the ones she loved. How they saw her, what they called her. Her friends, her exes, her sisters. He wanted to see her from every point of view.

Because from what he knew of her, he was well aware that there was more than meets the eye. She could be wild and free one moment—a competitive, funny tomboy. But the next second she could be the uptight, put-together businesswoman. She was an enigma.

He'd caught glimpses of what lay beneath, but he suspected the key to figuring it out lay in her past.

Leaning forward he rested his weight on his elbows. "Didn't you have any nicknames growing up?"

She opened her mouth as if to protest but then stopped, her eyes widening. She shook her head. "It was stupid…"

"What was it?"

She cleared her throat, and he caught the hint of a smile curving her lips. "Rose, when she was little…" She laughed softly. "I'd totally forgotten about it."

"Oh come on, you're killing me here, Lia." The nickname felt natural on his tongue, and she didn't even seem to notice.

"When Rose was little, she couldn't say my full name," Dahlia said, her eyes were trained on the cards, but her gaze was distant. "So she started calling me Dah-dah." She started to chuckle, and he did too. "As you can imagine, it sounded a lot like… like Dada."

His laughter trailed off. He didn't know the entirety of their story, but everyone in Aspire knew Frank O'Sullivan had abandoned his daughters.

Dahlia cleared her throat again, her smile a little strained but still there. "Anyway, I never really thought much of it, and Daisy didn't either. It was just what she called me, but…"

"But?"

"But then she got older, and she still kept calling me that. And I remember…" She stopped shuffling, her gaze focused somewhere in the distance. "It must have been second grade, maybe? Somewhere around there. They had parent-teacher conferences, you know? And sweet little Rose kept telling her teacher that Dada was coming."

"Oh no," he murmured.

"Oh yes." She burst out in a laugh that nearly broke his heart because it was so sweet and youthful, and yet that story…

That story was so freakin' sad.

She shook her head, clearly coming back to the present. "You can imagine the teacher's surprise when Dada showed up and it was a girl from junior high."

"Junior… What grade were you in?"

"Seventh." She nodded, her smile fading slightly. "The teacher kept asking where my mom was, but… she was having a bad week." She winced, like the memory was physically painful.

He watched her closely as she got back to the business of shuffling.

He'd wanted to see her in a new light, and that was exactly what he'd gotten. And this new view…

Well, it explained a whole lot.

"You were mom and dad for Rose as a kid, weren't you?"

She acted like she didn't hear him.

"I bet Daisy too," he mused, more to himself than anything as he put the pieces together from all he'd heard about the O'Sullivan sisters these past few months. "From the sounds of it, your twin isn't exactly the reliable sort."

She straightened, all hint of her previous smile gone as she peered over at him. "Are we going to play another game, or are you going to sit here and psychoanalyze my family?"

He just barely swallowed a sigh. He could practically see the fun tomboy disappearing behind that cold mask she wore so well.

Luckily for him, he'd gotten awfully good at teasing out the tomboy.

"Are sure you can handle another round?" he quipped. "I don't want you having a hissy fit when I win again."

"*When* you win?" She arched her brows, her eyes glinting with amusement. "Now who's trash-talking?"

"I'm just looking out for you, Lia." He put a hand to his heart. "If I'd known you were such a poor loser, I'd never have suggested poker."

She pinched her lips together, but he could see the smile forming.

"We could have had a nice game of Go Fish instead, unless…" He widened his eyes. "Unless Go Fish is too high stakes for you?"

She burst out laughing as she dealt the cards. "Okay, smack talker. Let's do this."

He reached for his cards.

"And I'm not a poor loser. I just don't think losing is fun. Unlike some weirdos." She added the last part under her breath, making him laugh.

"Aw, come on. Losing a few times makes the game a challenge… and you can't say a challenge isn't fun."

She rolled her eyes. "You have the ability to put a positive spin on everything. It's kinda annoying. Has anyone ever told you that?"

"All the time." He laughed. "That's exactly what Rena used to say."

His insides froze as soon as the words popped out. They seemed to echo in the air around them. And he couldn't breathe.

Rena? Really? Where did that come from? He hadn't said her name in years and it popped out now? In front of Dahlia?

He wanted to slap the back of his head for being such a careless idiot, but instead he fixed his gaze on the tabletop and their two little piles of jellybeans.

Red, blue, green, orange. He started counting candy colors, anything to keep his gaze off the beautiful woman across from him and the question he just knew was coming.

"Who's Rena?" she asked.

"An ex," he murmured, shuffling in his seat. He tried to think of any way to steer this conversation elsewhere, but Dahlia's gaze was fixed on him.

He risked a glance at her face and wished he hadn't.

Her eyes narrowed into thin slits. "Sounds like it was serious."

"Really?" He gave a snort of amusement. "You picked that up from two words?"

"I picked it up from your squirming and the way your neck is going bright red."

He cleared his throat. Crap. Why on earth had he said her name? It was one thing that Dahlia had proven so easy to talk to, but this?

This was not a conversation he wanted to have with anyone, least of all the woman he liked.

He glanced up at her again. There was no denying it. He did like her. He liked her a lot.

"Who was she?" Dahlia tapped her finger on the table. Waiting.

And he had a sinking feeling she'd wait all day if that was what it took.

JJ wished he could lie, but he couldn't. One lie now would cause a thousand problems later, and for some reason, he didn't want to risk this newfound friendship with Dahlia. He knew it couldn't go anywhere. He suspected she wouldn't want it to, even if she was sticking around. But he refused to ruin what they'd built between them with lies.

So, he blurted out the truth. "She was my wife."

Dahlia's eyes widened, her mouth hanging open until she gathered her wits enough to reply. "You've been married?"

"For a short time."

He could practically see the questions racing through her mind. He swallowed hard as he battled with how much to tell her. Where to even start.

"Here?" Dahlia said, her brows drawn together in confusion. "I mean, was she someone you met here in—"

"No." His tongue felt thick and heavy. This was why he never wanted to discuss his past. He had no idea how. He didn't have the words. And besides, no one ever tried to pry. They could sense immediately that he wouldn't go there.

But Dahlia was a different story. She wasn't the type to settle for some vague answers.

"So you were married… in South Carolina?"

He nodded.

"And then?" she prompted, an edge of impatience in

her tone. His Dahlia clearly had no patience for hedging or half-truths.

He swallowed hard. *His Dahlia?* When had he started thinking of her as his anything?

"And then…" he started. Oh heck, there was only one way to finish. "Then I left."

"You left," Dahlia repeated. Her whole demeanor shifted right in front of his eyes. This was no fun poker partner, and it wasn't even the fiery dragon her sisters seemed to see.

No, sir. This woman before him was pure ice.

"You left your wife?" Her tone was impossible to read, the hollow look in her eyes so much worse than her poker face.

He leaned forward. "It wasn't quite that simple. I—"

"No, I understand. It didn't work out. It got too hard, so you quit. It happens, right?"

She shot out of her chair before he could stop her.

And that was when he noticed that her chest was rising and falling too quickly, her hands clenched into fists at her sides.

Her extreme reaction rendered him speechless.

She was heading toward the door before he could get a word out.

"People always quit," she muttered. "It doesn't matter that she might have problems of her own. She's just too impossible to live with, was that it? Why suffer for the rest of your life when you can be free!"

He shook his head as he followed her, his own pain and anger lost in the sheer shock of her over-the-top reaction.

"Look, Lia, you don't even know what happened."

"I don't need to hear your story! It always ends the same!"

He gaped at her as she yanked open the door.

"What are you doing?" His voice was clipped with urgency.

"Leaving is always the easier option." She gave him a pointed look... and then stormed right out into the raging blizzard.

27

D ahlia knew it was a mistake the second the door slammed behind her. She wasn't even dressed for this weather. But she stepped into the snow anyway.

The wind whipped around her, but she didn't stop. She pushed forward, pressing into the wind, shutting her eyes against the sting of snow and the slap of her hair as it flew into her face.

It was stupid to storm off, even stupider to storm off into a snowstorm with zero protection against the elements. But she wasn't thinking.

She just had to get out of that cabin.

Away from that man.

The one she thought she knew but obviously didn't!

Her throat swelled, and she struggled to swallow as she staggered against the win. She wouldn't go far. She may be acting crazy, but she wasn't totally insane, just...

Oh heck, she didn't know what she was... other than angry.

No. It wasn't anger, it was hurt. Disappointment. Shock.

Maybe disillusionment?

JJ had been so perfect. She'd been struggling to fault him for anything more than an overly sunny outlook on life.

Why? Why did he have to be so freaking human after all?

She shook her head and swiped at the long dark locks that were blinding her. A bitter toxic sludge seemed to be making its way through her, coiling in her belly and sliding through her veins. She wrapped her arms tightly around herself as another strong gust hit her, cutting straight through her clothes.

She had to turn back. And she would…just as soon as she calmed down. Just as soon as she could face him again.

But she couldn't face JJ like this, not when her insides felt like he'd shredded them.

Then I left.

So simply stated like it wasn't a big deal. Then I bought milk. Then I did the laundry. Then *I left my wife.*

She gulped in air but it did nothing to cool the fire in her belly.

Why had she thought he was different?

Stupid, stupid Dahlia.

How many times would she have to learn that men did not stay? No one did. Her stomach churned even as some weak part of her mind tried to say, *But that's not fair.*

Her pulse roared as loudly as the wind. Stumbling forward a few steps, she sheltered beneath a tree. It groaned under the weight of the snow, but its trunk offered some protection from the wind.

She just needed a moment. She wouldn't stay out here for long.

But she couldn't spend another second in that tiny little cabin with that big mountain man.

That big, gorgeous man who left his wife!

Even as she thought it, she heard JJ bellowing for her.

Her heart slammed against her rib cage. He'd come after her? Into this blizzard?

And that meant… what?

A few minutes ago, she might've taken it to mean something real. That he was dependable. Responsible.

But responsible, trustworthy, loyal men didn't ditch their wives. They didn't come across the country and hide out in a cabin in the woods when they had a family back home waiting for them.

She squeezed her eyes shut as another gust of wind made her shiver. These boots weren't meant for this. She could already feel the snow saturating them. Her toes were going numb. Her body was starting to shake.

She crossed her arms around herself.

Stop feeling, Dahlia. Stop caring so much!

Why did she even care?

JJ wasn't her boyfriend. He wasn't anything to her except an airport chauffeur, and, okay, maybe a friend. He was her friend. Her ice fishing buddy.

She snorted and shook her head, not wanting to relive those happy memories when her insides were so raw and wounded.

Why did it hurt to know that he'd left his wife?

Tears burned her eyes, and she told herself it was the wind. The cold. The snow.

It couldn't be the fact that her heart felt like it was splitting in two.

If she cared this much, that could only mean one thing,

and she refused to believe it was true. She couldn't care this much about a man she'd only just met.

Her teeth started chattering as her boots and pants became soaked through. Snow clung to her inept clothes. Why hadn't she taken the time to grab a jacket?

She was such a fool!

The trees above her were groaning louder now, the storm having a field day as it whipped nature around like a taunting beast.

How fitting. A sob escaped. She felt whipped and battered herself, taunted by life on all sides. She'd been good, hadn't she? She'd spent her whole life working hard and caring for her family, and for what?

To go and fall for a man who was just like the rest of them.

She opened her eyes with a scowl. "I'm not falling for him."

But as soon as she whispered the words, she knew they were a lie. She was falling hard and fast…

And it was nothing at all like how she'd come to be with Brady. That hadn't been so much falling as… settling. Finding a person who needed her. Being the motherly nag he'd needed to keep his life together while he…

What had he done for her? Kept her company? Kept her from feeling the loneliness when Daisy ran off to pursue music and Rose moved out on her own?

She rubbed a hand over her chest. This was so much worse than what she'd felt with Brady. She'd never feared what they had, but what she was starting to feel for JJ?

The way a simple comment about his past relationship had taken out the floor from under her?

That was dangerous. If she let herself fall, JJ would have the power to completely destroy her.

She'd seen the way her mother had crumbled after their father left. She knew better than anyone how dangerous love could be.

"I can't fall," she whispered. "I don't want to fall."

Her heart ached as if it was trying to protest, but she shook her head and focused on the whirling snow.

JJ came into view. His boots were on, and he wore a coat over top of his sweater, because he was smarter than her. He also wore a look of fury so intense it should have made her quake.

But his anger didn't scare her.

He scared her.

Everything he could potentially make her fragile heart feel scared her senseless.

He stalked toward her. "What do you think you're doing?"

She ignored him. Humiliation was rapidly rising up alongside her anger and this idiotic sense of betrayal. She should go back in before they both froze out here.

"You're going to get yourself killed!" He was shouting, his expression darker than the clouds above.

A stubborn streak flashed through her, and she nearly told him to leave her alone. She was on the cusp of shouting, "Just go back inside!"

It was silly. Impractical.

But how could she return to the cabin now? He'd want an explanation for her senseless behavior, and she had no idea what to tell him.

Maybe it would be better just to freeze out here in the snow.

A heavy sigh rose within her as her logical brain told her all the reasons why she wasn't allowed to die.

So, as much as she didn't want to, she picked up her

numb foot and went to take a step toward him, toward the cabin—but she stopped when the tree's groaning grew as loud as thunder.

With a frown, she glanced up, her eyes bulging in horror as the limb above her gave a final crack and started to fall.

28

"Lia!" Panic surged through JJ, making him colder than the winter wind. His heart stopped beating, and for a moment, he froze, the sound of her scream still splitting the air.

But then adrenaline surged, and JJ was racing across the snowy drifts to get to her.

"Lia!" he shouted again. The wind blew his voice back at him, and his feet couldn't move fast enough to cut through this snow. "Lia!"

If she heard him, she wasn't shouting back, and his heart tripped and turned, making it hard to breathe. His mind was rushing ahead of him, trying to figure out what he'd do if she was seriously injured. He'd need to get her off this mountain and to a hospital...

Without a truck.

He alternated between cursing and praying as he fought the wind to reach her. When he did, his insides sank with relief when he saw her lying there in an embankment, her skin pale but her eyes open and looking right at him.

"I'm here," she was saying, like she'd been saying that all along, but he hadn't heard her. Her voice was more of a croak than a shout.

"Are you hurt?" He reached her side, bending over to check on her.

The answer was obvious when she winced. He glanced down to see that the tree limb was on her leg, trapping her.

"My ankle," she said through gritted teeth. "I don't think it's broken, but I can't get my foot out from under this thing."

Her voice was clipped but calm. Of course it was.

His Dahlia wouldn't panic or whimper in the face of pain.

He dropped his chin to his chest as relief made his muscles temporarily go limp.

She was alive and well.

Thank you, God.

For a second he wanted to take her face between his palms and kiss her senseless while another part of him wanted to shout at her for running out like that.

But then she shivered, her lips trembling before she pinched them tight.

A surge of protectiveness overrode all other urges.

"Here." He shed himself of the overcoat he'd thrown on and secured it around her. "Let's get you out of here."

"But you'll freeze," she started.

He shot her a glare as he knelt over the limb that was holding her hostage. "Now is not the time to argue."

The fact that she had no response to that had him more alarmed than anything. He tugged on the tree limb. Too heavy for him to lift much on his own. He'd have to make space below so when he lifted it by a couple inches, she could pull her foot free.

It only took him seconds to realize what had to be done, but in that time, she'd started to shake visibly, her fingers clutching the coat with white knuckles.

From this vantage point, it was clear that her clothes were soaked through. No doubt her boots too, since she'd been wearing Lizzy's, which were meant for staying warm by the fire, not trekking through the elements.

"I'll get you out of here in no time," he promised. "Just stay still, okay?"

She nodded as another violent shiver racked her frame.

He hadn't thought to put on gloves, and there was no time now, so with bare hands, he dug into the ice and snow packed in around her leg and ankle, trying to make some space so he could wiggle her foot free.

Every few seconds, he glanced back toward her face to make sure she hadn't passed out. Every time his gaze met hers, he felt a flicker of relief.

Dahlia was still awake and alert.

She wasn't a frail woman by any means, but lying here in the snow, she wasn't the big baddie she pretended to be either. Her jaw was clenched, her expression determined— but no amount of attitude could save a person from hypothermia.

His fingers hurt as he dug through the snow, but by the time he'd made a hole wide and deep enough around her foot and lower leg, he couldn't even feel them. He gave his hands a shake, frustrated by his own body's weakness in this cold.

"You ready?" He stood, spreading his feet for balance. "When I say so, try and pull your foot free, okay?"

She nodded as her teeth chattered violently.

Fear surged through him. He needed both hands to lift the limb, but what if she didn't have enough strength to pull her foot free?

Just lift the tree, JJ!

"Okay. One, two… three!" He grabbed the limb, his muscles straining as he lifted it away from her. Dahlia grunted as she used her hands to shove herself back. It was a struggle, and JJ was close to dropping the heavy wood, but Dahlia wrestled her foot free in the nick of time.

He dropped the limb and was rewarded with a sharp sting down the middle of his hand. He gripped his fingers into a fist. It felt like the mother of all splinters had found a home in his palm. It hurt, but he could deal with it later.

He had much bigger problems to solve first.

Dahlia was leaning over her ankle, her face a mask of pain.

He hoped she was right that it wasn't broken, but even so, she couldn't walk on it.

He bent over her, readjusting the coat as best he could. "I'm gonna lift you up." He started to slide a hand beneath her knees, but she slapped at his shoulders.

"I-I can walk," she said. "It'll be faster."

He wanted to argue with her, but he suspected she might be right. The ground was uneven, the snow thick and hard to manage. If he carried her, there was a good chance he'd lose his balance.

"You lean on me," he growled as he helped her up onto her good foot.

She nodded. "I can do this."

It would have been far more convincing if her voice wasn't trembling and her body shaking like an earthquake was ripping through her.

Fear blasted him as they started off slowly, his arm

around her waist as he tried to take as much of her weight as possible while still negotiating the peaks and valleys of the snowdrifts that blocked their path back to the cabin.

They were passing a tree when Dahlia lost her balance while limping against him. JJ reached out to grab the trunk for balance, and even through the frigid numbness that had his fingers feeling like icicles, he felt bark cut into his palm where it had already been scraped and battered. He grunted in pain.

"Are you okay?" Dahlia asked.

He looked down at her. With her face tipped up to look at him, her hair blowing around her, and those glazed eyes filled with concern…

His heart ached. Fear and worry and every protective instinct he hadn't even known he'd possessed reared up in him, and he tightened his grip on her waist.

"I'm fine." He nodded. "Can you keep going?"

Her face was so white it terrified him, and her shaking sent a new spike of desperation surging through his body. She managed a nod, and they set off again, stumbling and limping their way to the cabin door.

29

The blast of heat when they entered the cabin brought both bliss and pain.

Dahlia hissed as her throbbing foot brushed against the doorframe, but the second she was inside, she hobbled toward the fire.

JJ's hands were firm and sure on her waist as he helped her navigate into a chair. "We need to get you out of those wet clothes."

Her trembling grew worse in front of the fire, and she couldn't say if it was because of the cold, the heat of the flames, or the low rumble of his voice.

She shut her eyes. Now was not the time to be thinking about JJ's voice. Or his hands. Or notice the fact that he was currently… stripping?

Her eyes widened and her discomfort temporarily fled as she turned to see JJ pulling off his sweater and the flannel underneath. He yanked them over his head, exposing skin and muscle and—

Yep, she was right. JJ had a six-pack. Or maybe it was eight.

She really shouldn't be counting.

Darting her eyes away, she clasped her hands together and tried to stop shaking, but she couldn't. She also couldn't keep her gaze on the floor, and two seconds later, her eyes were tracking back to study the tall, muscular mountain man.

"Wet clothes will only make you colder," he started saying.

There was nothing at all seductive in his voice. He was in full survival mode.

Which… she should be too.

She shook her head and tried to pull her sweater off, but with hands so shaky, it took three times to get it over her head.

"I'll draw a hot bath." He disappeared through the bathroom door, and she closed her eyes.

A hot bath. Another full-body shiver racked her from head to toe. The thought was delicious.

Even sitting in front of the fire, she felt frozen to the bone. The fire's heat was scorching her skin, making her extremities burn as they came back to life.

She was suddenly overwhelmingly grateful that JJ had turned the water and electricity on so a bath was possible. She wasn't sure anything else would help.

His voice came from the bathroom, where the bathtub's faucet made a racket as it churned out water. "Lia, can you get those clothes off yourself, or do you need help?"

She winced as she stood, her throbbing ankle protesting. Her fingers trembled, but she managed to pull off her shirt. "I got it."

Her clothes fell onto the hardwood floor with a wet splat. It took a few tries, but she finally unbuttoned her jeans and shoved them down her thighs.

As she did, a towel landed on the floor next to her.

She wrapped it around herself, the shaking so violent now it nearly made her topple over. But she clutched the towel around herself tightly and managed to wiggle out of her underwear and bra.

She was still shivering like one of those wind-up toys that bounced around a table when JJ came out of the bathroom shirtless and scrubbing a hand through his damp locks. The flakes covering his dark hair had melted into his beard as well. He gave it a scratch as he quickly took her in.

His expression was grim as she stood there trembling before him.

She would never be warm again. At that point, it felt like a certainty.

JJ walked to her and within four easy strides was wrapping his arms around her body. "I know this is awkward, but do us both a favor and give me a hug. We need to get warm."

She tentatively wrapped her arms around him and had to fight the urge to rest her head on his shoulder and just breathe him in. He smelled so good. Like... well, like *him*. That unique combination, which at this moment was equally comforting and terrifying. And the feel of his arms around her, the way her head fit "just right" against his shoulder...

It was scary how *not* awkward it felt, like she was born to stand beside him, lean against him.

The occasional shiver shook his body as well, but he continued to rub her back and shoulders.

She clung to him, the whole ordeal starting to catch up with her as the shock faded away.

What an idiot.

She was solely responsible for this freezing state, not to mention her injury. She'd done this. And what was worse, she'd made *him* suffer too. If it wasn't for her, he wouldn't have hurt his hand.

She pulled back with a gasp. His hand!

"Are you okay?" she asked. At his frown of confusion, she added, "Your hand."

He shook his head like his own comfort wasn't even a concern. "I'll deal with it once we've defrosted." He led her into the bathroom and pointed at the old, cracked, and utilitarian tub. "Now get warm."

He walked out, closing the door behind him, and she took a seat, easing herself into the water and letting the liquid envelop her. As the blood in her veins started to circulate a little faster and fill her with warmth, she wondered how JJ was defrosting. Probably pacing by the fire. She winced and rested her forehead on her knees.

She couldn't believe he'd had to rescue her, that he even came after her. She'd been acting like a crazy person when she stormed out. She could admit that. But even so, he'd come after her, and she'd...

She groaned against her knees.

And then she'd turned into a damsel in distress. Ugh! Shame spiraled through her. Humiliation was hot on its heels.

She didn't want to be anybody's burden. That wasn't her. She was the one who took care of others. She didn't like anyone having to take care of her.

But here she was, curled up in a hot bath while the guy who rescued her shivered in front of the fire.

She sighed, sinking back against the tub's edge until her shoulders were immersed in the hot water.

She wished she could turn back time, but she couldn't. She couldn't undo her bad behavior.

Her fingers played over the top of the water, skimming the surface as the heat spread through her all the way to her toes. Her ankle still throbbed, but by the way it was lessening, she knew she'd been right. It wasn't broken. Badly bruised and potentially sprained, but not broken.

She'd survive. Thanks to JJ. She squeezed her eyes shut, but it was no use. All she could see was the fire in his eyes as he'd rushed toward her in the snow. The look of concern and anger and protectiveness.

She let out a shaky sigh. She'd never been one to harbor fantasies of knights in shining armor, and that gruff, unkempt mountain man out there didn't fit any of the images that descriptor called to mind.

But that was exactly how he'd acted. Like a hero to her ridiculous damsel in distress routine. Despite her crazy anger and her temper, he'd come after her and he'd rescued her and… and that was so sexy. So sweet. And so… lovable.

She frowned as the word filled her mind.

No, not lovable. Honorable.

She nodded decisively. It was sexy, sweet and honorable.

Honorable… which is a completely loveable trait.

She snapped her eyes shut and tried not to think.

As soon as she could feel her toes again, she jumped out and dried off. Just outside the door were a set of her clothes—dry, clean, and comfy. She pulled them on and ran her fingers through her hair. When she couldn't put it off any longer, she opened the bathroom door and inched back into the living area.

JJ didn't seem to hear her. He was sitting in front of the fire in new clothes, his head bent over his hand.

Her heart gave a weird little hitch at the sight of him frowning in concentration.

It looked like he was trying to fix his own injury, and without much success. He was struggling to hold the tweezers and grunting in frustration. His frown was endearing, and Dahlia was overcome with affection, attraction, tenderness, and... and...

Not love!

She swallowed hard, pressing one hand into her belly as if that could help squelch this surge of emotion.

Whatever it was she was feeling, she knew that even if she wanted to run and hide, she couldn't. JJ needed help, and she was the only person around to give it.

The thought had her straightening.

Taking care of people she could do. It was what she did best.

A new sense of purpose helped her to shove aside the confusing mix of emotions. She strode more confidently toward the fire. Toward JJ.

She might not know the first thing about love and romance.

But cleaning cuts and bandaging wounds?

That she could do.

3 0

J J heard her coming. Like a coward, he kept his head down for another moment. He didn't fear her anger or even her judgment about his past.

But the feelings she'd stirred when he'd held her in his arms?

Yeah. That had scared him witless.

He listened to her slow shuffle across the room. Her limp wasn't as pronounced as before, and a wave of relief flooded him. Her ankle was already on the mend.

When she was standing right in front of his chair, he finally looked up. He was relieved to see color back in her cheeks, but as for the rest of her…

He swallowed hard, his good hand clenching the tweezers in a fist as he fought a surge of heat so intense it rivaled the fire.

She'd never looked more beautiful than she did at this moment. With her hair all loose and messy, all he could think about was burying his fingers into it, drawing her close, and kissing those pink lips.

He swallowed and turned his attention back to his

hand. He highly doubted she'd want him now, not after the way she reacted to his divorce confession.

"Let me." Her voice was soft as she took the tweezers from his hand.

She knelt in front of his chair.

"But your ankle."

"It's okay," she murmured. "I'm comfortable down here." She held out her hand, silently asking for his.

It would have been fruitless to argue. A smile tugged at his lips as he laid his big, rough hand on top of hers. He watched her studying his palm. Her lips were pursed, and her gaze was focused.

So very focused and determined, his Dahlia.

He closed his eyes for a second. Not *his* Dahlia. He had to stop thinking like that.

Meticulously and with the utmost care, she pulled out the large splinter and the other small ones that were embedded in his skin.

It hurt a little, but he gritted his teeth, waiting out the tormenting silence. If he knew what to say to make things less awkward between them, he'd say it. But he had no idea how to fix things, especially since he was pretty sure it was his own admission that had broken this connection between them.

"I'm sorry," she finally whispered. "I shouldn't have run out like that. It was such an idiot move. I just... I..." She shook her head with a sigh. "I have no good excuse."

He waited until she glanced up and then gave her a little smile. He silently told her she was forgiven, and he enjoyed the soft blush on her cheeks.

"I didn't walk out on my wife," he murmured.

Dahlia stilled, her head slowly rising so she could look

him in the eye. A mortified frown crumpled her expression. "She left you?"

He lifted a shoulder. Suddenly he wished he hadn't kept silent on this topic for so many years. Maybe then he'd know how to talk about it. "We left each other. It was a mutual decision."

Her lips quivered a bit, and he could all but see her wanting to believe him. "That sounds like a line. It's never really mutual, is it?"

He sighed, looking up to the ceiling as he tried to find the words to explain. "Maybe not always. But by the time Rena and I split, we were both in agreement that it was a mistake."

"A mistake?"

He looked back down, and his heart ached at the vulnerability in her eyes. He didn't know for sure why she'd run out of here the way she had, but from what he'd learned of her history, he could guess.

He'd always known that prickly armor of hers hid a world of hurt, and he suspected that today he'd caught a glimpse of it.

Brushing a finger down her cheek, he leaned back and gazed at her. "Rena and I never should have gotten married in the first place. The truth is neither of us really wanted to. We'd known each other for years, started dating in high school, and the big plan was to graduate, see the world, then come home and settle down."

Her gaze searched his face when he paused. "You don't have to tell me. I get that it's too hard."

He'd only paused because he'd surprised himself by that torrent of words. Even more surprising was the fact that the moment he'd started talking, he'd realized that he *wanted* to tell her. He never dove deep into his past with anyone, but here in this isolated cabin, the story seemed to want to come out of him.

"I grew up in a very religious family, and Rena did too." He shifted uncomfortably. He'd never tried to put all this into words before. "Now, I'm a God-fearing man, and I've always done my best to walk the right path…"

She nodded, and somehow that simple acknowledgment put him at ease. It was important to him that she knew he'd never tried to shirk his responsibilities and that his faith and his beliefs were important to him.

"I think one of the reasons Rena and I were drawn to each other in the first place was because we both had these grand plans." He chuckled softly. Those days felt like a different lifetime. "We'd both been born and raised in Charleston, and our families assumed that we'd follow in their footsteps. But we were both a little rebellious, I guess."

He shrugged. In hindsight, after all he'd seen of the world, they weren't that rebellious at all. They were just two kids who'd wanted a taste of freedom.

"We used to daydream about traveling. Neither of us had ever seen anything outside our hometown, and we threw ourselves into planning all these adventures."

When he glanced down, he saw a hint of a smile on her lips.

"The problem came when graduation neared and we told our parents about these plans."

"They didn't approve?" she guessed when he paused.

He shook his head. "They wouldn't hear of us traveling together without being married. Even when we argued that we wouldn't be traveling like that. We didn't plan on sharing rooms or anything, but…" He shrugged. "I'm still not sure if they didn't trust us to keep our word, or if it wasn't about us at all."

"What do you mean?" she asked.

He met her gaze for a long moment. Her open honesty, the curiosity she didn't try to hide...

There was a strange sort of comfort in it.

"I mean..." He huffed as he ran his free hand over his hair. She was still holding his injured one even though all the splinters were out. "For my parents, in particular, it always seemed to be more about appearances than anything. Even if they believed we were just traveling as friends, they didn't want to raise eyebrows or ruffle feathers in our community."

"So they pressured you to marry?" she guessed.

He nodded. "To be fair, we could have changed our plans. We could have come up with some other way to see the world and follow our dreams..."

His heart ached again, this time for the kid he'd been. For the kid Rena had been. "Neither of us knew what we were getting into. Marriage seemed like such a simple solution at the time."

She leaned back, her gaze filled with concern. On his behalf. The thought had him smiling.

"So you got married just to make your parents happy?" she asked.

He sighed. It wasn't quite that simple. "We talked about it a lot, me and Rena. We prayed on it too. Neither of us had any experience dating anyone else. We had nothing to compare it to. We thought it must be love." He winced. "That sounds terrible, doesn't it?"

"No." She shook her head quickly. "It makes total sense. Brady was my first real boyfriend, and I felt the same way with him."

He stilled. He'd had the distinct misfortune of meeting her ex when he'd come to the ranch. A surge of jealousy washed over him at the idea of that jerk with Dahlia.

"I thought just because he was nice to me, because he needed me..." She shrugged with a little wince. "I was stupid."

He shook his head. "You were young, not stupid."

She arched a brow. "I guess the same goes for you and Rena, huh?"

He laughed under his breath. She was right, of course. But he'd never seen it that way... until right now.

How easy it was to let someone else off the hook for being young and naive when he'd spent the better part of a decade cursing himself for the same thing.

He sighed. "In the end, I guess Rena and I thought that having shared dreams was enough. That since we both wanted to travel and one day start a family, that was a good enough basis for marriage." He lifted his head to meet her gaze, his smile rueful. "It wasn't."

A silence descended. He supposed she had lots of questions. He knew there was more to say. But for a long moment they just sat quietly, lost in their own thoughts.

She got busy disinfecting his hand. He hissed at the burning antiseptic, but she didn't let up until the wound was cleaned.

"So, what happened? Why couldn't you stay married?" she finally asked when she was done torturing his poor palm.

He reached for a bandage and focused on the wound.

"Within a few months of traveling, we realized that dating and living together are two very different things. We just... we thought differently about so much stuff, and we were constantly biting at each other. Little spats turned

238

to full-on arguments, and then we started sleeping in separate rooms at the various places we stayed in. After a while, it just seemed silly that we were seeing the world together but alone." He shook his head with a sigh. "One night we met a group of fellow travelers, and she really hit it off with one guy in particular."

Dahlia's head shot up, her eyes wide. "Did she cheat on you?"

"No." He shook his head. "But she'd wanted to, and it made her realize that our marriage was a total farce, and it was holding us both back. I had to agree with her."

"How'd your parents react?" Dahlia cringed as if she already knew the answer.

"They weren't happy about it." His expression took on a hard edge; he could feel it. His emotions always got a little brittle when he remembered this part. "They were mortified. Told me I wasn't allowed to divorce my wife. They didn't care how hard it was. I'd made vows, and I had to keep 'em." He met Dahlia's gaze, wondering if she could see the pain traveling through him. "The thing is, if Rena wanted me to, I would have done just that. I didn't take my vows lightly, even if I regretted them."

Dahlia nodded, and he felt the vise around his lungs start to break.

"But Rena knew it was a mistake too. As she put it, it was a mistake she didn't want to spend a lifetime paying for." Dahlia winced, and he chuckled. "She wasn't trying to be mean. Just honest."

Dahlia nodded in understanding. "It must have been a tough time for you both."

"It was," he agreed. "But while Rena's parents eventually saw reason and supported the divorce, my parents dug in their heels."

He scratched the back of his head, wondering how much to tell her. Most people in Aspire would likely never guess that the bushy-bearded mountain man came from old money.

And he didn't relish admitting aloud that his parents used that wealth to try and control him, wielding it like puppet strings.

"Needless to say, they didn't exactly welcome me with open arms. So I left. I try my best to keep things civil these days. I check in regularly, mainly so my younger sisters don't forget I'm alive." He shot her a self-deprecating smile, but she frowned back at him with a concern that made his chest too tight. "I think if it were up to my father, he'd rather just forget that they once had a wayward son. Heck, they've probably written me out of their will."

She arched her brows. "Is that a big deal?"

He winced. "Money's never a big deal, but, uh... I probably kissed a couple hundred million dollars goodbye."

Dahlia gaped. "A hundred million?"

He scrubbed the back of his neck again at her open-mouthed stare. "My parents are quite... well off."

"Quite?" Dahlia let out a surprised laugh.

"At least I still had access to the money my grandparents left me in their will. I used that to buy this luxurious place." He swept a hand through the air, as if showing off his grand home.

They grinned at each other, and he felt it again, that strange connection like an invisible tether tying them to each other.

She looked away first, dipping her head to his injured hand, which still rested in hers. Lightly brushing her fingers around the bandage, she sent tendrils of pleasure racing up his arm before placing his hand back on his lap.

"After you left, what did you do?" She got busy packing away the first aid kit.

"I hitchhiked and walked from Charleston to Montana."

She stopped and turned. "Wow."

"I needed to. That whole experience, traveling with Rena and the collapse of our marriage…" He shrugged. "I had a lot to sort through. I stopped in North Dakota for a while. Got some seasonal work in the oil fields. By the time I hit Montana, I felt like I'd found my soul, and I didn't even know it'd been missin'."

Her eyes went glassy, and he brushed his thumb over her cheekbone before leaning back with a tender smile. "And now that I've bared mine, maybe you could tell me why you lost your head and thundered out that door." He pointed to the door she'd disappeared through, and she turned to look at it.

For a second, he thought she might not say anything, but then she looked back to him with that steely determination he loved so much… and she started to talk.

31

"You seem so put together—" Dahlia clamped her mouth shut.

What a ridiculous way to start. As if it was his fault she'd leapt to the wrong conclusions.

He arched his brows, a smile hovering over his lips. He didn't prompt her to continue, just sat there and watched her. Quiet. Patient. So freakin' kind.

She cleared her throat. "What I mean is... you seem like such a good man. A kind man. And..." Oh goodness, this was difficult. But he'd poured his secrets out to her, and it was only fair that she at least try to explain her over-reaction. "I just couldn't stand the thought of you betraying your wife or hurting her by walking out on the marriage."

"It didn't happen that way."

"I know," she quickly whispered. "And I should have let you explain. It's just..." She sighed and rubbed her forehead. "My dad left my mom. You know that, I'm sure."

He didn't try to deny it. Like it or not, O'Sullivan business was town gossip now that their father's will had brought his daughters to Aspire. Even if he didn't pay attention to gossip, he'd likely heard an earful from Emma and Lizzy these past few months.

"He walked away for good after Rose was born," she said. "I guess my mother's postpartum depression was the final straw for Frank. Or maybe he just didn't want another daughter."

She shrugged, but there was no hiding the bitter hurt in her voice. She hadn't bothered to try.

"But really, he'd walked away a hundred times before that. He came and went as it suited him." She wrapped her arms around her knees. She couldn't quite bring herself to meet JJ's soft, kind gaze. "I don't remember much of it. I was only five when Rose was born, but some of my earliest memories are of Frank leaving. Walking out that door like we meant nothing to him. And I waited, you know? I waited for him to come back like he usually would." She shook her head and could barely get the words out. "But he never did."

She narrowed her eyes as she tried to summon up actual images, but like always, her earliest memories were just emotions. Fragments of a child's perspective. "Even when I was little I knew my mother was sick a lot. It wasn't until I was older that I realized 'sick' was my grandmother's way of saying mentally unbalanced."

She hitched her lips to the side, shifting slightly so she could see the fire. The crackle and glow were hypnotic. And for a second, she let herself believe that this was a moment out of time. She could speak the truth here and now, without worrying about Rose's feelings or Daisy's response.

"My mother's staying with a family in Canada these

days, and I don't know that she's ever gotten the treatment she deserves. All I know is that back then, she didn't want anyone's help, and so while I can guess that maybe she was bipolar, she was never officially diagnosed."

He leaned forward and reached for her hand, holding hers like she'd held his while he'd talked.

"Every time she was 'sick,' as my grandma put it, Frank left." Anger, tight and painful, clawed at her chest. "He just... left. He left me and Daisy to deal with our bedridden mother who didn't care if we slept or ate, let alone if we got dressed or brushed our teeth. Thankfully my grandmother was still alive back then. She brought some normalcy and structure to the house."

She fell silent, lost in a dark sea of memories from those early days. Memories that felt too hazy to pin down, but they were real, and they still hurt.

"When did your grandmother pass away?" he asked.

"Just before Rose started preschool." Her voice turned to a squeak, but then she cleared her throat, regaining control. "I was in the fourth grade."

"And there was no one else around to help you?"

She stiffened defensively, even though she knew the reaction was silly. "We managed."

His smile was tender. "I'm sure you did."

"My mother wasn't sick all the time. And when she was good, she was—" Her breath caught, a laugh bubbling up at the memories of their mother when she was flying high. "Well, I guess doctors would say she was manic." She shrugged. "All I know is, when she was doing well, we all felt like we were flying high." She swallowed hard. Just thinking about that time in their lives made her chest tighten with anxiety. "Except the thing was... the older I got, the more aware I became. I knew those highs would end. And I found myself just…" She shook her head. "Just bracing for it, you know?"

He nodded, even though he couldn't know. He couldn't possibly know.

"I tried to be like my grandmother," she hurried on. "I wanted to take her place after she passed. I tried to be the rock in the storm, so to speak." She smiled a bit at her own naivete when she'd made that decision. "My grandmother was practical, so I followed her lead, focusing on the logistics of the household. The laundry, the bedtimes, making sure everyone brushed their teeth and did their homework."

She shook her head with another rueful laugh. She'd been an overbearing tyrant even back then.

"Mom was up and down like a roller coaster. Bubbly one minute, depressed the next. Working like a maniac one week and then barely able to get out of bed." She tugged her hand from his. "Somebody had to be levelheaded."

JJ winced. "That must have been really hard."

She gritted her teeth. She hated pity, yet that wasn't what he was offering, and she knew it. But even his gentle understanding was difficult to swallow. It made her want to feel sorry for herself, and that was something she tried never to do.

"When my dad walked away that last time after Rose was born… When he left and didn't come back…" She took a deep breath, fighting waves of pain and anger so intense it was like she was a child all over again. "I don't really remember him, but I remember what happened after. I *know* his leaving sent my mother into the worst spiral I'd ever seen. And every time she was down, she talked about him. Blamed him." Dahlia's hands clenched into fists. "And he never came back! So I grew up hating him."

"He never tried to keep in touch?" JJ asked after a long silence.

"He sent cards." Her voice was brittle with a bitterness she couldn't disguise. "Every Christmas and most birthdays, although sometimes he forgot. I tore those cards up and deposited the money into bank accounts for Daisy and Rose. I didn't want his lame attempt at trying to make himself feel like he did something for us. He walked away." Her voice was getting sharp and snappy, so she licked her lips to try and cool off.

JJ's voice was a breezy balm. "Do you still blame him?"

She swallowed. "To some degree, I guess. I still hate him for leaving us like that, but as I got older, I started to see the reality of our situation more clearly. I started to realize that my mom was really hard work."

She felt a stab of guilt just saying it.

"I mean, I found her nearly impossible, so I can only imagine what being married to her must have been like. When she was down, she was so cold and detached. She didn't want affection or..." Dahlia shook her head, fighting tears. "Neither did my grandma, but for different reasons. That woman was so practical." She let out a short, hard laugh. "She did a good job taking care of us, but she was also... cold. Stern. All that mattered was making sure we were fed and in bed on time."

Guilt was nearly drowning her now, and she looked away from JJ with a sigh. "Not that I'm criticizing either of them. My mother was sick. She should have gotten help. And my grandmother tried her best, but she'd never asked to be a mother three times over when she should have been enjoying retirement, you know?"

She was babbling and forced herself to stop. To breathe.

But it was too late. The floodgates she'd kept sealed were open, and more words tumbled out of her mouth. "I so didn't want to grow up to be like either of them, but that's exactly what I've done. I've become the kind of woman any man in his right mind would walk away from. And so I can never... have that, you know? I'll never have the wedding or the marriage."

Her lungs felt far too tight, and she was keenly aware of JJ's eyes on her.

Stop talking. Just... stop.

But her mouth seemed to have a mind of its own, and her heart felt like it was purging every dark thought. Every fear she'd been steadfastly refusing to face. "I can't be a mother. There's no point, because I'm too much work. And I won't be in a position where I'm left with three little kids and a broken heart—"

"Hey." JJ reached out, touching her chin until she looked at him. "You are not your mother. And you're not your grandmother either."

She tugged away from his touch. It was too tempting to sink into it. To let him reassure her. But she knew the truth about herself. She knew what she'd become, and she didn't need to overhear herself being called the dragon to know that everyone else saw it too.

She wasn't loveable. She wasn't fun like Daisy or sweet like Rose. She was practical. Logical.

"I guess I've always thought..." She swallowed hard as more vile truths bubbled up. "If they need you, they can't leave, right? That's what I thought when it came to Brady. He was like an overgrown child, and he needed me, and that... that I could do. I mean, I lost Daisy a long time ago, but Rose... she needed me." Her smile was sad and bitter. "Until she didn't. She doesn't need me anymore."

JJ leaned forward until she was forced to look at him. "Rose might not need you, but I have it on good authority that she loves you something fierce."

Dahlia's eyes stung, and her heart ached. Why did she need this man to tell her that? It made no sense. But even so, she clutched the words close like a treasure. "Thank you."

He studied her long and hard. "There are a lot of people in this world who love you, or who would love you if you just let them."

The sting of tears was so painful now she knew it was only a matter of time before she lost the battle. Thank goodness she was leaving. She had no idea how she was going to face JJ again after he'd heard all this.

But just as quickly as she felt grateful for the fact that she was leaving, she was swamped with a wave of sorrow at the thought of walking away from him.

She sucked in a shaky breath, desperate to regain her control, but she couldn't hold back the tears.

Gently taking her face, JJ studied her with a look of complete anguish.

"You're wrong," he whispered, brushing the tears off her cheeks. "You're wrong about all of it. You're not emotionally fragile like your mother, but you're not made of ice either. You have a heart, Lia. You're just afraid to let people see it."

She sniffled and shook her head, but before she could argue, he spoke again, and his voice was filled with feeling. "I wish you could see what I see."

Her entire body stilled as she gazed into his eyes. They were a tractor beam—mesmerizing, drawing her in.

"I see strength, determination, and a heart that wants to give and serve and take care of the people around her. You have no idea how incredible you are."

She tried to shake her head, to deny his words, but he held her still.

"You are so worthy," he whispered, leaning toward her, so close she could feel his breath on her cheek. "You're worthy of every good thing."

She couldn't help but touch him. Lightly running her fingers down his beard, she tried to resist her thundering heart, but it was no use.

His power over her was too strong to fight.

Impulse pulled her forward, and she pressed her mouth to his like it was the only thing she was born to do.

32

For all the years JJ spent searching for a home, he never expected to find it in a kiss.

But the moment Dahlia pressed her lips to his, that was exactly what he found. Her lips were soft and warm, and they fit against his like they were born to be there.

For a second, he couldn't breathe. He couldn't move. His entire life came down to this moment, this feeling of her heat pressed against him, of her lips molding to his.

It wasn't until a heartbeat later, when he felt her warm breath against his parted lips, that his body overtook his stunned state. He reached out to grip her shoulders before she could pull away, and this time he sought her lips for a harder kiss—one that was deep and sweet and that he hoped said all he wanted to say.

She gasped at the urgency of it, so much harder and fiercer than her sweet, almost chaste kiss. But she wound her arms around his neck as he tilted his head, fitting his mouth to hers.

Slowly, he learned the taste of her. With all the patience

he could muster, he savored the feel of her lips against his, the way they moved, nipped, and clung.

But this angle wouldn't do. She was still on her knees before him, and he was bending over her...

In one quick move, he reached for her waist, hauling her up and into his lap. He pulled back just long enough to look down at her ankle. "Does this hurt?"

The stunned look in her eyes as she gazed back at him made him smile. "Hmm?"

He chuckled. He couldn't help it. She was too adorable when she was studying him like this. Desire and affection were clear in her eyes.

"I guess that's my answer," he murmured.

Her gaze was on his lips, and her glazed awe perfectly matched the way he was feeling. He was reeling, truth be told, but in the very best way. Like planets were repositioning in the sky, and the ground was shifting below, and the whole world was realigning into place like pieces of a jigsaw puzzle.

And all because of a kiss that felt more right than anything he'd ever known.

He swallowed hard, his eyes skimming her lips. "I'm going to kiss you again," he whispered, his voice husky.

It wasn't a question but a mere statement of fact. He had to kiss her. There was nothing else he could do. Thankfully, she nodded.

He leaned in slower this time, savoring every second, from the slight rasp of her breathing to the feel of her breath on his lips right before they met. Her arms wrapped tighter around him, and the weight of her against him was like nothing he'd ever felt before.

She was everything he'd never known he'd wanted,

this riddle in his arms. Soft and tough, solid and fragile. And the way she kissed him back…

He'd never again believe her to be an ice queen, not when she was pure fire in his arms.

Though every part of him wanted to claim her fully, to tell her there was no going back now—that she was his—he also knew he had to go slow. Because that was not what this kiss was about.

The kiss deepened slowly, perfectly. Each of them exploring and learning.

There's no rush, he told himself when he pulled back to catch his breath and let her do the same.

Her breathing was shaky, and she dropped her hands to clutch his shirt, her hands fisting the material as another shiver raced through her. But this one, he knew, had nothing to do with the cold.

She'd laid herself bare just now, and nothing had ever been more beautiful. He moved his hands to do what he'd been dying to do before. Delving his fingers into her long, still-damp locks, he held her still so she had to meet his gaze.

"Tell me you know I'm right," he whispered.

There wasn't even a flicker of confusion in her eyes. She knew precisely what he meant.

That she was worthy. Deserving of marriage and kids, and anything else she might dream of. But mostly, she was deserving of love.

She didn't answer, and he hadn't really expected her to. No one could convince someone of that sort of thing. It needed to be experienced. Proven.

And as his lips sought out hers again, he did his best to show her with his touch just how perfect she was.

Flawed? Yes. But who wasn't? Her imperfections made her human.

They made her perfect for him.

And he tried to show her that as his hands roamed into her hair, skimmed across her neck, and trailed down her back. His lips rained kisses on her dainty nose and her elegant cheekbones and across the length of her stubborn little jaw.

All of it as perfect as she was.

And he wanted to hurt the people who'd ever made her doubt it. He wished he could bring Frank O'Sullivan back from the dead just to account for all the ways he'd let his daughter down.

But none of those people mattered now. Because here in this cabin, it was just him and her. And he wanted it to stay that way forever.

The thought brought with it a flare of shock, a flicker of terror—but then she lost patience with his gentle trail of kisses and claimed his mouth in a searing kiss that burned away anything but the here and now.

Once more, life came down to Dahlia in his arms.

The fire crackled as the wind outside roared. But she was safe, and they were here, and with his kiss, he did his best to tell her everything she refused to believe.

He had no idea how much time passed in this blissful piece of heaven before she pulled back, settling in his arms like she was just as at home as he felt.

"Wow," she murmured, a grin stealing over her face and taking his heart right along with it.

"You can say that again."

Her eyes flickered with laughter. "Wow," she teased.

He groaned at the silly joke.

She reached out and touched his beard.

"Am I giving you beard burn?" As soon as he asked, he saw she was a little red around the mouth.

She shook her head but then said, "I like it."

He grinned. "And I like you."

Her blush matched the beard burn, and he couldn't resist pulling her into his chest for a tight hug as his heart swelled painfully.

She hugged him back, her fingers toying with the long hair that curled over his collar. "Thank you," she whispered. "For… for everything."

He swallowed hard against another wave of emotion. But when he pulled back to face her, he didn't try to hide it. "I could kiss you all day."

She blushed as she laughed. "You're pretty good at it."

"Only pretty good?" He feigned insult. "You mustn't have been paying proper attention. Here, let me show you again."

She giggled, and he captured the sweet sound with his mouth, sinking back into another long, luxurious kiss.

33

D ahlia couldn't stop smiling.

Honestly, it was becoming a problem.

"Well, Ms. O'Sullivan?" JJ leaned forward over the table with a little grin that made her heart dance. "What do you think of this fine cuisine?"

She just barely managed to squelch a giggle before it escaped.

Goodness, she didn't recognize herself right now.

She eyed her oatmeal dinner with feigned thoughtfulness. "This might be the finest bowl of oats I've ever eaten."

He leaned back in his seat, his grin widening. "Bet you say that to all the men you're stranded in snowstorms with."

She couldn't have stopped the smile that split her face if she'd tried. "Only the ones who rescue me from fallen tree limbs."

He chuckled, and the sound was warmer than the fire that still crackled and popped in the fireplace nearby.

All afternoon it had been like this. Smiles, laughter, and

easy chatter as they tended to the fire and sorted through the food options.

Dahlia would have thought that spilling all her deepest, darkest fears and insecurities would have made her wary around JJ. She'd expected to be embarrassed. To not be able to meet his gaze.

But the exact opposite happened. The way he'd responded, the way he'd kissed her after seeing all her worst flaws on full display…

It was cathartic. She'd felt reborn by the time they'd reluctantly ended their make-out session.

Both of them knew full well where it would lead if they'd continued, and that wasn't what this was about. What was happening between them now was a different sort of intimacy. One she'd never experienced before.

It was the giggling, fizzy joy of a first crush. It was the much deeper connection of a newfound friendship. It was attraction and respect and reveling in each other's company and…

Oh gosh, she didn't know what this was.

As she grinned around the next bite of bland oatmeal, her chest felt like it might explode from happiness.

Whatever this was, it was a first for her…

And she didn't want it to end.

She shoved the thought aside. It would end. It had to. But she didn't want to think about that right now. These moments they had together felt precious. Maybe it was being cut off from the rest of civilization with no access to phone or email or even a way back into town, but this day had felt like a moment out of time.

They'd been cast in a spell where the clock had stopped and the world ceased spinning. It was just the two of them in a perfect little bubble.

"What are you thinking about right now?" he asked, his voice soft, his gaze tender.

She swallowed hard. *Reality. How this is going to end.*

Once more she shook off the thoughts. Of course she knew this time together had an end, but that didn't mean she couldn't enjoy every second while she had it.

She'd drown in this happiness while she could, and when she was back in her apartment in New York, alone and stressed out over work, she'd have these memories to call upon to keep her warm.

The thought was bittersweet, but it helped her shove aside that worry of it ending once and for all. She leaned forward, making a show of thinking over her response. "What am I thinking about? Hmmm…" She tapped her spoon to her lips.

He'd asked her that several times already. Every time she went quiet or got lost in her head, he'd gently draw her out again. And he'd watch her, just like this, while he waited for a response… with his gaze and his attention riveted on her, like he really wanted to know. Like he needed to know each and every thought that crossed her mind.

And for the most part, she'd been utterly honest in her responses. But right now…

Well, she didn't want to bring him down by talking about how this magical moment would have to end. But she couldn't bring herself to lie to him either. So she smiled as she spoke a version of the truth. "I'm thinking about fairy tales."

His brows shot up. "Fairy tales, huh?" A smile tugged at his lips.

It seemed neither of them could go more than a few seconds without grinning like lovesick fools.

He shifted in his seat, tilting his head as if to study her from a different angle. "You don't strike me as the fairy-tale type."

She gave a snort of amusement at that. "That's because I'm not. But that doesn't mean I'm not well versed in all things Disney princess." She pointed her spoon in his direction with an arched brow. "Two sisters, remember?"

"I bet Rose was a big fan of *Beauty and the Beast*. What with the library and all."

Dahlia's lips parted, a huff of delighted amusement slipping out.

JJ pointed his spoon in her direction. "Two sisters, remember?"

She burst out laughing. "I bet you were a great older brother."

He shrugged, his smile growing a touch sad. Just enough regret evident in his gaze that she felt it like it was her own. "I *was*, I guess. But these days a phone call every now and again is the best I can do."

She nodded, swallowing hard.

Maybe it was because Dahlia was so reticent to open up to others, but she was realizing here with JJ that no one ever really opened up to her either. She was never the first person Daisy or Rose turned to with heartaches and hurt feelings. She was the one they came to for Band-Aids and advice on student loans.

She set her spoon down carefully, the weight of responsibility settling over her. There was no being sarcastic or flippant when someone shared something real like JJ had.

Like she had.

He was gentle with her, and she wanted to be the same for him.

"I bet you're doing all you can," she said finally. "And no one can ask for more than that."

His gaze was uncharacteristically serious for a moment before he gave her a small smile of gratitude that made her heart clench. "Thanks, Lia."

Her answering smile felt watery. She cleared her throat and forced a bright tone. "To answer your question, no. Rose was always more into reading books than watching movies. She liked the Disney movies well enough as a kid, but it was Daisy who was obsessed." She rolled her eyes at the memory, and JJ laughed.

"What was her favorite?"

She gave another huff of amusement. "What wasn't? So long as it had music, and a princess, and a happily ever after, she was into it. And Rose and I would hear her rendition of every song over and over and over...." She trailed off when JJ started to laugh a little louder.

"That's right, she's the musician, isn't she?"

Dahlia nodded, a little annoyed with herself for bringing up her twin. She didn't want any more family drama tainting the joyful afternoon they'd been having.

"I hope I get to meet her someday." JJ's eyes sparkled with amusement.

She nodded. "I hope so too."

But I doubt it.

That would require Daisy to come to Aspire. And while Daisy loved to travel, she was a pro when it came to avoiding messy emotions. And a newfound family? An estranged father's inheritance? The ranch and its inhabitants were about as messy as it got.

JJ seemed to be waiting for her to say more, so she added, "You'll love her."

"Oh yeah?"

"Everyone loves Daisy."

And that was the truth. Daisy was fun to be around. Lively, vivacious, and comical—basically everything Dahlia was not.

JJ leaned forward, his eyes sparking with a heat that burned away any of the resentment and hurt that always came up when she thought about Daisy. "Well, if she's anything like her sister, I'm sure I'll love her."

Dahlia's chest lit up like he'd set off fireworks. But she couldn't help a snort. "She's nothing like me. But I guarantee you'll still love her."

His sexy lopsided smile and that heat in his eyes made her forget everything but him and this cabin and this perfect day. "I'll take your word for it."

For a long moment, they went back to the goofy grins and swoony gazes. All thoughts of sisters and families and responsibilities and jobs were out the window.

Tomorrow she could think about all that. For today...

Today she'd rack up the memories. "So, how do you think we should entertain ourselves this evening?" She arched a brow, shifting her gaze to the abandoned deck of cards.

JJ chuckled as he slid his empty bowl to the edge of the table and reached for the cards.

"Want to let me beat you at cards again?" JJ asked with a cheeky grin.

She tilted her head to the side as if to think it over. "Or I could beat you."

His eyebrow arched. "Well, you could *try*."

"Challenge accepted, sir." She burst out laughing.

And as JJ dealt her a hand, she found herself wondering how she could make this night last. Preferably forever.

JJ shifted on the couch, rolling onto his left side as if maybe by some magic, he would fit better on this dang lumpy sofa.

Not that he really minded that so much. He was used to sleeping in tents and campers. He didn't need more than a pillow under his head to find sleep.

Typically.

But he didn't typically have a heart-achingly beautiful woman lying just across the room when he was trying to drift off.

She'd been quiet in the bed for so long he was sure she must be asleep. He flipped onto his back and folded his arms beneath his head.

Good. She needed her sleep. That was why when she'd tried to insist on taking the couch, he wouldn't hear of it.

She'd had a scare today, which must have wiped her out. Not to mention the emotional upheaval and her sore ankle. It'd seemed better by the end of the evening, but when she pulled back her sock to examine the bruising, it still looked kind of nasty. But at least it wasn't swollen or immobile. She'd no doubt be walking on it normally by the time the snowstorm had blown through.

His heart slammed against his rib cage just thinking about it all. How close he'd come to losing her if that limb had fallen just a second earlier or if she hadn't thrown herself back to try and avoid it. Then how much she'd let him in by opening up about her parents.

Even the way he'd spilled his own secrets. He kept waiting for some sort of repercussion. Some guilt or weirdness over the woman he liked finding out about his past after he'd held it close to his chest for so long.

But that never happened. If anything, he felt... relief.

Her acceptance of his story, and the way she'd somehow managed to ease some of the guilt he felt toward his sisters...

All in all, today felt like some sort of miracle.

And while he wasn't sure he deserved it, he treasured it all the same.

The wind howled fiercely outside the window, so harsh it shook the cabin's frame. The sound of it made him smile. Maybe it was wrong, but he was grateful the storm still raged outside.

Oh, he knew it couldn't last forever. And he shouldn't want it to.

He glanced toward Dahlia's still form. The fire lit the lump in the bed with a soft glow. She was curled under the covers, hopefully snug, warm, and dancing through dreamland.

Tucked in here away from all the drama with her family and the reminders of her life in New York. This storm was keeping her from all that.

But he couldn't forget that she'd be leaving just as soon as this storm passed.

He shifted and stretched. All the more reason to enjoy this time with her while he had it.

And after?

He shoved the thought aside. He'd never been a worrier. He'd never seen much point in fretting over matters that were out of his control. And while some part of his mind itched to go there—to try and find ways to make this thing between them last—he resisted the urge.

For the tenth time since he'd bid Dahlia good night, JJ shut his eyes with every intention of falling asleep.

And just like every other time, his eyes opened again, as if they had a mind of their own. And just like every other time, he found his gaze drifting toward the bed.

What was she dreaming about?

He couldn't wait to hear her stories in the morning.

He gave a soft huff of laughter. What had come over him? He was a man obsessed. He felt this crazy curiosity around Dahlia, and he couldn't seem to get enough of her. He wanted to see every little facet of her personality. Heck, if she was cranky first thing in the morning, he wanted to know.

And then he'd do everything in his power to make her smile.

She must have thought him nuts with all his questions about what she was thinking. But he couldn't help himself. The more he found out about her, the more she let him see, the more he wanted to know of her.

There was a bottomless pit inside him when it came to Dahlia O'Sullivan. And he wasn't sure he'd ever get enough.

One day in a cabin definitely wouldn't cut it.

And there his mind went again, trying to fix a problem he couldn't do anything about.

For long moments, he let his brain settle in the silence. He let the memories of the day slide through his mind's eye. He let himself linger on Dahlia's smile, the quirk of her lips, the curve of her chin, the way her fingers felt as they gripped his shirt...

The way she'd kissed him with such passion.

Those thoughts had nearly lulled him into sleep when he heard it. A sound coming from the bed. He stilled, waiting to hear it again, confirming what he suspected.

Yep. There it was.

A soft shiver. Lightly chattering teeth.

Coming to stand, he padded quietly toward the bed. "Are you all right?"

"Just a little cold," Dahlia murmured. Her voice was quiet and sleepy, and JJ's heart faltered, affection sweeping through him faster than he could stand it.

Without hesitating, he headed to the couch and grabbed his blanket, walking it over to the bed to add an extra layer.

She turned onto her back, her eyes darker than night in the flickering light of the fire. Her features were cast in an ethereal hue, and she looked like an angel in his bed, all delicate and sweet without her armor on.

"Is this your blanket?" She fingered the material. "But... what are you going to use?"

"Well..." He paused. He hadn't actually thought it through. All that mattered was Dahlia's comfort. "Don't you worry about it."

Her answer was a huff of amusement as she sat up. "Don't worry about it? You do know who you're talking to, right?"

He chuckled as he leaned over her, tucking her in. "I'll be fine until morning."

She sighed. "JJ, I'm not going to be able to sleep if I think you're freezing over there on the couch."

He smiled down at her. Did anyone else in the world know how big her heart was aside from him?

He certainly hoped so. This woman had so much love to give.

The silence stretched and widened as they gazed at one another. That feeling he'd had all day—this sensation that it was just the two of them, alone in this little world they'd created—it was stronger than ever here in the dark and the firelight.

It made him want to whisper every secret and ask for hers in return. He swallowed hard and looked away. Toward the uncomfortable and soon-to-be-frigid couch. He winced.

There was one solution.

One obvious answer to their problems...

He puffed out his cheeks and then scratched the back of his neck as he turned the idea over in his mind. Finally, he blurted it out. "Maybe we could share the bed, and I could keep you warm."

She studied him for a long moment. He didn't need to see her eyes to feel her gaze. His skin burned wherever her eyes landed.

"I promise to be the perfect gentleman," he added.

A slow smile pulled her lips wide, and he suspected that was the confirmation she'd needed. He could understand that. Kissing her had been the best thing he'd ever done. One of the best moments of his life. One he'd treasure forever.

But to take things any further...

Well, that meant thinking about the future. And right now they seemed to be of one mind about that topic.

They'd both been content to revel in the present all day, and he wasn't about to mess with perfection.

After a brief silence, she flipped the covers down and scooted over. "That'd be nice. Thanks."

He climbed in beside her, and for a moment, his senses were overwhelmed by the intimacy of it—her scent, her warmth, the softness of her body as she rolled into him, letting him wrap his arm around her.

She burrowed into his body with another shiver before sighing her contentment as her head nestled against his shoulder.

"That's much better," she whispered.

He smiled and rubbed her arms and back, trying to get her even warmer. Her head was tucked beneath his chin, and he tipped down to kiss her forehead. "Get some sleep, Lia. You've had quite a day."

He felt her smile against his shoulder, and her breath was warm on his neck. "I've had the best day."

His heart stopped for a beat before kicking and slamming its way back into action against his ribs.

Her voice had been so soft and sleepy, he wasn't sure she'd even meant to say it aloud.

"Me too, Lia," he murmured, even though he knew by the way her breathing slowed that she'd drifted off to sleep already. His arms tightened around her, and he kissed the top of her head. "I've had the best day of my life."

And with that, he drifted off himself.

When he woke, the cabin was bright with sunlight, and the smell of coffee filled the air. He rolled over, disappointed to find the bed empty. But a second later, Dahlia's voice called out to him.

"Morning, sleepyhead."

He propped himself up on his elbows and grinned at the sight of her. Now he knew—Dahlia was a morning person.

He also now knew that tousled bedhead was an excellent look on her, and without makeup and her face scrubbed clean, she was the prettiest woman on the planet.

And as she came toward him with a steaming mug, padding along in socks on the hardwood floor and drowning in one of his woolen sweaters, one other thing became clear.

He was absolutely smitten.

"Black, just the way you like it." She grinned, sitting on the bed beside him as he took the mug from her with a grateful smile.

"How long have you been up?" he asked.

She shrugged, her gaze roaming toward the couch where her laptop was sitting open. "Long enough to do all the work I could offline." Her features screwed up. "Which wasn't a lot."

He chuckled, shaking his head with a tsk. "Haven't you realized yet that being disconnected from the rest of the world is the best part of being in the wilderness?"

She pulled her knees up to her chin as she perched beside him. "Yeah," she agreed slowly. "I think I'm starting to get the appeal."

The blush that stole into her cheeks as she peeked over at him made his chest ache again.

He rubbed a hand over his heart as he sipped the coffee. This woman would be the death of him.

But what a good way to go.

"How's it look outside?" he asked.

"Still snowing."

Her tone gave nothing away. He hoped like heck she

was just as happy about that as he was.

He gestured toward the laptop. "You done with work?"

She nodded. "There's nothing else I can do right now."

"Good." He set his mug on the side table and threw his feet over the side. "Then let the learning begin."

A couple hours later, Dahlia was laughing harder than he'd ever seen as she sat beside him in front of the fire. She held up the mess of twine in her hands. "How is this so hard?"

"Tying knots is no joke," he teased. "I told you it would be harder than you thought."

She rolled her eyes, but she was still grinning. "Okay, Bear Grylls, what's next on the survival training list?"

"Hmm…" He pretended to ponder. There was no real list; he'd been making it up as he went along. But just like he'd suspected, Dahlia thrived while learning new tasks and tackling challenges.

She'd thrown herself into learning mundane things about the cabin, like how the winterizing process worked and how he maintained the old roof. She'd marveled over the history when he'd shown her the places where past inhabitants had marked their kids' heights against the wall, and she'd grown a little sad as he'd pointed out the place where the family who'd owned it before him were buried.

He'd shown her how to cook the sausages they'd thawed the day before over the fire for lunch, and they'd even braved the snow so she could try her hand at chopping wood. Her ankle had improved enough to attempt the task, but he made sure it was a short session. The first time she toppled over with the ax blade stuck in a hunk of wood, he picked her up and forced her back inside.

Her protests about being carried like a princess were absolutely worth it, and he didn't set her down until they were back beside the fire and he could kiss her complaints away.

In between it all, they'd drunk too much coffee and settled in for long chats about everything and nothing. They touched on serious topics but also had a hearty debate over the merits of *Star Wars* versus *Star Trek*.

He'd told her all about how his fascination with wilderness and the wild west had come about, and she'd made him laugh his butt off with a story about the time she'd been kicked out of a Rangers game for getting too rowdy.

In her defense, she'd been sticking up for the nice old lady beside her.

By the time the sun was setting and the stars were beginning to show overhead, JJ knew two things for certain.

The storm had nearly run its course...

And he needed to find a way to keep Dahlia in his life.

Not just as Rose's sister. Not as one of the owners of the ranch. But as his woman.

How he'd make that happen when she was mere days away from leaving, he had no idea.

But as he wrapped his arms around Dahlia again that night and listened to her breathing deepen as she fell asleep against his chest, he knew letting her out of his life wasn't an option.

He needed Dahlia. He wanted her.

He just needed to make sure that was what she wanted too.

And then he had to figure out how to make that work.

3 5

W aking up for a second morning in the cabin was as perfect as the first.

There was nothing better than coming to in JJ's arms. For a moment, Dahlia lay still, absorbing the feel of his heat wrapped around her. It was so intimate even though they'd done nothing more than kiss. And even with kissing, they stopped before it could get too heated.

She knew why she'd put the brakes on anything physical, and she suspected it was the same for JJ. A kiss here and there, the occasional holding of hands, and yes, even cuddling for warmth—they were just this side of some invisible line that neither wanted to cross.

Or... She shifted slightly to stare up at the wood beams on the ceiling. It wasn't that she didn't want to cross that line. It was just that once past that line, things would get complicated.

And this time in the cabin was anything but complicated. It had all been so simple. So easy.

As her mind woke from the fog of sleep, another realization struck.

It was also… over.

She didn't even have to look out the window to know the storm had passed. The incessant howling wind had ceased, and the silence in its wake was deafening.

She shifted away from JJ with subtle movements in the hopes that he'd stay asleep. She wasn't entirely ready to face the day yet and all that would come with it.

Coffee would help. And yet…

She found herself lying there for far too long, unwilling to stay in JJ's arms—that would prolong the torture of having to leave—but not quite ready to get out of bed either.

Stuck in limbo, she thought as a wave of emotions made her lips quiver. Caught in an untenable situation, she couldn't stay, but she dreaded leaving.

Her fingers itched to reach out and touch JJ's beard. For a man so burly and gruff, he was awfully adorable when asleep. He looked younger. Softer. The hard edges of all his years of searching and working melted away when he was relaxed like this.

She rolled onto her side, giving up the pretense that she was doing anything other than gawking at JJ.

But she had to take the opportunity while she could, right? There were no more mornings waking up in each other's arms to look forward to.

She swallowed hard, her insides sinking as reality settled over her.

This was it. *Time's up*.

After one more lingering look, she forced herself upright and then off the bed. She went about making a pot of coffee as quietly as possible, and while it brewed, she moved to the window to confirm what she'd already guessed.

The storm was over. Outside, the sun was shining, the sky was blue, and the snow glimmered in the early morning light.

It was beautiful, really.

Beautiful and so freakin' sad.

Dahlia's head fell against the window with a thud as she drew in a deep breath and told herself to pull it together. She'd known it couldn't last.

With another deep inhale, she walked away from the window and poured herself a mug of coffee. She was in the bathroom, brushing her teeth and packing up her toiletries, when she heard JJ stir.

"The sun is shining, sunshine," he called in a gravelly morning voice that made her insides quiver. It was almost as good as that low, husky voice he used at night when he was tired and nearly asleep.

She paused in the middle of packing up her toiletry case, a stab of pain rendering her temporarily frozen. She quickly tamped down that sensation, but her fingers wouldn't stop shaking as she tried to shove her toothbrush away.

She'd meant it when she'd said she'd never been interested in fairy tales. She'd never believed in magical happy endings, and one snowstorm didn't change that.

She met her gaze in the mirror before picking up her toiletry bag, bracing herself with a smile, and heading out to face the inevitable.

"Morning," she said.

He was already up and pouring himself a mug. Leaning against the kitchen counter, he had an adorably disheveled look about him. As she took him in, his gaze raked over her, doing the same.

He lowered his mug as a slow, sexy smile slid over his face. "How do you do it?"

"Do what?"

He took a step toward her. "How do you look more beautiful with each passing day?"

Her lungs hitched, and what came out was half laugh, half sob.

She didn't know what it was. All she knew was that this look of reverence in his eyes, the way he was staring at her like she truly was beautiful, like she was the center of his world and always would be...

She looked away with a hard swallow. For the first time in ages, she felt flustered around him. Nervous, even. "I, uh... I started packing," she said. "I'm guessing it won't be long before help arrives."

He was quiet for a beat too long. "You're right about that. I'd bet Cody's already on his way."

She nodded, still not looking at him. "I'll, uh... I'll start cleaning up the kitchen so we're ready to leave when he gets here."

"Your ankle okay to do that?"

"Yeah." She held out her foot, rotating it back and forth for him. It still hurt just a touch at certain angles, but it was healing quickly, and she was confident she'd be strutting around in heels soon enough. "I'm all good." Her voice was raspy, and she swallowed, shuffling past him to get busy. She needed the work to keep her sane and had a feeling the cabin's kitchen would be near sparkling by the time she was done with it.

He didn't say much of anything after that, but they worked together in companionable silence. Every time she peeked his way, he seemed just as lost in thought as she was.

Was he sad to see this little adventure come to an end?

She shook her head as she washed some dishes and put them away.

That was likely wishful thinking on her part. But even if he was disappointed, it didn't mean anything.

Cody arrived even sooner than either of them expected. The crunch of his truck's tires could be heard long before he pulled into view, parking next to JJ's truck.

Dahlia opened the door for him, and Cody greeted her with a warm, if shy smile. "Dahlia, it sure is good to see you. Your sisters have been awfully worried. Kit and Nash have had to work overtime trying to reassure them you were in good hands, but…" He paused to shake JJ's hand as he strode into the cabin. "Well, they'll all be relieved to see you healthy and well."

Surprise had her lips parting, and she wasn't sure how to respond. All of them? She'd thought maybe Rose would worry about her, but it was a shock to hear that Emma and Lizzy were worried too.

"Why would anyone worry when she was with me?" JJ feigned offense. He turned to Dahlia with a wink. "Guess they haven't seen how handy I am with an ax."

She gave a snort of amusement. "Your ax skills? Please. Just wait until they get a load of my knots."

He grinned, and they shared another goofy smile that faded much too fast.

"Well…" Cody looked between them, obviously picking up whatever vibe was pulsing in the air. "I think they'll all just be happy to know you're safe." His smile turned impish. "And that neither of you killed the other."

"Well, things got real dicey there for a while," JJ drawled.

For a second, Dahlia thought he was going to tell Cody

about the tree limb and her ankle. But then he added, "Turns out our dear Dahlia is not keen on losing at poker. Can you imagine?"

Cody laughed. "You know, I can." He turned to her with a wink. "I've seen her play darts."

"Exactly," Dahlia added. "He knows I'm a natural born winner. I never lose."

"Except at poker," JJ mumbled loudly enough for them to hear.

Dahlia pretended to be mad, and the teasing continued as they followed Cody out to his truck to get the parts.

The teasing felt a little forced, like it was for Cody's sake more than anything, but Dahlia was still a little relieved. Having Cody around broke the tension and made her feel like she could breathe when she went back inside to finish cleaning up while the guys worked on the truck.

When her chores were done, and the kitchen was sparkling, she went back out. But the sight of JJ working under the hood was too enticing. Was there anything this man couldn't do? And while Cody's presence took the edge off, it was still too hard not to think about what had happened. Or what was to come.

Goodbye, that's what's to come.

She shut that voice down before she did something stupid… like cry.

Instead, she pulled a book off the stack in the screened-in patio and started to read. Or she pretended to read.

Focus wasn't really happening. Her attention kept drifting back to the handsome mountain man outside. And before she could stop herself, she was watching him from the window, hugging the book to her chest, and doing anything but reading it.

The morning seemed to stretch, time alternately flying by too fast and then inching along at a crawl.

On the one hand, she was impatient to leave. To get this pain over with. But on the other...

On the other, she wasn't sure she'd ever be ready to say goodbye to JJ.

But she would. She had to.

Didn't she?

She gave her head a shake as she turned away from the window with a huff.

Yes, of course she did.

36

Dahlia's silence in the passenger seat was killing him.

He tapped his fingers on the steering wheel as they wound their way down the mountain. Cody had left before them, but with everything all packed and Dahlia handling most of the re-winterizing while he worked on the truck, they'd left not long after.

He drew in a deep breath as she fiddled with the radio dial. "She's running good as new now," he said.

"Mmm."

Mmm. That was the most he'd gotten from her since they'd set off five minutes ago.

Typically, he loved silence. Talking, in general, was highly overrated. But right now, Dahlia's silence was putting him on edge. She'd been acting strangely all morning, but he'd thought—or he'd *hoped*—that was because she was just as reluctant to part as he was.

But now...

He shifted in his seat as he watched her switch off the static-filled station and turn away to look out the window.

The powder-white terrain around them was breathtaking. He gazed over the quiet earth. It was always so still and peaceful after a storm. The blue sky was a stunning contrast to the white gleam of snow, and he'd usually be sucking in a satisfied sigh and smiling in gratitude.

But he couldn't muster a smile right now.

He glanced at the back of Dahlia's head.

What are you thinking about?

He'd asked her that countless times over the last two days, but right now he wasn't sure he wanted to know. Besides, he was the one who ought to be talking. He knew precisely what he meant to say.

And yet they both sat in stilted silence for another few minutes.

Aw heck, emotions had never been easy for him to talk about, but this weekend he'd had no problem pouring his heart out. Now wasn't the time to be a coward.

He cleared his throat. "Lia, I just wanted to say…" He trailed off with a frown. Was that his voice?

He sounded so formal.

She shifted in her seat. "Yes?"

"Uh, the thing is…" Why did he suddenly feel fourteen again? Like he was asking a girl out for the very first time. "I had a real nice time at the cabin." He glanced over. "With you."

He winced inwardly and shot another sidelong look her way. He wouldn't have blamed her if she was laughing at him and his awkwardness, but her response…

It was worse.

She flashed him a smile that was polite but distant. There was none of the humor he'd come to recognize in her eyes, and none of the warmth that he wasn't sure he could live without now that he'd experienced it.

She looked hard. Untouchable. She might as well have been covered with scales and had smoke pouring out of her nose, because this right here was the dragon.

He finally understood why Lizzy had named her that.

He knew it wasn't true. Heck, even Lizzy had caught on that the fire-breathing routine was all an act. But right now, that hard, prickly armor wrapped all around her…

Yeah, he could see the likeness.

"I'm not saying it was anyone's dream vacation," he said, aiming for lightheartedness. "I could have done without the injuries and the scare out in the storm…"

Nothing. He wasn't exactly performing a stand-up comedy act over here, but he'd thought maybe he'd get a chuckle. A real smile, at the very least.

"But I, uh…" He cleared his throat again. "I just wanted you to know that I really enjoyed our time together, and—"

"JJ, stop. You don't have to do this," she interrupted.

He blinked in surprise. "Do what?"

She shifted to face him, her gaze shuttered, her expression blank. "We had fun, yes. And the kissing and the cuddling… it was nice. Really. But I'm a big girl, JJ." Her chin came up as she clasped her hands in her lap. "I don't expect it to lead to anything more."

His head jerked back like she'd just struck him, and he turned his focus to the winding road ahead of him as she continued.

"You're going back to the ranch, and I'll be heading to the airport for the next flight out." When he glanced over, her smile made his chest turn to ice. "We don't have to have 'the talk.'"

She used air quotes, as if her cynical tone wasn't enough.

"The talk?" he echoed as his brain tried to keep up.

But he knew what she meant. The "it's been fun, but..." talk. The "it's not you, it's me" talk. That was where she thought he'd been going with this?

He turned his head and arched his brows in disbelief. "You think I'm trying to *end* things?"

She lifted a shoulder and faced forward, her lips a little too pinched for her apathetic shrug to be believable.

She might be acting like she didn't care. But she did.

That was enough to give him a fresh wave of courage.

"Look at me, Lia."

She resisted for a second, staring out the front window as she drew in a deep breath. Then she turned to him on a sharp exhale, like she was steeling herself for battle. Her brows arched in challenge, as if she was baiting him to prove her wrong.

Oh good Lord, save me from this woman's stubborn pride.

He might've actually laughed if he wasn't still reeling. "Lia, that wasn't what I was going to say at all."

Her brows dropped, a hint of confusion and vulnerability slipping past her armor before she went all icy on him again. "Then what were you going to say?"

He huffed in exasperation. "I was trying to say that I had such a great time with you that I was hoping... that is, if you're up for it... I thought maybe we could see more of each other going forward."

Ah heck. There he went sounding all stiff and formal again.

He glanced over to see Dahlia staring at him in clear confusion. "How?"

Valid question. He drew in another deep breath. "Well, I know we'll be apart for a while, but I do have a phone.

And don't tell anyone, but we actually have Wi-Fi out there in the bunkhouse."

He shot her a teasing smile, but her frown never wavered.

Right. Okay, then.

"And besides, Emma and Nash's wedding is about six weeks away. I assume you're going, and..." He glanced over, but she didn't react. "I'd like you to be my date."

Silence.

It seemed to echo in the truck's cab. He stole another glance, but she'd turned away from him.

When he couldn't take it anymore, he asked, "Well, what do you think? Will you be my date to the wedding?"

She shook her head, her face still turned away. "I wasn't planning on..." She sighed, her head still shaking. "I can't, JJ. You shouldn't even be asking me."

Her words pricked at his pride, and the rejection burrowed into his chest, threatening to pop that bubble of hope he'd been holding on to. But he wasn't done yet. He hadn't honestly expected this to be an easy conversation. "Why not?"

"Because... what's the point?" She turned to him, anger, or maybe fear, sparking in her eyes.

"The point is I'd get to have you on my arm," he argued. "The point is we could dance together and laugh and talk and... and have a proper date."

"A proper..." She sighed loudly. "And then what? Then I'd go back to New York again and not come back until the baby is born in June. So what's the plan there? Say we have a nice time together at the wedding. Is our second date going to be in June?" Her tone dripped with sarcasm. "Are we going to start dating on a quarterly basis? Is that the plan?"

He winced. "Honestly, I don't know." He shrugged. "I'm not sure how this would work, but I'm just asking that we take it one step at a time." He turned his head to meet her gaze. "Take that first step with me, Lia. And we can deal with the rest as it comes."

His heart was in his throat. *Take my hand. Say you want this too.*

Between them they could figure this out if she said yes. He had to believe that.

"I appreciate the offer," she said, her voice so stilted he barely recognized it, "but Emma's wedding? That's… that's not a good idea."

"Why not?" he repeated, his tone growing harder now too.

She threw her hands up. "Because everyone will be there. My family, the entire town. It's like making this big statement."

"And what if I want to do that?" he shot back. "What if I want everyone to know how I feel about you?"

"Why would you when we have no future together?"

He stilled, his hands tightening on the wheel as the main road came into view. They'd reached the fork in the road—literally and figuratively.

Any other time, the thought might have made him laugh.

As it was, his voice sounded low and gruff as disappointment threatened to drown him. "No future, huh? Is that what you really think?"

"Come on, JJ," she sighed. "I live in New York. You're not about to become a city boy just for me. You would hate it, and it's not like I can move my life here."

"Why not?" The words were out before he could stop them.

"Because I have a job in New York," she started.

"A job you hate."

"I don't hate it."

He told himself to stop, but the words came tumbling out. "You don't love it either. You're underappreciated. You're worth way more than their assistant."

It was true and she knew it. But even so, he felt a sharp kick of guilt. Was he actually trying to convince her to stay? That hadn't been part of the plan.

They hadn't been dating nearly long enough for him to ask for that sort of commitment.

He wanted that. More than anything in the world, he wished she'd move to Aspire… for him. But he wasn't so selfish that he'd ask that of her.

And yet that was basically what he'd been insinuating. He winced, trying to backpedal with his thoughts. To get them back on track. "Look, Lia, I'm not asking you to drop everything and move—"

"And I'm not offering," she snapped.

Another tense silence followed.

She broke it first. "This is a ridiculous conversation to be having," she muttered. "We spent two days in a cabin together, and suddenly we're pretending we're in love?"

He flinched at the bitterness in her tone.

"It doesn't work like that. And you know better than anyone the stupidity of rushing into things and being with someone for the wrong reasons."

His breath hissed out of his lungs as her blow hit him right where it hurt.

He didn't try to argue. How could he? She was right. He knew better than to rush into a commitment.

But this is different. This is real. What we have is—

He shut down the thoughts before they could go any

further. Was it? Right now he felt like he was sitting next to a stranger. He couldn't catch a single glimpse of the woman who'd stolen his heart.

She was in there, but in this moment, he couldn't help but wonder if he'd made her up. His dream woman. Because right now, she was nowhere to be found.

So he forced the thoughts of love and romance out of his mind. She didn't want to hear it. And maybe she had a point.

Maybe he was asking for too much.

Maybe what he wanted was a pipe dream, and what they had was never meant to last.

Either way, he kept his mouth shut, and they rode in silence the rest of the way back to the ranch.

37

D ahlia was certain the silence would kill her.

But she survived. And when they drove up to the ranch house and she opened the passenger side door, she took her first full breath in nearly an hour.

JJ wouldn't look at her as they both moved mechanically to get her bags out of the back.

"I got it." He snagged the handle of her luggage before she could.

She pulled her hand back quickly so they couldn't touch. He noticed. She could tell by the way he stiffened.

Her throat tightened so badly she couldn't speak.

I'm sorry!

She wanted to grab his wrist and make him look at her. She wanted to beg him to understand.

But he was gone, walking through the front door with her luggage as all three of her sisters rushed out to greet her.

Rose reached her first, throwing her arms around her shoulders. "I was so worried!"

Emma and Lizzy followed right after, and Dahlia

patted them awkwardly as they joined in the hug until they were an unwieldy medley of tangled arms.

"I'm so glad you're okay," Lizzy said.

"Thank goodness you were with JJ," Emma added.

Not one of them even thought to tease her about being trapped alone with the guy they clearly knew she was smitten over. If only they knew how much her feelings had grown in such a short time.

The fact that they weren't saying anything about it told her how worried they'd been.

She forced a smile as they all pulled back to check her over for injuries, but her throat was still much too tight.

Tears had already been so close, and this sudden realization that even her newfound sisters might actually care about her…

She sniffled, tears hovering on her lashes.

Her sisters watched her in horror.

"Are you okay?" Lizzy asked. "JJ called earlier to say you'd been hurt. Are you in pain right now?"

"Dex is on his way," Rose quickly added.

"I'm fine," she managed. "It was just…"

She had no idea how to finish.

Emma winced, wrapping an arm around her shoulders and squeezing her like she was a child. "It must have been quite an ordeal. Let's get you inside."

"I'll make some tea." Lizzy was already leading the way.

Dahlia nodded, letting Emma guide her inside as Rose took her hand and squeezed.

The tears were abating, thank heavens. But she didn't offer up an explanation. Let them think it was because of her ankle.

Let them believe being stranded had truly been an

ordeal... and not the best time of her life. It would be easier if she didn't have to explain.

The next twenty minutes passed in a blur as her sisters fussed around her in the kitchen. Emma insisted on cooking her a hot meal while Lizzy brought her a warm sweater and Rose poured her tea.

"I appreciate the concern," she finally said with a laugh, "but I swear I'm not an invalid. JJ and I did just fine."

We did better than fine.

Kit and Nash showed up to welcome her back, but JJ didn't appear in the kitchen with them.

Dahlia tried not to feel the disappointment that swelled.

What did she expect? She'd shot him down. And she'd do it again if she had to. She tried to convince herself of this as she snuck another glance toward the back door.

He was probably at the bunkhouse, or maybe he'd leapt straight into work.

For the best, really. It would be better for everyone if she left here without another run-in with JJ.

There was no changing her mind. She'd watched what'd happened when her mother based her life on a man. It had destroyed her.

And besides, New York was her home.

"I'm so relieved you're here." Rose interrupted her thoughts when she rested her head on Dahlia's shoulder. "I'd better text Daisy. She was worried too."

Dahlia couldn't help her snort of disbelief.

Rose straightened with a frown. "She was worried. You know she loves you."

Dahlia nodded as guilt swelled. "I know she does. And you're right, she cares about us in her own way."

Rose smiled, shifting out of her seat. "I'm not kidding that she was worried." She paused and widened her eyes. "*She* actually called *me* to check in on how you were doing."

Dahlia widened her eyes in mock shock. "No way."

Rose giggled. "It's true."

She slipped out to get her phone as the back door opened. Dahlia jerked much too quickly, spinning to see...

Dex.

Her heart faltered and fell. She recovered quickly enough to flash him a smile. "Sorry they called you all the way over here for nothing. See? It's fine." She pointed down at her ankle, which barely even ached anymore.

And soon enough her heart would stop aching too. She hoped.

Dex grinned as he knelt in front of her. "Why don't you let me be the judge of that?"

"Can I grab you some water or tea, Dr. Dex?" Emma called from the stove. Whatever she was heating up for Dahlia smelled delicious.

"No, thanks," he said.

Lizzy surprised Dahlia by coming up behind her and wrapping her arms around her neck. "I've got to get to the store. I'm working today. But I'm so glad you're back safe and sound."

Dahlia patted her arms as Lizzy gave her a squeeze. "Thanks, Lizzy. I'll be heading out soon, so... I guess I'll see you next time I'm back?"

"You bet." Lizzy moved away and shot her a wink from the door. "You'd better fly in early. I expect you to be at the bachelorette party. It's a sisterly requirement."

Dahlia's mouth went dry while Lizzy let out a girlish giggle.

She thinks I'm coming back for the wedding.

She didn't have the heart to tell her the truth. She didn't want to kill Lizzy's grin or have to handle a conversation about why she wouldn't be there. An uncharacteristic weakness stole over her, and instead she settled for an awkward smile and ambiguous nod.

Dex was gingerly removing her boot and rolling down her sock.

"I can do that, Dex. And I swear, it's fine."

He ignored her.

Emma came over with a full plate just as Rose reentered with her phone held up as proof. "See? Daisy even texted to nag me for an update."

Dahlia chuckled.

"Hey, beautiful," Dex greeted Rose.

She came to stand beside him. "How's our patient?"

Dahlia rolled her eyes, making Emma giggle. "She's right here, and she's fine!"

Dex ignored her, talking to Rose instead as he prodded her ankle. "It doesn't seem swollen, just badly bruised."

Dahlia shared a look with a laughing, sympathetic Emma. "Just let him do his job, Dahlia," she said. "We'll all feel better if he signs off on your good health."

Dahlia sighed. "JJ is the one who could use Dex's help. You should go check on his hand before—"

Dex's laughter had her stopping short.

"What's so funny?"

He grinned up at her. "Just that this is *déjà vu*." At her frown, he continued. "I ran into JJ on my way in. I saw his bandaged hand and told him I'd take a look. But he shooed me away, saying I had to check on you first."

Dahlia bit the inside of her lip, commanding herself not to cry. She would not be some stupid weeping girly girl.

Of course he'd been more concerned about her ankle. That was JJ for you. He'd never put himself first.

And yet he wants you to give up your entire life to fit in with his.

She frowned down at the table. That didn't sound right. And he hadn't actually *asked* her to make any sacrifices. But that was the only way it would work, right? JJ was happy here in Aspire. He'd be miserable in the big city. So inevitably it would come down to her sacrificing everything and—

"Dahlia?" Dex's voice was gentle. "Did I hurt you?"

She swallowed hard. The dang tears were becoming a real nuisance. She sniffed. "No, not at all." She tugged her ankle out of his hands. "I'm fine, just… just tired."

His gaze said he didn't believe her, but he nodded.

She looked away from his understanding gaze. He couldn't possibly get it.

Emma was giving her an equally painful look of sympathy. It wasn't pity, but it was much too close.

She looked away and found Rose watching her thoughtfully.

"I'd better go check on JJ before I head back to the clinic," Dex said, breaking what was about to become an awkward silence as everyone pretended that Dahlia wasn't fighting back tears.

"I'll walk you out," Emma murmured.

When Dahlia was alone with Rose, she turned to her little sister, her heart lodged in her throat. "Can you take me to the airport?"

"Now?" Rose's eyes widened when Dahlia nodded.

She couldn't stay here a second longer. Not when at any moment JJ could walk through those doors. She wasn't sure she trusted herself to have another encounter. Because if he asked her to stay…

Oh heck, she'd be so very tempted to say yes.

"But…" Rose frowned. "When's the next flight?"

"I don't know, but I'm just going to stay there until I can go." Rose looked like she was about to protest, so she hurried on. "I'll fly standby if I have to. I'll take the next flight out to a major hub, and there's bound to be flights leaving for New York, and…" She faltered in the face of Rose's clear concern. "Rose, I just… I have to get home."

Her little sister still looked like she might argue, but she clamped her lips shut with a nod. A second later, she was up and reaching for her car keys. "Let me just text Dex to tell him where I'm going."

Dahlia nodded. "I'll get my luggage."

The trip home was long and miserable. It probably would have been just as bad even if she'd had a seat and didn't have two lengthy layovers. But eventually she got home.

And her apartment had never felt lonelier.

For long hours that night, she sat up, looking out the window at all the apartment lights on the street around her. The sight used to comfort her. She was alone in a crowd, but there were people around.

Now it just made her feel more alone than ever.

She told herself that going back to work would help. She needed to get back into her routine, that was all.

But the next morning, she was exhausted thanks to the time change and a bad night's sleep. Her coworkers greeted her politely, but she couldn't help wondering if they were actually disappointed to have her back. Awkward smiles and polite nods abounded as she strode to her office, then went to check in with Jason and Marian.

Her bosses each made jokes about her being stranded in Nowheresville.

The jokes weren't funny, and the way they spoke of the people in Aspire—calling them local yokels and acting like they weren't as intelligent just because they didn't take public transportation—it made her hackles rise.

They were talking about Rose now, she kept thinking. They were talking about Rose, and Emma, and Lizzy, and Nash...

And JJ.

They were talking about a place they'd never been and people they'd never met. But that didn't stop them from making all kinds of assumptions.

"You must be glad to finally be back, huh?" Jason said when she was leaving his office with an armful of files to sort and notes to type up.

Yeah, of course. So grateful to be back.

All the words she should have said died on her tongue, and she only just managed a smile and a nod before she shut the door behind her with a click.

38

Three weeks had never felt so long.

"... isn't that right, JJ?" Kit said.

JJ looked across the stables to where Kit, Nash, Cody, and Boone were all hanging out.

There were still chores to be done and work to do during the dead of winter—work never really stopped on a ranch—but as this was the down season, there was far more time for the crew to hangout.

Normally JJ loved that about this time of year.

These last three weeks? Not so much.

He'd prefer to be riding the range alone than fending off his friends' well-intentioned attempts to cheer him up.

"Sorry, what was that?" he asked.

"Bernice is running a pool competition this weekend at the tavern," Cody said. "We're placing bets on which one of us will win. You in?"

He shook his head. "Nah. Not this time. I've got plans this weekend."

Not big plans. Not *good* plans. But chopping wood up

at the cabin was as good a way as any to tire him out so he could sleep through the night.

Besides, the thought of playing pool only reminded him of that time he'd spent with Dahlia at the bar. The night where she'd cheered on the Rangers and showed him a side of herself that he'd never seen before.

A stupid smile started to form at the memory before he squashed it.

"You sure, man?" Kit said. "You haven't gone out with us in a while. Your hermit qualities are starting to show. Not sure it's that good for ya."

Three weeks. That wasn't *a while*, but it felt like an age.

It'd been three weeks since he'd even attempted to have fun. Three weeks since he'd gotten back from showering up and having his hand tended to. Three weeks since he'd walked into the ranch house, set on talking things through with Dahlia, only to find that she'd already left for the airport.

Without even a goodbye.

He headed toward his friends. "Yeah, I'm sure you're right. Thanks for the offer, but… I'm just not up for it, I guess."

His friends exchanged glances that weren't difficult to read.

They were worried about him.

"If you want to talk…" Nash started.

The others all grimaced, which made JJ chuckle. These fellas were the best friends a guy could ask for, but this was not a crew that did touchy-feely chats all that often.

In fact, they typically avoided it like the plague.

"Right," Nash sighed with a good-natured shrug. "Can't blame a guy for trying."

"Look," Boone said. "We're all done for the day, right?

298

Why don't we head into town for a late lunch at Mama's Kitchen?"

All eyes were on him. JJ took a deep breath.

"I'm buying," Nash added, arching a brow.

Now the pressure was on as everyone waited for his response. He dipped his head with a rueful chuckle. "All right, fine. Let's go eat."

A little while later, the group trekked through the snow toward Mama's Kitchen. A weekday and the dead of winter, the sidewalks of Main Street were largely empty except for a few locals.

JJ waved to Norman and his pals, who were sitting in the coffee shop, watching out the window as if today might be the day that something interesting happened. They called out a greeting to Kit and Cody's mom, who was heading to work at the flower shop.

When they got to the diner, there were only a few tables empty, and they grabbed one by Levi. The sheriff was in uniform as he sipped a coffee.

"Lunch break, Sheriff?" Kit asked.

"Yeah. Just waiting on Dex, as usual." He shook his head. "Probably caught up with one of his patients. Oh hey, Nash, I got your invite in the mail, and I'm looking forward to it."

Nash grinned, like he always did whenever anyone mentioned his upcoming nuptials. His sister, Casey, kept teasing him about being more excited about his wedding day than she had been about hers.

Even now, he couldn't stop smiling like a fool as Kit and Cody filled Levi in on the bachelor party plans and the other pre-wedding shenanigans they had in the works.

JJ focused on the menu in his hands as if he didn't have the dang thing memorized.

He was happy for Nash and Emma, but every mention of the wedding had him fixating on the plus-one he did not have.

The only plus-one he wanted.

His knuckles turned white as he gripped the menu tighter.

The plus-one who'd run away before he'd even had a chance to say goodbye.

"There's Dex now," Kit pointed out.

JJ lifted his head, greeting Dex along with the others. But yet again, Dex's mere presence was enough to stir up memories.

"She did a good job with your hand," he'd said that day when they'd returned. "It'll heal just fine."

If only he could say the same about his dang heart.

Just after the food arrived, Kit was the one who finally broached the topic. "JJ, man, do you want to tell us what's going on?"

"You haven't been acting like yourself lately," Cody added when JJ continued to eat his Monster Burger in silence.

His friends all looked to one another before Nash chimed in. "We get it that you're not big on sharing. But none of us like to see you so low."

JJ swallowed his burger. "It's not that I don't trust you guys. It's just..." He shrugged. "There's nothing you can do to help."

"Sometimes talking it out helps," Boone said. He grinned when everyone stared at him. "What? I'm an evolved man. I know things."

They all chuckled at that.

"Maybe talking does help some people. But in this

case, the person I need to talk to is on the other side of the country," JJ admitted.

More looks were shared, nods exchanged.

Aw heck. This was why he never opened his trap around these guys. Now they'd want to help. But how could they?

He wasn't even sure what he'd say to Dahlia if he had the chance.

"What did that O'Sullivan sister do to you out at that cabin?" Cody teased, his smile good-natured.

"Seriously," Kit added. "I thought I'd had it rough with Lizzy, but from the looks of it, Dahlia's dragging you over the coals."

JJ dipped his head, trying to chuckle and failing. He knew they meant well. This was their not-so-subtle way of getting him to talk. And he supposed it was working. "She didn't do anything wrong. I just... I don't like how we ended things, that's all."

I don't like that we ended things. Period.

There was a gaping hole in his chest every time he thought of a future without Dahlia in it. "The problem is that... she made a good point about something. And I don't know if she's right."

Silence followed this. Not surprisingly. They all knew he'd been married, but that was all they knew. They didn't know how he'd made a commitment for the wrong reasons. Her parting shot still stung, but he wasn't hurt, just... worried she was right.

Was he trying to rush things just because she'd been leaving?

No. He didn't think so.

He frowned down at his burger that he left half finished as his appetite fled.

He tried to imagine a different scenario. One in which she'd already agreed to live in Aspire. He'd have asked her to the wedding.

Then he would have asked her out again. And again.

One date would flow into another, and before he knew it, she'd be his girlfriend... and maybe a while after that, she just might be his fiancée... and then his wife.

He blinked, the idea surprising him. Did he really want to get married again someday?

To the right woman? Why not?

Was Dahlia the right woman?

A soft smile bloomed inside him.

It was a no-brainer. He could imagine a life with Dahlia. And trying to imagine a life without her wasn't just painful, it was impossible.

He shifted in his seat, all too aware of his friends' stares.

"Look, JJ," Nash started. "I don't know what Dahlia said, but I wouldn't let it torture you. I'll admit, I'm starting to come around to liking her more after this last stay. I think Emma was right all along. Dahlia's got a good heart and a lot of love, especially for Rose. She just has a different way of showing it."

JJ stared down at the table, his gut churning with emotion. "You don't know the half of it."

There was a long silence.

"Yeah, we sorta figured that," Kit murmured.

JJ arched a brow.

Kit shrugged. "Lizzy and Emma are convinced that she's just as heartbroken as you are, from what Rose has told them about their phone conversations."

"Is she..." He cleared his throat. "Is she okay?"

Kit nodded, uncharacteristically serious. "Physically? Yes. But Rose is worried about her."

"Did she… say anything?" He winced and shot a chuckling Boone a glare. He sounded lame, needy, desperate even. And he knew it.

"She's been as tight-lipped as you." Nash shook his head. "Rose has been talking a lot about vibes and how Dahlia seems to be sending off a bunch of negative ones. She's been snippier than usual, but not so bossy. It's really worrying the girls."

"Maybe that's why they're such a good match," Cody murmured.

The others chuckled.

"That's right," Boone said, nudging JJ's elbow. "She's the strong and silent type, just like you."

JJ shot Boone another withering glare. He liked Nash's young cousin, but right now he was not in the mood for his easygoing laughter.

Strong and silent? Dahlia? Hardly.

"She's not, though," he muttered.

He hadn't meant to say it aloud, but maybe some part of him actually did need to talk it out.

Not that he'd ever tell Boone he was right.

"She's not what?" Kit asked.

JJ shrugged. "Strong." He frowned. No, that wasn't right. "I mean, she is. For other people she's a pillar of strength…" He frowned down at the table as he tried to explain it. "She's been through a lot, you know? And she's had to be brave and step up. But that's also left her…"

"Vulnerable?" Nash offered.

Kit sighed. "I knew all along that whole dragon routine was a ruse."

Cody elbowed him. "You did not."

JJ ignored their banter. He was too busy thinking about Dahlia. About how she'd acted in the truck. That hadn't been her, not the real Dahlia he'd come to know. She'd activated every dang defense she had...

But why?

The answer was so clear it nearly winded him.

Because she liked him too. She'd fallen just as hard as he had... and it terrified her.

His heart twisted with affection for that complicated, sweet, loving, irritating woman.

But Nash was right too. She was vulnerable. He'd known from the first time he'd met her that she was like a spooked colt. It had taken an age to get past her prickly armor, and the fact that he had must have scared her senseless.

Because...

He gripped the table's edge as realization struck.

Because he could hurt her.

And while he wished he could say he wouldn't— much as he knew he didn't want to—that didn't change the fact that he could, whether he intended to or not.

Hadn't his marriage to Rena taught him that? Good intentions meant little in the grand scheme of things.

But this wasn't the same as that. This was something totally different.

He'd cared for Rena. She was his first crush, his high school sweetheart. But what he felt for Dahlia was something completely different.

It was rich and deep and—

He pushed his chair back so quickly it scraped the linoleum.

"Where are you going?" Nash asked.

"I've got to head back. I've got some thinking to do." He stopped as he started to leave. "But thanks."

He headed out to his truck and got back to the ranch in record time. Once there, he took Zion out of the stables and rode. He rode with no clear destination in mind, and it wasn't until he reached the lake where they'd gone ice fishing that he stopped.

Steam billowed up from Zion's nostrils as flurries landed on them both. From where they'd stopped, he had an epic view of the sun sinking behind the mountaintop, a burnt orange hue painting the sky.

After all that riding, one thing had become clear.

He wasn't the kid he'd been when he'd married Rena. Sure, he was still human, and he could make mistakes, but he knew himself now. He knew what he wanted.

He knew *who* he wanted.

He took a deep breath as the sun sank lower. He loved it here. This town, these people, and this view. But none of that could fill his heart the way Dahlia had.

He'd choose a life of love and laughter over simple and uncomplicated any day.

Heck, he could live anywhere if it meant being with Dahlia. And if it really was just location keeping them apart, then he could be flexible.

He'd do whatever it took just to be with her.

And if that wasn't love, if that wasn't the basis for commitment... then he didn't know what was.

As he tugged the reins and spurred Zion back toward the stables, he leaned over to talk to his stallion. "You gotta be good for Nash and the others while I'm gone, you hear? See, I've got a trip to make."

The horse made a huffing sound.

"That's right. I'm off to get my girl."

39

The snow was worse in New York than Montana.

She gritted her teeth and ducked her head as she barreled through a wave of oncoming pedestrians on her way back from the deli where she'd taken a quick lunch.

One of the oncoming walkers brushed against her, jostling her. She bumped into the man on her right.

"Sorry," she muttered.

"Look where you're going," he snapped.

She gripped the bag with her lunch as another snowflake hit her nose. It looked pretty coming down, but the instant the flakes touched the sidewalks and streets, they turned gray.

The piles of snow on the corners near the crosswalks were black in places and yellow in others. There was nothing beautiful about it.

And there you go again.

She snapped her brain out of comparison mode, something she'd had a bad habit of slipping into ever since her return nearly a month before.

The lack of silence, the crush of people, and now the

dirty snow... It seemed some part of her, at least, was intent on holding the two places side by side.

Manhattan almost never came out the winner.

When she reached her office building's lobby, she snagged one of the tables in the public atrium and pulled out her sandwich. While she nibbled on that, she called up Daisy.

It was all part of this new routine. She'd been working like a dog since her return—first playing catchup and then just because she couldn't seem to stop. Work was grueling, but even being snapped at by her bosses was better than being home alone in her apartment.

And so she'd settled into a new routine. She got up and arrived at the office earlier than everyone else and called to check in on her sisters every other day during her lunch break. Daisy answered every other time; Rose always answered. She stayed late, always the last to leave the office, then went to the gym to run until she wore herself out.

Only then did she return home, make herself a simple dinner before falling into bed exhausted.

It's not much of a life, she thought as she ate. The phone rang for the third time. But she was surviving. And maybe someday... maybe someday soon, even, she'd be able to make it through a single hour without wondering what JJ was doing or reminiscing about something he said or did back in that cabin.

She was just about to hang up when Daisy answered.

"Hey, D." She sounded distracted, her voice lacking the bubbly joyfulness that was so uniquely hers.

"Hey, how are things?" Dahlia asked, then clamped her mouth shut before she could ask about the band again. Last time, Daisy had bitten her head off.

Clearly not a good topic.

"Fine. Did you need something?" Daisy asked.

"No, just… checking in."

"Oh, yeah, I'm fine. We're good. Things are… they're okay."

"Okay"? Dahlia straightened, her mom radar on full alert. An "okay" from Daisy was a "terrible" from anyone else. "Are you all right? Do you need to talk ab—"

"Nope. I'm all good."

If that wasn't a clear shutdown, Dahlia didn't know what was.

"Okay, well, I won't keep you, then."

Daisy covered the receiver, but Dahlia still heard her snap at someone, "I said I'm coming!" To Dahlia, she added, "Yeah, sorry, sis. It's just super busy right now. I'll call you soon, though, 'kay?"

"Okay, b—"

Daisy had hung up before she could even say bye. Taking a big bite of her sandwich, she moved on to Rose.

"Hey, Dahlia!" Rose, at least, sounded happy to hear from her. "We were just talking about you."

"We?" She took another bite. It would either be Dex, Emma, or Lizzy. They were the people Rose hung out with the most.

"Me and the guys," she said.

Ah. Or "the guys," which were the group of old men who seemingly resided at the coffee shop.

"They were just asking me if you'd be back for the wedding."

"Um, I'm not sure yet," she hedged.

Her belly formed knots faster than she could take a deep breath. All mention of Emma's wedding made her think of JJ. Of that conversation.

Of how she'd just… left.

She squeezed her eyes shut. "It's just… work's pretty chaotic, and I've already had so much time away."

Rose's voice grew quiet. "It's only a weekend, Dahlia."

"I know, but I can't afford to get stuck there again." She swallowed a hysterical laugh at that understatement. She wasn't sure she'd survive leaving JJ a second time.

"Dahlia, if this is because…" Rose sighed. "Never mind. I'm still putting your name on the list, just in case you change your mind. Emma is completely fine with that."

Dahlia smiled. "That's nice of her."

"But I hope you'll make it," Rose added.

"Duly noted. Now, tell me everything about you and the baby," she commanded. Then she took a big bite and settled into her seat to listen with a smile as Rose regaled her with all the latest.

She could feel the baby kicking now and was over the moon about that. And then there was the fact that Dex had mentioned marriage.

She'd known this already because Dex had called the week after she'd returned to New York to get her permission. Which had left Dahlia torn between being enraged at the archaic patriarchal custom while also making her weepy with relief that her little sister had found someone so old-fashioned and sweet.

"What's the latest on that?" she asked.

"We've come up with a compromise."

Dahlia could practically see her sister's beaming smile as she spoke.

"I know you'll think it's silly, but I really do want a big wedding with all the bells and whistles—"

"I don't think that's silly," Dahlia murmured. She had

to force herself to swallow, because for a second there, she'd gotten a flash of her own wedding. Hypothetical, of course. Just a daydream.

And featuring one very kind, very burly, very perfect mountain man. She could just picture him waiting at the end of the aisle for her, dressed in a suit, his hair combed into a short ponytail and his beard neatly trimmed. It sent a shiver running right through her.

"But we both want to be married before the baby's born, so we've decided to do a simple ceremony at the courthouse first and then have a big celebration after the baby."

She blinked, taking a moment to catch up with her sister's words. And then she smiled. "Oh, Rose, I think that's a great idea."

"Yeah? Okay, good. Because... well, I was sort of hoping that I could convince you to come back to be a witness for the courthouse ceremony..."

She trailed off, and Dahlia's mouth went dry. "Oh, um... maybe? Can I, uh... can I take a look at my calendar?"

"Yeah, of course." Rose's voice dropped with disappointment.

Dahlia was pretty sure they both knew she was just putting off the inevitable no.

And while work definitely was a factor, Dahlia hated the fact that it wasn't the biggest deterrent.

She just wasn't sure she could face JJ again. It'd be impossible to fly back and not see him, right? Unless she just met Rose and Dex at the courthouse, but that would probably offend everybody at the ranch if she came all the way and didn't pop in for a visit.

Shutting her eyes, she rested her fingers on her forehead.

JJ was too tempting. Even now, what he'd said in the truck tugged at her, pulling at her heart and twisting all her plans. It had her reevaluating her life choices and second-guessing what she'd always believed to be her fate.

In short, he'd messed with her head in a very big way.

And if that were all, she might be able to move on.

But he'd messed with her heart too. And she had no idea how to fix it.

"I'll do my best, Rosie," she offered.

"I know. You always do." But Rose's tone was still sad as they hung up.

After three long minutes of sitting there staring at her half-eaten sandwich, Dahlia got up and threw the rest away.

Her heart felt like ashes in her chest as she rode the elevator up to her office. Her mind was a swirl of thoughts. None of them good. All of them about her family, about JJ, about the decision she'd made when she was much too young that she'd never marry…

Her head was such a disaster and her spirits so low that she barely noticed when the elevator stopped at her floor. She got off just before the doors closed again and shuffled through the reception area with her head down, her gaze unfocused.

The receptionist cleared her throat.

Dahlia glanced up. "Hey, Megan. What's the plan for—"

She stopped talking when she realized the receptionist was grinning at her like a lunatic. Her eyes were wide and her smile knowing as she nodded meaningfully to something behind Dahlia.

Dahlia frowned but turned to see what the other woman was so excited about. And then she froze.

Sitting on the plush couch against the reception wall in faded jeans, boots, and a flannel shirt sat the sexiest cowboy Dahlia had ever seen.

"JJ?" she said. Or rather, she whispered.

And when he stood and smiled at her, that grin which had never *not* made her belly flip and her heart flutter… well, it made everything inside her come alive.

For the first time in weeks, she felt her heart start to beat again.

40

After wondering for hours if this trip was a good idea, JJ now had his answer.

Joy exploded in his chest at Dahlia's expression. In the span of seconds, he saw everything in her eyes, plain as day.

Her happiness that he was here. How much she'd missed him.

The feelings she had for him that she couldn't deny.

Her lips wobbled as her eyes filled with tears. Meanwhile, a satisfied grin curved his lips.

He couldn't help it—relief coursed through him right alongside this overwhelming warmth at seeing her again.

Any doubts he'd been struggling with as he'd navigated airports and taxis to get here were banished.

He was exactly where he was supposed to be. With his Dahlia.

The fact that they were in a reception area in a stuffy corporate office didn't even matter.

To him, at least.

He saw the moment Dahlia recalled where she was.

She straightened like a soldier, her shoulders going back, her face morphing into one of bland professionalism.

It was a sight to behold. But his Dahlia couldn't fool him any longer.

She'd missed him.

With a nod toward the hallway behind her, Dahlia murmured, "Come with me, please." Like he was here for an interview or some kind of marketing meeting.

He chuckled as he fell into step behind her, nodding at the grinning receptionist as he left. He sauntered after Dahlia, admiring her classic business clothes and how they hugged her body in all the right places. Those heels sure did make her stocking-covered legs look good. But so did skinny jeans and UGG boots. Heck, she could be sporting a pair of tartan pajamas and she'd still look sexy.

He scored himself a bunch of looks and stares from the gallery of paper pushers in the cubicles they passed.

Dahlia's cheeks were burning by the time they walked into her office and she quickly shut the door. The office was tiny. More like a cubicle but with higher walls. There was barely enough room for her desk, but that didn't stop her from standing behind it and crossing her arms as she faced him. "What are you doing here?"

He just grinned. Wasn't it obvious?

She huffed. "Yes, but why? Why are you here to see me?"

"Because I couldn't stand another day of not seeing you," he said. "I miss you, Lia."

She stared at him, her eyes wide, her lips parting like she was desperate for a snappy comeback but couldn't find one.

"Don't look at me like that. I know you missed me too, so I'm visiting for the weekend."

Her lips trembled with a smile like she wanted to give into her joy but couldn't let herself. "I don't finish work for another couple hours."

"No problem." He took a seat in the small chair wedged into the corner and pulled a tattered novel from his bag. "I'll just read until you're ready."

She watched him for a long moment, but when he held his novel up with arched brows as if to say "Do you mind? I'm trying to read here," she gave her head a shake and sat down at her desk.

The minutes ticked by slowly as he tried to read. It was useless. No matter how hard he stared at the book in his hands, his mind was constantly on the woman before him. He was painfully aware of her every movement, her every glance.

And oh how she glanced. Nearly every time he peeked up from his book, he caught her stealing glimpses of him.

Every time, he grinned.

And every time, she ducked her head with an adorable little blush.

After a while, it was like no time had passed at all since she'd left the ranch. They could have been sitting in silence in the cabin instead of a sterile office for all the sweet, lingering looks and the secretive, knowing smiles.

The air thickened, and that intangible connection that had always been between them was once more undeniable. As real as that annoying clock over his head that ticked loudly with each interminable second.

Watching Dahlia try to tuck those cute little smiles away, to don her professional demeanor and then lose the battle all over again a few minutes later...

Well, this was the best entertainment he'd had in weeks.

Still, he was relieved when she finally turned off her computer and started to pack up her things.

He stuck his book in his bag and watched her get ready, even though she avoided eye contact all the while.

Finally, she had her jacket on and was leading the way out of the office. Once more, he filed past a bunch of gawking employees and a grinning receptionist. She gave him a wave and a wink as he followed Dahlia out the door.

They waited for the elevator in silence.

He had loads to say, even more that he hoped to hear. But this was her workplace, and he respected that. Even though his hands itched to reach for her, and his arms ached to hold her, he was determined to act like a mature professional until they left the building.

The elevator doors opened with a ding. Dahlia walked in first, then him. She punched the button for the ground floor, and the doors slid shut in front of them.

Before the elevator even began to move, she turned to face him. He turned as well, studying her for less than a beat before she launched herself into his arms.

He caught her with a groan, holding her close as their lips met, colliding and reuniting in a kiss so heated it stole all his strength. It took everything in him not to lift her off the ground and push her back against the elevator wall.

His heart was slamming against his chest by the time they reached the ground floor, but still they kissed with an urgency that was heady and undeniable.

He poured every ounce of his heartache from the last few weeks into that kiss. Every bit of his joy at seeing her again.

And when her soft, warm mouth molded to his and

she leaned into his embrace, he felt her misery and her relief. The bittersweet ache of reuniting.

She pulled back just as the doors dinged.

And when they opened to a crowded lobby, she was once more Miss Professional.

But his grin was as wide as Manhattan as he followed her this time, his strut more like a swagger.

Oh yeah, she'd missed him.

And coming here to win his girl?

This was the best decision he'd ever made.

41

T he subway was no place for a real conversation.

It wasn't an ideal spot for kissing either.

But that didn't stop them from trying both.

"JJ, not here," she giggled as he nuzzled her neck, his arms wrapped around her from behind.

He was braced in the doorway of the subway car while she stood in front of him. It wasn't the most packed she'd ever seen the F train, but it was far too crowded for this sort of PDA.

"Are we there yet?" he teased, his voice a low rumble in her ear as the train stopped and let out a stream of passengers.

Even more piled on.

"Not yet." She giggled again, because apparently three weeks away had left her more susceptible than ever to JJ's unique charms. She playfully slapped his hand, which was situated at her waist. "Two more stops. Be good."

"Yes, ma'am," he sighed.

But she could hear the laughter in his voice.

Her smile made her cheeks ache, and some part of her

brain was desperately trying to shut down this crazy well-spring of joy.

It won't last. It can't last. You're only going to be more hurt in the end…

She swallowed hard and shut her eyes. Her insides were at war. Her heart happy, her mind a whirl of terror, and her body…

Well, her body was too busy melting to putty in his arms to have much of a say in the matter.

"This doesn't change things, you know."

"No talking," he joked. "Subway rules. See?"

He nodded to the row of seats beside them where everyone sat in silence, either engrossed in their phones or listening to something on their earbuds.

"I'm serious." She shifted to face him. It suddenly felt urgent that she at least acknowledge reality before giving in to the sheer joy of having him at her side. "I'm happy to see you—"

He leaned down and gave her a quick peck on the lips. "Same here, Lia."

"But…" She suspected her silly grin was spoiling her attempt at seriousness. "This is still a bad idea."

"Noted."

"No, I mean it." She started to turn in his arms, but he stopped her by burrowing his face in her neck and holding her even tighter.

"Lia, I know you're scared and that sharp mind of yours wants to figure everything out right this second…"

She went still, her heart rate quickening. She both loved and hated how easily he read her.

"But I came here because I need you to know that I don't care where you are. You are more important to me than Zion, or the ranch… or even my cabin."

Her heart stopped, her lungs hitching dangerously. But before the emotions could swallow her whole, he hurried on in a more casual tone. "Now, I've never been to this big city, so I'm hoping you'll show me around."

She hesitated for a moment, her lips quirking with the urge to smile. "You'll hate it."

He chuckled. "Is that a challenge?"

"Maybe."

He kissed the top of her head. "Bring it, Lia. All I care about is being with you. What we do or where, that's up to you."

Dahlia latched on to the challenge. Maybe it was her competitive side coming out, or maybe... maybe she just couldn't let herself believe it might be possible. No man would give up everything just to be with her.

Not even JJ, with his big heart and his kind soul, would sacrifice the life he loved just to be with her.

And so...

"Game on," she whispered as the subway slid into her station and the doors opened.

On the short walk to her apartment building, she called up the restaurant that her bosses regularly chose to wine and dine clients. They knew Dahlia well because of all the reservations she'd made with them, and thanks to that, they slipped her in for a late dinner.

She turned to JJ with a grin as they climbed the steps to her apartment. "Hope you brought something nice to wear, country mouse. This restaurant has a strict 'no muck boots' policy."

His laughter made her grin, but she still experienced a surge of nerves when she unlocked her apartment door and ushered him inside.

He stopped short in the entryway. Her apartment was so small that he could see most of it just standing there.

Dahlia squinted slightly, trying to look at it from his point of view.

She instantly wished she hadn't. Her insides sank at the sight before her—so familiar, and yet right now it felt like she was seeing it for the first time.

Since she didn't own it, she hadn't done much to the place, just a few cheap framed pictures she'd found at a secondhand shop. A few fake plants because she worked too much to keep even a cactus alive. The furniture was all serviceable… and beige.

Everything in her apartment was a neutral color, a fact that had never bothered her before. Neutral was easy to match and could easily be replaced. But she found herself frowning as she stepped in front of him to give him the quick tour, ending with her tiny closet of a bedroom.

They both stared at the bed for far too long before awkwardly backing out.

"I didn't come here expecting…" He winced and scrubbed the back of his neck. "I came here so we could figure things out. I don't want to make the situation more complicated for you."

She nodded, swallowing hard. There was nothing to figure out. Nothing had changed. He might think he could leave Aspire behind for her, but she knew without a doubt that by the end of this weekend he'd realize how wrong he was.

"I appreciate that," she managed.

He grinned. "So I guess what I'm saying is I'll take the couch."

She nodded, swallowing a laugh at his ease with all this while she felt like a kid who'd never been on a single date. Clearing her throat, she glanced toward her closet. "If you want to freshen up in the bathroom first, I'll get changed."

"Sounds good." He leaned over and pecked her cheek as he squeezed her hands in his. "Thank you for letting me stay."

Her throat was too tight to respond. *It's fine. You won't be here long.*

She hated that she knew that.

Hated it even more that it fell to her to prove it to him.

A little while later, they were both cleaned up and looking nice.

Correction: she looked nice. He looked… edible.

She kept casting glances his way, unable to stop herself from admiring how he looked with his beard trimmed and his hair tied back in a neat, stubby ponytail. He still wore jeans and boots, but the boots were polished, and the button-down shirt wasn't a flannel. It wasn't even checkered.

"What?" he teased when he caught her looking. "Did you think I was raised by wolves?"

She started to laugh. "As a matter of fact…"

He reached for her hand and tugged her against his side, feigning indignation. "I'll have you know I can get gussied up with the best of 'em."

"Gussied, huh?" she teased. "Sometimes I forget you're from the South, and then you go and say something like that."

He chuckled, reaching for the door of the restaurant and pulling it open for her with a little bow that cracked her up. "After you, ma'am."

The restaurant was dark, intimate… and fancy as all get-out. JJ was the first to point it out.

Truthfully, Dahlia was a little on edge in this place. She'd been in this world long enough to know the proper etiquette, but she still felt like a fraud when she ordered wine, which she didn't actually enjoy, or tried to pronounce the French dishes without sounding ridiculous.

Meanwhile, JJ looked to be doing just fine.

She frowned a bit as she watched him converse with the sommelier about what wine would pair well with their meal.

She'd chosen this place to try and show him just how out of place he was. So why was he the one who seemed at ease and she felt like a kid playing grown-ups?

He caught her frown when the sommelier walked away. "What's that frown for?" He arched a brow. "Are you impressed by my knowledge of wines?"

He waggled his brows, and she burst out in a laugh.

"I am, a little."

"You forget I was raised by rich folks?"

"Charleston elite," she muttered, shaking her head. She *had* forgotten. "Is there anything you can't do?"

"Persuade you to do something you don't want to?" He winked, and she couldn't fight her grin. "Don't worry, I'm taking on the challenge with gusto."

She groaned, but her smile tempered it. What a conundrum. On the one hand, she desperately wanted him to fight for her. On the other, this would all be far less painful in the long run if he just walked away now. Because with each passing second, she was losing more and more of her heart.

When the wine was served, she took a tiny sip and watched him do the same.

There was a very good chance that by the end of this weekend, she'd have lost her heart for good.

He'd walk away. He'd go back to the ranch where he belonged. It wasn't even a debate in her mind. He might be able to fit in here, but he shouldn't have to. This place would make him miserable.

There was still no question that he'd leave, and if he didn't want to, she'd make him for his own good.

Just like there was no question that when he left, he'd leave with a good portion of her soul.

J J leaned over the railing of the ice skating rink in Rockefeller Center as he and Dahlia watched the skaters below. He scratched his jaw and turned to Dahlia. "Do you think these people know there are real lakes in the world?"

Dahlia burst out laughing. As she'd been in the middle of sipping on a hot coffee, she had to clap a hand over her mouth.

He grinned, turning to take in her profile. Her winter gear here was far more stylish than the oversized service-able jacket she'd had to sport in Montana, but she looked no less adorable in her gray ski cap and that fancy cash-mere scarf.

She leaned in toward him and lowered her voice. "Don't tell anyone. The powers that be don't want anyone knowing there's life beyond Manhattan."

He grinned, the warmth in his chest entirely unrelated to the coffee in his hand.

It'd been like this all day. Easy. Fun.

No, he didn't enjoy the constant crowds bustling

around him or the frantic pace, but he now knew he could put up with just about anything so long as Dahlia was smiling at him like she was right now.

She leaned in to him, resting lightly against his side.

This had become the norm too—the light touches, the easy familiarity, the way they kept being drawn together like they were a couple of magnets.

He'd never understood the whole hand-holding thing until now. Until this trip. And now he couldn't seem to walk more than a block without reaching for her fingers and linking their hands together.

"I wish the tree was still up," she said. "It was a sight to behold."

He leaned down to talk softly in her ear. "You're a sight to behold."

She giggled and playfully elbowed him in the belly. "Stop that."

"Nope." He'd been doing it all day. And all last night too. He couldn't resist any chance to tell her how beautiful she was, or how clever and kind and warm and… perfect.

After dinner last night, they'd taken a stroll through some of Dahlia's favorite neighborhoods. The weather wasn't as cold as Montana, but the wind cutting through the cross streets had them shivering by the time they'd reached Central Park.

He'd discovered that while Dahlia liked admiring the poor horses who were stuck pulling carriages through the park, she'd never actually ridden in one. And so, bundled up under blankets, they'd taken a ride, Dahlia cuddled against him as she'd pointed out all the landmark buildings in sight.

No stars were visible thanks to the light, but it was still a magical evening.

They'd stayed up late, chatting about everything and nothing as if they were still in that cabin with nothing better to do than learn each other's every whim and foible.

She'd discovered his insatiable love of old dime-store Western novels—part of the reason he'd headed west after his divorce. He'd found out that she'd always wanted to travel but hadn't been able to. He answered all her questions about the places he'd been, and together they went online and researched her dream trip—an African safari.

When they'd been too tired to keep their eyes open any longer, he'd given her a good-night kiss he'd never forget, and they'd fallen asleep.

Luckily they'd slept well, because first thing this morning, they'd set off on a city adventure. First stop, her favorite coffee shop. And after that, she'd hauled him around to every one of the touristy destinations he'd read about, and a bunch of hidden gems he'd never heard of.

"What do you want to do next?" she asked. "I've still got loads to show you."

"I think my feet may fall off if we pound any more pavement today." He chuckled.

She tipped her head to grin up at him, and he slid an arm around her waist. It was torture to be this close and not touch her, so he'd given up the battle. Occasionally he'd even given in to temptation and stolen a kiss.

He'd been trying his best to be a gentleman, not just because that was how she deserved to be treated but because he knew they still had a world of issues to sort through, and he didn't want to muddle the situation any more than it already was.

But then again...

He leaned down and claimed a kiss that made her gasp, her free hand fluttering up to settle against his chest.

Then again, he needed her to be clear on the fact that he wasn't looking for friendship. Of course, he'd take it if that was all she could offer. But he wanted more. So much more.

He wanted everything with this woman.

She turned to face him, twisting her hand in his so their gloved fingers snuggled up together. "What do you say we stop walking for a while and grab a bite to eat?"

He nodded, letting her lead the way out of the busy tourist spot. "Do we need to stop home and change?" He glanced down at his admittedly rough-around-the-edges attire. "This isn't another froufrou place so you can scare me off, is it?"

She flinched as she glanced over at him. "Not scare you off, just… just trying to show you that you wouldn't like it here if you stuck around."

He dipped his head, hoping she wouldn't see how much that stung. Truthfully, he didn't want to stick around. He was already missing Zion, not to mention his friends on the ranch. Mostly he was missing the fresh air and the wide-open spaces.

A taxi honked, and JJ winced.

Silence. He really, really missed the silence. But even as he thought it, he gripped her hand tighter, loving the little smile she tossed his way.

No amount of noise, crowds, or impeded views would keep him away from this woman—that much he knew.

Just so long as she wanted him to stay.

"No froufrou places," she was saying as they crossed a busy intersection. "I was thinking tonight we could keep it casual." The shy glance she cast in his direction stole his heart. "This is where I go for comfort food."

"It's not Mama's Kitchen, is it?" he teased. "Because if

we hop on a plane right now, we might be able to—"

She smacked his arm, laughing as she did so. "Don't be ridiculous. I'm not hopping on a plane to Aspire with you right this second."

He smiled and kept his mouth shut. He'd been doing his best not to push the issue, but he was set to fly back out tomorrow afternoon, and he couldn't put this off forever.

The thought of heading back to Montana without her was unbearable. He at least wanted to have something settled between them. A date for when he'd get to see her again, at the very least.

He let the conversation drop, and soon enough she was dragging him into a warm, delicious-smelling pizza shop.

"Uncle Joey's Pizzeria," he read the sign with a grin.

"No other pizza will ever compare. I promise you."

She laughed as she dragged him into the tiny eatery. Cramped and dirty, it didn't look like much, but as they took two seats at the counter and she ordered them a large pepperoni, he couldn't keep the dopey smile off his face.

As soon as they were served, he grabbed a slice, groaning in ecstasy after only one mouthful.

"There's nothing like New York pizza," she murmured.

His heart pounded with pure love at her satisfied smile. He reached out and brushed away a string of cheese from her chin, and they both burst out laughing like they were a couple kids.

"Much better than the French place last night," he agreed.

"That's an understatement."

He grunted his agreement, his mouth too full to speak.

After their early dinner, he followed her into the subway, not bothering to ask where they were headed. It wasn't like he knew one neighborhood from the next.

When they got out, he caught her pinching her lips together like she was holding back a laugh.

"You look like the cat that ate the canary. Where exactly are you taking me?"

Her grin was mischievous and adorable. "I thought of a place where you might fit in."

"Uh-oh," he muttered, making her giggle.

When they turned a corner and the neon sign came into view, he stopped, froze… and then burst out laughing. "What on earth is The Lumberjack?"

She was laughing too as they took in the sign, which had two axes crossed over the door. "It's an ax bar."

"An ax what now?"

She took his hand and pulled. "Apparently there's a local league and everything." She shot him a coy smile. "It's highly competitive."

"It is, huh?" He followed her in and let a hostess show them to a booth in the back, where their table was located directly across from an ax-throwing alley. Hatchets and axes of varying sizes were lined up, and after signing their lives away in release forms, they were left to throw axes and drink beers.

"Like this?" she asked an hour later.

JJ chuckled, the grin on his face starting to feel like a permanent fixture. He took a second to just revel in how cute she looked when her gaze was narrowed in concentration, her lips pursed like she had a personal vendetta against the block of wood they were aiming for.

He adjusted her arm, mostly because her form was off, but also because he couldn't resist the urge to touch her whenever possible. "Okay, let 'er rip, Lia."

She threw the hatchet, and it spun blade over handle, landing perfectly with a thud that had Dahlia whooping and dancing around before he pulled her in for a hug. "Nice work, beautiful." He kissed the tip of her nose. "But I'm up next."

Her head fell back with a laugh. "No fair. I shouldn't have to compete against a professional."

He arched a brow, feigning haughty indignation. "You do know I don't spend my days on the ranch tossing axes around for fun, right?"

She took a sip of her drink with a wave of her hand as if to say, *Yeah, yeah. Get on with it.*

Another hour later, they were laughing so hard they stumbled out of the ax bar, clutching each other to stay upright.

"You did not," she said.

"I most certainly did. My little sisters never teased me again after that."

She wrinkled her nose. "But a real live snake? That's disgusting."

He turned to face her. "Tell me you've never done something gross to torment your sisters."

She rolled her eyes. "I didn't have to do something gross. Tormenting them was my full-time job."

He chuckled, a new warmth stealing over him at her rueful grin.

Ever since she'd told him about her childhood, she'd been more laid-back about mentioning it. Even making the odd joke, like now.

He knew for certain the memories still stung, but he was grateful that she'd gotten comfortable talking about it. For his part, now that the bad memories of his marriage's bleak ending were in the open—with Dahlia, at least—it took away some of its power. He supposed airing out the dark past was rather like shining a light into the shadows.

"Where to next, city girl?" he teased as he wrapped an arm around her shoulders.

"Well…" She bit her lip and cast him a quick sidelong glance. "There's a game on, so if you don't mind heading back…"

"Mind?" he echoed, already heading toward the street where taxis were whizzing by. "What are we waiting for?"

A little while later, they were curled up on Dahlia's couch. She'd changed into pajama bottoms, and they'd picked up some beer and chips from a corner market. He was warm and cozy with Dahlia curled up against his side.

She cheered for something that happened in the game —he didn't know, he was barely paying attention. All his focus was on the woman in his arms.

He meant to savor every second he had with her. With that thought, he dropped a kiss on the top of her head.

The move tore her attention from the game, and she smiled up at him as a commercial came on. "So, what do you think of the city?"

He didn't hesitate. "It's a concrete jungle."

She winced. "Cold and hard like me, huh?"

"No. Not at all like you." He shook his head. Frustration lanced through him. She was joking… mostly. But he hated the joke. It felt like she was verbally pushing him away. "Why do you say things like that?"

"Because it's true." She leaned away with a sigh. "I'm no forest. I'm not warm and colorful. I'm practical and organized." She shrugged and reached for her bottle of beer, swigging it back before licking her lips and murmuring, "I don't know how to be anything different."

"Not true," he argued. "You feel more deeply than anyone I know."

Her frown was confused and kind of adorable. She really had no idea.

He grinned. "You're just really good at hiding it." He pulled her toward him, trailing kissing up her neck and along her jawline. "I love that you're so strong. That you care so much."

He felt her still in his arms. There was an awkward beat.

And then she said it.

"Please don't fall in love with me," she whispered.

He jerked back, pain searing through his chest at the words that sounded like they'd been torn out of her.

The light from her lamp was casting a haunting shadow across her face, but he searched her eyes, hoping she could read his mind... his heart.

Licking his lips, he reached forward and turned off the TV.

She didn't even complain.

She just sat there, staring at him with a look he didn't want to decipher.

"Too late," he croaked. "It's too late, Lia. I *am* falling in love with you."

"We can't... I can't." Her eyes were wide and... panicked.

He knew her well enough to recognize that gaze. She was scared, plain and simple. "You can't love me... or you won't?"

"I won't." She tried to move off the couch, but he wouldn't let her.

Gently holding her wrists, he kept her seated. "What are you so afraid of?"

She shook her head, staring down at their physical connection. "Love doesn't work, JJ. Not for me. I'm not built like that. I can't… I can't let myself go. I never could and… I never can."

"Maybe you just haven't met anyone you trusted enough before," he started.

She didn't let him finish. "JJ, I don't know how to love you." She wasn't quite meeting his gaze, and the frustration was back, tightening his gut. Anger too, but not toward Dahlia.

He wished he could go back in time and knock some sense into the father who abandoned her, the mother who didn't get the help she needed… even the grandmother who hadn't known how to show affection.

He wished he could go back and show her just how wonderful she was. How much she deserved. But he couldn't change her past.

He only had the here and now, and if she'd just listen…

If she'd just let him in…

Maybe he could be her future.

"You're afraid, Lia. I get that. But—"

"Of course I'm afraid," she cut him off. "This thing between us, it won't last. Love never lasts. And I don't want you to hurt me." She squeaked out the last few words, her chest rising and falling too quickly, her face pale as she clamped her lips shut.

He suspected she hadn't even meant to say all that aloud.

His heart ached for her. For himself.

She was so terrified, and he wished he knew what to say or do to get through to her. For the first time in his life, he wished he was a man of words.

But he wasn't an eloquent talker, and besides…

Dahlia didn't like pretty words. She liked action… and honesty.

338

With a sad smile, he brushed his knuckle down her cheek and decided to go for the raw, unedited truth. "I'm gonna hurt you, Lia."

Her lips parted on a gasp, her eyes wide. But her gaze collided with his.

He'd shocked her enough to at least get her attention.

He smiled to soften the blow. "It's inevitable that at some point, I'm gonna hurt your feelings, and I'm gonna annoy you, and I'm gonna make you cry." She jerked away from him, but he dropped his voice to a low hum and kept going. "But I'm also going to make you laugh, and I'm going to make you feel safe." He brushed her hair behind her shoulder, lightly touching her neck. His thumb skimmed her jawline and rested just below her ear. "You're gonna call me an idiot and you're gonna call me 'my love,' because that's the journey… and I want to walk it with *you*."

Gently coaxing her forward, he pulled her into a kiss, and any hesitancy she might have shown melted away the moment their lips touched. She sank into a kiss that grew deep and passionate. It was heavy with emotion and nearly impossible to pull out of.

But he did.

He leaned back long enough to whisper, "Let me be that for you. Let me be your man."

Her tearful gaze met his, and he saw a world of emotions. Fear, yes, but also want and need and… and love.

He knew for a fact that she loved him… or at least, she wanted to love him.

She wanted this as much as he did.

But would she find the courage to admit it?

D ahlia's apartment had never felt so small.

She could hear JJ getting changed in the other room the next morning as she fussed with the coffee maker.

Once again, time seemed warped as their goodbye drew near. The seconds flew by too quickly as the hour of his flight grew close. But at the same time, the wait felt interminable.

It was a countdown to another goodbye.

It was the last moments before the inevitable.

She leaned forward until her forehead rested against the cabinets as the pot filled. The smell of fresh coffee wafted up her nose as the sound of it brewing drowned out the noises of JJ moving around in the other room.

She'd ordered a car for him, and he ought to be packed any moment now. It wasn't like he'd brought much for such a short visit.

The pot was full by the time he came out. His hands were tucked in his pockets, and while he was often quiet, his silence as he leaned against the counter beside her felt... wrong.

There was something heavy and strained about it.

She reached for a mug and filled it for him. "Have you packed?"

He shifted beside her. "Not quite."

She glanced at the clock on her wall. "JJ, you're gonna be late. You don't know what New York traffic can be like."

"Hey, I've watched movies." He gave her a halfhearted smile as he took the steaming mug from her.

She snickered and shook her head. "Go get your stuff."

His smile fell, his expression uncharacteristically serious. "I don't want to."

"What? What do you mean?" She blinked up at him.

Leaning in toward her, his gaze grew intense, and the air between them thickened with emotion. "I want to stay here. With you."

For a moment, time stopped. The roar of blood past her ears was the only sound as his words reverberated through her.

He meant it. He would do that... for her.

She shook her head. "JJ, you can't. You're... you're a mountain man. This city will shrivel you up like a dried raisin."

She felt a wave of guilt just thinking of him leaving Aspire behind. The ranch, his horse, the cabin...

She shook her head again. "I can't let you do that."

A muscle in his jaw ticked, his throat working as he set his coffee down. "Then come back with me." His voice held a desperate edge that should not have been endearing. But it was. It curled around her heart, coaxing, begging, trying to cajole. "Come on, Lia. Aspire could be your home. Your family's there. They love you."

"They tolerate me."

"They *love* you," he countered. "You just need to let them."

She pressed her lips together and crossed her arms, trying to force her mind into blankness. Her heart was beating frantically, like it could somehow escape being hurt if only it could find its way out of its cage.

"Lia, please. I know you say you don't belong in Aspire, but here's the thing. You belong with me. I know what I want, and it's you."

She opened her mouth to protest, but she couldn't manage to say all the ugly thoughts pushing into her mind.

You shouldn't waste your energy wanting me. Even if you do now, it won't last.

What made him believe it would last?

It would end. It always ended. He would leave her once this chemistry fizzled out. And then where would she be?

"No," she croaked out before her throat grew too tight.

He took a step toward her, crowding her body and filling her senses. "I'm not a young fool anymore, and being with you isn't a rushed decision made for all the wrong reasons. I want to be with you because you make me happy and I love being around you. You challenge me, excite me. *You* make my life warm and colorful. And I don't care if we have to live in outer Siberia if that's what it takes for us to be together. I'll move for you. I'll move here for you."

She shook her head.

His voice grew painfully gruff. "I know you love me, Lia."

She couldn't deny it. Her heart felt like it was splitting in two at the thought of sending him away.

But she had to... for both their sakes.

Reaching for his hands, she was fighting tears as she smiled at him. "Because I love you, I can't ask you to move here for me." She sniffed and went up on her tiptoes to grab his face and kiss him. "But I'm not ready to move to Aspire for you. I'm sorry."

She kissed him again and he let her, but she felt him pull away.

She knew how much she'd just hurt him.

44

J J nudged Zion faster, one hand on the reins, the other on the phone in his hand.

The useless phone.

He scowled at the space where bars should be. Was it only weeks ago that he'd thought having spotty reception out on the range was a good thing?

He supposed it had been before he'd met the love of his life. And before the love of his life had become a modern-day pen pal.

"Stupid son of a gun," he muttered as he gave his phone a shake.

The shake didn't help, but Zion snickered.

JJ patted the horse's neck absently. "Not talking to you, Z. Just waiting for a response from my girl."

He paused. *My girl.* Was he allowed to call her that after the way they'd ended things? He suspected not. She might have admitted that she loved him, but then she'd all but shoved him out the door.

He sighed, sticking the phone back into his pocket as he steered Zion toward the stables.

She wasn't his girl, but she was his friend. He tried to be grateful for that. They'd exchanged texts every couple days since he'd left two weeks before. They'd even had a few phone calls.

But it wasn't the same, and not just because they were on opposite sides of the country. There was a wall between them. Or many walls, maybe. All erected by Dahlia, and seemingly made of steel.

The L-word hadn't come up again. And she either didn't respond or fell quiet on those rare moments when he gave in to temptation and told her how much he missed her.

The only thing that gave him hope was that she seemed just as miserable as he was.

Not that this was a good thing. He didn't want Dahlia to be miserable... but it did give him hope that maybe someday she'd come to her senses.

He muttered another curse under his breath when they rode into an area where he had reception... and there was no text.

He hoped she'd come to her senses sooner rather than later, because much more of this pining from afar and he might just lose his mind.

He got Zion back into his stall and cleaned up, all the while pondering what he ought to do.

Every day he went through this battle. Should he go back or give her space? Tell her he loved her every dang day or let her be so she could come around to it in her own time?

Zion huffed at him as he left.

Even the horse was tired of his brooding.

He ran into Nash in the office that he rarely used. It was attached to the main barn. As best he could, Nash tried to keep his work out of the ranch house. And now, the typically easygoing cowboy was smacking the old desktop computer in the corner like that was gonna help.

"Technical troubles?" he asked.

"Always," Nash muttered.

JJ gave a huff of amusement. Nash was an excellent cow boss, and he knew how to treat his men, the buyers, and not to mention the cattle, but when it came to crunching the numbers and sorting out the taxes and whatnot, Nash turned grumpy.

"Shouldn't you be in a better mood?" JJ leaned against the doorframe. "With being an almost-married man and all?"

Sure enough, Nash's frown morphed into a silly smile.

Mentioning Emma or the wedding had proven to be a surefire way to cheer up the boss whenever he was stressed about the finances and logistics of running this operation.

He sighed as he leaned back in the chair. "It can't get here soon enough."

JJ smiled, ignoring the twinge of unease. If talk of the wedding made Nash over the moon, it served as a reminder to JJ just how badly his trip to New York had ended.

Maybe he'd been overly optimistic to think a weekend together on her turf would solve everything. But all he knew was he still had no plus-one for the wedding. And the woman he wanted to be "the one" had rejected him.

He'd like to think he could accept the rejection if he thought it would make her happy.

No, he knew he could. If being in New York and at that job made her happy, then he wouldn't just accept her rejection. He'd move there and live right alongside her.

347

It wasn't like she could keep him from moving to that city.

But the thing was she wasn't happy. Only two nights before, they'd been talking, and with every mention of her job, he could hear it. It sounded like the life was being drained right out of her.

A lifetime of giving and serving and never being acknowledged or thanked...

Well, maybe it made sense, then, that she'd gravitated to a job where that was the norm.

What would it take for her to realize she was worth more? Not just at work but in life? That it was time to stop worrying about everyone else and let herself be taken care of?

It was time to let herself be loved.

"Did you need something?" Nash asked.

JJ shook his head, bringing him back to the moment with a start. There he'd gone, brooding again like he was some angsty teenager.

"Nope, just, uh..." Aw heck, why had he come in here? He was losin' his dang mind over this woman. "Just seeing if there was anything you needed help with. I'm guessing you've got a full plate with the celebrations coming up."

And I am desperate for distraction.

Nash sighed wearily. "You'd guess right. That's why I'm trying to get this stuff done. I want to leave for my honeymoon and not give this another thought."

JJ crossed his arms. "You know the place is in safe hands while you're gone, right?"

Nash glanced up. "Of course I do."

"Good. We'll take real good care of her for you and Emma and all those other O'Sullivan sisters. Don't you worry."

"I know. Thanks." Nash paused with a sympathetic smile. "How you holdin' up?"

JJ didn't know how to respond, so he just tipped his hat with a forced smile. "Better get back to it."

Nash nodded and let him go.

That was one of the things he liked about his friends here on the ranch. The townsfolk might live for gossip, and they might love to pester a man with questions. But here on the ranch, Nash and Cody and the others, they respected his privacy.

They seemed to understand that he didn't want to talk about what had happened in New York. Even Rose, Emma, and Lizzy hadn't pried, though they'd each made it clear that they were there for him if he wanted to talk.

He knew they'd be there for Dahlia too if she needed them. But did she know that?

Did she have any idea how much her sisters would love to be there for her like she'd been there for Rose and Daisy all those years?

His heart felt too heavy in his chest as he walked toward the bunkhouse.

Not that he was one to talk, he supposed. He wasn't exactly the chatty sort when it came to matters of the heart. It wasn't like he'd been going to Nash or Kit or any of the O'Sullivans for advice on how to win over his stubborn woman.

But then again, they wouldn't know. He didn't think any of them knew her as well as he did. Not even Rose.

And it was precisely because he knew her—because he loved her—that he had to let her face this on her own. He'd said his piece. He'd shown her his heart, and he'd offered to compromise.

There was nothing left for him to do except love her as

best he could and hope that one day she'd realize that love can be a place of safety. Love can last. Love can be trusted.

But she needed more than courage to take that first leap. Bravery and strength alone weren't enough—not if she didn't have faith.

ahlia's apartment was just as tiny as ever... but it felt like a cavern without JJ filling up space and making it feel all warm and cozy.

Every sound seemed to echo as she cleaned up after her dinner. It was too empty. Too loud. Too cold.

She reached for a throw blanket on the sofa with a frown. Not even the thought of watching the game tonight could cheer her because it just wasn't the same watching the game by herself.

For weeks now, she couldn't seem to get comfortable. Her routine, which she normally could immerse herself in when she was feeling low, just felt monotonous.

Pointless, even. What was the point of working so hard when no one even noticed?

And what was the point of rushing home after a long, grueling day only to sit here alone and in silence?

Dahlia nearly jumped off the couch at the sound of her phone's ringer. She leapt for the device with an eagerness that would have been pathetic if there'd been anyone there to see.

But she was alone, of course, so no one did see her overly eager lunge... or the crestfallen look on her face when it wasn't JJ's name flashing on her screen.

She swallowed down the disappointment and cleared her throat. "Rosie, hey. Is everything okay?"

"Of course."

She held the phone away from her ear in honest confusion. "Do you have any updates on the baby? Are you and Dex all right, or—"

"Dahlia," she interrupted.

"Yes?"

"Everything is fine. I just..." She went quiet for a moment. "I was thinking about how you're always checking up on Daisy and me and thought maybe I should check up on you sometimes too."

"Oh." Dahlia leaned back into the couch cushions as her tensions eased. "That's nice of you."

"How've you been?" Rose asked.

But Dahlia tensed all over again at the simple, benign question. Rose hid her concern well, and she'd been really great about not asking too many questions about JJ's visit, but Dahlia knew that was what had prompted this call.

"Oh, you know... same old, same old." She hurried on to questions about Rose and the baby before her sister could ask anything that would hurt too badly to answer.

Rose seemed content to do most of the talking, and Dahlia curled up on the couch, finding some comfort in not feeling so alone for the first time in weeks.

"Hey, Dahlia?" Rose said after a lengthy pause.

"Yeah?"

"I really love you."

Dahlia lost her breath. Rose sounded so genuine, her

sweet voice pure and confident. Dahlia didn't know how to reply.

"I know we don't say that kind of thing to each other very often, but I just… I was praying for my little baby girl, and I just got this overwhelming urge to call and tell you." She paused, and Dahlia could hear the smile in her voice. "I want you to know that I really love you, and I wouldn't be where I am today without you."

Rose's speech was so unexpected, so sudden, that Dahlia didn't stand a chance against the crashing wave of emotions that had tears welling in her eyes.

"You raised me and cared for me," Rose continued. "You gave up so much for me… even going to community college instead of moving away when you could have gotten a scholarship to any school you wanted. But you stayed close so I could still rely on you."

The silence that followed was filled with the sound of Dahlia's sniffles.

"Where's this coming from?" she finally managed to whisper. Her throat was so thick it was hard to speak properly. "Did JJ put you up to this?"

"No." Rose sounded confused. "Why would JJ—"

"Nothing. No reason." She winced. But what did it matter? It wasn't some great secret that something had happened between them. It wasn't as if Rose and the others back at the ranch didn't already know there was something going on there.

Not anymore.

So why was she still waiting desperately for his phone calls? Why was she forever checking to see if he'd texted? Why did she keep hoping against hope that she'd see him again in her office's reception area, or waiting outside her apartment door?

It was stupid. Futile. He'd left—

No. He hadn't left. She'd sent him away.

Guilt and shame mixed with heartache as she and her little sister sat in silence on the phone.

Rose sighed when the silence grew too long. "Truth is, as I prepare for motherhood and think about the daunting task ahead of me, it's starting to make me realize how much you did when you were only a kid yourself." Her voice started to tremble with tears. "And I never thanked you. I never appreciated you the way I should have. You held us together. You sacrificed so much and I... I really love you." Rose sniffed, and Dahlia started losing the battle with her own tears. "I just hope you know how amazing you are."

Dahlia couldn't speak. Tears slipped down her face, her insides rattling with emotion.

Sucking in a breath, she suddenly blurted, "When are you and Dex planning on getting married? Just the little courthouse one."

"Oh. Uh... maybe the weekend after Emma and Nash's wedding? We don't want to encroach on their special day, and I was kind of waiting to see if you..." Her voice trailed off, and Dahlia easily filled the space.

"Tomorrow, at work, I'm gonna ask for a few days off so I can come back and be a witness for you and Dex, okay?"

"Really?"

"Yeah. I don't want to hold you back from your life. Your marriage. I just want you to be happy. I really love you too, Rosie."

They broke into this weird wobbling, laughing kind of cry, sounding ridiculous as they dealt with all this emotion together.

Then Rose sucked in a breath, and her tone grew wary. "Hey, can I ask you something?"

"Sure."

"Well, now that I'm a grown-up and all, you know you don't have to keep sacrificing your own happiness anymore... right?"

Dahlia sighed. "Rosie, I didn't forfeit my life for you. I'm happy."

"Are you?"

She opened her mouth to respond but couldn't.

"I guess..." Rose's voice grew timid. It often did when she was challenging someone. "Well, I... I want to understand."

Dahlia's insides went cold. "Understand what?"

"Whatever it is you're trying to prove? Can you seriously say you're happy in New York? I mean... what's keeping you there?"

"It's my home."

Rose let out a soft, disbelieving laugh. "There's this great saying that home is where the heart is. And I don't think your heart's in New York."

Dahlia plucked at the blanket, torn between the urge to stubbornly argue... and a desire to be convinced. "What would I do in Aspire?"

"I don't know. Be my daughter's aunt? Be my sister? I mean, I don't want you to move for me. I want you to do what makes you happy. If staying in New York is what you need, then go for it. But... if your heart's someplace else, then you need to follow it."

There was truly no subtlety in what Rose was trying to say. And if Dahlia were a different sort of woman, a different sort of sister... she might have given in to the not-so-subtle nudges to talk about her relationship with JJ.

But what was there to say? She'd gone and fallen in love, but she didn't trust—

What? What don't you trust? She frowned as a nagging voice challenged her. *Him? You don't trust JJ?*

She shifted in her seat. That wasn't right. She did trust him. He was the most loyal, generous, and trustworthy man she'd ever met.

She didn't trust love.

She swallowed hard, her frown aimed at the blanket in her hand. But love wasn't some monster in the night. It wasn't the boogeyman. It was two people and how they felt about each other.

She might not have had good experiences with love, but trust…

She could trust JJ.

And herself? She swallowed hard. Could she trust herself not to lose her identity and sense of self if she surrendered to these feelings?

"If you need to talk, I'm here, okay?" Rose offered.

Dahlia nodded even though her sister couldn't see. "Good night, Rose."

Her sister sighed. "G'night."

Dahlia hung up and stared at the blank TV screen long after the call ended. Rose's words swam in her head, like sharks circling their weakening prey.

She just got schooled by the baby of her family, and Dahlia couldn't help letting out an astonished laugh. Tipping her head back, she gazed up at the ceiling and shouted, breaking the silence of this cold, empty apartment with a bellow that wouldn't endear her to her neighbors.

It was part joy, part anguish. It was an explosion of emotion that she had no idea what to do with.

You can trust this love, Dahlia.

That gentle whisper moved through her.

She didn't know that voice in her head, but it stirred and called to her. Its soft, peaceful tone was in complete contrast to her raging emotions, and it made her stop. It made her listen.

This love won't leave you or forsake you.

She frowned. Where had she heard those words before? And why was she suddenly thinking about that sermon she heard in Aspire? The one that gave her the worst hay fever… those tear-inducing allergies.

She snickered at herself, shaking her head and staring back at the blank TV screen again.

It was the sermon about that woman, the adulteress, who Jesus didn't judge. He showed mercy. When everyone else wanted to hate her, *kill* her even, he showed her love.

Because love heals.

Wasn't that what the pastor said?

"Love heals," she whispered.

And if love healed, why did she need to fear it?

Closing her eyes and letting more tears slip free, she let those words, that question, churn through her over and over again.

Dahlia walked to the subway's entrance the next morning, but as a stream of people pushed by her to go down, she stood there at the top of the steps. Finally, she turned and started to walk.

When was the last time she'd walked to work?

It had been an age. Not because she didn't like walking but because it took up time, and she'd always been anxious about getting in early.

But this morning, she couldn't quite muster up that sense of urgency that normally drove her out of the apartment and onto the subway.

And so she walked. The weather was nice enough, though snow was still piled up on heaps at every crosswalk. But the sun was shining, and the wind wasn't bad, and she needed fresh air more than she needed to get to work on time.

She wrapped her coat around herself tighter as she reached an intersection and waited for the walk sign. As she stood there, she took it in. All of it—the people, the skyscrapers, the sounds, and the traffic.

She didn't hate it. In fact, she felt a swell of affection in her heart for this place that had been such a part of her for so long. How many times had she lost that feeling of loneliness because she'd been swallowed up by a crowd?

More than she could count.

In stadiums, at Madison Square Garden, but also on sidewalks like this one when she felt like she was part of this city—a small but integral cog in the wheel, so to speak.

Something bittersweet rose up in her as she looked around. Once upon a time, she used to swear that she could see the energy that pulsed through the streets and seemed to vibrate overhead.

It fed her, made her feel connected.

She stopped just across the street from her office building.

But did it anymore? Just because she'd needed this place once, did that mean it was where she had to be forever?

Was it still what she needed?

Her thoughts grew bittersweet as memory after memory of her life here with her sisters hit her anew. One after the other, some good and some bad.

Someone jostled her elbow, and that was when she realized she'd been so lost in memories, she'd nearly missed the sign that it was time to move.

And that was it, wasn't it? She blinked dazedly as she kept walking. It had been so hard to make things work for so long that when she'd found what worked, she'd stuck with it. Right or wrong, good or bad, she'd clung to what was working in her life.

Even if she'd been miserable.

Even if Daisy had gone off on tour and Rose had fled to Montana.

Even if all the reasons she'd put down roots here were gone.

"Dahlia, are you coming?" The receptionist paused beside Dahlia on the street, fixing her with a curious look as she glanced toward the front door.

"Oh. Yeah. Um… I forgot my coffee. I'll be in soon."

The receptionist shot her a quizzical frown but walked inside.

It wasn't just rare for Dahlia to stand outside her office building. It would be weird for anyone to stand still in the city. If you stayed still for too long, you'd get run over.

So she'd moved. She'd hustled. She'd spent the last decade doing nothing but spinning wheels, trying to keep her head afloat so she could be a rock for her sisters.

And she was tired.

She nearly sank down onto the curb as it hit her. She was bone weary, and she hadn't even realized it until she'd been forced to stop. Until she'd been stuck in a cabin and forced to relearn what it meant to relax. To talk. To laugh. To enjoy all the simple things.

She walked in a daze to the coffee kiosk nearby and ordered a cup. Black. "Like my soul," she'd once joked to JJ. He'd rolled his eyes and given her that lopsided grin that said she was full of it.

The memory made her chest ache, which was nothing new.

She'd been aching for weeks now, and it kept getting worse instead of better with each passing day.

The sweeping landscape and wide-open spaces of Montana had taken her breath away. She loved the rugged mountains, raw in their beauty, unforgiving in their presence. They stood tall and strong the way she always wanted to.

But that wasn't what she loved about that ranch or Aspire.

It was the people.

The *people* had her heart.

So why was she denying herself the joy of being around them?

The coffee cup paused halfway to her lips as the question sank in. She turned to face her office building with a start.

So… what?

What did that mean?

She stood like a statue, unable to drink, unable to take a step forward.

It meant she wanted to go back to Montana, that was what. It meant she missed JJ, yes, but…

She looked around her with new eyes.

Because now she'd seen another way of life. And maybe she no longer needed this world of strangers and crowds to feel like she belonged.

Maybe she'd needed this place once, but maybe she'd changed.

Maybe she wanted to change.

And maybe, finally, she wasn't afraid to do it.

She headed toward the office building again, and this time she didn't stop. She wasn't entirely sure what she intended to say, but she'd know it when the time came.

Walking to her office, she dumped her stuff on the desk and smoothed down her dress.

Time to go for it.

That soft voice was in her head again.

She drew in a breath and held it.

You can do this. Trust yourself. Trust your heart.

Laying a hand on her chest, she let herself breathe in and out a couple more times.

She was no closer to having figured it all out, but those quiet words propelled her out of her office. She knocked firmly on her bosses' door and pushed it open the moment she was invited in.

Marian was sitting behind the desk, Jason just beside her. They looked annoyed by the interruption.

"Hey, guys. Can I have a minute?" Dahlia asked.

Jason's eyebrows dipped together, but he nodded. "What's up?"

Irritation flared at their dismissive looks, the irritation they didn't even try to hide.

She pictured JJ's smile and the way his face lit up whenever he was around her, and she felt a surge of strength.

Clearing her throat, she started by saying, "I'd like to request a few days off to head back to Montana."

Jason tutted. "Are you kidding me? You've already had so much time."

"Well, I've had days away, but I was still working throughout. I want actual vacation time. My sister's getting married, and I've never taken my allocated vaca—"

"No."

She blinked. "Excuse me?"

They looked at each other before Jason spoke again. "Permission denied. We're coming into a really busy patch, and we need you here."

She worked her jaw to the side, trying to keep her cool. "You know, if you'd taken my suggestions and that

proposal I sent you a couple months ago into considera-
tion, the next few weeks wouldn't be quite so busy."

They hit her with dual glares, their expressions stony
and unimpressed.

Their silence only fueled her anger. "I work late for
you. I come in early for you. I do everything you ask
of me."

They looked at each other with clear exasperation. Like
she was a child having a tantrum.

"I haven't asked for overtime or extra leave, but—"

"But what?" Marian interrupted. "You're doing your
job. Do you expect a trophy just because you've gone
above and beyond once or twice?"

"Once or…" Dahlia trailed off, her mouth gaping open
in disbelief. Did they really have so little appreciation for
all she'd done? Did they really not see how much she'd
given this company? "You never say thank you."

"Excuse me?" Jason drawled.

"You never acknowledge anything I do, and I feel
totally underappreciated."

"Oh, so we're talking about feelings now?" Marian
huffed." If you want to do that, you can run on down
to HR."

"I'm *so* over this." Dahlia shook her head. "I'm so over
trying to make you guys happy." She threw her hands up.
"And I'm worth so much more than this."

That made her stop. She'd never thought of herself that
way. She'd always served, provided for, and cared for
others. But now there was someone out there who wanted
to care for *her*. There were people out there who loved her
without demanding or expecting anything. She didn't
have to earn their love; it was automatic.

The thought made her laugh, which in turn made her bosses frown.

"Oh my gosh." She let out another joyous whoop and grinned at them, feeling completely liberated.

She didn't need this. She didn't need them. Everything she'd fought for, everything she'd wanted—the love, the family, the life—it was all hers for the taking.

She just had to be brave enough to reach for it.

Her bosses looked at her like she'd gone insane, and she just laughed again, her shoulders going back and her chin tilting up.

"I quit." Her voice was cheerful and confident. "I'm so done."

Their faces dropped. "You can't leave now. We're coming into a really busy time of year."

"Not my problem." Dahlia shrugged and then had to say it again. "That is not my problem." She laughed and spun on her heel, heading for the door. Just before grabbing the handle, she turned back with an impish grin. She just couldn't help herself. "By the way, good luck finding someone to replace me. You guys have no idea how lucky you've been."

And with that, she walked out of the office, shutting the door on their protests and feeling lighter than she ever had before.

47

Cody left early to do his ushering duties at the church, which left JJ alone in the bunkhouse to get ready.

It was nearly impossible to keep his gaze away from his phone on the nightstand as he donned his nicest suit and made himself as neat and tidy as a burly mountain man could be. Which wasn't all that neat. And definitely not tidy.

He was relieved Nash hadn't asked him to be a groomsman. He didn't know if he was up for standing in front of a big crowd while the loved-up couple shared their vows. Thankfully, his boss and the lovely Emma had decided to go for a small party of Lizzy on one side and Kit on the other.

Chloe was, of course, the flower girl, and little Corbin was taking his duties as the ring bearer with utmost seriousness.

JJ's lips twitched as he reached for a tie. He wished Dahlia was here to see it all. She was on his mind more than ever, and not just because he yearned for her like she was a missing limb, her very absence an ache he could feel. But also, he was worried about her.

They all were. Rose and the others up at the main house, Kit and Lizzy. Dex had even stopped him in town the other day to see if he'd heard from her recently.

Miss Strong and Steady was hurting, and everyone knew it, but no one knew how to help her. He'd given in to the urge to call her the night before, though he'd been doing his best to respect her need for space.

She hadn't answered.

That, more than anything, was what had him scowling at the phone as he knotted his tie.

Up until last night, she'd at least seemed glad to hear from him. She might have sounded sad, but she'd always answered. He picked up his phone to make sure there were bars.

There were.

So there was no reason why she shouldn't have at least responded to his texts last night, and again this morning.

"She's turned me into a nag," he muttered. Any other time, the thought might have made him grin. But right now he was too worried to find the humor in this situation.

He was too worried to go to a wedding, but there was no way out of it. No matter how much his heart was aching, and no matter how worried he was for his woman, one of his closest friends was about to tie the knot, and he had to pull it together to celebrate.

There was a knock on the door while he was cussing and muttering over the stupid dang tie. It'd been a long time since he'd had to tie one of these things, and he didn't recall them being so difficult.

"Come in," he called out.

It was probably Cody coming back because he forgot something. Or maybe Boone coming to keep him company before they left for the church.

He kept his gaze focused on the mirror as the door creaked open, and then his heart dropped into his stomach when he heard the voice behind him. "Wow. Aren't you a sight for sore eyes?"

He whipped around, his heart doing a full-blown tap dance as he drank in Dahlia. His girl. His woman.

She looked absolutely stunning all dressed up for the wedding. Her dark hair fell in pretty waves around her face, softening her features. And whatever she'd done with her makeup made her look like she was glowing in that pale blue dress.

But honestly, she could have been wearing a burlap sack and a mud mask and his insides would have still turned to putty.

Her presence caught him so off guard, he found himself speechless.

Her expression was uncharacteristically shy as she clasped her hands in front of her, hovering by the doorway to his room. "I heard you needed a plus-one for the wedding."

His heart squeezed so hard he lost the ability to breathe. For one long moment, he actually wondered if he was imagining this. If he'd finally lost it for good and was full-on hallucinating about Dahlia.

But there was nothing imaginary about that sweet vulnerability in her eyes, and not even in his best, most vivid dreams could he have conjured the perfection that stood before him right now.

Finally, he let out an awed laugh, and he caught her lips curving up in a tremulous smile in return.

Slowly walking toward her, he rested his hand on her waist, heartened when she didn't move away. Some part of him was still worried she'd come back here for Emma's sake alone. That she was here in this bunkhouse as his friend.

He leaned his head down, making sure to hold her gaze. "I'm actually looking for a plus-one for life, Lia."

As soon as he said it, his insides knotted. He was half expecting her to bolt out the door. Lightly tightening his hold on her, he held his breath and prayed.

She swallowed hard, her eyes brimming with tears.

Those tears nearly took him out at the knees. This was it. This was the moment that she rejected him once and for all.

He only barely stopped himself from dropping to her feet to beg.

But then she reached up to touch him. She ran her fingers down his beard before winding her arms around his neck and playing with his stubby ponytail. Her gaze lifted, and when it met his, he felt that jolt of a connection all the way to his pounding heart.

"I can be that," she whispered. "I can be your plus-one... for life."

The words set off an explosion of fireworks in his chest. "Really?"

She smiled as she nodded. "Yeah. You see... it turns out that home is actually where your heart is." Her voice took on a teasing lilt. "Were you aware of that?"

A laugh caught him off guard. "I think I've heard that sentiment before, yeah."

Her laughter mixed with a sob of relief. "Well, since you own my heart, I guess this is home."

Aw heck. He was done for. He hadn't thought he could

love this woman more than he already did, but then she had to go and say that.

"You sure?" His voice was little more than a rumble, but he had to ask. He wasn't sure his heart could take it if she changed her mind. "Not New York?"

Her smile grew a little bigger, her eyes shining with tears. "*You're* my New York. You're my Amsterdam. You're my Paris, my Dubai, my outer Siberia. You're my African safari." She laughed. "I could live anywhere, JJ, as long as you're there too."

He leaned down to kiss her. It wasn't some chaste brush of the lips but a deep touching of souls. The kind of kiss he could pour his every fiber into. It was sweeter than anything he'd ever experienced in his life. She kissed him back with an urgency that made his heart kick. She kissed him like she could *show* him how much she meant what she'd said.

Lifting her off her feet, he pulled her into a bear hug while she laughed and cried. The next kiss they shared was warm and tender and filled with love.

That kiss, with the woman of his heart in his arms and the sound of her laughter still ringing in his ears...

It was home.

This kiss, this woman...

It was his future.

48

Rose leaned in to Dahlia as the crowd around them burst into applause. "You're not allowed to cry more than me," she said as she giggled through her tears. "I'm the hormonal one, remember?"

Dahlia laughed too, a hiccupy sound escaping that was thankfully swallowed by the cheering and laughter around them as the guests greeted the new bride and groom.

Emma and Nash paraded down the aisle, beaming and happy, as they led the wedding party toward the back. Lizzy was halfway down the aisle when she turned to Dahlia and Rose, giving them two thumbs up, which had Dahlia laughing all over again.

And crying.

"I don't know what's wrong with me," she whispered to JJ, who hadn't let go of her hand on the entire ride into town or throughout the ceremony.

She had a feeling he'd never let her go again if he could help it.

And she couldn't say she minded one bit.

He leaned over and kissed the top of her head. "You cry all you want, sweetheart. You've been through so much these past weeks. You are absolutely entitled."

She nodded, her lips quivering all over again.

"Have I mentioned how proud I am of you?" he murmured.

She tipped her head up to give him a wobbly smile. These dang tears were just irritating at this point. She was happy. She'd never been happier.

And she didn't have a single regret.

The look on JJ's face when she told him she'd quit her job… she'd hold that in her heart forever.

She'd known she was making the right decision as she'd boarded the plane to Montana. But when JJ had pulled her into his arms…

Well, nothing in her life had ever felt so right.

Dahlia was dimly aware of Rose and Dex whispering beside her. She caught Dex saying her name.

"What's that about?" she asked Rose.

Rose pressed her lips together, but a giggle escaped as she turned bright pink. "He was wondering if maybe you might be pregnant too."

Dahlia's jaw dropped, and the surprise was enough to stop her tears. *Thank goodness.*

"No!" she finally yelped, turning to see JJ scrubbing a hand over his mouth, trying to hide a grin.

Now her cheeks were turning red too as she murmured, "That's an impossibility."

"For now," JJ added under his breath as he slid a hand around her waist, steering her toward the aisle, where the guests were beginning to file out to head to the reception.

For now.

Dahlia's head felt much too light, and she was grateful

for JJ's arm helping to hold her weight. All at once, all the dreams she'd denied herself, the future she'd thought she couldn't have…

She would have tripped if JJ hadn't caught her and held her to his side. "You all right?" he asked. "Is it your shoes? Because I can carry you if you need—"

She stopped him with a kiss, not caring who saw. "It's not my shoes."

His brows drew together in a question, but there was laughter in his eyes. "Was it my comment about kids?"

She nodded, a warmth unfurling in her chest so sweet and so precious, she wasn't sure if she could put it into words. "I think I want that," she whispered. "With you. All of it."

And because he was JJ, and he'd always been able to understand her even better than she understood herself, he got it. There was nothing but love in his eyes as he leaned down, his voice low in her ear. "And you deserve it all, Lia. You deserve everything."

He pulled back, his gaze expectant as if to ask, *Do you know that now? Do you understand?*

She nodded and was rewarded with a grin.

"What do you say we get to that reception?" he said as he took her hand. "We can show 'em how it's done."

She laughed as she let him lead her into the crowd. "Don't tell me you can dance too. Is there anything you can't do?"

"I guess you'll just have to find out."

The reception room was a converted barn decked out to be the most stunning venue Dahlia had ever seen. Lizzy had pulled out all the stops, and Dahlia smiled up at the lights hanging from the rafters. The tables were swathed in white linen with glowing centerpieces that gave the space a magical quality. They'd taken this rustic place and turned it into a fairy tale.

Musicians were starting to play on the far side, and a handful of kids were already on the dance floor, chasing each other around in a circle.

"I'm afraid to say at least one of those little devils is mine," a voice said from behind them.

They both turned, and JJ grinned. "Levi! Good to see you, brother."

The dark-haired man was slightly older and had a weary look about him, but his smile was kind as he turned to Dahlia. "Welcome back. I didn't think you were gonna make it for the wedding."

"I had a change of plans." She smiled at JJ while he wound his arm around her waist.

His smile couldn't have been brighter. "Yes, siree, you're gonna be seeing a lot more of my plus-one around here."

"Oh really?" He shared a look with JJ and started to chuckle. "Well, can I just say… I'm a little jealous. My plus-one is off sulking somewhere because I wouldn't let her wear a skintight dress that barely covered her butt."

Dahlia followed his gaze to a pretty, sullen teenager nearby. She was decked out in a modest red gown that looked beautiful on her, but yes, she was indeed pouting. Dahlia winced. "I know a thing or two about raising teen girls, so you have all my sympathy."

"Dahlia! Over here!" Lizzy's voice interrupted them. She was waving at them from a round table in the corner.

"We'll see you around, Levi." JJ navigated them through the crowd to join Lizzy, Kit, Cody, Rose, and Dex.

Dahlia also recognized Nash's sister and her husband standing nearby, along with Nash's parents, who were in deep conversation with another couple that she had to assume were Lizzy's folks.

Dahlia hesitated next to Lizzy. "Isn't this section for the wedding party?"

"And family." Lizzy nudged her with her hip.

"Maybe JJ and I should go—"

"You're not going anywhere," Lizzy interrupted. "What do you think you are? You're our sister, which means you're family."

Oh heck. Dahlia clamped her lips shut as she fought yet another surge of emotions.

Lizzy still caught it though, and she leaned in with a sweet smile. "I know we didn't hit it off right away, but I wanted to say I'm glad you're here. Not just at the wedding, but… here. In Aspire."

She had to swallow hard before she could manage, "Thanks, Lizzy. I'm glad I'm here too."

Lizzy pulled her in for a hug, and Dahlia caught Rose dabbing at her eyes as she looked on from where she sat. Emma was smiling over at them too, and her eyes were shiny with tears as she blew a kiss in their direction and mouthed, "Welcome to the family, sis."

"Welp, now I'm gonna be a puffy-eyed mess all night," she muttered when Lizzy let her go.

Lizzy laughed. "Join the club. This family has been through a lot this year. And something tells me the drama is far from over."

Dahlia took a deep breath as she nodded, thoughts of Daisy bringing a wave of guilt and regret. She should be here too. She missed her fun-loving sister something fierce right now.

"You're probably right," she said as JJ pulled her against his side in a protective move. "But for tonight, I say we enjoy this wedding that you so excellently helped plan."

Lizzy made them all laugh as she tossed her hair. "What, this? It was nothing."

"It was everything," Emma said as she joined them. Nash was right behind her, gazing at his bride like she was the most beautiful thing the world had ever known.

She looked absolutely stunning in her white gown. It was a masterpiece of tulle and satin with a sweetheart neckline and shoestring straps. Dahlia didn't know how she wasn't freezing. She was probably too hopped up on pure joy to feel anything but that.

Reaching for her sister, she took her hand and gave it a squeeze. "She's right, Lizzy. We can't thank you enough for your help with the wedding."

"You seriously could go pro as a wedding planner," Dahlia added.

"Ooh." Rose perked up. "Could you help with mine?"

Dex was grinning at her like a lovesick fool, and for once, Dahlia didn't mind seeing everyone around her so happy in love.

Probably because she was a lovesick fool herself.

"I'd love to help." Lizzy touched her chest like she was about to give a speech for the Oscars. "We should talk color schemes—"

"Later," Kit cut in. He wrapped his arms around his wife's waist. "The twins are dancing with Grandma and Grandpa, which means this dance is just for you and me."

Lizzy giggled as she turned into his arms, calling to Rose over her shoulder. "We'll talk color schemes later... after a dance."

Rose laughed, leaning in to Dex, who was giving her lower back a rub.

"Do you want to dance?" he asked.

She wrinkled her nose. "Could we just sit here and relax a bit? I think my back and feet could use a rest."

"Of course." He kissed her temple. "There's no place I'd rather be."

Emma laughed as she turned to Dahlia. "Are Nash and I that sickening?"

"You're worse." Dahlia grinned.

Emma's head fell back with a loud laugh. "That's what I thought. Come on, hubby, let's dance."

"As you wish, my lovely wife," Nash said with a grin.

JJ's arm tightened around them. "Well, Lia? You want to dance?"

"I'd love to." She winked at him as she led the way to the dance floor. "If you're half as good at dancing as you are at throwing an ax, I'm one lucky lady."

He was laughing as he joined her amid the other dancers, and just as he reached her side, the musicians switched to a ballad.

"It's my lucky day," he murmured as he took her into his arms and they swayed in time to the music.

"I'd say it's *my* lucky day," she argued.

"I'll fight you for it," he deadpanned.

She started to laugh, but his kiss made her forget all about her giggles, and she sighed dreamily instead.

"Here's to our first dance as an official couple," he murmured.

She tightened her arms around his neck and rested her head against his chest. "And here's to countless more."

49

Nearly a week later, JJ glared at the phone in his hand before bringing it back to his ear. Frustration rippled off him as he tried to keep his cool. "I hear what you're saying, Mr. Masterson, but I don't think you're listening—"

The voice on the other end wouldn't quit.

It didn't help that the computer wasn't doing anything it was supposed to. He hit a tab in the corner and managed to lose everything he'd just done.

His muttered curse didn't stop the supplier haranguing him on the other end of the line.

"I will not be supplying you one more thing until I receive full payment for my last—"

"We did pay him! I know that invoice is in there somewhere." Kit was hovering over the desk with his hands on his hips, glowering at the computer like he could intimidate it into submission.

JJ set the phone down, a moment's reprieve from the bleating in his ear. "Where's Cody? Maybe he knows how to work this dang thing."

Kit shook his head. "Sent him into town for supplies."

JJ frowned.

"Should we call Nash?" Kit asked.

JJ shook his head. "And interrupt his honeymoon? No, sir."

"Right." Kit sat on the edge of the desk with a sigh. "We can figure this out. After all, we promised Nash we'd keep things running without a hitch. We just need to find that invoice. That has to be proof enough for this stubborn jerk. I knew Nash had reservations about switching over to him, but when Willard retired, we kind of ran out of options."

"Are you even listening to me!" The voice from the phone got louder, and they both flinched.

Just then the office door swung open, and a smiling Dahlia walked in, her hands full of coffee mugs. "Hey, guys, I brought…"

She trailed off with a frown as she took in JJ's expression, the computer, a scowling Kit, and the phone on the desk. "What's going on?"

JJ's insides leapt with hope, and he looked at Kit. "Dahlia knows this stuff. You know computers, right, baby? You know numbers?"

She arched her brows, looking on the verge of a giggle, but she must have picked up on his desperation, because she didn't even pause before setting down the mugs and shooing him out of the office chair. "What's the problem?"

His blood turned to lava. Goodness, she was gorgeous when she went into business mode. In a few sentences he laid out the issue at hand. Nash was a stickler about paying invoices on time and had never once missed a payment. But this new supplier on the line was trying to convince them they owed that plus more, and—

Dahlia cut him off before he could even finish. "Give the phone to me."

JJ lifted the phone to his ear. "Mr. Masterson, I'm just gonna pass you over to the ranch's, uh…"

Kit and Dahlia gave him expectant looks.

"Our business manager." JJ winced at the off-the-cuff lie.

Dahlia rolled her eyes, but she looked like she was trying not to laugh as she stole the phone from him.

"Mr. Masterson, Dahlia O'Sullivan here."

Kit wasn't even trying to hide his amusement. "You're a terrible liar, JJ."

He shushed his friend, wanting to capture every second of this as Dahlia clicked a few keys and called up an entirely new screen in the accounting software.

"I can't find the dang payment," JJ whispered as her sharp gaze flicked left to right over the screen, taking in all the numbers as if she was reading the alphabet.

"I know it's been made," JJ continued. "I think he's trying to dupe us."

Dahlia gave him a little wink, pulled her shoulders back, and spoke into the receiver. "So what seems to be the problem?"

Her voice was so in control and professional that JJ blinked at her in disbelief. He'd started to get so used to this new Dahlia who was quickly finding a home for herself on this ranch that sometimes he forgot the suit-wearing bossbabe she'd been in New York.

She made a few murmurs of acknowledgment as the supplier kept talking on the other line. All the while, she was flicking through screens and reading the data.

Finally, when there was a pause on the other end, she spoke smoothly. "I don't think so, Mr. Masterson. You can't double-charge us and then slap on extra interest without giving us the chance to prove that payment has been made." Dahlia let out a withering snicker that had Kit staring at her wide-eyed, maybe a little scared. "Nice try, buddy."

JJ beamed with pride as her eyebrows lifted. Whatever Mr. Masterson just said was making Dahlia's nostrils flare.

She let out a short, disbelieving laugh before cutting the bullheaded man down to size. "I take it from your comment that you don't value your business in the town of Aspire."

JJ's fists curled, and Kit looked ready for a smackdown when the voice at the other end cut in, clearly shouting at Dahlia.

"My turn again," JJ growled, reaching for the phone.

"I'll tell him where he can get off," Kit sneered.

But Dahlia ignored them both, clearing her throat and looking unperturbed. "Bark at me as much as you like, sir, but I can assure you that if you don't treat us fairly, every ranch in the surrounding area of this town will drop you faster than you can say boo."

Even JJ could hear the man sputtering on the other end of the line.

"Just because you're the new supplier doesn't make you the only one. This is the O'Sullivan Ranch, and we are highly respected in our community. Now if you want to keep your business alive, I suggest you start being a little nicer to me."

JJ snickered in awe, sharing a glance with Kit, who held up a hand to high-five him.

"This place is in good hands, my friend." Kit gave JJ a friendly pat on the back as they shared another grin.

Who would have thought that not only was Dahlia exactly what he needed…

But maybe she was what this ranch needed as well.

"Yes, I can agree to that." Dahlia nodded. "I will find you that invoice, no problem, and I appreciate the 10 percent discount you'll give us next time we use your services."

There was more sputtering as Dahlia feigned surprise.

"You didn't? Oh, well, maybe that's something you'd like to consider if you're set on keeping your good name here Aspire. I'm sure it would go a long way toward proving your excellent customer service." She grinned and shook her head. "If that's how you want to play it. But as I said before, you are not the only supplier available to us, and I have no problem taking our business elsewhere."

She paused, obviously waiting for a response as she glanced at JJ and gave him a cute little wink. His blood stirred again—a mix of desire and admiration coursing through him.

A broad smile stretched her mouth wide. "Good thinking, Mr. Masterson. We look forward to doing future business with you."

When she hung up the phone, JJ pulled her out of the chair and into his arms. "You are the coolest person I've ever met. You know that?"

She laughed, and the merry sound filled the office and shot straight into his heart.

C al's Coffee Shop was a blessed relief after a long morning helping Rose move.

"You two lovely ladies look like you could use a piece of cake to go with that coffee and tea." Dr. Bob, the local veterinarian, had stopped by on his way to join the other members of their little coffee crew. He'd set down a piece of cake he'd bought up at the counter with an affectionate grin. "Gluten-free too." He winked at Rose, and she clapped her hands together with a delighted laugh.

"Thank you!" Leaning forward, she called up to the counter, "And thank you, chef!"

A soft holler came from the back. "I finally found a recipe that works. Anything for you, sweet Rosie."

Dahlia stifled a laugh. Every time she came here with Rose, the old men who gathered at this place treated her to something new.

Rose dug in with relish. "If Cal and his wife keep coming up with gluten-free treats for me, I'm going to turn into a whale."

Dahlia grinned. "A little thing like you? Never."

Rose rubbed her round belly with a laugh and pushed the plate toward her. "It's delicious. Try some."

"Oh, I don't know…"

Rose rolled her eyes. "Dahlia, you've been busting your butt to help me move into Dex's place all morning. I think you've earned yourself a little sweet treat."

Dahlia laughed. "Okay, if you insist."

For a long moment, they made each other laugh with their over-the-top moans of delight every time they took a bite. Between making each other giggle and eavesdropping on the coffee crew, Dahlia was highly entertained.

"Do they really gossip like this every day?" she asked.

Rose nodded, her eyes wide with amusement. "Every. Day." She popped a forkful of cake in her mouth with a dramatic flair.

Dahlia giggled. She and Rose had been having so much fun together these past few weeks since she'd officially moved to Aspire. What had once been a tense, almost mother-daughter relationship had rapidly been turning into a real friendship.

She could say the same about her relationships with Emma and Lizzy too. They'd all been spending a lot of time together recently, especially now that Dahlia had found a way to help out at the ranch.

When Emma and Nash returned from their honeymoon, they moved into the upstairs master bedroom, which freed up the downstairs area for Dahlia. With Rose moving out as well, she now had two whole rooms plus the office space. She was quickly turning it into a happy home, although she spent more time up at the bunkhouse than she cared to admit. She just loved how rustic and rowdy it was. Dart nights and poker games were becoming a regular thing, and she loved every moment of it.

"Oh no…" Rose gave a mock pout. "Poor Mikayla."

Dahlia wiped a crumb off the edge of her mouth. "Who?"

Rose nodded toward the men who were listening as Norman told a story about Levi's teen daughter and how he'd caught her ditching school.

"Did you tell Levi?" Chicken Joe asked.

"Nah. I didn't want to get the girl in trouble. You know how strict he can be. I gave her a good talking to, though." Norman took a sip of his coffee. "I don't think she likes me very much."

The men chuckled while Dahlia and Rose shared a wink.

"Do you remember how much Daisy used to ditch?" Dahlia grinned. She could laugh about it now, but it had caused her no end of headaches back then. Trying to keep her twin sister in line had nearly caused World War III on multiple occasions.

"She never actually left school." Rose snickered. "She played hooky in the music room."

They both laughed.

"I think she had a crush on the music teacher." Rose tipped her head in thought. "Do you remember how he'd always let her stay, even if it was breaking the rules?"

"Ugh. That guy was such a softie. And luckily happily married, because you're right, Daisy definitely had a crush on the guy." Dahlia shook her head. "She's always had a thing for older men."

Dahlia pulled a face, which made Rose laugh. She took another sip of tea before scraping icing off the plate with the tip of her finger.

"Have you told Daisy yet that you've found a job working for the family ranch?" Rose asked.

Dahlia tipped her head from side to side. "I mentioned it, but you know how it is with Daisy. I couldn't tell if she was really paying attention."

Rose nodded in understanding. "But this business manager thing is working out okay?"

Dahlia couldn't stop a grin that spread from ear to ear. "I love it. And I think Nash is just as happy about it as I am, so I don't feel like I'm stepping on his toes or anything."

Rose laughed. "I talked to Emma about it. He's over the moon to let you handle the books."

Dahlia shrugged. "I'm good with numbers and Nash hates them, so it's a perfect fit."

Not to mention she got to spend her days near JJ and their weekends at the cabin. But the best part about the job was that she got to use her skills and was appreciated for her hard work.

Plus, as a part owner, she actually benefited directly. She'd already made an appointment to meet with a business manager and see where they could take the ranch in the future. She had a feeling they could be doing way more than just keeping things ticking over. The possibilities were there, just waiting to be uncovered.

Rose took her hand and gave it a squeeze. "So, I take it you've changed your mind about the whole selling the ranch thing?"

She nodded. "Yeah, I think so. But..." She pointed a forkful of cake at Rose. "I will understand if the others don't feel the same way. But until then, we might as well make the most of things."

Rose smiled. "I know. We'll just have to take it one step at a time."

"Or one sister at a time," Dahlia corrected with a laugh.

"Exactly."

A police siren outside the coffee shop had them looking out the window. The coffee crew grew silent as everyone in the shop watched Levi get out of his cruiser and approach the Volkswagen Beetle.

A scratched-up, pale blue Beetle.

Dahlia's lips parted, and a glance at Rose saw that she recognized it too.

"Is that... *Daisy*?"

Rose giggled. "Being pulled over for speeding, no doubt."

Levi wore a frown and hitched his belt as the window rolled down to reveal a gorgeous blonde with long, wild locks and an unapologetic smile.

"What is she doing here?" Dahlia stood and walked toward the window.

"Sweet-talking her way out of a ticket, by the looks of things." Rose laughed, one hand on her belly as she got to her feet as well.

"You know that girl?" Chicken Joe called over to them.

Rose answered. "That's our sister, Daisy."

"Oh brother," Norman muttered. "Another O'Sullivan? Lord help us."

Rose giggled and kissed Norman's cheek while Dahlia walked outside to find out why her sister, who was supposed to be doing some recording deal in LA, was actually sitting in the little town of Aspire.

EPILOGUE

Dahlia stared up at their lodgings with an open mouth.

She could feel JJ beside her, shifting from one foot to the other and watching her with the eager excitement of a young child.

Or a nervous mountain man.

"Well? What do you think? Is it too weird or—"

Before he could finish, she leapt into his arms and kissed him. "I love it."

"Yeah?"

"I love it so much!" She wrapped her arms around his neck for a quick squeeze before letting him take in some more. "It's a tree house!" She clapped a hand over her mouth with a laugh. "In the safari!"

He chuckled as he scratched the back of his head, looking unbearably adorable and boyish as he watched her. "Yeah, well, I couldn't afford a trip to Africa just yet, so…"

"So you found a safari on the West Coast," she finished. "It's perfect."

And it was. The conservation retreat had giraffes and other wildlife that they could check out on expeditions into the "wilderness."

"It's a little less rustic than the cabin," JJ murmured as he scratched his beard and looked up at their luxury tent, which was set up on a platform in the trees.

"Somehow I think we'll manage with a little luxury in our camping experience," she teased.

Though truthfully, she'd become a fan of roughing it, both out at the cabin and tent camping now that the weather had finally grown warm enough in Aspire.

"I figured we'd both need a little reprieve after a few nights in the big city," he said.

She nodded. "You were right." Turning to him, she added quickly, "Don't think I didn't appreciate the city portion of this trip, though. I don't think I realized how much I'd missed ethnic food and culture until we got to San Francisco."

"Mmm, was it the museums and food you missed or the sporting events?" he teased as he came up behind her, wrapping his arms around her waist.

She laughed. "Okay, fine. You caught me. The highlight was getting to see the Giants play at Oracle Park."

He grinned. "That was fun for me too. I thought watching you holler at the TV was entertaining, but seeing you do the wave..." He arched his brows like he didn't even have the words for how much he'd loved it.

She leaned into him with a laugh. "You were such a good sport in the city. But you're right, a few days of dealing with the crowds and the noise and I was ready to get back to nature." She pursed her lips and looked around them at this crazy safari in the middle of wine country just north of a major city. "Or the closest thing to it."

He laughed as he picked up their luggage and headed toward the stairs of their new abode. "One day I'll take you all over the world, my love. But until then, I'll do my best to bring the world to you."

Her heart was in her throat as she followed him up, and when they found themselves in a magical tree hut with green all around and sounds of wildlife filling the air, she reached for his hand. "You are my world, JJ. I love that you brought me here, but you know that, right? You know I don't care when we can travel or where we go, just so long as you're by my side."

The look of love on his face made her want to weep all over again.

Turned out that once Dahlia learned how to let her armor down and her family and boyfriend into her heart, she was actually kind of a softie.

And much to her horror, she was an emotional one at that.

But luckily, JJ didn't seem to mind her newfound need to cry at the drop of a hat. If anything, it always had him looking at her with this soft tenderness that spoke of adoration and love more eloquently than any words ever could.

"I'm actually really glad you said that," he said as he took her hands in his. "That's exactly the opening I was hoping for."

Her brows drew together in confusion, but then...

She gasped when he dropped to one knee before her.

He grinned up at her. "Lia, my love, I know we've both had a lot to learn about love and relationships and what makes for a true partnership. But I think we've helped each other get to a place where a lifelong commitment isn't scary but a joy to imagine."

His hands squeezed hers as her heart beat so loud and fast that it rivaled the sound of drums they'd heard when they'd first pulled into this safari retreat.

"I want to have every adventure with you from here on out," he said, his eyes burning with love and sincerity. "From making a home together to traveling the world to starting a family. I want it all. And I want it with you."

She made a noise that was part laughter, part sob as she joined him down on the ground so she could kiss his beard, his cheeks, and his nose.

He was laughing as he finished. "Will you do me the greatest honor of my life and marry—"

"Yes!" She threw her arms around him and knocked them both over onto the rug. "Yes, yes, yes!"

He laughed and hugged her tight before going up on one elbow, his eyes shining with emotion. "Lia, you've made me the happiest—"

A loud snorting sound interrupted him, and they both gaped at each other.

"What was that?" she whispered, laughter bubbling inside her.

"If I had to guess, I'd say the warthogs," he managed.

And then they both burst out laughing so hard, their heads tipping back as JJ's romantic proposal was turned into a comedy-fest. He kept trying to finish what he was going to say, but laughter would snag him, and they'd start giggling all over again.

Honestly, they were like two dopey kids who couldn't control themselves.

Finally, after much throat clearing and a few deep

breaths, he managed to say, "Well, that was unexpected, but…" He dug into his pocket.

"No. That was perfect." She fingered the buttons on his shirt, her belly still shaking with the remnants of her laughter.

He nodded, his gaze softening as he held up a diamond engagement ring. "Can I put this on you now?"

"Yes." She could barely whisper the word as she held out her hand and watched him slide the ring onto her trembling finger. It was beautiful. It could have been a hunk of coal and it still would have been beautiful. Because it was a statement of love from JJ to her. A promise.

She beamed down at it before looking up at him. Resting her hand on his face, she could barely speak past her riotous emotions. "I love you."

"Always and forever," he whispered, pulling her into another kiss.

Thank you so much for reading JJ & Dahlia's romance. I've been waiting to write their story since the moment I met JJ. I knew he'd be perfect for the sassy city girl.

But who will be perfect for her sister, Daisy?

There might just be a certain sheriff in town who could use a little of her sunshine. And in return, she just might need his protection…

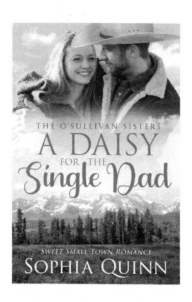

THE O'SULLIVAN SISTERS

A DAISY

FOR THE

Single Dad

SWEET SMALL TOWN ROMANCE

SOPHIA QUINN

He's a small-town sheriff who likes to follow the rules. She's a wayward singer who lives by the seat of her pants. But a broken taillight is about to bring them together and their lives will never be the same again...

A single father to the three kids, plus Aspire's lawman, Levi Baker knows the only way to survive is to live by the rules and have a strict routine. There's no time for fun when he's trying to keep his community and beloved family safe. He gave up fun the day his wife died and he's not about to get distracted by the ball of blonde sunshine who just burst into his life... or is he?

Daisy never planned on coming to Aspire, but when the record deal she thought was in the bag fell through and the band she trusted completely betrayed her, she fled to be with her sisters. She just needs some money—okay, a lot of money—to pay back the huge amounts of debt she racked up supporting the band while they toured the country. She'll lay low, earn some cash and then be on her way. But life has other plans…

Daisy never meant to get pulled over by the gruff sheriff, but something about him tugged at her heartstrings. And then she met his kids. Forming a quick attachment with his surly thirteen-year-old daughter, Daisy soon finds herself drawn into the Baker's home.

In spite of his attempts to resist her, Levi's dark clouds are burned away by Daisy's sunlight and her inability to stay-put is tested to the limits as she falls hard and fast for this single father and his adorable family.

But buried hurts and Daisy's secrets can't stay hidden forever and when rules are broken, this unlikely couple are put to the ultimate test...

AVAILABLE IN SEPTEMBER 2022

ACKNOWLEDGMENTS

Dear reader,

JJ & Dahlia's story touched me in a really deep way. I cried a lot of tears while working on those cabin scenes and anytime Dahlia was brave enough to open up and share her deepest fears with JJ. His unconditional love was everything she needed to bloom like a flower in the springtime. Her character growth was the highlight of this book for me. Love has the power to transform and heal. I'm so grateful for that.

If you enjoyed the book, I'd like to encourage you to leave a review on Amazon and/or Goodreads. Reviews and ratings help to validate the book. They also assist other readers in making a choice over whether to purchase or not. Your honest review is a huge help to everyone.

And speaking of help, no book is complete without a team of people, so I'd like to thank Deborah for this perfect cover, Kristin for being such a wonderful copy-editor, my proofreaders who caught those last few mistakes and gave me suggestions for how to make the story even better, and my amazing review team who have helped promote the book and left reviews that gave me all the feels.

Thank you, my reader, for hanging out in the O'Sullivan Sisters world. It's a very special place and I'm excited for you to return there again with Daisy's story.

And just before I go, I'd like to thank God for his unconditional love. He sacrificed everything so that we might live in eternity with him, surrounded by his love and grace. What a privilege that is.

ABOUT THE AUTHOR

Sophia Quinn is the pen-name of writing buddies Maggie Dallen and Melissa Pearl Guyan (Forever Love Publishing Ltd). Between them, they have been writing romance for 10 years and have published over 200 novels. They are having so much fun writing sweet small-town romance together and have a large collection of stories they are looking forward to producing. Get ready for idyllic small towns, characters you can fall in love with and romance that will capture your heart.

www.foreverlovepublishing/sophiaquinn

Made in the USA
Middletown, DE
05 December 2022

16910467R00241